AXIOM II
TWO TRIALS. TWO HEARTS. TWO DEATHS.

MADISON ROSE

First paperback edition November 2024

Cover design by Rebecca-Ira @rebecacovers

ISBN (Paperback) 978-1-7637440-0-4

ISBN (ebook) 978-1-7637440-1-1

Map design by Molly Renkin-Holloway

madisonrosebooks.com

Before diving into AXIOM II, make sure you experience Amrey's journey from the beginning. Discover how she made it this far by reading;

AXIOM

One test. One serum. One truth.

N
W
E
S
AXIOM CITY
THE BUNKER

THE SKI LIFT
THE CABIN
THE DEFIANCE ENTRANCE
THE DEFIANCE
REPOSITORY
COMMAND CENTRE
TRAINING CENTRE
DISPENSARY
AMERY'S ROOM
CAFETERIA
LIVING QUARTERS

For everyone who read Axiom and wanted more of Amrey's story,
this is for you.

A note for you

Hi, lovely reader!

This is just a quick disclaimer to let you know that *Axiom II* has been written and published in UK English. If you're from the US, you might notice a few spelling quirks, like *'re'* instead of *'er'*.

And while it might be jarring to see words like *centre* or *realise* spelt that way, rest assured, this isn't a typo or a sign of my literary demise—it's simply how we Aussies roll!

With that said, please enjoy *Axiom II* with all the extra *'U's* and *'S's* over *'Z's* it entails. Happy reading!

CHAPTER ONE

I broke the rules. I escaped my marriage.
Now, as lies and truth bleed into one, with my heart tied and my
hands stained, I fight to protect what's mine. The prison I knew
will burn to the ground.

No one tells you that you don't need to die to be dead. I achieved it while still breathing. The person I was before died, and in her place, I've become someone else—a new, inescapable self.

I remember who I was often, what I wanted, who I wanted. It all feels like a very distant memory now. I was dragged away from Axiom, and though I made it back to the Defiance, who I was stayed behind. She died along with Mum. With everyone else who didn't make it out. Trapped behind the walls with my father and Sacha. And though I don't miss who I was, I miss what she had: a mum who was alive. A boy who looked at her with hope. And a brother who didn't blame her.

Three weeks have passed since then. And I've felt every damn second of them. Every moment I've looked at Henry or Mags. Every time Jaxon avoids me or Kale tries to make me smile. I don't know how to act. I'm not the same, but everyone's expecting me to be. And that's why I find myself in the cafeteria more days than not. Kale found the Defiance's stash of cider and though liquor isn't something that was ever in my home growing up in Axiom, deciding to drink it was easy. Deciding to keep drinking it was easier.

"You two are needed in the command centre." I draw in a quick breath and turn to see Jaxon standing in the doorway. He carries a scruffy look these days. Dishevelled. Hopeless. He used to be cut clean. Sharp. There were no rough edges about him. Now I see the hollowness in his eyes, the pain on his face. And I'm sure his jaw hurts from holding it so tight. He won't cry in front of me, though I know he does.

"Let me guess, bad news." I challenge, not lifting my lips from the rim of the glass, the smell of cider filling my nose. Jaxon doesn't answer, but the look he wears gives me everything I need. The mission was unsuccessful. I take another sip of my drink.

"Regardless, you're needed," Jaxon repeats.

"Eye, eye captain. We'll hop to it," Kale slurs, raising his cup and saluting Jaxon before clanking it against mine. It's not a surprise for Jaxon to find us both here. It's the only place we've been since being removed from rescue missions. We would be training, but then we'd have to give up drinking, and neither of us is prepared for that.

I take another sip, finishing what's left in my cup. Kale begins to pour himself another, though I don't see it because Jaxon's eyes have a firm hold on me. And for reasons I can never explain to Kale, let alone myself, I push my cup away and get up. Jaxon nods once, then turns and leaves. Kale unsteadily rises from his seat, calling, "wait up, Captain." But he won't wait, not for me. He gave up on that weeks ago.

AS WE EXIT THE CAFETERIA, a group of kids rushes past, knocking Kale flat against the wall. A string of curse words follows. Space is hard to come by these days. Since our battle against Dane, the number of residents in the Defiance has doubled. Many citizens managed to escape Axiom and join us, but others didn't. And some never even got the chance.

We walk down the same narrow corridor to the command centre, a routine that occurs almost daily. Briefs, updates, missions, and scoutings. All of it is usually useless. None of it ever successful.

"Maybe Captain Jax just has a good poker face," Kale says, looping his arm with mine. "Who knows, this time it could have worked." I let him guide me forward, maintaining a neutral expression, even though the heat of his skin against mine is fogging my senses. Drinking may help me think less, but when Kale touches me, my mind goes completely blank. It's a dangerous line to cross.

I step out of his hold when we reach the door. If it bothers Kale, he's never said. We are what we are in private: an escape, a relief, white noise to drum away our demons. But when the drinks wear off and we stand face to face with the others, I reel it back in.

"After you," Kale says, opening the door. I muster a smile and step inside. New faces have taken over the command centre, replacing those we lost. Blane now takes his new stand at the front, but not as head of training or defence. He takes his position as head of the Defiance. My father's place. A decision made by a vote I wasn't a part of. It was made the same day we were brought back, and I would have been there if it wasn't for me breaking the news about Mum to Henry.

"Nice of you to make it," Blane comments, eyeing me as I walk to the far left corner. He may have his new post, but I prefer the back until my words need to be heard.

Kale stands beside me, away from the table where Jaxon,

Griffin and Owen sit. There's a spare chair, but no one dares to take it. Owen gives me a small nod as Archer walks in, his face hollow and sleepless. He sees me and the sourness in his expression doubles. I avoid his stare. It's been two weeks. And though people tell me what happened wasn't my fault, Archer believes it was and so do I.

"I won't deride you with fake sentiments." Blane begins, stepping forward with his hands clasped behind his back. "We all know why we're here. Let's just get to it." He then signals to Archer who moves to the front of the room, filling in the spot that Sacha once held. But I refuse to think about her because thinking about her makes me think of Mum and I can't handle those emotions right now.

"We didn't even make it past the first border this time." Archer's face is unvarying as he speaks. "More guards line the edges of the trees. Dane's pushing us out."

The roll in my eyes doesn't escape Blane's attention.

"If you have something to say, say it." He shoots me a challenging glare. I step forward, pining my shoulders back. Though speaking my mind often provokes everyone, for some reason, Blane never denies me the chance. I don't know if it's a favour to my father or me or if he's generally interested. Regardless, I take the opportunity every time.

"I told you this would happen. I warned you," I say with a bite in my tone, the cider still burning in the back of my throat. "We had a small window, and now it's gone."

"The window you're referring to, was a day after we barely escaped with the people we did. And if I'm correct, we did follow your lead, and it failed," Blanes replies coolly.

"How many failed attempts have there been? And you can't even breach the walls? I at least got us back in. If you gave me another chance, we could have-"

"You could have what? Got more people taken?" Archer

snaps, and instantly, Blane draws his gaze on him, rendering him silent.

"Amrey, I know you have a strong opinion on this matter, but just because I let you express it, doesn't mean it holds any merit in this conversation. You've made it quite clear what you think is the right approach, but we tried it your way, and it cost us one of our own."

The room suddenly feels three sizes smaller, and though no one's directly looking at me, the weight of their silence sits heavy on my chest, especially Archer's.

"I never wanted-" I begin.

"It's not the place," Kale whispers, sliding his hand over my arm, and despite the urge to defend myself, I hold my breath and bite my tongue, letting my words dissipate. Blane accepts my silence and moves on. I don't dare look at him again, but Jaxon is there, looking at me. I feel like I've lost the ability to tell what he's thinking, or maybe I fooled myself into thinking I ever could. But the way he's staring at me makes my blood run cold.

Archer and Blane are still talking logistics and possible strategies when Rowan walks in. The room hushes instantly, eyes trained on the small tablet she's carrying. The brightly lit screen is directed solely at Blane. Rowan doesn't see Kale, but he sees her, and that's enough. Within seconds he leaves the room.

When I found out Dad was alive—that he faked his death and left me—I didn't think there was a way to forgive that. And even now, I'm still figuring it out. Kale is too, in his own way. But so far, he's avoided Rowan and Magnus at every turn. I've not even seen them interact. Though, it's not like he ever leaves my side. If we're not here listening to briefings, we're in the cafeteria drinking or in one of our rooms, not talking. And while I want him to have a relationship with his parents, I'm also not ready to be alone. So, I don't push him on it.

"What is it?" Blane asks, looking at the tablet none of us can see.

"It's our security cameras; they're back on."

"How? I thought Dane had disabled them all?" Blane's shoulders stiffen. Since escaping Axiom, Dane shut us out. He took down every camera he could find, and then he hacked our system and disabled the others.

"It took time," Rowan says matter-of-factly. "I had to edge my way past their disablers, but as of exactly five minutes ago, I got through."

Curious glances are shared around the room as Rowan plugs in the tablet and the monitor behind us lights up. "It's blurry and a little glitchy, but I believe it's the camera we posted right over Axiom's boundary. They mustn't have found this one." Rowan motions to the screen, and every one of us watches as it glitches, static filling the picture, until, after several moments, it clicks clear. It's the city centre. The screen glitches again, but the picture holds.

"What are we looking at?" Owen asks.

"It's not what we're looking at, but what we should be looking for." Rowan's voice is ominous, and immediately I feel stiff. She's right. The city centre itself is empty, but there are movements in the far corners, people on the streets that just cut into the frame.

"Why are they dressed like that?" My question peeks out of the darkness from the back of the room. Rowan's eyes meet mine, a smile on her lips.

"That is what I'm wondering."

With a curt nod, she taps on the corner of the frame and enlarges it, until there's no denying what we're seeing: hundreds of Axiom citizens dressed in uniforms – grey, plain, prison-like, marching in sync. A far cry from the Axiom guard we're used to seeing.

"A cult," Owen mutters.

"An army," Archer pales. And the weight of his words fills

the space. "It's why we can't breach the walls anymore, Dane has them posted up everywhere."

"They look like robots."

"That's because they are," I answer. "If they're under his serum, then their free will is gone. Dane will have them programmed like he did Orias. They're all injected, all victims—hundreds of Axiom citizens under his control." My words open a portal for the room to stare into. "It's what he wanted. He got my DNA, and he got his army." I feel the burden of everyone's gaze, their need for an answer, for some sprout of hope. But I ran out of that weeks ago.

"So he wanted an army, but for what? What does this mean?" Owen leans forward in his chair.

"It means we've run out of time," Jaxon speaks to the room, but he may as well have just been talking to me. He knows as well as I do – now that Dane has his army, our chances of saving our people have become slight. That's why I wanted to get in early, to save them before this happened. But it failed. I failed.

"I'll see if I can get another camera working and get a better vantage point."

The monitor glitches and I find my eyes glued to it once again; I stare at the torpid bodies marching mindlessly, unaware that they're even being controlled.

"Wait," I stammer, stopping Rowan from disconnecting the screen as I hurry to the front of the room. I no longer know how to breathe as I press my hand against the monitor, ignoring the voices that question me.

"It's him," I choke, "It's Emeric."

He's alive.

CHAPTER TWO

Uproar breaks out in the command centre. When we lost Emeric, we also lost all communication from inside Axiom. No one knew what happened. We assumed he was dead. This is the first time we've seen him, the first bit of hope we've had in weeks.

"What's the plan? There has to be a plan." Archer is the first to rationalise.

"Having sight into Axiom doesn't change the facts. Dane has complete control of the guard. Right now Axiom is one giant prison cell." Blane directs the attention back to him. "And as long as he has Xavier and Sacha, he has an endless supply of Subversive blood to produce his serum."

My heart aches. I knew the second Mum died that not everyone was making it out. I just never expected them to be the ones left behind.

"We'll make a deal," my voice interrupts the room. "Me for Emeric."

"Don't be ridiculous, Amrey. We will not give Dane the exact thing he wants. Having you is our only power against him."

"I'm not saying hand me over." Even though I would trade my life in a heartbeat for Emeric's, for anyone I love. "I know giving Dane my blood would only give him more control. But that doesn't mean we can't use me."

"What exactly are you suggesting?" Blane locks his eyes on mine, our usual game of cat and mouse. He lets me speak. But will he pounce and shut down my plan? Or let me run with it?

"Use me as bait."

The room is unusually quiet. It seems no one knows whether to agree or contest.

"Even if you use yourself as bait. How do we even know that Sacha and Xavier are still alive? You could be risking your life for nothing," Owen asks.

"It wouldn't be for nothing. It was my plan that failed. Emeric was caught because of me. He's there because of me." *They all are.* "And I should be the one to bring him back."

For a beat, the only sound is Blane's inhale. The only person seeming eager to agree is Archer. And then there's Jaxon, his jaw clenched so tight, I see the veins popping in his neck.

"It will be discussed," Blane says sharply.

"Blane, you can't be serious." Jaxon rises from his chair, the metal legs screeching against the concrete. Owen stands too, only to calm him. And Blane ignores them both.

"But Amrey. Next time you want your plan to be considered I suggest not coming straight from the bar; you reek of cider. Enough wallowing. Quit the drinking and get back to training. Maybe then your words will hold more weight." My face hardens with every breath, but I don't let him rattle me. This could be my chance. For weeks, I've ached to go back. And now it seems like Blane might finally be listening to me.

"Briefing's over. No one breathes a mention of this to anyone outside this room. It stays between us until we have a plan."

"Blane, a word," Jaxon growls.

"No," Blane says briskly. "Training started five minutes ago.

Your rookies will be waiting." Jaxon bites down his unsaid words and turns to follow the rest of us out of the command centre. Blane's eyes press against mine a final time. I reply with a curt nod. The game is far from over.

THE SECOND I reach the hallway, I turn away from everyone. It might be time for training, but knowing Kale, he's back in the cafeteria, downing another cider. I'm hoping after what I tell him, he'll sober up enough to train with me. I don't want to face Jaxon and the guys alone, not after that.

"Hurry up!"

"Come on!"

Kids voices echo down the hall. It's the middle of the day, lunchtime, meaning I need to beat the rush to the cafeteria. The last thing I need is for them to see Kale. A drunk Kale is no stranger to me, but when his mum is involved, it's worse.

The room is only just starting to fill up with people when I get there. However, the smell of cider is still thick in the air.

"Kale?" I call into the kitchen, not surprised to see a fresh bottle in his hand.

"Check this out. I found more of the stash." The cooks at the Defiance brew their own cider. But that doesn't mean we have an unlimited supply, and lately, Kale and I have been finding it harder and harder to get our hands on it.

"That's great, but we've got to go." I take the bottle from his hands and pull him to his feet. "We have to train."

Kale looks at me like I was hit on the head. "Since when?"

"Since they might be sending me back in. And you too, if you want?" I watch him study me for several seconds. He was there that day Emeric was taken. He knows how badly I want to go back and fix it. To save them all.

"Come on."

Kale sways back on his heels before sliding to the ground and swiping the bottle from my hands. "No. I'm good."

"Seriously?"

"Amrey, be realistic. There is no way Blane's sending you back in. The chances of you saving Xavier and the others are slight. And even if you do, Xavier will kill Blane the second he finds out he let you go back. So yeah, I'm pretty sure he's just saying what you want to hear."

I stand there for a moment, stung by the truth of his words. But Kale wasn't in the room. He didn't see Emeric in the footage; he didn't see Blane's face. I think he means it this time.

"You're wrong. I'm going to train, with or without you."

"Without."

I watch him pour the contents of the bottle down his throat, half the cider missing his mouth and drenching his shirt. A rush of kids enters the cafeteria then.

"Looks like happy hour's over."

Kale's eyes meet mine. "We could go back to my room?"

My feet hesitate at the door. There's so much sadness and anger shared between us that it's hard to escape sometimes. Drinking helps. It would be all too easy to say yes to him right now. I have before. Instead, I slowly edge my body out of the kitchen, past the kids swarming the cafeteria and make my way to the training centre. Kale doesn't stop me.

When I round the corner to the arena, I'm not the only one there. A small group of kids stand at the door, dressed in exercise gear and eager to enter. Only a handful were allowed to start training, and right until this moment, I hadn't realised Henry was one of them.

He sees me before I see him, and I watch him walk over, closing the few metres between us.

"You're here to train?" His voice is curious. I could ask him the same question.

"I am." I smile, but Henry barely looks at me.

"Why? I thought you thought it was stupid."

I recoil, watching his little face crease. He's angry at me, and I don't blame him. Henry's been forced to grow up so fast. Forced to deal with everything, and I haven't been the sister he needed. Especially last week, when he snuck out after curfew and discovered Kale and I in the cafeteria, drunk on cider and not in the mood for a lecture. I barely registered it was Henry before I yelled, and he ran. I thought about chasing him, apologising, but my feet didn't move. Only my hand did, to lift the glass back to my lips. I found him the next day and apologised. But it seems, just like everyone's attempts at lecturing me, my apology didn't find its home in Henry either.

"I never said that. I just took a break," I try to level with him.

"Whatever." He bites, and before I can say anything else, he turns and walks away. I should call after him, but the words never come.

"Don't take it personally. He's just dealing with stuff in his own way."

I turn to see Jaxon standing behind me. His anger's gone, though I can tell the morning's briefing has set him on edge.

"He's angry at me."

"He's young. He needs someone to blame. He'll get over it." I didn't expect Jaxon to be the one comforting me today. And I don't think he expected it either. "But he's also not stupid, and if I can smell the cider on your breath, so can he."

Embarrassment flames my cheeks, and I fight the urge to step back. It's no secret that I've found ways to keep myself busy these last weeks. I don't hide it, but that doesn't mean I like being called out for it.

"So where's your best friend? I'm surprised he's not here; I never see you two apart these days."

I roll my eyes. "I'm fully capable of training on my own."

"Are you sure?" Jaxon eyes me over. "Because, Amrey, you're a mess. You might think you're holding your shit together, but it's clear by just looking at you how checked out you are. Things aren't going your way and you hate it. But going back to Axiom, the place you fought so hard to leave, is not the solution."

His words slap me in the face. Jaxon, the person who used to warm me up, now feels as cold as ice.

"Don't tell me I'm checked out. I might be abusing my time while I wait on orders, but at least I'm still fighting to go back. I'm still fighting to do something. You're the one that's checked out. You've turned into this combat robot with no feelings, grunting and growling all over the place. I know we all went through shit. But don't go judging my coping methods before dealing with your own."

Jaxon's jaw twitches, but for once, he doesn't open it to argue or yell. Instead, he simply turns and walks into the training centre.

"Don't bother coming in."

It's the last thing I hear before the door shuts in my face, leaving me in the hall alone, staring at the metal in front of me.

I'm too stunned to move, and instead, I'm forced to look at my reflection for the first time in weeks. I can avoid mirrors, but I can't avoid what's looking back at me right now. It's a bleary view, but the truth lies in it. My hair is knotted in a bun. My uniform, once form-fitting, is loose. I've lost muscle. I've lost weight. You can see it in my face, my tighter cheeks. You don't need to eat as much when you're full of guilt and cider.

I touch my face, feeling the hollowness. My eyes carry bags greater than I ever saw on Mum – a woman who worked and raised two kids on her own. I look deflated. I look tired. I don't look ready to face the people on the other side of this door. So, letting the reflection of myself go, I turn and walk away. Maybe tomorrow I'll train. Right now, I need a drink.

I BARELY MAKE it a few metres when Mags steps out of the shadows. She's dressed in scrubs, most likely on her way to the dispensary to help Cynthia.

"Mags, hi," I stammer, hoping she doesn't question my steps. "How's Cynthia?"

"Hey Amrey, she's good… managing." I'm glad the subject of Cynthia is at least a lot easier to broach with her than Jaxon. Mags doesn't care for grudges or resentment. I love that about her and envy it all the same.

"What about you?" I ask, "Sorry, I haven't checked in for a while. I've been meaning to, I've just been a little distracted." My words are mumbled, my feet suddenly very interesting to look at.

"Amrey, please don't apologise. You lost your mum, and Dane has-" She doesn't finish that sentence.

"I guess we're all dealing with our own stuff," I finish.

"Yeah." Mag's offers a small smile. She doesn't mention Sam, and I don't ask. She told me once that she knew the risks of following her family back to the Defiance. It cost her Sam. I reach out and squeeze her hand. I don't think she was ever in love with him, but he was her partner. He was there for her when I wasn't. And to know, that given the choice he didn't follow her. That would hurt anyone, no matter the relationship behind it.

"Enough of that," Mags says, straightening up. "I should get going, and you've got training…" It's more an unfinished sentence than a question. But the interest is there.

I lift my face to hers. "Yes, I should get going too."

Not an answer. Not a lie. And though Mags isn't one to judge, the look she gives is worse than any lecture or verbal slap I've received today. I respond to her unspoken message: "Don't say it, I know. I just can't, okay? I can't face them. Not yet."

Mag's face softens. "Amrey, I know I've said this to you already, but what happened isn't your fault. Everyone knew the stakes of that mission. Emeric especially. And though I didn't

know him very well, from what I learnt, he would hate for you to
be sitting around blaming yourself."

I don't have anything to say, so I just accept her hug and
watch as she disappears down the hall.

"TRAINING LASTED LONG." Kale's eyes barely lift from the bottle
as I open the door to his room. I don't know who between us is
the least surprised to find me here.

"Shut up," I snap, taking the bottle from his hand and
drinking it. He's lying on his bed, legs stretched out, hands
behind his head. I slump down on the end, kicking off my shoes.

"Your boyfriend wasn't happy to see you?"

I punch him in the leg. "He's not my boyfriend. You of all
people would know that."

"Mmm, I don't know… According to the rumour mill, he
was about to be…"

"Talking to Owen does not count as a rumour mill. Besides,
if you're talking to anyone, shouldn't it be your parents? Have
you even sought them out yet? You know Rowan is stationed in
the tech room."

Kale's stare hardens like he's trying to figure out if I'm
digging for a reason or to be a dick. He chooses the latter.

"If I wanted parenting advice, I'd talk to someone with
parents."

"Ouch," I wince. Even though I know he's being a prick on
purpose, it doesn't make the comment sting any less. And at that,
Kale sits up, edging closer to me on the bed. His fingers play
with the fray of my pants.

"I'm sorry, that was harsh," he murmurs, and I glare at him
over the rim of the bottle, his eyes now on my lips. I feel that
look race over my entire body, my senses heightening as I curl

my toes. Just when I'm about to do something about it, Kale breaks the tension.

"We should play a game." He grins.

"A game?" I question.

"Yeah, why not. We're always so serious. Let's do something fun." I don't look convinced, but Kale keeps going, "I ask you a question. Answer or drink." Kale reaches for the bottle, I pull it further away, watching as he eyes it hungrily.

"Fine." I smirk. "But I have a better idea. Answer the question or no drink."

Kale shakes his head. "You've always got to be in control, don't you?"

"It's a lot more fun," I taunt.

"On the contrary. I'd say losing control is where the real fun starts. But fine, Amrey. I'll play by your rules. So, tell me, what's your first question?"

I look him over, watching him shift slightly under my gaze. There is one thing I've thought a lot about. Something I'm not even sure I'd know how to answer myself.

"If you could go back in time, knowing what you know now. Would you still catch me after I fell in combat class?"

Kale's gaze burns with something I want to call curiosity, but the shadow in his eyes makes me hesitant. "You think that's our defining moment?"

I let my silence answer.

"Well, then I disagree. Whether or not I caught you that day would have played no effect on our future Amrey. Wish as we might, we've been fated since birth with our freaky subversive DNA."

I'm at a loss for words. It's not an answer. Not completely. Though, I don't stop him as he takes the bottle from my hand and swallows several mouthfuls of cider.

"My turn then." Kale presses forward, resting the bottle between us, one hand still clamped around its neck. He pretends to mull the question over for a while, but the devilish smile returns as his eyes land on mine. "Who would you rather sleep with, Owen or Blane?"

My whole face pinches. "Seriously, that's your question? That's what you're rolling with after what I just asked?"

"Yep," Kale quips. "I think it's rather informative. Your answer will say a lot about you."

I stare at him for several beats, judging his seriousness. And then, with a grunt, I push the bottle back to him.

Kale remains smug and takes another sip.

"Fine, if you're gonna be a prick. Tell me, who would you rather sleep with? Owen or Blane."

A wide grin slips over Kale's lips. I expect him to laugh it off. Instead, he says, "Owen, obviously. That guy could laugh anyone into bed."

My eyes roll to the back of my head.

"My turn," Kale groans.

I snatch the bottle back. "I don't think so. You evaded my first question, this time I want a real answer." Kale looks at me with a raised expression but bridles his comment.

"Alright, Amrey, give it to me."

I contemplate, relaxing into the bed and edging away, ever slightly. "What did you think of me the first time we met?"

Kale visibly scoffs. "Such a girl thing to ask."

"Hey!" I scowl. "Don't act like you're not curious about what I think of you."

"I already know what you think of me." Kale bites his lip, lowering his gaze to my legs and back again.

"Dammit, Kale, just answer the question."

"Fine." The seconds linger as he presses closer. "Do you remember that night in Axiom? When I saved you from the blizzard?"

I roll my eyes. "I remember that a little differently, but yes."

That night was the first we spoke, the first time I met Kale. If only I'd known what fate awaited us then.

"You asked me what I wanted from you?" Kale moves even closer, lifting onto his knees.

"I remember." My breath hitches, and the next thing I know, the bottle is on the ground, and Kale is on top of me. His face hovering an inch from mine, his chest pressed against me as I lay flat on the bed. His elbows sit on either side of my head.

"I'd seen girls as you'd seen boys. But none had held my mind captive like yours. I told you, you intrigued me, and I meant it. But what I really wanted to say."

I hold my breath, waiting for his answer, unable to tear my eyes from his.

"What?" I finally quiver.

Kale's reply isn't with words.

In a moment, his lips are on mine, his hands tangled in my hair. Our legs wrap together as we tussle over the bed until I'm on top. Kale breaks away.

"You have to be in charge, even now?" he asks, but it's more of a grunt, and then his lips are on mine, and he has me on my back again.

THE HALL LIGHTS are dim when I leave Kale's room. That happens in the old section; power needs to be saved somehow. This part of the Defiance, which used to be closed off, has been renovated to accommodate all the new people from Axiom. The rooms are fashioned from thin drywall and whatever bedding we could find. It's not much, but it works.

I creep down the hall, mad at myself for missing dinner. We fell asleep. Kale and I don't talk too deeply, so when the kissing stops and the drinks finish, sleep is inevitable. I just wish I managed to stay that way, because this is the time of the day I hate the most – when the Defiance rests, and there's nothing to keep me distracted. I don't know what to do with myself. I could find Henry and make sure he's alright, but I doubt he cares to see me. Besides, he's in good hands with Cynthia and Makin.

That leaves bed. My bed. But that is the last place I want to be right now, so I keep walking the halls. One foot in front of the other, until more light floods my path and I'm standing in front of the training centre.

I edge towards the door slowly. Training finished hours ago; it'll be empty now. The last time I was inside was before we left to save Henry. I didn't know if I'd make it back. I didn't think I'd live to. Yet, here I am.

Drawing in a breath, I open the door.

The same feeling of awe fills my chest, just like it did the first time I saw the training arena. It's hard to believe that we're sitting in the chamber of a cave, covered in snow, hundreds of feet below the earth. If it weren't for the dome roof I wouldn't believe it. Made of glass, it fills the whole space with the magic of the night. I walk down closer to the lake and sit on the bank. The stars reflect off the water, casting me in their glow.

When I was younger, I used to sit in the kitchen with my mum and watch the stars from the window. The world seemed so much smaller then.

"Amrey?"

No. I curse under my breath. I wasn't expecting company.

"I thought I saw you walking in here." Wiping my wet cheeks, I turn around to see Owen. I don't bother replying. I don't invite him over. The only move I make is to turn and look back up at the sky, but still Owen sits next to me. I'm not sure if he can see my tears or if he's just choosing to ignore them. Regardless, I'm grateful.

"What are you thinking about?" he asks softly.

"Does the moon seem brighter to you?" The words leave my lips before I know what I'm asking, but I don't take them back.

"What do you mean?"

"The moon is a lot brighter here than it ever was in Axiom. The stars are even clearer."

Owen gives me a look I can't quite see but then he leans back on his elbows and watches the sky.

"Mum would have thought so. She would have liked it here." I don't know why I keep talking. Or why I brought her up. Owen and I haven't spoken much, not alone and not like this. But for some reason, I feel very safe in his silence. Even as my voice breaks when I say her name and the tears start again.

"To be honest, I reckon you're seeing things, Sub, but I've learnt better than to tell you you're wrong, so I'll just keep that opinion to myself."

And like that, I'm laughing. "It's an important lesson to learn," I tease.

"Emeric never really mastered it, though. He seems to think he can put everyone in his place. It's like he believes himself a bloody good Samaritan or something." Owen's laughing, but since the moment he mentioned Emeric's name, I've been frozen. And now he's noticed.

"Amrey, what happened to Emeric was shit. A total screw up. But it wasn't just yours, and the blame doesn't only lie on your shoulders. Even though I know you like to let it."

"Archer seems to think so."

"Archer doesn't know how to handle his emotions. Hopefully, Griffin can sort him out."

I grin a little at that. Griffin and Archer together still boggles me, only for the fact that they're completely opposite in nearly every way. But that seems to be the thing they love the most.

"Besides, Emeric's not gone. You saw him on that camera. He's alive, and we're going to get him back."

A giant part of me has been feeling guilty for so long because of what happened with Emeric. I've hated myself for being so consumed in hurting Dane, in getting our people back, that I forgot about the ones I had with me. Emeric wanted to scout ahead. It was his suggestion, one I let him take. I let him go and take a stupid risk. It was my call, my mission, and I let him get taken. That's on me. Every day since I've prayed he is alive. That he is okay. And today, I finally felt that relief. I didn't get one of the best people I know killed. I can get him back. I have to.

"You need to come to training." Apparently, Owen isn't one for skipping out on hard topics. Sitting up and making me look at him he continues, "We miss you. We need you. And Jaxon wants you there too. Even if he won't admit it. He's just going through his own shit right now, but I see it when he looks at you. Whenever you're in the same room together. He's dying for things to go back to normal. We want the team back together. And that means coming to training so we can get our shit sorted and save Emeric."

I have no rebuttal in me. Owen's right. I just don't know if I'm ready to leave the bubble of guilt and mourning I've created for myself. So, instead, I nod and turn back to the lake.

Owen sits with me a while longer, until the clouds start to roll through and the Arena darkens.

"We should probably get some sleep." He yawns, and I feel him move away, the space next to me suddenly colder.

"You go. I'm going to stay a little while."

"Are you sure? I can stay."

"No, I'm good, I just want to watch the moon a bit longer."

"Alright, Sub, but get some sleep. We have training early tomorrow, and I better see you there. It's been a while since I've kicked your arse."

"The only arse being kicked will be yours." I smirk.

Owen laughs, the light from the moon reflecting off his eyes. "I'm gonna hold you to that."

Then I watch him walk away. Owen was the last thing I expected tonight. But if anything, it made me realise the people I do have here. People I wish Mum had had the chance to meet.

I lay back on the bank, watching the stars.

"Wait, I think I know why it's brighter." Owen's voice carries through the Arena. "It's because your mum's there now." My laugh can probably be heard in the halls through the Defiance, but I don't mind. That may be the dumbest thing he's said, but for some reason, it carries the greatest comfort in the world, and as I look back up at the moon, I find a smile on my lips.

"Hi Mum, I've missed you."

CHAPTER THREE

My hands are sticky with blood. My ears ringing from the crack of the bullet as I stare down at her body.

"Mum," I plead, but there's no answer.

Her body's still warm in my arms. How can she be warm and not breathing?

This isn't fair.

I stare at her white, lace-up shoes, the only thing not bloodied, not ruined.

"Mum." My voice is barely a whimper now, my throat thick with pain and words I can't say. This shouldn't be happening. Mum should be alive. She should be breathing.

A weight, mountains heavy, bears down on my chest. My lungs cave in, my body drawing closer to the ground. All I can hear is Dane's voice—his vile laugh stings like acid, burning my skin, melting me down.

"Mum, come back, mum." More whispers, more pleas that go unanswered. And then my hands are scraping along the ground, and I'm standing, charging at Dane. Until arms pull me back, tightening over my waist and dragging me away.

Shots ring in the distance. Screams claw at my ears. People

break out into a violent fight against Dane's guards. I want to help. I have to.

"Let me go. Let me go!" I writhe in a crazy fit against the strong arms around me. "Mum, Mum!" Her body disappears from view as I collapse into the black.

I WAKE up in a cold sweat, my heart hammering against my chest. Plying myself from my bed, I walk into the bathroom and splash water on my face. The cold slaps my skin, sharpening my sight, but still, it doesn't chase away the lingering fragments. Scenes embedded in my mind. I might be awake, but my mind is stuck in that nightmare. And I hate that it's not just a nightmare but a memory that now lives in the buried corners of my brain, resurfacing in my dreams to haunt me.

At least today, I can get some release. I can finally hit something.

"HEY," Kale smirks as I reach the end of the hall. He's had his eyes on me since I left my room, leaning against the wall, just waiting until I came close enough.

"Don't you have anything better to do than watch me?" I groan, rubbing my face. I'm too tired to care about being rude and too sensitive to talk about it.

"Not particularly."

I roll my eyes as he falls into step next to me.

"So you changed your mind?" I ask.

"Nope. I'd much rather be in bed, but I figured someone has to be there to keep you in check. Don't need your boyfriend kicking you out a second time."

"One day, you're going to stop calling him that."

"The same day I believe it," he says, and I can see out of the corner of my eye, his lips quirk into a grin. My cheeks are hot under his gaze. Kale's been like this since I got back – flirty, but mostly restrained. He knows what to say to rile me up, but I know better than to bite. Most of the time. Behind closed doors is another story. I know he says things about Jaxon to bug me, but deep down, I think he does want an answer. And I think that's why it bothers me so much. Because I don't have one. When Kale and Jaxon dragged me out of Axiom, I didn't speak to either of them for days, not until we had a plan to save the others. And after everything that happened on that mission, Kale was the only person I could bear to be around besides Mags. Kale didn't know Emeric. I didn't feel so guilty with him, so sad and horrible. I could barely look Jaxon in the eye. Emeric is his best friend. So, I avoided him and instead started to find myself in Kale's room. It's quiet there. He keeps my mind busy.

WHEN WE FINALLY REACH THE door to the Arena, I hesitate.

"After you," Kale says, opening it for me.

"Thanks," I breathe, unsure if I even spoke.

"Woah!" Kale's eyebrows raise as we walk in, "why didn't you tell me the Arena looked like this? I would have quit ditching it weeks ago."

It takes me a second to realise that this is the first time he's been inside. And I understand the reaction. This place is special. Even better in the day when you can see it all. I loved it when I first saw it. I love it still. The only difference is the sheer volume of people now using it. And instead of Blane kicking my arse, it's Jaxon.

The door slams shut behind us, blowing my hair forward. And my stomach is in my throat. Everyone is looking at me. I swallow hard and take a step, picking up the pace as I walk past the running track, past the kids stretching on the far side, and head straight to the sparring mats in the middle. The whole time, Jaxon's eyes don't leave mine, and I refuse to be the one to look away. I won't let him see me scared.

I come to a stop on the padded ground in front of him. He doesn't say anything, not even when Kale makes a comment about his brooding stare. He does, however, look away. And that's when I glance past Jaxon to the lake and the rocky wall behind it. I haven't missed that climb or that jump. The small ledge still sits at the top. The mere sight of it makes my stomach twist. You'd think with all the heights and falls I've had to face recently, it wouldn't bother me. But I guess that's the thing about fear–conquering it doesn't necessarily mean it's gone, just that it hasn't killed you, yet.

"So, what's the go, captain? You gonna make us run laps, or can I start kicking Amrey X's butt over here?" Kale bumps his hip against mine. Jaxon's face hardens.

"We're waiting for the others. But by all means, if you're bored, you can leave." Testosterone is filling the air faster than my breath can draw it back.

"Who else is coming?" I ask, only to fill the tense silence. Jaxon just nods to the space behind me and I turn around to see Owen, Archer, Griffin and Mags walking down.

"You came!?" I say, almost in disbelief. Last night, after Owen ever so calmly put me in my place, I realised Mags should be training too. If anything, it would be some fun for her. I slipped a note under her door, but I didn't know if she'd come.

"The promise to let me kick your arse was a hard one to pass," Mags smirks.

"So, she's going around promising everyone that hey," Kale mocks. "You know I'm starting to think you've just lost your edge, Amrey, and this is your way of not having to show face."

I kick him in the back of the knee, and he stumbles forward.

"Keep talking, and I'll show you who has to save face."

"You two done flirting? Or should we leave you to find a

room so we can train?" Jaxon's voice snaps through the air and makes my cheeks burn red. He's glaring at me. Everyone else is now too. Kale doesn't seem fazed at all. If anything, he's more amused. He loves pressing Jaxon's buttons, for reasons I don't care to think too much about. But I hate being called out, especially by Jaxon. I get that he's pissed at me, but I'll be damned if I'm his punching bag.

Twenty minutes and ten sets of sprints later, Jaxon has us stretching in preparation for sparring.

"Who is that?" Mags asks, dipping her head to the left. I look past her to a group of kids doing drills near the running track.

"The kids?"

"No, the guy teaching them."

All I see is his back until he turns around.

"Oh, that's James," I say, though I'm slightly confused to see him here myself. I knew Blane pardoned him, but I hadn't expected him to be around kids.

"Excuse me," I say, storming over to Jaxon and interrupting his conversation with Archer. "What's he doing here?"

"You'll have to be more specific." He arches his eyes as I turn and point in James' direction. "Wasn't my call." He directs his eyes back to me, but I can tell from his expression the idea of having James around the kids is just as unsettling to him.

"Hang on, I thought you were all for him being pardoned? Aren't you like school buddies or something?" Archer snubs. I pinch my face, hoping he can sense the finger I'm giving him with this look.

"I wanted him pardoned. I didn't want him around kids."

Archer glares at me. "You mean Henry?"

"He is a kid."

"Well, maybe you should go over there and babysit. Don't want someone else getting hurt on your watch."

My fist goes flying before he even finishes his last word.

Jaxon catches it.

Archer didn't even flinch. Instead, he grins.

"Is that all you got?"

"Enough!" Jaxon steams. "If you two wanna start this fight again, you can do it on the mat."

"Now, this will be fun," Kale's voice occupies the last of the silence.

CHAPTER FOUR

I'M NO STRANGER TO SCRIMMAGING WITH ARCHER, BUT TODAY feels different. It's been a while since I've had the chance to fight, and I'd be lying if I said I wasn't aching for one. My fingers tingle with the anticipation to swing again. As we circle each other, Archer's eyes piercing mine, I can tell we both need this. And I, for one, am looking forward to it.

Archer pounces first. I feel the air move with him, but he doesn't follow through. It was a test, and I flinched. A smile draws over his lips.

"If you're scared, Sub, you can walk away. No one will judge you."

Prick.

I square my gaze, steadying myself. "I'd judge you," I snide, "Now, are you going to make a move, or will you keep running your mouth?"

Archer's lips twist. I clench my fist.

"Shit, this is going to be good," Owen says, "I knew we missed you at training." And just like that, Archer lunges for me. He's fast and manages to get a hit on my shoulder. I rip myself back and duck before his next swing hits me in the face. My heel punches the back of his leg, and he stumbles forward but doesn't fall. Pivoting back around, he's on one side of the mat, and I'm on the other. We're standing face to face again. His eyes locked on mine. It's a waiting game.

Archer's face is taut. I watch him crack his knuckles, drawing his hands back into fists, while stretching his neck. But he doesn't make another move towards me. He's putting on a show.

Strike hard, strike fast.

The words I've lived by. It's about time I put them back into practice.

Without letting the decision show in my eyes, I pounce forward. Archer doesn't have time to anticipate my swing before I strike him in the ribs. He swats me back and immediately starts on the attack, throwing fists at my face and jabbing punches. I block them all, but with every swipe, my feet slide closer to the edge of the mat.

He's boxing me out.

I have to find a way to break out of his attack before this fight ends with a technicality. He's just punching so fast, too hard for me to give up defence. And with every move I block, my lungs constrict tighter. I'm winded already. I'm realising now how weak I've become. Two weeks of drinking, of slumming it with Kale, and this is the result.

I can't lose. Not this early, and not to Archer.

Lowering my arm, I let him get a shot in. His fist collides with my shoulder, sending a splintering pain down my arm. Archer pulls back, expecting me to cave, but I don't take a second to dwell on the pain. Instead, I use my window and charge right at him. His arms fly up. I'm on the attack now. But where Archer thinks I'm going to punch, I kick. My foot collides with his knee, and he falters. My fist collides with his jaw, and his hands meet the mat. I take a few steps back, desperately gasping for air. My stare lands on Mags, and I notice the eyes of our small group are no longer the only ones on us. Nearly everyone in the arena has walked over to watch.

Archer slowly rises to his feet, spitting blood from his split lip, a menacing look in his eyes. My bated breath is ripped from my lungs as he takes no time charging across the space towards me. I put my hands up to block, but he's not aiming to hit me. Before I realise what's happening, his hands meet my shoulders, and his body throws mine on the ground. His legs trap mine beneath his. His fingers dig into the skin of my collarbone. This isn't the combat we've been taught. This is animal.

Archer must sense the shock that's taken hold of me because as I look up at him hovering above, his face shifts. The hating look he wore before now morphs into something more daring. More fun. And I'm down to play.

Archer punches. I move quickly, but his fist catches my cheek, burning the soft skin. The moment his knuckles collide with the ground, I launch my hips up, bucking him off my torso, then I bring my knee up and drive it into a place that makes his eyes grow wide and his face turn white. He rolls off me in clear pain. I swivel out of his grip and find my feet again, leaning onto my knees as he pulls himself off the ground. When his gaze meets mine, the challenge is still there, but now he's pissed, and game or not, he wants to make this hurt.

The usual chill in the air is gone as the sun beats down, heating the glass roof and cooking us inside the cave. I watch Archer cautiously, ready for round two. When he runs forward, I punch him hard in the chest. Except his arms reach out and grip the back of my neck as he draws his knees into my gut, over and over. I try to block them. I'm successful for a moment. This pain is one I haven't missed, but the adrenaline flooding my veins is addicting, and I use all the energy I have to push at his chest. His fingers slip on my neck, and he stumbles back. I kick him in the stomach. He stumbles further. I kick again, and he falls on his back. I don't wait to see if he'll get up this time. Instead, I jump on top of him. My legs straddle his, my arms pinning his above his head as our chests rise and fall against each other. Our positions have swapped, but the dare in our eyes is still there. Archer locks his gaze with mine, our bodies drawing in the air like we have none left. And then, something I would never have guessed ten minutes ago happens. Archer smiles at me, and I smile back. Then I slide off him and stand up. Reaching my hand down, Archer takes it and finds his footing next to me. No words are exchanged, but it's in the look we share. It's in the way we both nod and move off the mat together. The fight's over. There is no clear winner. But neither of us cares. We did what we wanted to. And I feel it. The animosity shared between us for months is gone. Beaten down by our punches.

Jaxon meets my gaze then, only briefly, and for the first time in weeks, he doesn't look disgraced by my presence. He seems, almost, impressed.

"Interesting," Kale murmurs as I fall in line next to him.

"What?" I whisper against the sound of Jaxon shouting his next orders.

"Oh, nothing," he goads, and though we're both looking ahead, I can feel the taunting grin on his lips.

"If it's nothing, drop the smirk," I snap.

"Woah, that's a lot of bite for someone who just gave away her win."

"What are you on about?" I turn to face him now.

Kale looks at me with a deadpan expression. "It's just interesting that you'll beat up James to impress Dane, but you'll forfeit Archer to impress captain brown eyes."

I feel the anger in my chest – still simmering from my fight – begin to boil over again. Kale's long list of curly nicknames for Jaxon is getting on my last nerve. As is whatever vendetta he has against him. It's dumb. It's stupid. And now it's pissing me off.

I'm about to say "enough," but the word doesn't have time to leave my mouth.

Whipping my head around, I come face to face with Jaxon. He's standing in front of both of us, but his eyes are purely on Kale. "If you don't want to be here, you can leave."

Heat creeps up the back my neck, fanning over my cheeks. Everyone's eyes are on me once again.

"We were just discussing Amrey's lack of aggression," Kale taunts, not at all fazed by Jaxon hovering over him. Jaxon doesn't bite back. Instead, he rests on his heels, urging Kale on. "You see, you might be Mr instructor in here, but we've dealt with Dane. Or at least I did. He was my combat instructor for three years. I know how he works. I know how he fights. And after that display..." Kale looks past Jaxon and nudges his head towards the mat, towards Archer and me. "Friendly competition won't save you."

Silence.

Seconds of delayed silence.

"What are you saying?" Jaxon says, standing taller.

My lungs – my entire chest – tighten at the question. I know where this is going. And it isn't going to end well.

"Kale, shut it," I mouth, but it's of no use. The boys have moved into a different world, one where my words don't penetrate and only their competing egos live.

I brace myself as Kale puffs out his chest. "I think I'd be better at your job."

And like that, Jaxon swings his fist at Kale.

Or at least, that's what I was expecting.

Seconds turn to minutes as everyone waits to see what Jaxon will say, what he'll do. No one's more surprised than me when he walks over to the mat and ushers Kale to join him.

"You won't mind if we put that to the test, do you?"

The tension in the room rises irately with each step Kale takes towards the mat. The echo of his footsteps provides cadence to the stillness. Owen shoots me a look, and I raise my shoulders in defeat. I want to stop this. This won't end well, but even Owen knows I have no power here. I watch as they circle each other. Mags moves next to me.

"This isn't going to be good, is it?" Her voice is as trepid as my breath. I shake my head. Mag's squeezes my hand. These two have been at odds since Kale arrived. I put a lot of that on me. I could have handled things better, but no words I say now will deflate this situation. This fight is happening. I just hope they don't kill each other in the process.

Kale lunges first, which doesn't surprise me. We both learnt to fight in Axiom. "Strike first and hard" isn't just my motto, but the entire guard's, Dane's included. Jaxon also doesn't look surprised by Kale's attack, blocking his first hit with ease and spinning out of his orbit. Kale didn't like that. Stopping for no amount of air, he attacks again, and this time, he doesn't miss. Jaxon takes a punch to the ribs but catches himself mid-stumble. Stepping into Kale's hold, he hits him hard in the shoulder, driving his knee into his gut. Kale falters, but only just. With a grunt, he charges at Jaxon harder, faster. In Defiance training, though we fight to win, we've always done it with slight restraint. Don't maim your opponent if you can help it.

Kale doesn't respond to that rule.

Aiming high, his fists fly at Jaxon's face. He just manages to defend them, but only slightly, and while putting up a block he loses his footing slightly. But that's all it takes Kale. He jumps on Jaxon, who just manages to roll out from under him, repositioning himself on top. But as quick as he gets leverage, he loses it to Kale again, and the two of them keep fighting it out over and over. I watch them wrestle for power, neither of them conceding. It's clear the fight has gone from technique to a show of strength. And it's not ending anytime soon.

Owen's eyes meet mine, asking for permission. I look at the boys, still wrangling each other on the ground and give a small nod. With that, Owen taps Archer and the two storm the mat and break them up. Kale attempts to shake them off, leading Griffin to step in.

"Enough!" I shout, making them all stop and look at me. Jaxon eventually shrugs off Owen's grip, and they all straighten up.

"Look, your defence is solid," Kale says, ignoring my glare, "but your attacks are weak. Because of that, you'll lose against Dane."

Jaxon's frustration is visible.

"Thank you for your opinion." He replies tightly. "But we are not Dane, and we won't fight like him. If you don't like that, you're free to train on your own."

Kale turns his head to me, he knows I'll kill him if he tries to fight again, so instead, he shrugs his shoulders. "I gave my advice, if you don't want it, that's on you. Come on Amrey, let's go." Kale turns around and leaves. And I'm stuck. Caught in between.

Jaxon turns his face to me. "It's up to you. If you want to fight like that, I won't stop you. But it's not what Blane or your dad would want."

I don't know if it's the mention of my father or Blane that ushers me to speak, but suddenly I find my voice.

"It doesn't matter what they want. Maybe Kale didn't go about it the best way, but he's right. Dane was his combat instructor for years. He knows how he fights. How the guards in his army will fight. We'd be stupid not to utilise that. Even if it's not how we normally do things. We all know first-hand that Dane doesn't fight fair. We can't keep fighting with respect and expecting that our opponents will have the same." The air between us turns taut. Not even Archer breathes a word. Jaxon's face remains firm, but with another beat, he lets his shoulders drop.

"I think you better go with him," he says coarsely. His words hit like a punch in the gut. I wasn't expecting it. But I should have. Getting him to agree with Kale was never going to be that easy. I hold his gaze for a second longer, then nod and leave the arena.

"And to think I was doubting you'd follow me." Kale smirks as I enter the hall, leaning against the wall with one foot propped up and his arms folded.

I roll my eyes, brushing past him.

"You just had to fight him."

"I was proving a point." Kale pushes off the wall and follows me.

"And you had to fight him to do that?"

Kale mulls on my words for only a second before puckering his lips. "No, I guess not, but it was more fun that way. Don't you think?"

"What I think is that you just wanted to mess with Jaxon because you knew it would upset me. And to be honest, Kale, I'm over playing games with you. We've kept each other distracted for a while, and it's been nice, but I was serious when I told you I wanted to right my wrongs. I want to train. I want to be taken seriously again. And for that to happen, I can't keep slacking off with you. I want to fight with them."

Kale grabs my wrist, spinning me to face him before pushing me up against the wall. 'Fight with me instead,' he whispers, pinning back a piece of my hair while his other hand remains firm on my hip.

"Kale, this isn't a joke." I bat his hand away, but he still holds me in place, his eyes darkening.

"If you want to be taken seriously, play training isn't the way to do it. Fighting like that won't help you against Dane." He's breathing heavily against me. I lift my chin, locking my gaze with his.

"You seem to forget you're not the only one who has fought Dane. Just because I don't like how you handled yourself, doesn't mean I don't agree with you. I know we have to be smarter, to fight better. But there's a way to do that."

"I'm sorry to break it to you, but your buddies don't agree."

"Not true. You didn't give them a chance. You just attacked and expected them to follow you. That's not how it works around here. If we go back in together, if you apologise, we can work something out. We can all learn from each other-"

"Not gonna happen." Kale interrupts.

"And why not?"

"Because, Amrey, I'm not a polite Defiance soldier. Just because you know what it's like to fight Dane doesn't mean you know what I went through. I didn't just learn to fight under Dane, I was trapped by him, tortured. I learnt to think like him. I'm your best bet at defeating him, and you know it."

It's hard to stay stern with Kale when he brings up his past. I still hold so much guilt for what happened to him. I wish I could take back what he went through, take his memories of that time away, his pain. But I can't. I can only help him move forward. Slowly, I draw my hand up his chest, resting it over his heart.

"I haven't forgotten what you went through. And I know I only experienced a fraction of what you did. But you've got it wrong. We don't have to train to be cruel like Dane. We can't. We have to show restraint. We need to. Or we're only going to end up like him."

Kale sighs, his face softening, his hold on me slipping. "That's the thing, Amrey. I'm afraid I'm already too much like him." Then he pushes off me and walks away. I don't know what just happened. But I know he can't mean that.

My chest is heaving deeply when I finally turn around, right into Jaxon's waiting gaze. "Are you okay?" he asks. I suck in a deep breath as he moves to stand beside me, his eyes trained on the space Kale just left.

"I'm fine," I say with a shake of my head, hoping he can't

read between the stress lines on my face, because "fine" is a deep stretch from what I'm actually feeling.

"Owen told me to find you. He said I was too harsh. Do you want to come back in?" He nudges his head towards the door but doesn't take his eyes off me. There are so many unsaid words hanging in the space between us. Hopefully, one day, I'll say them. But for now, I remain silent, and follow Jaxon back into the arena, where I find Mags and spend the rest of the day with her.

I don't blame Kale for how he acted. And I understand why Jaxon did what he did. It's easy to forget sometimes how young we are. I know for a fact, that most of us haven't even processed dealing with the fallout from Axiom. We're all just doing our best to get through every day. To figure it out. I just hope that by the time we do, it's not too late.

CHAPTER FIVE

Blood. So much blood.

It covers my hands. Her body. She's drowning in it, and there's nothing I can do. Something hard and strong wraps around my chest, collapsing my lungs against my heart. I squeeze Mum harder; it's all I can do to keep from falling apart. "Mum, wake up! Wake up! Wake up. Wake up…"

"Amrey, wake up!"

I jolt awake in a gasp. A gloss of sweat covers me from head to toe.

"We need to go."

"Jaxon?" I blink, my eyes stinging as I stare against the light. He's in my room, sitting on my bed. "What are you doing here?" My mind struggles to come back to reality, fragments still lingering in my nightmare. Jaxon watches me tentatively for a moment. How long has he been here? Was I thrashing in my sleep? Can he tell I've just come back from the dark?

My answer is given quickly.

"We have to go," he says, his voice vibrating through the mattress and into my chest. My pulse quickens. "Blane told me to get to the command centre. I stopped here first." His reason doesn't explain why he's waking me up instead of Kale or Owen, but I don't have time to question it.

I sit up and Jaxon's eyes fall to my stomach. I quickly pull my top down. With each second that passes, the reality of this moment hits me harder. Jaxon, out of breath, dressed only in a thin white top, is sitting on my bed. In my room. In the middle of the night.

My body starts feeling things it shouldn't. I can't help it. He's just sitting there, staring down at me, and I feel that stare everywhere. My face. My stomach. My bare legs. A chill spreads over my skin, and I push myself up.

"Give me a second," I manage to say with a steady voice.

"No time. Here." Jaxon throws me a pair of pants, not bothering to turn around as I slip them on. Then, jumping off the bed, I follow him out the door and down the hall.

"Jaxon, wait," I say as we reach the command centre.

"What is it?" He asks, inspecting my eyes before letting his gaze trail down my body. He thinks something's wrong.

"How did you get into my room?" I swear his face blushes three shades of red before he chokes it down and flattens his expression.

"I have a key." That much is obvious, but he doesn't offer anything more.

"How did you get it?" I prompt. Jaxon looks at me like this answer is as obvious as the last. It's not. "However you got it, take it back. You can't just have access to my room whenever you want."

Jaxon's brows rise, my words seeming to incite a challenge. "And what if I didn't have a key? Who would save you while you're sound asleep?" I don't have an answer for that. Jaxon knows it. And instead of waiting for me to come up with words, he turns and walks into the room. I hate when he does that. But it's no use fighting now. More people rush past me into the command centre, and I follow them inside.

Immediately I'm engulfed in the frenzy. No one in the room is properly dressed, and everyone wears the same tight expression.

"Do we sound it?" I hear someone ask.

"They're not close enough yet. They could turn around." That voice I recognise. Blane's. Before I can ask what's going on, I feel a body creep up behind me.

"Nice outfit," Kale's voice tickles the bare skin of my neck, and I turn around, nearly slamming into his chest. "Nice to see you too," he says, reaching out to steady me. "And to think, I thought you'd be mad after how we left things last night. But I see your anger is reserved for someone else today." I turn to follow his gaze. He's staring at Jaxon. "You and lover boy quarrelling?"

"What are you talking about?" I snap. A wrinkle creases my forehead. Did he see Jaxon and me walk here together? The thought has guilt pinching my stomach, and I feel a spell of confusion I can't begin to dissect. Kale loves to tease, but there's something else hidden in his eyes—a hint of anger? I doubt it. But there's something.

"Your mind is too much sometimes," Kale says, watching me sift through my thoughts. Just when he's about to speak again, a piercing alarm sounds.

The siren continues to run for several minutes as the entire Defiance goes into lockdown. The front display lights up, flashing views from each of our security cameras. More people rush in and out of the room. I train my eyes on the screens until I spot Henry with Cynthia, Mags and Makin as they join the rest of their section and lock themselves in the cafeteria.

I keep scanning the feeds, darting from monitor to monitor, watching as one by one, each section of the Defiance locks down. Not a single person is left in the halls. Not a sound can be heard over the alarm. And then suddenly, it stops and all the lights go out, sending the entire base into dark silence.

For a long moment, no one moves or talks. All that's heard is the inhale and exhale of breath—a room of hearts beating as fast as mine. A low drumming begins shortly after, and gradually, the edges of the room begin to glow, providing some light. The front display turns back on, showing the camera views of the Defiance. I can see it's not just the command centre that's lit back up. A soft glow lines the walls of nearly every room in the Defiance. I can no longer make out clear faces, only the outline of bodies, but everyone remains still. The cafeteria holds the most people, and a part of me sighs with relief knowing that Henry is with Mags.

Everyone in the room watches as the last sections come back to life on the screen, and then all heads turn towards Blane.

"What is going on?" I'm the first to speak, my stern voice breaking the nervous silence. Blane regards me for several seconds before moving to the front of the room.

"Four intruders were seen pushing closer to our boundary line. I didn't think it was of concern, but we just got word they have crossed it. If they continue on their trajectory, they'll be on top of us within a quarter of an hour." The air seems to escape everyone's lungs. I don't gasp, but I do narrow my eyes on Blane.

"What's the plan?"

"We're in lockdown. We have no reason to worry just yet. They could walk right over us."

I square my gaze, "This isn't a plan. Have you forgotten about the giant glass roof on the Arena? That's not something you walk past and miss."

"Amrey," Jaxon moves to my side and points to the screens, specifically the one displaying the arena, and I realise the roof is gone—no, concealed—in a material that resembles the colour of stone.

"Thank you," Blane nods to Jaxon before addressing me again. "We've closed off the roof. Hopefully, it'll blend right into the outside surroundings."

"Hopefully," I repeat. The edges of Blane's eyes harden. He opens his mouth to scorn me, I'm sure, but one of the screens begins to flash red.

"They're nearly here," a voice calls, and we all watch as four figures emerge onto the monitor. It's too dark to make out their features, but from their builds, it looks like two women and two men, one of them limping. Their clothes flap against the wind, looking torn and flimsy. One of the women is barely dressed. They don't look like they're going to hurt us. They look like they need saving.

I creep closer to the screen.

"What is it?" Jaxon is at my side again, his voice barely a whisper.

I don't reply. Instead, I keep watching one of the women. It's so dark, but I can just see it. The flash of red. And that's all I need to start running. I rush out of the command centre before anyone can stop me.

"Open the doors!" I scream as my feet pummel over the ground. Jaxon's right on my heels, and when I reach the repository room, he grabs my elbow before I can open the door. I realise now they're still locked. No one listened.

"Amrey, stop!" His voice is sharp, and his grip on me stings as he jolts me to a stop in front of him. My breath is frantic. "It's them, it's Sacha and Dad. I know it's them." Right as the words leave my lips, Kale enters the room, his eyes square on Jaxon. Specifically, his hand which still holds me.

"Is everything okay?" he asks me solely.

"It's them," I repeat, "It's Sacha."

Kale's lip quirks into the slightest grin, "I thought I saw red." However, the relief doesn't meet his eyes.

"I'm sorry, but red hair isn't enough," Jaxon says as he releases my arm, but his stance only hardens.

"The hell it isn't." I move towards the door, but it's no use, it's bolted shut. I don't have the authority to override the system. But Jaxon does.

"Please. You saw them! Even if I'm wrong, they aren't going to harm us. They can barely keep themselves standing."

"It's not my call." He doesn't say I'm wrong or that he doesn't believe me. Only that he can't do what I'm asking. I don't know why that aggravates me more.

"They'll die out there." I'm no longer talking quietly. The repository room is surface level with the ground, hidden only by a few layers of snow. If I wanted, I could scream loud enough for them to hear me. Jaxon seems to see the decision in my eyes. And right as the cry rips from my throat, Blane bursts into the room.

"Blane, you have to open the door!" I whirl at him.

"I know," he cuts me off right as the lights turn on, and the locks on the door disengage.

Jaxon's eyes dart to Blane, "You can't be sure?"

"Rowan managed to get us a closer look. It's them."

Time slows down, but I'm watching everything happen at warp speed. People, faces, rush into the room, gear up and file out into the snow one at a time. I begin to follow them, but Jaxon holds me back, looking down at my legs, my bare feet. I relax in his grip and wait.

The first thing I see is a black boot—or what's left of one. Purpled, blemished skin peeks through a torn, grey uniform. Whether the discolouration is from bruises or the cold, I can't be sure. One leg carries more weight than the other, and blood stains line the tears in the fabric clinging to his torso. I drag my eyes up the rest of the body and suck in a breath.

It's been three weeks since I last saw him. Since he saved me and sacrificed himself. But he looks so different now, so haunted. His face is hollower, his skin three shades too pale, and he has a beard, overgrown and wispy. But his eyes, his eyes are still the same. His dark glowering eyes. Eyes that have watched me grow. Watched me fail. Watched me run. They're the same. And when they meet mine, my whole body stops working.

For just a second, I freeze.

The room continues to move around us, people in and out, covering Dad in blankets and patching up his cuts. As he stands there, accepting the help, his eyes never leave mine, not for a second. I stay unmoving, watching him, like a picture behind glass, too delicate to touch, too scared to see if it's real.

The movement through the door is the only thing to pull my gaze away. Her red hair is the first thing I see, the colour staining nearly every part of her. Sacha's eyes are darker than Dad's, and her arm is cradled against her chest. She winces when her footing slips, and Dad reaches out to steady her, his own legs barely holding him upright. As they lean on one another, their bodies forming a portrait of pain, everything suddenly comes rushing back: Mum's words, Dane's laugh. The ringing of the gun. It all flashes through my mind, pulling me back to that moment. And it's paralysing.

I feel the brush of a body against mine, a blur in my vision, and then it's Henry. I don't know who went to get him. I suspect Owen. I watch from where I stand as he runs right past me, through the crowd of people and straight into Dad's arms.

Everyone in the room watches as they hug. Tears escape Dad's eyes as he bends down and picks Henry up, holding him so tight, I think he might break a rib. He was barely able to hold himself up moments ago and now, it's as if all his pain leaves. It's heartbreaking and heartwarming all at once. The whole room can feel it.

When Dad finally puts him down, his eyes land on me again;

fear prickles my skin, my palms flat against my side. Henry hasn't seen Dad in four years. Three of them he spent thinking Dad was dead. Yet, he ran straight to him without any trepidation. So why can't I?

I can feel Jaxon watching me, Kale too. Everyone is waiting to see what I'll do, and I have no idea.

"Amrey," I hear someone speak my name, but it doesn't come from Dad's mouth, or Henry's.

The voice rips through all the guilt inside me and bursts the floodgates open. Emeric stands at the door, his giant goofy smile, just as deep as before. His skin might look a little weathered, his face tighter, his eyes duller, but it's him. This time I run right into his arms. He wraps them around me. I bury my head into his chest, mumbling "sorry" over and over. He tells me to be quiet. I keep apologising until Emeric pulls me back, hands gripping my shoulders, and then wipes away my tears.

"I'm not going to say I forgive you because there's nothing to forgive. I made my decision to follow you. It was my choice to go in blind. And no matter how much power you think you have over me, I'm sorry to break it to you, but you're not that special." I choke on my tears, a small laugh escaping my throat. "I never once blamed you, Amrey. Now, would you stop the crying, Sub? I'm alright. I just need a drink."

Most people in the room are either laughing or crying now, including the guys, who are each swarming Emeric with hugs. I finally let the relief wash over me, and some of the guilt begins to settle. He's okay. They're okay.

"Let's go get you some food," Owen says, helping Emeric stand.

"I've got it," he grovels, stumbling slightly.

"Yeah, yeah, I know you're strong and tough, but just take our help, will ya." Archer slaps his back, sliding his arm under his other shoulder. Emeric rolls his eyes but just as quickly scans the room.

"Where'd she go?" he says, but not to me or the guys. Emeric turns to Sacha and Dad, and they both look just as perplexed.

"I'm here," a girl's voice breaks through the confusion, and everyone in the room turns towards the door for the final time.

"Elle?"

CHAPTER SIX

I'LL ADMIT IT TAKES ME A MOMENT TO SEE THE RESEMBLANCE. The last time I saw Elle, she was slipping away into the darkness of Axiom's cells. Now she stands in front of me, hands trembling, body swaying, with so much blood mixed into her hair the blond has turned orange. The girl from my memories now stares back at me, her eyes growing big as she takes in all the people watching her. For a moment, she looks like the same scared 12-year-old girl who failed the Axiom test all those years ago.

To my surprise, Kale is the first to rush to her side, his expression unreadable as he speaks close to her ear. I have no idea what he's saying, but Elle seems startled.

"Who's that?" Jaxon asks, sliding into the space beside me. His eyes follow mine to Elle and Kale, still entwined in hushed conversation. I can't help but notice how Kale looks at her—*surprised*, I think. *Protective*. I remember that he knows her. I try not to dwell on it as I watch them talk, but the way he studies her uncoils something in me, and I tear my eyes away.

"She's from Axiom. She was trapped in the cells too."

Jaxons gaze sharpens. "Can we trust her?"

"I don't know, but she is James' sister, so he should be there when the decision's made."

It becomes impossible to hear my own thoughts as more people flood the room. Finally, Blane orders everyone out, instructing them to reconvene in the command centre in an hour.

Jaxon takes it upon himself to find James. Everyone else leaves except Kale, who is now wrapping a blanket around Elle's shoulders. The burning in my chest is still there as I walk into the hallway.

"Amrey!" Henry calls, and I hesitate before turning around.

"Hey, bud," I wince, unable to make eye contact with Dad or Sacha, whose hands seem permanently linked to Henry's.

"Stay with us," he says firmly, like he can sense my objection already coming. He knows me too well for a seven-year-old. I look down at him, and for the first time in weeks, he looks like the little boy I left, full of questions and hope.

"It's okay, Dad and Sacha need to eat and get cleaned up. I'll see them later."

Henry's about to protest when Dad places a hand on his arm.

"She's right, buddy. Amrey probably has a lot of prep to do before the briefing. We'll catch up after." Henry drops his shoulders in defeat, and I hate that I'm disappointing him again. While I'm more relieved than words can describe that they're safe, that doesn't mean I'm ready for family time just yet.

It doesn't mean I'm ready for *her* just yet.

Dad guides Henry away, leaning on him for support, but Sacha idles back.

"Amrey," she says, and my stomach tightens. My name sounds like a prayer on her lips, like it's something she thought she wouldn't get to say again. Something that now holds a whole new meaning. Mum's last words changed everything forever. And I hope Sacha can see in my eyes that I'm not ready to open that wound.

"I'm glad you're okay." That is all I manage to say before

turning and leaving the room. Another drop of guilt slides down my chest.

I'M the only one in the command centre when I hear the door open behind me.

"Having a staring contest with the wall, are you?" I tear my gaze from the dark spot in the corner and face Jaxon.

"I was just thinking," I hum, too tired to put emphasis on meaningless words.

"The silence helps with that," he notes.

"Probably why I've been avoiding it."

Jaxon only looks at me.

"My brain hasn't been a place I've wanted to visit lately."

"Hence the cider," he says, like it's an answer to an invisible question.

"Cider helps quiet thoughts."

"What about Kale? Doesn't he keep you distracted?" It's not a light question, not by any means. Jaxon's smart; he knows what he's asking. Though I won't lie to him about Kale, it doesn't mean I'll answer him either. Jaxon must realise that. Biting into the silence, he sighs and leans against the wall.

"The guilt you wanted to escape from, was that over Emeric?"

I mimic his movements, resting my head back to stare at the ceiling. "It's still there. Even after what he said. I don't think it will ever go away."

"Maybe not, but Emeric was right. What happened was as much our fault as it was yours and his. I'm sorry if I ever made you feel otherwise."

"You didn't," I say quietly, because it's true. Jaxon was never the one who made me feel worse than I already did. I hadn't needed an apology from him, nor had I expected one.

"But thank you. I'm sure I'll believe it one day."

"You will."

I turn to look at Jaxon at the same moment he looks at me. Neither of us says anything more, just taking in the silence and each other. It's the closest we've been since before Mum died. It's the most we've talked since he saved me, and I had forgotten just how much I missed it.

"Jaxon I-" but my words are cut short as the door swings open.

The command centre fills up quickly. It's the early hours of the morning, and judging from the look on everyone's faces, they're hanging on for sleep. Everyone stands around the table, with a map of Axiom in the middle, and the only camera view we have projected on the screen behind us.

Blane stands at the front, next to Dad and Sacha. Emeric and Elle also join them, and James, who now appears glued to Elle's side. The four of them look worse for wear, but at least their cuts have been cleaned and their wounds bandaged up. Dad's right ankle is strapped as he leans on a cane. Sacha's arm is in a sling, and Emeric's face is swollen purple, but Elle looks relatively fine considering.

"It's nice to have you back," Blane says first.

"We are lucky. One more day and we wouldn't have been." There's a long pause after that. Then, Dad leans across the table, pointing to a spot on the map: the cells under the Governor's building. A place I'm all too familiar with. I feel Kale flinch next to me as Dad circles it.

"We were kept here." There's a low deafness that comes after he speaks, one I believe only Kale and I sense.

"What did they do to you?" The whisper of a question comes from somewhere in the back of the room. But Dad doesn't respond. Instead, his eyes meet mine, and Sacha holds herself tighter.

"The details don't matter now. He wanted our blood, our DNA, and he had ways to get it." I shudder at the memory. I hate that Dad and Sacha now share it too.

"We suspected yours would only suffice for so long," Blane comments.

"You would be right. Dane took our blood for a while, but eventually, he stopped. Our DNA isn't what he wants."

"Mine is," I speak up for the first time, grabbing the attention of the room.

"Yes," Dad agrees, meeting my gaze once again. "Amrey is a child of two subversive parents."

My chest tightens. That's the first time he's admitted it. The first time I've heard it be mentioned out loud since Mum. I sense Jaxon looking, but I don't falter my gaze from the front.

"Her DNA is the strongest. It holds the missing component he needs for his serum to work. It's not strong enough without it. We saw it first-hand." Dad looks at Emeric and I suck in my breath, remembering how only days ago we watched him on the screen, marching like a mind-controlled soldier.

Emeric steps forward, "I was kept in the cells at first," he takes a breath, "until they drugged me, or at least that's what it felt like to begin with. It was as if I was floating in my body, and I had no control over it. They ordered me to march, to fight. To carry out tasks, and no matter how much I detested, I still did it."

My stomach clenches. I've had my share of experience with Dane's serums, and I know firsthand what it's like to lose control of your body. It's the worst kind of fear. For me, it only lasted minutes; for Emeric, it was days.

"Eventually, it started to wear off," Emeric continues. "I found myself slowly becoming more in control. It started with being able to change the direction I was walking, to being able to ignore orders. I knew then I had an advantage. And that's when Elle found me."

Elle steps forward, her hair swinging with her steps, her face no longer covered in blood. All that remains is a single gnash above her right eyebrow, three small pieces of tape, pressing it closed. James moves with her like a shadow. Her eyes meet Kale's first, then mine. I wish I could tell what she's not saying.

"I've been kept in the cells since I was twelve," Elle says. You can feel the air sucked out of the room. "After a few years, Dane no longer wanted my blood. I thought that was it for me, but he kept me around. He kept me doing other things." Kale falls stiff at my side. Elle doesn't fill us in on what those things were, but I can tell from the faces in the room that we're all very curious.

"When he finally achieved his mind control serum, I thought that was it. I'd be a droid like the rest of his guard. But he never used it on me. I knew then he had mistaken my fear for loyalty. I could find a way to leave. And I did. I just never took it." She looks at me then, as does everyone. "Even when you came and rescued people from the cells, I didn't go with you. I convinced myself if I did, there'd be no one left to help the others. When in fact, what came next terrified me more than any fate with Dane." I watch Elle fidget under the room's gaze. Up until now, it's the question I've always wondered. Why did she stay? And I'm not sure if I believe this answer.

"After your attack on Axiom, Dane just snapped. He became unhinged in a way I'd never seen him. He killed all the governors and began capturing anyone, even those who weren't subversive. The cells filled up again. I started talking to prisoners, and that's when I found Xavier and Sacha. When they told me who they were to you, Amrey, I knew Dane would want them dead. I had to get them out. And this time, I was going too.

"Being Dane's pawn did come with one benefit. I knew the

guards and their schedules. And with some little help from the faulty wiring, sneaking out of the cells was doable."

My thoughts fade to the memory of escaping with Kale, the blackout Elle caused to free us.

"Getting through Axiom unseen posed the real problem." Elle continues, "we needed a guard on our side, someone to make our act look plausible if we got caught. That's where Emeric came in. One of the jobs Dane delegated to me was administering the serum. I hated it, but it also allowed me to see things. The serum should turn you into a mindless drone, devoid of fear and most emotions. We call it a zombie state. Yet Emeric still flinched at every injection. His eyes still tracked mine when we spoke. It was clear Emeric was subversive. And that's when I started faking his injections."

"It doesn't quite add up though," Archer hums, grabbing everyone's attention.

Emeric shares a look with Elle and says, "She's telling the truth."

"Then explain how we spent weeks attempting to breach Axiom's borders," Archer continues. "They're locked down with guards. You were caught as a result. So forgive me for feeling a little apprehensive that you were just able to sneak out." We all watch as Archer slowly walks over to the table. And though the question was directed at Emeric, his gaze is focused solely on Elle.

"I don't know what you're insinuating," Elle bites.

Archer's eyes rise in a challenge. "I'm not insinuating anything. Yet." The emphasis on his last word is clear.

"My sister saved them from being killed, and you're questioning her?!" James rebuffs, moving to stand in front of Elle. "All you should be saying is thank you."

"She might be your sister, but she said it herself, she's been trapped down there for six years. How do we know where her loyalties lie?" Jaxon's voice surprises me. I look over at him, his back still pressed against the wall, his emotions stoic. Conversations of conflict are not something he usually indulges in unless it's to end them.

"Guys, I know you mean well, but Elle saved us. She got us out and if it wasn't for her, we'd all probably be dead," Emeric comes to her defence, and while I admit I want to as well, I can't dismiss the questions. I don't know Elle all that well. She saved me once, but she stayed behind. While I'll always be grateful to her, I'm not fully convinced there isn't more to her story.

"That's probably what she wants," Archer says, looking at Elle, "for you to be indebted to her."

Elle recoils as if she was slapped in the face. Archer's words have done more than sting; they've thrown a web of doubt over their rescue, and no one seems fully certain anymore.

"Enough," Dad barks, and the room falls prey to the silence, but the tension is palpable. "You will all drop this. Elle saved us. We owe her for that. And we have bigger problems."

I watch Sacha straighten up before she says, "It's not long until Dane has the entirety of Axiom under his control. Our first advantage is that, without Amrey, his serum isn't as strong and needs to be re-administered to hold its effect." Her voice is steady despite the slight shake in her stance. "But by now, he'll have discovered we escaped. We need to tighten our perimeters and double our watches. He'll be coming for us."

Dad's sigh is tight. "And our second advantage is that he doesn't know where we are." His words skate along my nerves, a whisper of chills racing over my spine.

Yet.

I breathe.

Dane doesn't know where we are, *yet*.

CHAPTER SEVEN

IT'S THE EARLY HOURS OF THE MORNING WHEN THE MEETING finally ends. Sleep is long overdue. Everyone disappears to their respective dormitories. I do the same. Reaching my room, I practically stumble through the threshold. I managed to grab a jacket earlier but I'm still shoeless and dressed in slacks, and my room lies in shambles from when I rushed out the door. It feels like days since Jaxon woke me up. Since the alarm went off. But it was only hours ago.

The light turns on.

"Didn't mean to startle you," Kale's voice comes from behind me, and I reach for the wall to steady myself.

"Of course, you didn't," I drawl, not bothering to stay and chat. Leaving him in the doorway I walk to my room. Kale takes that as his invitation to stay. His footsteps approach my bed as the door clicks shut in the background.

"I noticed you didn't stick around to talk to your dad. Or Sacha. They looked like they wanted to chat."

"I'm tired."

"And that's why you're making your bed right now?" Kale tweaks his eyes at me, and I stop and stare at my hands. I hadn't even realised I was pulling up my covers. Letting the blankets slip from my fingers, I sit on the bed.

"I don't want to talk about it."

Kale moves to sit next to me. "Wanna not talk about it together?" He smirks, tilting his head closer. His lips hover in front of mine, teasing, waiting for me to take it. Kale kisses me lightly, his nose grazing mine. My breath becomes heavy, my skin heating up. And suddenly, my hands are in his hair, pulling him in deeper, and the second his tongue touches mine, I'm swallowed by silence.

Kale's hands slide up my back, wrapping around my waist. He presses into me, laying me on the bed, shifting his weight until he rests on top of me. Within the space of five seconds, our kiss goes from sweet to desperate, our limbs a tangle of words our mouths won't speak—eager to quiet our minds.

This has become regular for us. Our lips prevail where our words fail. But this moment feels more intense, and for some reason, I find myself pulling back. Kale looks just as confused when I force us both to sit up. Our lips swollen, and our breaths laboured.

"Why'd you stop the fun?"

"Do you believe Elle's story?"

Kales takes in the question, shifting to a more comfortable position on the bed. "What's not to believe?" he asks, and I can't tell if he's being sardonic or not.

"You know her, don't you?"

Kale's jaw twitches, and he grows silent for several seconds. "I met her in the cells." He breathes finally. "She kept me company from time to time. But no, I don't know her that well."

"So you trust her?"

"Trust isn't something thrown around lightly these days."

"So you don't?"

"I trust what I know. And the truth is Elle could have left when she rescued us. She didn't. It makes me question."

Kale's answer leaves me at a loss. I knew Elle's story was odd, but she saved me and the others. Why would she do that if she was working for Dane? It doesn't make sense. Though, I'm realising, when it comes to Dane, nothing does.

"Regardless, she's here now. All we can do is watch her, and if she's not who she says she is, we'll find out," Kale finishes. I only nod, still wrapped up in my head. So many theories. So many questions.

"But enough of that. We need to get some sleep, and I have just the thing to help," he says. I sit and watch as Kale reaches next to the bed for a bag I didn't even notice he came with and pulls out two bottles of cider. Cider is the last thing I need or necessarily care for, but he's popped open the bottles and has poured me a cup before I can refuse.

Kale places the glass in my hands and clinks his own against it.

"To silencing the voices." And with that reminder, I'm more inclined to drink.

"To silence," I say back, the cider burning my throat on the way down.

When I wake up, my mind's cloudy, and there's a searing pain coming from my right shoulder. But at least no nightmares last night. I roll over on the bed. Kale's gone. The small clock I fixed to the nightstand says it's mid-morning. I've slept too long. I jump up, the pain in my shoulder intensifies, and I grab the wall to steady myself. It must be the cider or the quick movement because the blood rushes from my head faster than I can handle, and the room drops out of focus.

By the time I shower and skull some water, my head isn't ringing so loud, though my shoulder is still stiff. I must have slept on it wrong, but I don't even remember falling asleep. The two bottles of cider sit on my kitchen bench in answer. *Idiot*, I mutter, sweeping them into the bin and walking into my room to collect the glasses. Once they're washed and my room's clean, I head out. Training was pushed back because of last night's events, so I haven't missed it, but I did miss breakfast. Not a good impression to make the day your father returns.

"Cider helps quiet thoughts," I had said to Jaxon.

And it has.

When Emeric was taken and Kale slipped the cider in my hand for the first time, I didn't know what to expect. But the bitter liquor shut my mind off. It numbed the pain. Only I'm not sure I need it any longer and I'm getting over the lingering fogginess it causes.

Out of curiosity, I decide to visit the command centre before going to the arena. When I arrive, there's a meeting happening inside, but I don't enter. I simply lean against the door and listen quietly to the voices. They're muttering about extended patrols and perimeter checks, but I hear nothing of my plan. After Elle's ramblings and Dad's insistence on tightening our perimeter, I spoke my mind. We should be going after Dane, weakening his defences, and for once, I think Blane might have agreed with me. Though, like usual, my words were left to be thought over. *Discussed*. And it seems there's still no decision. So, I bite my tongue and continue to the arena. By the end of the day, I'll have an answer, and until then, I'll train.

The smell of the arena is always pungent: earth, mud, must, and the dew from the cave walls. It's beautiful in its simplicity. I missed it—more than I realised. Though it seems Henry has become accustomed to this place in my absence. I spot him stretching with the other kids and try to make eye contact, but he doesn't spare a glance in my direction. I guess it will take more than just having Dad back for him to forgive me. And now that Dad is back in charge, I'm not overly surprised to see Blane in the arena—back in his role of head of defence, and our ass-kicking.

"I guess Jaxon's no longer leading training," I say, reaching Mags. She startles slightly, tearing her gaze from Blane and the boys. "This isn't Axiom, Mags. Stare all you want."

Caught out, her cheeks bloom pink, but then she whispers, "Maybe I will," and her gaze finds the boys again. My gaze finds Emeric, who winks at me. I'm not surprised to see him here. Besides looking a little tired, he seems perfectly fine. Though, I'm pretty certain he was told to sit training out. I shake my head at that, then stop, surprised by the figures approaching. Elle is currently walking over with James. I'm about to intercept them when the door slams shut, the bang echoing through the cave chamber.

Kale saunters over, looking rugged and a little tired.

"Where were you this morning?" I ask when he reaches me.

"Just thought I'd take a page from your book and leave while you're asleep. Why? Did ya miss me?"

I roll my eyes.

"Thought so." He smirks, just as Blane takes command of the arena.

"Welcome to today's Battle Games."

"The what?" Kale looks at me like this is something I've done. My expression shows him it's not and my stare finds Jaxon's from across the group. He only shrugs his shoulders.

"In light of recent events, I've decided it's time for a shake-up. Each of you shares one thing in common. You want to defend the Defiance. But today, instead of just training to fight, I think it's time you all get to know each other better. To realise exactly who it is you're fighting for. Therefore, today's games will be competed in teams." Blane turns to Griffin, who hands him three different colour ties. Black, red and white. "Your teams will face off in three challenges, testing your skill, endurance and perception."

"Who picks the teams?" Kale asks. Blane releases a tensed breath, his face still primed tight as he holds the ties in his hand. "I do."

He does. After ten minutes, the teams are decided.

The white team consists of Mags, Griffin, Emeric and Griffin's younger sister, Helena. I didn't realise the twins had a younger sister, but she seems to be hanging out with Henry, which makes me happy. I'm in the red team with Owen, Archer and Henry. I know Blane did that on purpose.

The final team, the black team, is the most polarising, consisting of Kale, a young boy named Tobias, Jaxon, James and Elle—who remains glued to James' side like he's a shield. Blane didn't seem convinced that Elle should even participate, but this was the compromise, leaving the black team with five members.

"You will each be assigned one of the kids to mentor during the games."

I look over at Henry, Helena and Tobias. They look so young, so innocent. "It will either be your strength or your weakness but only you can determine which." Blane then tilts his head and motions the kids forward with a nudge of his chin. Henry barely looks at me as he strides over.

Everyone is given a coloured piece of ripped fabric. I tie mine around my wrist. Owen wraps his around his head and swipes some dirt on his cheeks. Henry copies, putting two stripes of mud under his eyes. Archer helps him fix his tie the same. I offer to help, but he just ignores me.

The other teams also seem to be getting into it. I try to make eye contact with Mags, but she's too busy fastening Emeric's and her ties around their respective arms.

"The first game is *water run.*"

We all look towards the narrow part of the cavern at the lake resting on its fringe. "Each team will have 15 minutes to fill their drum with water." Blane walks over to the edge of the bank and we all follow.

"Fill the big bowl with water. Sounds easy enough," Owen jeers, nudging Archer in the arm. He doesn't return the amused expression.

Blane looks blankly past all our faces, his gaze drawn to the mud crawl, where a single beam has been placed one metre above it. I follow, noticing the opening of the arena and the three tall drums that now sit there.

"Or maybe not so easy," Owen hums. Archer rolls his eyes.

"The drum is ten gallons in size. You will need to collect your water from here, using whatever you can find. And carry it over the mud to your drum." Blane continues. "The team who fills theirs the most in the allocated time, wins the advantage for the second game."

When his words settle, so does everyone's previous enthusiasm.

And this is only the first challenge.

I notice Henry fidgeting nervously beside me. The other kids look much the same. We all take our places on the bank, the water already lapping at my ankles. When Blane calls for time to begin, Archer shoots into action. He told us he knew where the buckets were; I was fine with him handling that portion. I watch the other groups. It seems they also have the same idea. Both Griffin and Jaxon chase Archer, and the three of them race it out to the weapons shed by the entrance. Buckets aren't something I'd expect to find there, but sure enough, a minute later, Archer springs back towards us, a bucket hanging from each of his hands. Jaxon and Griffin are on his tail. When he reaches the bank, he doesn't bother for a handoff. Running straight into the lake, he dunks the buckets under, choking them with water before hauling himself back towards the top of the arena.

Archer moves quickly, and within minutes, he's made it to the mud pool and onto the balance beam. And even though Jaxon's nipping at his heels. His steps don't slow one bit. His movement is controlled as he strides over the beam and down the steps. I'll admit, it's impressive. But Archer has always been competitive, his focus is unfaltering, and his dedication to the challenge is intense. At least this time, it's in my favour.

Our drum is painted red. It looks smaller from here, but when Archer reaches it, it stands nearly as tall as him. And I realise now, that filling it up in fifteen minutes isn't as achievable as I might have thought. But that doesn't mean we can't fill it up the most.

Archer barely stops for a breath as he tosses the water into the drum and speeds back towards us. Owen nudges me forward when he sees Archer approaching, and I take that as, "you're up," but my heart is in my chest when I notice Emeric is also lining up to start. I can't race him. I can't try to beat him, not after everything.

"I know what you're thinking," Owen says, placing a hand on my shoulder. "But doing anything less than your best right now would be an insult to Emeric. He's not weak, and that's all you'd be implying." My jaw is tight, but I nod and brace myself for Archer's impact.

The buckets are barely in my hands when my feet leave for the water. I engulf them under the surface seconds later. If my count is right, we still have ten minutes, long enough for Archer to have a second run. I just have to be quick. But as soon as the buckets are full, my arms fall like logs to my side. I hadn't realised watching Archer that the flimsy things must fill to at least three litres each, heavier than I've carried in a long time. But despite the burn in my arms, I don't stop, only looking up as my feet carry me out of the water and off the bank. The entrance of the arena is 200 yards away, which isn't too far, except when you're carrying six litres of water. By the time I reach the mud, I'm exhausted. Sucking in a breath, I tense my stomach, holding myself together as I climb the steps to the beam. My forearms are so taut they could snap off at any moment, but I don't hesitate. Without a second thought, I place my foot on the wood, digging my toes into the panel, trying to keep my balance and the water from spilling.

"Better hurry up there, Sub."

My heart lurches as Emeric comes up behind me. I know he wants to win, and after everything, I want that for him. But Owen's voice is clear in my mind. Emeric wouldn't want me to throw the challenge. It would be an insult if I did. So, I need to push forward. I need to move.

Taking one deep breath, I focus on the steps off the beam and run—one foot after the other. Squeezing my muscles tight, I keep moving, not leaving my feet down long enough to wobble. And when I reach the steps, I finally let myself breathe, the shakiness pouring out of me as I climb down. My knees almost give way as I run, but I managed not to lose too much water, and by the time I've emptied both buckets, our drum is a little over a third full. I look over at the black team, the water line is not as high. I grin obnoxiously, turning around and sprinting as fast as I can back to the bank, collapsing into Owen as I swing the buckets to Henry.

"You got this!" I wheeze, but he's already taken off running to the water. I watch him fill them both to the top. Three litres on each arm is too much for him to carry. I yell just that, but he swats my words away with a jarring stare.

"Telling him what to do won't help him," Owen says next to me. "You have to let him figure this out for himself." I look over at Helena and Tobias, struggling the same, and I realise he's right. So, I let him go, his steps swaying as his arms hang like dead weights at his side, his fingers coiled tightly around the bucket handles. His feet stagger and slow, but Henry makes it to the mud first. I hold my breath as he climbs the steps to the beam.

"Balance. One foot in front of the other," I find myself whispering. "That's it, one step at a time. Slower, slower, steady, STEADY." He makes it halfway across the beam before he falls. My heart drops to my stomach as he scrambles up, fetching the now empty buckets and charging back towards the water. He repeats his steps faster than the first time. He's barely behind when he reaches the beam again, all three kids attempting to cross it.

I listen to Mags and Emeric's voices ring through the arena as they encourage Helena forward. I think about doing the same, but stop myself. I don't want to distract him. Jaxon has the same tactic, watching Tobias keenly across from me, though Kale only looks at the ground, bored.

"Straighten up!" Owen yells, and my eyes dart back to Henry. His feet teeter on the beam. I watch him bend and sway, fighting gravity to stand upright. The buckets dip, water splashing over the edge. Helena has now made it off her beam and begins to walk over to the white drum, but her steps are slow. Henry can still make it, he just needs to hurry. His feet continue to wobble, and now I know he needs more than my silent thoughts. Leaving Owen's side, I run up to the mud; he's managed to stabilise himself, but he's barely moved a step when I get there.

"Stop looking down," I say. Henry pinches his face, but he doesn't look at me.

"I'm fine," he bites, stammering as he moves forward a step. His grip on the buckets looks painful. "It's okay if you lose water," I tell him, stepping closer to the beam. "Just focus on crossing, one step at a time, contract your muscles, eyes ahead." I don't know if Henry's even taking in my words, for he offers nothing in response. But from the corner of my eyes, I see Tobias straighten his shoulders and tilt his gaze ahead as he takes a few more steps. At least someone is listening.

Henry sways again. I wince, but he manages to hold himself steady.

"Stop looking down," I say again, and this time, Henry does hear me. With a growling breath, he whips his head in my direction.

"I don't want your help," he snaps, his eyes flashing with an anger I've never seen—built up, simmering, and targeted at me. "You're making it worse." And with that, his feet wobble again. Henry grunts.

"Hey buddy, you've got this. Shoulders back, look straight ahead!" Owen suddenly appears at my side, his hand on my arm as he tugs me back. "We'll be waiting for you on the bank." I try not to look too stunned as I turn around and let Owen guide me.

Henry doesn't want my help. He doesn't want anything to do with me. I wish I was more surprised, more hurt, but Henry's anger towards me isn't a surprise. Since the moment I escaped, I had a choice. Henry needed me by his side to help him get through everything, but Dane had just murdered our mother, who turned out not to be my biological mother. The hatred I bore then was not one I wanted around Henry. I needed to keep him away —from the missions, from the truth. He didn't need to know how bad it was. It didn't matter if I thought I was protecting him. He only saw it as me staying away, ignoring him. That's all I see when I look in his eyes now. He just turned seven, but time has aged him years.

I watch from the bank as Henry finally crosses the beam. He did well despite my apparent distraction. Owen squeezes my arm. "He's just young. He'll come around." I nod. When Henry makes it back, flinging the buckets at Owen, I remain silent, waiting for him to catch his breath, to acknowledge my presence or say something. But he doesn't.

"You did great," I say hesitantly.

Henry's shoulders tighten as he replies, "no thanks to you."

I refrain from reacting. Instead, I swallow my spite and grin through it. "I was only trying to help."

"Why? It's not like you care about me or our family." Henry's words shock me silent for a good ten seconds. He's wrong. I have to tell him he's wrong. But the words fail to form on my lips, and instead, I stand mute as he walks away.

"Family trouble?" Archer says with a bemused look. I glare in return, turning to watch as Owen makes it to the beam.

"Are you kidding?" Archer slaps his leg in frustration, as Owen drops the buckets and circles back to the bank. "He did that on purpose to let Griffin win, I just know it."

I watch Archer closely. "And that bothers you?"

He regards me for a moment, "My relationship doesn't pay favour over my team. I want to win. If we're bested, it better be because we suck, not because Owen gives it away."

I only nod. Time is almost up when Owen reaches the bank. He must realise this too, for instead of running back into the water again, he simply drops the buckets and waits for Blane to call time.

We come in last which is no surprise to any of us except maybe Blane whose stare pierces me like a disapproving parent. I shake it off and follow everyone back to the top of the arena.

"Well, that was a bust," Owen says, clearing his throat.

"Only because you dropped the buckets," Archer scowls.

"Calm down buddy," Owen slaps him on the back. "It's only one challenge; we still have two more." The tension between the two of them is thick, and Archer storms ahead. It seems that no matter the friendship nothing should come between Archer and winning.

"What was that?" I hiss at Owen when both Archer and Henry are out of earshot.

"What do you mean?"

"Archer says you dropped the buckets on purpose so Griffin would win. Did you?" Owen looks appalled.

"Now come on, Sub, do you really think that's something I'd do? Besides, if I did, it wouldn't be for my brother." That puzzles me. I take a step back, watching where his gaze lands. On the white team, on Mags. Of course.

"You're ridiculous, you know that," I sigh, giving him an eye-roll so big it makes me dizzy.

"I don't know what you're talking about," Owen laughs.

"Say what you want, but so you know, Mags wouldn't be impressed with flattery. Especially if you think giving the win to her is a nice gesture."

Owen's mouth hangs open, looking at me stupefied. He decides to keep whatever sarcastic comment he has on his tongue to himself. Biting it down, he just nods. "Noted."

"For most of you, that game was easy. But for some reason, I find that nearly all of you failed except for the white team." Blane looks over at Mags and Griffin. Emeric and Helena. The winning team. "They won the first challenge, not because they were faster or more skilled, but because they worked as a team. They encouraged each other and repositioned their weaknesses to make them strengths." I look over at them sourly. I'm not jealous they won. I'm envious of their amity, something our team is lacking.

"Now, as promised, the winners get an advantage." We all watch as Emeric walks over to Blane, a devilish grin spreading across his face as he learns the second challenge.

CHAPTER EIGHT

The second game is Cypher Seek.

Blane circles around us, his hands clasped behind his back. The objective: solve the riddle and bring him the answer. After the last game, I'm itching for the win, especially as the white team has already been given the riddle and is whispering off to the side.

"What is it, buddy?" Owen asks as Henry races back over to us. Blane had picked him and Tobias as the team representatives to receive the riddle, making me even more nervous.

"Um..." Henry swallows, closing his eyes, his little face scrunched as he speaks carefully. "I'm needed all the time, but you often forget. I can give life and take it with one breath. I'm a body without a soul, a necessity for survival. But lay claim to my clutches, and death awaits your arrival."

When Henry finishes, his big eyes open, and he meets my gaze first.

"Good job," I whisper, but he ignores it, turning to Owen to repeat the riddle. Tobias is doing the same to the black team. I steal a glance at Kale, who winks at me, puckering his lips. I roll my eyes, shaking it off and see Blane make his way to the front of the arena, where I assume he'll wait for an answer. By the looks of it, he'll be waiting a while. Not one team seems to be getting it, not even the white team with the head start.

Archer repeats the riddle a few more times as if the mere act of it will make the answer appear.

"He has to be talking about an object," Owen says a little too loudly, and Archer slaps him on the back.

"Next time, why don't you just walk over and give them the answer?" he whines. I peek over at the others. Thankfully, none of the groups have figured it out yet, which gives me some hope.

"It could be food?" I suggest.

"No," says Henry.

"A lighter?" Owen throws out. This time Archer and I join Henry.

"No," we say in unison. Owen rolls his eyes.

"Then what?"

"I don't know," Archer hums, "but it has to be something we can hold. Blane said to bring it to him. Maybe something we use to fight, that we forget we need, but can be used to kill, meaning survival?"

"Yeah, that has a body?" Owen jokes, but the second the words leave his lips, something in Henry's eyes sparks to life, and before I can ask what he's thinking, he pivots on his heels and is running. We all follow him to the weapons shed as he scrambles around.

"What is it, buddy? What are you looking for?"

"A knife," he pants, digging through a box of vests, some riddled with bullet holes. The sight brings back a memory. Those trials seem like another lifetime ago, back when I wanted so badly to prove myself worthy, to save Henry and Mum. Despite all that has changed, my need to protect Henry hasn't.

Something metal clatters on the ground, jarring me from the thought.

"Here!" I say, fetching a dummy knife from the wall and

handing it to Henry. "But are you sure it's the answer?" He snatches it up, ignoring my comment and runs out of the shed. The three of us follow him over to Blane. Henry holds out his hand with the blunt blade in his palm.

"This is the answer. A knife." His tiny chest heaves in a few breaths as he waits for Blane to accept the blade and name him the winner.

Except he doesn't.

"I'm sorry, but that is not the answer. Keep searching."

Henry goes still for a few seconds, his hand still distended in front of him. His eyes grow big, but he doesn't cry. Sometimes I forget he's only seven. He's so mature for his age. He's grown up years in only months. I hate that for him.

Archer interrupts the silence with a grunt and shake of his head and stalks back to the bank where the other groups are. Henry's outburst had caused a commotion, but they all quickly went back to trying to decipher the riddle.

"It's all right buddy," Owen says, taking the knife from Henry's open hand. "We'll just keep looking." He moves to return the blade to the shed, leaving me with Henry. I reach for his shoulder to guide him back towards the bank, but he shakes my hand off and storms ahead. Watching the smile fade from Henry's face is crushing, and I can't take it anymore.

"Henry," I call, hurrying to catch up.

"What?" He grunts, stopping to face me.

I pause for a moment. I guess part of me didn't expect him to give me the chance to speak, and now I find myself at a loss for words. I want to say it will get better, that this is just a game. But those facts don't matter to a seven-year-old. They won't mean anything to Henry. And there's something else I need to say that's long overdue.

"I'm sorry." I sigh. "For everything. You have every right to be mad at me. I know I've sucked as a big sister lately. I've been selfish and distant, but I'm going to be better. I promise."

Henry's face softens, just slightly, the tiniest, slyest hint of a smile playing at the corners of his lips. "You have sucked." Then, he turns back around and keeps walking towards the edge of the bank. "Well," he calls behind him. "Aren't you going to help me figure this out?"

We walk the rim of the water for a few minutes, both of us replaying the riddle over and over. During that time, the white team brought Blane a match and a lighter. Owen eyed us dangerously as we waited to see if they were correct. Archer would have hated it if Owen's suggestion was the answer.

Thankfully, it wasn't.

"So, why did you think it was the knife?" I ask after the white team returns to their search. Henry looks at me like the answer is obvious. "I'm sorry, but you know I'm not good with puzzles."

"This is a riddle, Ry. Not a puzzle." My heart does a flip when he uses my nickname, and I try not to scare him away with my giant smile. Luckily, he's too busy looking at the water.

"I thought it was a knife because it has a body, and you need it to hunt food, and you need food to survive. It kills animals but gives food to humans."

"And its clutches make you await death's arrival?" I ask curiously.

"The knife is the clutch. It's a weapon. The blade is sharp and can kill you. So, you meet death." Henry kicks at the water. I can see the cogs in his brain ticking over. He's so smart for his age, too smart for his own good sometimes. A part of me wishes he wasn't, that he would just be a kid and do mindless things, but that's not Henry. It wasn't me either. It doesn't run in our blood.

"That makes sense," I finally say.

"I was so sure…" Henry groans, "but now I don't know what other object it could be."

"Technically," I say, slowing my steps. "Blane never said it was an object, just that we had to bring it to him."

"But if it's not an object, then what is it?" Henry huffs. His frustration is palpable, and I don't want to see him lose another round of this game.

"Hey, why don't we stop and go get a drink?" I ask softly. "I'm thirsty and could use a break before the next round of whatever Blane has in store." I thought my subtle attempt at diverting Henry from another defeat was well intended. But he doesn't register it at all. Instead, he stops completely in his tracks, the abruptness causing the water to splash over both our ankles.

"What did you say?" he mumbles.

"That we should take a break?" Confusion creases my face as I watch Henry's small eyes beam wide. And then he's running again.

"What does he think it is now?" Archer moans, both he and Owen walking over to join me.

"I don't know, but be nice if he's wrong," I throw a stern look at Archer, right as Henry comes back with a bucket.

"I don't think-" but before I can finish, Henry throws the bucket in the water and fills it up.

"We've finished that game buddy," Owen says gently.

"It's water," Henry wheezes, seeming to be taking his first breath since he ran off with the bucket.

"This," he says, pointing at the lake. "Is a body of water. Water is something we can't live without, but we always forget to drink it. It can give life or take it with a breath. And if you can't swim, you lay claim to its clutches."

"You drown," I finish his sentence.

"And death awaits your arrival," Owen says and we all stare at each other with wide eyes.

"You're right," Archer beams, taking the bucket from Henry's hand as Owen picks him up.

"Let's go!"

The four of us, Henry on Owen's back, race towards Blane with giant smiles on our faces. Henry laughs with every bump and jump. It's the most fun I've ever had sprinting in this arena. And when we make it to Blane, Archer gives Henry the bucket, his little hand gripping it so tightly as he hands it over.

"The answer is water," he says confidently.

Blane's eyes narrow at the corner, and he presses his lips into a smile. "That is correct."

"Yes! We won!" Owen bellows, picking up Henry and swinging him around. "Sub, your brother is a little genius."

"He is," I laugh, pulling him in for a hug once Owen sets him back on the ground. Henry wraps his arms around me and a million tiny weights lift off my chest.

"So what did we win? What's our advantage for the next game?" Archer asks, and Blane looks at him studiously.

"Nothing." His tone is ominous.

"But I got it right?" Henry stammers, looking at Blane through slitted eyes, his long lashes tinged with tears. The child I often miss in him comes out. Blane's expression softens only just.

"You did, but you weren't the first team to solve the riddle. The black team was."

"Hell yeah!" James triumphs, high-fiving Kale. The memory flashes then, back to Axiom, back to our final combat exam. Kale had sought to protect me from my fight with James, and in that gesture, I mistook their relationship for enemies, when, in actuality, they had been friends.

James' haughty laugh echoes through the arena, the white team making their way over. Archer is looking at James with the same glare of annoyance I feel. James hasn't done anything outrightly wrong, except for trying to kill us all when he worked for Dane. But it seems Blane's moved past that. Elle, however, still stands at his side, looking shaken.

"Alright then," Blane's voice cracks through the air. "Who's ready for the final game?"

CHAPTER NINE

PELLETS FLY AT MY HEAD AS I DIVE UNDER THE BARRICADE WE made of old crates and a torn-up tarp.

"Watch out!" Owen shouts. I dust off my pants, giving him a piercing stare. I feel for the gun saddled to my side as I peek through the small wedged gap of my barricade and look out over the arena. In the space of an hour, Blane had it turned into a battlefield.

I duck my head as mud pellets smash against the crate, just missing me. "Mudball," as Blane called it, started 15 minutes ago. So far, four people have been hit: Elle and the kids. It's tough, but they were easy targets, and we're a competitive bunch.

"Amrey!" I turn towards Archer and Owen, crouched behind the water drum we used in the first game. "Look." They signal towards the bank where Emeric and Mags are shooting at me.

"I know," I mouth, throwing my hands in the air, "But I'm a bit stuck."

The objective is to be the last team standing. Or the last one. The winning team only needs one representative, so we have a three-in-nine chance. Archer's genius plan is to target one team at a time, starting with the white, hence why I'm currently crouched under a crate, deflecting mud pellets. My job is to be the moving target, a distraction for all the teams to shoot at while Archer and Owen make their move, beginning with Griffin. They just haven't made it yet.

"Hurry up!" I curse at them, letting off a round of pellets, trying to draw fire away from me. The pellets might be made of mud, but at the speed they're flying, I'm not in any way excited to be hit by one.

"We've got you!" Owen calls right as he and Archer fire at Griffin, who had taken up post next to the weapons shed. Griffin falls to the ground, cradling his now muddied knee. Poor guy never saw them coming.

The arena is still ringing with the sound of shots while I watch Griffin hobble over to the other eliminated team members. He's the fifth person out, but the look he gives the boys makes me think he's not so sad about it.

"Amrey!" Owen calls, drawing me back into the game. "GO!"

"Got it!" I grimace, scrambling into a better position. Then, training my gun through a gap in the crate, I start firing wildly at the bank. It's not at anyone in particular, but the erratic pellets cause both teams to stop shooting for a moment, long enough for Owen and Archer to move out behind the small protection of the drums and next to me.

"That was close," Owen wheezes.

"You took down Griffin pretty harshly," I say.

"It worked, didn't it," Archer replies flatly, and I raise my brows, resisting the urge to comment.

"Remind me never to get on your bad side," Owen mutters.

Archer smirks, "Oh, I will. Now who do we target next?"

Five minutes later, it seems we've made an ally of the Black team. After targeting Griffin, they caught onto our idea and turned their guns away from us and solely on Mags and Emeric —the only two left in the white team. From our vantage point, I can see James circling behind them as we shoot from the front. Mags and Emeric are completely unaware of James, and a part of me wants to give them a heads-up, but this is a game, and Archer will shoot me out the moment I do. So, instead, I watch anxiously from behind our cover as James fires two shots, eliminating Emeric and Mags, leaving only six of us in the game.

Black vs Red.

"Time," Blane calls, signalling for dead air—meaning no shots fired in the next two minutes. Time to reset.

"What's the plan?" I whisper to Archer, refilling pellets in my gun. He has taken point in this game, and his tactics have proven useful so far, so I'm happy to oblige.

Archer holds a finger to his lips as he peeks out from behind the crate and looks over at the other team. "Jaxon and Kale are stationed on the bank behind a set of crates, and James is flanking their left."

"We need to draw them out," Owen says.

"Yes, but James is on his own. We need to go for him first," Archer's voice is so sharp that neither Owen nor me test it.

"How do we do that from here? All my shots just bounce off the crates," I huff, trying to get a better look at the Black team.

"Well..." Archer hums, sharing a smirk with Owen. I look between the pair.

"You want me to be bait again, don't you?"

"It worked with Griffin," Owen cowers sheepishly. I shake my head with a sigh.

"Fine, but you better not let me get shot. I do not feel like getting a giant bruise today."

"Yes ma'am," The boys salute. I roll my eyes, punching their arms right as Blane's voice bites the air. Go time.

Within seconds, the stillness of the arena breaks, and pellets begin smashing against our cover. Archer, Owen and I hunch closer together in the small protections of our makeshift fort, three singular crates stacked together. None of us have fired off a shot yet. But the black team's tactic seems to be shoot and don't stop. James, though, has started calling out absurdities through the arena, and Owen's and my hands eagerly tighten over our guns, aching to shut him up.

"Wait," Archer warns, "He's just trying to goad us. Don't listen to him." But the more James says, the more I want to smack the words from his lips, and I'm not the only one.

"Oh, that's it," Archer grinds, looking past me, through the gaps in the crate at James. A sweetly dangerous smile dances across his lips as he says, "This is going to be fun."

All three of us load off a round of pellets.

One after the other, they crack through the air like a storm, and the entire black team cower behind their barricade. That's when I make my move. Ducking out from behind the crates, I make a run for it. I know I only have a few seconds before they're shooting again. Owen and Archer keep firing from behind me as I sprint past the mud crawl, towards the far-left side of the bank. It's a far run to the barricade—that we hammered together using pieces of old wood and planks—but it backs onto the cave wall, leaving me well protected, and a hard shot for anyone in the black team. James will have to come out of hiding to get a hit anywhere near me, which is exactly what we want. I just have to make it there first. And I almost do, when Kale spots me.

I dive.

My arms are outstretched in front of my head as I slam onto the ground, sliding into the side of the cave with a thud. My body burns as it skids against the cold stone, and I feel layers of skin peel back as my uniform tears under the jutted rock. But I'm mud-free. The pellets missed me by just an inch, mud splattered around my ankles and knees. I hear Owen wallop a cheer, and I can't help but smile fiercely, even as blood begins seeping from my grazes. Time for phase two.

MY STARE MEETS Jaxon's from across the bank. He narrows his eyes thoughtfully, then raises his gun, both our weapons pointed at each other. My finger resting on the trigger.

"Amrey, make the shot," I can hear Archer's grunts in my ears, though he's nowhere near me. Tearing my eyes from Jaxon's I fire.

It misses.

Or, in other words, Jaxon ducks.

"Dammit!" Owen's curse pierces the arena as his pellets also miss Kale. But it doesn't matter; our shots have done their job—distracting them. While the boys duck for cover, Archer has made his way closer to the bank, crouched behind two casks we rolled out from the shed, directly opposite me on the other side. We have them flanked. Archer gives me a thumbs up from across the bank, and I think we might actually have this in the bag.

NO ONE HAS MADE a move in minutes, though I can hear the distant sound of voices whispering. I'm closer to the black team than my own. And while I strain my ears to make out a few words, I know our gambit's paying off. To win, one of them has to shoot me. Meaning, someone has to come out of hiding long enough to get a good hit. The closest to me is James. He is our target. And right on cue, I see him slip out from behind his cover and move closer to me on the bank. Archer and Owen both have better vantage points on James. I just have to give them the moment to shoot. Which, in other terms, is called being bait. Something much harder said than done.

I hear James creeping closer, his feet grating louder on the stone. But I don't shoot. I don't move. I pretend I don't hear him. I pretend to be looking somewhere else. My fingers coiled tightly around the trigger. James dips behind another cover, but that is his last. To shoot me he has to be in the open, and that should be all the time the guys need.

Seconds feel like milliseconds as I wait for James to make his move.

I barely have time to squeeze my eyes shut when he steps out from behind his cover, and a round of pellets flies through the air. I throw myself against the ground, but I'm not hit. Slowly crawling up, I hear James groan as he rolls over on the stone, covered in mud and holding his leg.

"Yes!" I shriek. Peaking my head out to smile at Owen and Archer, except Owen's not smiling, he's on the ground. And out of the corner of my eye, I see Kale, gleaming.

Dammit.

"Amrey," Archer calls, getting my attention before ducking just in time to avoid Jaxon's pellets. I don't know what he's trying to say, but I have to keep my wits about me. There are only two of us left now. We might be flanking them, but this is still anyone's game, and Jaxon and Kale have the upper hand by being together. Though, they don't appear to be communicating at all and neither of them seems to be shooting at me. I guess they haven't decided who will be taking that shot. Who will risk being out in the open? Or maybe neither of them will. I watch them target Archer, instantly realising what they're thinking. Or what Jaxon is. They're gonna pick him off, then corner me. And I'll be damned if I let that happen.

Archer's taking all the heat right now, and while I feel bad, we only need one person standing from our team at the end to win. I've just decided that's going to be me.

So, with Kale and Jackson's back turned, it's my chance to get a better vantage point. Not waiting for a break in the pellet fire, I stand up and make a break for it. Archer's eyes meet mine briefly, and he sprays the air with pellets as I run. I don't stop until I'm safely behind James' old cover—two metal drums that keep me low to the ground. It's only then I allow myself a second to breathe and look out at the arena. That's when I see Archer's muddied clothes.

He's shot.

I'm the only one left in the red team.

I'm stuck on the battlefield with Jaxon and Kale.

Lords help me.

The best thing about my current position isn't just that it's diagonally behind them. It's that they don't know I'm here. I've been lying flat on the ground, watching them through the slit in the drums, while their eyes stay fixed on the old wooden crate I'm no longer behind. Neither of them wavers or makes a move to shoot my way. Instead, Jaxon looks harder at Kale.

"Amrey's better than this," he says, like what he's referring to is obvious. Like they've had this conversation before.

"Maybe," Kale mutters, scanning the arena. I hold my breath for a second, but with how casually they're speaking, I don't think they know I can hear them.

"You're dragging her down a dark hole," Jaxon watches Kale fiercely.

"Hate to break it to you, but if you think I'm dragging Amrey anywhere, you don't know her well enough. I might not have a saviour influence like you but I'm not making her do anything she doesn't want to," Kale says, coolly.

"You might be right. But you could put a stop to it." Jaxon's expression is unreadable. He's become good at hiding his emotions.

"And why would I want to do that? What we do in private is our business."

"You're not good for her."

"Jealousy is not a good look on you," Kale says, sounding

pleased with himself. Jaxon looks away, unamused. All the while my pulse is racing, and not from the game.

"My feelings don't matter. But Amrey's a smart girl. She'll figure you out eventually, and when she does, I'll be here like I always have been." Jaxon's words rip the air from my chest. I feel almost guilty for hiding, for listening for so long. I should move, break away before they notice me. But then I see Kale. He looks mutinous, and before I know it, he lunges at Jaxon.

The shock jolts me to my feet as I watch the boys, tussling and clawing at each other on the ground. My pulse quickens as I come up behind them, hoping my presence will snap them out of it. It doesn't.

"Stop!" I shout. They don't listen. I yell louder, but my words don't pierce their ears. It's useless. So, raising my gun, I aim it straight and shoot them both in the chest.

Game over.

CHAPTER TEN

WHEN THE INITIAL SHOCK OF MY STUNT WEARS OFF, THE BOYS rise to their feet. Their eyes fixed on me.

"What was that?" Blane questions, a nip to his voice. He's not impressed.

"They got distracted," I shrug, "so I took my shot. Maybe next time, boys, you should pay more attention to who's sneaking up behind you." Both Kale and Jaxon's eyes pin me in place. Reading between the lines, they know I heard them, and yet, neither of us moves to address it.

"Very well," Blane says with a short, inverted nod, "it seems the red team has won Mudball."

"Yeah, we did!" Owen says, lunging forward and sweeping me up in his arms. Henry is next to pull me in for a hug, taking me a little by surprise. Archer and I share a look that is an inch further from disdain and closer to admiration, which is more than I would dare expect from him.

"Perhaps," Blane interjects, "but the games aren't over." I lift my gaze as he turns to face me, his voice daring, making my stomach churn. "Your final challenge, should you choose to accept it, is to fight me."

The arena falls silent for several seconds.

Sweat prickles down my spine, and my fingers twitch. Blane's already flattened me in a fight once. On my very first day of training at the Defiance, I was determined to prove myself, and I'm still harbouring that impulse now. A part of me thinks if anyone else had been the last standing after mudball, this fight wouldn't be happening, but Blane wants to test me. That much is obvious. I've been a walking problem for him these last weeks. My mission nearly got Emeric killed, landed him in Dane's grip and made me vengeful and careless. Blane sees me for my impulsiveness and insubordination. But Emeric's back now, and if he wants me to prove myself, then I will. I'll play his games. I'll follow his rules and use his fighting technique. I'll show up. I won't give him any more reasons to doubt me. Now that those I love are safe, Dane's retribution is coming, and I refuse to be on the side lines when that happens.

"Sorry, but is the challenge posed to our team or Amrey?" Archer interjects, "Because if it's our team, we should be able to pick our strongest fighter." My face burns as his commentary slices through me. Just when I thought we were making ground.

"Why waste the time," I smirk, "When I've already been picked."

"She has you there, pretty boy," Emeric laughs, nudging Archer.

"Okay then," I release a deep, shaky breath and swallow down my nerves. "How many rounds?"

"THIS SEEMS LIKE A WASTE OF TIME," James says, looking densely at me. Everyone is gathered around the sparring ground, squaring off an area for the fight. "Surely, we can call it a day. I'm hungry." Elle overhears and nudges James in the ribs, who appears to have resumed some semblance of his former arrogant self.

"No one's forcing you to stay, James," Blane's voice is intimidating even when he stands amongst us. "Though if you do go, you can report to the dispensary before dinner and let Cynthia know she'll have another helping hand tomorrow." James' face pales instantly. I bite my lip to fight the urge to laugh.

"I'll stay," he says, though it's more of an inaudible grunt. Owen, who stands next to him, thumps him on the back.

"You're an idiot," he laughs, and James turns beat red.

"Okay, enough taunts," Blane calls, tightening the strap on his shoulder. "Despite his whining, James is right about food. I'd like to get this done with enough time to eat if that suits Amrey." He cocks his head in my direction, and I manage a tight-lipped nod.

"Then let's begin."

Squaring my footing, I stare past Blane at Henry who gives me an encouraging smile, his hand held tightly in Mags'. Blane takes his position on the mat. I try not to shrink under his pinned glare, but his intimidation feels waves heavier from this close. My pulse races against my breath.

He smirks at me with a playful look, the late afternoon light shining on his face, making him appear almost adolescent. I often forget his age, and though he has years on me, it's not as many as my parents. I wonder about the life he had before this, if he was born a fighter or made into one.

"Now, Amrey, don't hold back," his words hit the air, and the game is on.

I don't bother circling him to figure out his strategy like I do to the others. Vying for an advantage isn't going to happen in this match. This is Blane. He knows how I fight and he especially knows my weaknesses. Any advantage there is, he has, and he knows it. With a wink, Blane dives, moving with blinding speed until his body is towering over mine. I stumble back. His hand snaps over my wrist, steadying me, before using his other arm to swing at my gut. I block it just in time, only to be dealt another handful of punches. I manage to throw my arms up in defence, but I don't have enough time to push back. I need to get out of his orbit.

Before he can swing again, I drop to my knees and sweep my leg at his feet. He stumbles but doesn't fall. The falter's all I need. Scrambling to the other side of the mat, I put space between us and earn myself a few seconds to come up with a plan.

Blane lunges at me the moment he's back on his feet. His arm swings high. I block the hit with my forearm and drive my other hand into his gut. He snickers, but not maliciously, almost like he's impressed. The smile throws me off, and I'm too slow to react to his next attack. Blane lands a hard knock to my chest, forcing me back a step and into his vantage point. He then lands three more punches, my head winging back with every hit. In the seconds I have before he knocks me again, I notice Mags looking away, Henry's head buried into her side. Blane takes my arms then, practically shaking me awake.

"Fight," he grunts.

I thought I had been.

His grip tightens, and the pain in my arms intensifies until he throws me back, and my head collides with the ground.

The world turns blurry for several seconds. Figures and shapes. Lights and colours in and out of my vision in a cloudy haze. My face stings where it was hit. Water leeches from my eyes as I wipe the blood from my lip with the back of my arm. My eyes lock with Henry. I see the pain I feel printed on his face in a wince. Jaxon's eyes meet mine briefly from where he stands. His jaw is tight. He looks unimpressed. But when I look at Kale, he seems wildly entertained.

"Get up," Blane orders. I recoil at his words, anger rising in me. Heat trickles up the back of my neck, through my muscles and out of my hands as I push against the mat and rise to my feet.

Blane stands on the corner of the mat, watching me with an impassive expression. I can't read him. Yet there's an edge to every heavy breath he heaves. He's pushing me. That much I do know.

"I thought we agreed on one round?" I ask, using the moment to catch my breath, though it only grows sharper as the seconds pass. The pain from all the knocks I've taken setting in. My cracked lip stings, sweat drips down my cheeks, and my jaw throbs with each inhale.

"The round's not finished," Blane says finally, with much assuredness. It feels like those seconds of hesitation were for my benefit. His eyes scan me from head to toe, his fists clenching tighter, but this time, I'm determined to make the first move.

Without a flicker of indecision, I leap from my corner and hurtle straight towards him. He isn't surprised but he also isn't expecting me to pull back at the last second. When Blane throws up his hands to block, I bend my height, ramming my shoulder into his stomach and knocking him flat on his back.

It's the first time I've ever bested Blane, and the silence in the arena proves just how rare it is. He doesn't stay down for long. Before I even have time to make my next move, Blane has my wrists in his hands and is throwing me around on my back.

But I won't go easy.

Ramming my knee into places that hurt him far more than they'd hurt me, I use his moment of pain to slip out of his grip and jump to my feet. As I do, Blane's hand locks onto my ankle, and with a twist, he has me spinning in the air before landing outstretched on my back. Completely winded.

I cough once and then twice. My mouth bites at the air, struggling to grasp any. Darkness teases to take over, but I push it back and find my breath again. My head stops spinning, voices entering my consciousness, and when my eyes finally graze open, hovering over me is Blane.

Unexpectedly, he's not glowering.

Instead, he smiles. Not greatly. Not even jovially. No, Blane's smile is subtle and understated, and if you were anyone but me, lying on the ground beneath him, you wouldn't even see it. The corners of his lips tweak with an emotion I'm too nervous to call pride.

"That was better than the first time," he says, extending his hand towards me.

"So the red team wins?" I grin, taking it.

"They win," he nods, pulling me up. But as soon as he tugs me to my feet, a spike of pain shoots through my hand, and I flinch, grabbing my wrist.

"You should get that checked." Archer points out unhelpfully. I side-eye him, cradling my arm. "But good job," he adds after Griffin elbows him in the back.

Both Jaxon and Kale don't move to say anything. James practically has one foot out of the arena already with Elle strapped to his side. None of them matter. Trailing my eyes over everyone, I don't stop until I see Henry. His smile could lift all my pain away. If only he were looking at me.

In Axiom, Henry never saw me fight. He always saw the bruises and the battle wounds but never the cause of them. Until now. All Henry's seen recently is me fighting and disappearing. After today, I thought we could be okay again, but it will take more than one day to fix the reputation I've set for myself.

Mags gives me a sympathetic look, and Blane, having had enough of the awkwardness, orders me to get my wrist checked before dinner.

"Everyone else," he adds, "Make sure to get rest tonight. If you think today was challenging, wait until you see what I have planned for tomorrow."

W̲ʜᴇɴ I ʀᴇᴀᴄʜ ᴛʜᴇ ᴅɪsᴘᴇɴsᴀʀʏ, I'm enveloped by the smell of disinfected air, chemicals burning the skin beneath my nose. The room is bleached clean, with rows of beds lining the walls—the same ones I woke up in when I arrived here. The room was empty then; it rarely is now. Our escape from Axiom left only a few unscathed. The rest are frequent visitors. Usually, Mags would be here helping with the intake. She'll probably be here later.

Walking over to a free bed, I wait for Cynthia to finish up with the boy across from me, whose knees are scraped raw. He winces as she bandages him up before sending him on his way.

"Hi, Cynthia." I say.

"Amrey," she gasps, stopping dead in her tracks, "you scared me."

"Sorry," I mumble, manoeuvring myself into a more comfortable position. "I didn't want to interrupt."

Cynthia shakes her head, grabbing a new pair of silicone gloves before walking to my side. "It's fine, sweetheart, I was half expecting a visit from you after Blane mentioned today's games. I'm surprised there's not more of you here."

"They might come later. I think the guys are a little too proud right now. But everyone's going to be very bruised tomorrow."

"I have a cream for that," she says while looking me over. "Oh, Amrey, you're pretty banged up." I notice the scrapes running down my legs, the blood dried and scabby now.

"Ah, that's nothing. It's my wrist that's really bothering me."

"Alright, let's get you fixed up."

Cynthia makes quick work of my cuts and scrapes before tackling my wrist. "Does this hurt?" she asks, slightly twisting it. I shake my head. "What about this?" Taking my hand, she extends and flexes it gently, though the movement makes me wince.

"Is it bad?" I ask, though I almost don't want to know.

"No, you've just over-exerted it. Your muscles are probably not used to holding a gun for hours. I will bandage it up, but make sure to go easy on it the next few days, and you'll be fine."

"Oh good," I sigh, "Thank you."

Cynthia gets up to retrieve a white cloth from one of the cupboards and when she returns, I notice her eyes darting around the room, her face sewn tight. She looks lost in thought. Or just a little lost. She doesn't say anything else as she works on strapping up my wrist, but the longer the silence draws out, the more uncomfortable I feel.

"Is everything okay?" I ask finally. Cynthia pauses.

"Nothing gets by you, does it?"

I just shrug. For a moment, Cynthia watches me, her hands still securing the bandage. It's not until she's done that she asks, "How's Mags doing?"

The first time I saw her in the Defiance, she asked me that very thing. How things have changed since then.

"She likes it here," I smile truthfully, though I'll admit, talking about Mags was easier when she was in Axiom. Now it feels odd, like we're secretly conferring about her when Cynthia could just ask Mags herself.

"And Jaxon?" Her voice is small. I hold her gaze.

"We haven't spoken a whole lot lately. But I'd say he's okay."

"That's good," she hums, her lips pressed together but not smiling.

"You should talk to him."

"He doesn't seem to want to talk to me much these days." There's raw pain in Cynthia's voice. And I find my good hand squeezing hers. I feel for her. But if I were Jaxon, I can't say I'd be acting any differently. I'm doing the same with my family.

"I don't blame him for distancing himself. I only wish he could understand why I did it," Cynthia confesses. "When we found him, lost, with no memory, I was gutted. I knew it was my fault. He ran away from Axiom because of me. And I panicked. I wanted to protect him. I didn't want him running back, or worse, being locked up here because he threatened to. Going home to Axiom was never an option. He didn't need to mourn something he couldn't get back. I wanted to save him from that pain. Trust me, it's an awful burden." Her voice is merely a whisper when she's finished. My heart goes out to her.

"I don't think I'm the one you should be explaining this to," I say.

Cynthia shuffles closer. "Do you think I'm wrong for what I did?" She watches me with bated breath, her hands trembling. I feel inclined to tell her the truth.

"I can't say yes or no to that because I don't know what choice I would have made in your position. But I can tell you that though Jaxon put on a good front, he wasn't handling every-thing well. The freedom you thought you gave him by not telling him what he lost only trapped him. He kept so much to himself, he was locked up, and I think he still is. And this could just be me, but sometimes all we want as kids is to be told the truth. That's the one thing Axiom promised to give us. And even that was a lie."

Cynthia rests back on the stool she's perched on, her hand slipping from mine. She looks awfully still, very pale, and I want to take back everything I've said.

"I'm sorry," I stutter, moving to stand.

"No, don't be. You're right." Cynthia stands with me. "I was trying," she begins, then corrects herself, "I was a coward to Axiom. To the rules, to Orias. I was a coward for so many years. And then I was given a choice, and I came here, only to be a coward to the truth again. If I could take it back, I would." I don't know what to say, so instead, I find myself hugging her. Cynthia startles, but then I feel her arms wrap around my back.

"Jaxon will come around," I whisper, "Just give him time." Her hands find my shoulders, and she steps back, studying my face.

"You know, you should talk to your dad, too."

Suddenly I feel claustrophobic despite being in an open room.

"Don't worry, I'm not going to lecture you. But I did notice you avoiding him last night at the meeting." I step back, finding interest in the floor. Cynthia sighs deeply. "Being parents, you have so much riding on every move you make. And truth be told, we make the wrong ones more than we'd like. No one prepares you for the enormous pressure that comes with having a child. Suddenly everything you do is analysed under a microscope. I'm not making excuses for my actions or your father's, but if I could offer you any wisdom, it would be to see them in a more forgiving light. No one is made perfectly. We all learn, even at our age. At the end of the day, the only foundation we need is the love we hold for each other, and as long as that's there, the rest will figure itself out. Remember that."

"I will," I say graciously. I don't know whether she said that last part for me or herself, but it seems we both needed to hear it.

As I move to leave, a flicker of hesitation passes across Cynthia's face.

"Amrey." I stop under the door frame. "I loved your mother. And I know Sacha will never replace her, but I also know Genevieve would want you to give her a chance." I'm still for a second longer. I've tried hard not to think about what my mum said right before she died. I've pushed it down and refused to let it sink in. But the fact is, they were her last words for a reason. Mum did want that. She didn't want me to be alone. She wanted me to have Sacha. But how can I want someone who never wanted me to begin with?

I thank Cynthia then turn and walk away.

93

CHAPTER ELEVEN

When I walk into the cafeteria, the room is alive. It's the most spirited I've seen it in weeks, and it's nice to see.

"Hey," I tease, pinching Henry's waist as I join him in the line.

"Amrey!" he squeals. "How's your arm?"

"It's okay," I smile, pushing him up in the line. "Cynthia said it's just a strain, and I should be all healed in a few days."

"That's good then," but he says it like it's not, and I know seeing me fight Blane today has gotten to him.

"Hey," I whisper, turning him to face me. "I know you don't like the idea of me fighting, but that's what I do. It's what I love to do. And I want to fight for us. For the Defiance and our family."

"I know," he pouts.

"Don't be so down," I nudge him in the arm, but he doesn't look at me. "Today was fun. Our team won, and we couldn't have done that without you."

"Really?"

"You were great Henry. Really great."

"Thanks, Ry." I squeeze him in a hug.

After we get our food, I walk Henry over to the table with the other kids, and he slides into a seat and begins chatting away without missing a beat. It's nice to see him like that—happy, carefree. I rarely saw that side of him in Axiom. I never saw him with his friends. Tobias, the little boy next to Henry came from Axiom too. His family didn't have any affiliation with the Defiance, but they knew something was special about Tobias. For a seven-year-old, he asked a lot of questions and spoke way more freely than was allowed, something I hadn't even really begun to question about Henry. But it makes sense. Many kids would be subversive. I have no doubt Henry is too, at least to some degree, and I'm glad it's something he'll never have to worry about.

"Spying on the kids, hey?" Emeric startles me from behind, his tray digging into my back as I turn around.

"Not spying. Just watching," I point over at Henry, who's leaning in to whisper something to Helena.

"Ahh young love."

My face heats up, and I hit Emeric on the arm.

"That's not what I meant!"

"I'm only messing. It must be nice though, to have your brother back."

"It is." I take one last look at Henry before focusing on Emeric. "And you, how's it being back?" I try to keep the question light, but my voice sounds weak.

"I'm good, it's great," Emeric beams. Some might say he's putting on a face, but I know Emeric, and he's telling the truth, which only makes me feel worse. He should never have been gone in the first place.

"Emeric. I know I've already said this. But you have to know, if I could go back-"

"Stop," Emeric sterns, cutting me off. "Amrey, you have to let this go. I have. I'm fine. I'm better than fine actually." Emeric's eyes trail over to Mags, laughing with Owen. "I know you have this whole self-righteous thing going, and you feel you have to be to blame for everyone's misgivings. But we all make our own choices. Like I told you, I made mine. What happened to me happened. It's over now. So let's forget about it and move on, okay?" Emeric rests his hand on my shoulder, lifting my gaze to his. "Okay?"

"Fine," I shake my head, "when you put it like that. How can I argue?"

"Exactly," Emeric nudges my arm, "Now come on, let's eat."

When we reach the table, Emeric slips in between Owen and Mags. The boys wrestle for space until Mags offers me a seat next to her, but Owen shoots me a look, and I decline. Instead, I sit on the other side of the table, next to Jaxon. Kale walks over with Archer then, and I half expect them to sit at the top end of the table, but of course, Kale walks all the way around and sits right next to me. Mags gives me a look straight away. I don't say anything.

"Remind me never to get on your bad side again," Kale taunts as I shuffle over to make room for him. I half cough, half squeak, as his hand squeezes my thigh.

"Kale's right. You and Blane looked like you wanted to murder each other for a second there," Griffin says, raising his fork at me.

"We did?" I say into my food. "I didn't think so."

"I mean, your wrist is strapped up, so I'd say yeah," Owen flicks my hand from across the table. I throw him a piercing glare, but then we both laugh.

"How is your wrist?" Jaxon's voice slices through the chatter like a blade. And I feel the gaze of everyone on the table pinning me down.

"It's fine," I smile, "Just a strain. Should be back to good in a day or two." Jaxon nods, returning his interest to his food. Why is he being so coy with me?

"Well that's good, because I'll be requesting a re-match of those games," Emeric hoots, sharing a look with Mags.

"Aw, Emeric, just take this as good practice for you. Not everyone can be a winner. The losers have their place too," Archer snarls, and I'm pretty sure Griffin kicks him under the table because he curses under his breath before muttering an apology. That ends with the couple looking dopey eyed and giddy.

"Get a room, you two!" Owen pretends to barf, causing the pair to blush red. I can't help but smile. I've missed this. Everything seemed so broken when we came back from Axiom. In a way, I'm still broken, though moments like this make me forget

"So, who wants to place bets on what they'll decide to do about Axiom?" Owen jeers.

"This isn't a game," Jaxon scowls, quieting the table. "People are getting seriously hurt over there."

"You're right. Sorry man."

"I think," Archer begins, heedless of Jaxon's warning, "with Xavier back, there's no doubt we'll be heading off in a few days."

"I wouldn't be so sure about that," Kale says under his breath.

"Do you wanna explain what you mean?" Emeric asks.

"I mean, I've only been here for a few weeks, but it doesn't seem like the Defiance is the type of place to rush into battle on a whim, even with your people back."

"He's got a point," Griffin interrupts.

"Yeah, you remember last time? It took them forever to agree to let us go when we did, and besides, it's not like we can blindly believe what that Elle girl says." Owen's voice is casual, but it seems to singe something in Emeric, who places down his fork and bores his eyes at him across the table—the same table which has now fallen silent.

Owen meets Emeric's gaze and continues, "Hey mate, I know the girl saved you, and I'm happy she did! But even you have to admit, her story doesn't check out. The fact that she just happened to be there. To find Amrey's parents." I flinch at the term, shifting my eyes from Owen's to the only other pair at the table not looking at him, Jaxon's.

"And she just happened to notice you were subversive to the serum, and could sneak you out without a guard noticing. Don't get me wrong, I'm grateful you're safe, but I'm not wrong in saying, something doesn't add up." Owen finishes his speculations by shovelling more food into his mouth. The rest of the table is at a loss for words, but I'll admit, his reasoning had crossed my mind.

With a sigh, Emeric's shoulders drop, "Look, I get how it looks. I do, but what can I say? I was there. Elle looked just as scared and tortured as the rest of us. Coincidence or not, she's the only reason we got out alive. And if it's any solace, it appeared to me like that wasn't the first time she'd tried to escape. I think she's been trying for years, and she was just as surprised when it worked as the rest of us." As Emeric finishes speaking, I notice Mags inching closer to him, her hand sliding over his under the table. Everyone absorbs Emeric's words, including Owen, who then murmurs, "Still, I think we should all be careful around her."

"And I think we should continue this another time," Griffin interjects, tilting his head over his shoulder. We all blanch noticing the same thing: Elle and James, walking right towards us.

Minutes later, James has joined the boys in their string of complaints at Griffin for his cooking skills, but Elle remains quiet. The sleeves of her uniform hang loose on her arms, her cheekbones pointier than mine or Mags's. I watch as she plays with the vegetables on her plate, barely eating. She's probably not used to having a lot of food. My stomach tightens at the thought. I want to talk to her, but I'm afraid my words will scare her. I don't think she's said more than two words to anyone since the night she arrived.

Meanwhile, James, who risked so much to find her, seems oddly complacent with her now. His shoulder is tucked slightly away from her and towards the rest of us, unconsciously blocking her from the group, keeping her just out of reach of accessible conversation. It's as if her presence has disappointed him in some way.

I try to make eye contact with her, but she seems worlds away, lost in her thoughts.

"Are you okay?" Mags' foot taps mine under the table.

"Yeah," I grin at her, reaching for my drink. "You?" She only smiles and shoots the quickest look at Emeric before her cheeks turn pink. I laugh into my cup.

"What are you two laughing about?" Emeric asks, and suddenly, the whole table is clued into the conversation. Mags' face has turned from pink to red, her big eyes pleading with mine to come up with an excuse.

"It's nothing," I stutter, holding the cup over my mouth to repress my laugh.

"Really?" Jaxon says this time. His head rests on his hand, but when he talks, he angles it slightly towards me. I only look back, raising my eyebrows in answer to his question.

"I have a question you can answer," Kale interrupts, biting the silence.

"Shoot," Emeric replies, drawing his eyes from Mags to him.

"After Amrey was so easily kicked on her arse today, I was wondering who else here has gone up against the mighty Blane and won? Or is he the type of teacher who doesn't like it when the student surpasses them?" The table eyeballs Kale. That was a fully loaded question that I'm not even sure Emeric could tackle impartially. Luckily, James is like Kale and has no trouble butting into conversations.

"Seems like the latter," he sneers, "and that's not a good sign. I mean at least we gave Dane a run for his money when he decided to whoop our arse. And Blane's not half the fighter he is."

"That's because Dane fights to maim and kill," Griffin groans, "while Blane fights to teach."

"Maybe so, but we are going up against Dane," James flatlines, and this time, Griffin doesn't argue against it.

"This is the exact point I was trying to make in training when Captain' Jaxon kicked me out," Kale jeers. Jaxon ignores him. No one at the table seems to know what to say, not even Mags or Emeric, who usually have words to filter every situation. Kale takes that to his advantage.

"Amrey agrees with me."

I kick him under the table.

"Is that true?" I look at Jaxon, currently hating that he's right next to me. "Do you think we should be learning to fight like Dane?"

"I already spoke to you about it. It's not like-" my voice cuts off as I struggle to skate around the truth. Jaxon's stare deepens.

"Just be honest," Kale encourages, his voice brushing the side of my neck, unsettling me even more.

"Fine, in a way, I do." Instantly, I feel the heat from Jaxon grow, his legs stiffening next to mine.

"Why?" This time I'm surprised by the voice. Mags, out of everyone, is not who I expected to be taking the other side.

"It's not that I think we should be fighting to kill," I begin, unsure where I even aim to finish. The others at the table don't seem to know either. "Look," I finally sigh, setting down my fork. "You guys were there. You saw how Dane works. He doesn't train the guards to fight fair. They carry guns for a reason. This isn't some specialised combat training camp we're preparing for. Emeric was already taken once. My mum was killed. I just think we should be taking it a little more seriously than mudball fights and riddles, that's all."

"I think you're ignoring the purpose of what today was supposed to be about," Jaxon says cooly.

"Yeah, you know Blane; he loves to give us those philosophical team-building lessons," Owen chimes in.

"I don't doubt Blane's teachings. I just think we would also be ignorant not to utilise what we have now."

"And what is that exactly?" Archer raises his eyes along with his fork as he takes a slow bite of food.

"Kale and James. They know Dane. They trained with him." I'm resistant to even mention James, but I know only leaving Kale's name hanging in the air won't further help my case.

"She's right. You could all learn a lot from us," James interrupts, and instantly I regret mentioning him.

"I wouldn't go that far," Griffin interrupts. But James doesn't back down, and within a breath, the table has broken out into a heated discussion—exactly what I was trying to avoid.

"Enough!" Emeric shouts. The whole cafeteria seems to quiet down at that.

"We get the point. It's not as simple as one way or the other. You have your reasons. And whether or not we agree," he says the last words sharply, pointing his stare at only Kale, "the decision is not ours to make. So let's forget about it and move on. I'm sure we can think of something a little more mundane to talk about." He looks over his shoulder at Mags, who's finishing the last of her apple.

"Oh right, yes," she chokes out, and I can't help it, I laugh.

"What do you suggest we talk about then Ric? It's not like we have graduations or dances around here," Kale's voice is slick as he speaks. Emeric narrows his eyes on him.

"How about a game?" Owen suggests. I'm not the only one who looks at him blankly. "Jeesh, I was just trying to have some fun, but by the looks on your faces, you'd think I just killed someone's cat."

"I think we played enough games today," Jaxon says, and I notice the slight twinge of his jaw when he looks at Kale.

"I don't know what Owen is on about," Archer points his fork in the air until it's angled straight at me, "but I have a question for Amrey… I want to know," his words spike through the air with a heavy weight, "If Xavier lets you decide—and let's be real, he will—who's your pick? Who's on your team? Better yet, who's the one by your side?"

I meet his eyes from across the table, recognising the challenge in them. Archer has a knack for unsettling me, and I usually bite. But he knows, like I do, what he's just asked.

The entire table has fallen prey to the tension his words created, Jaxon and Kale specifically. There's no way I'll answer the question. Even if I wanted to, just to spite Archer, I don't know what I'd say. So, instead, I play his game. With a raise of my brows, I take a bite of my sandwich and chew it slowly. Only when I've swallowed it, do I dare take my eyes off Archer.

"Why don't you tell me who's by yours first?"

Archer's lips turn sly, widening into a slick smirk as he rests back in his chair and takes the last bite of his food. With his gaze still caught on mine, he gives me a touché look. We both know that despite loving Griffin, when it comes to fighting, he prefers to go it alone, and that's exactly why he doesn't answer either. Instead, with the slightest raise of his glass, barely lifting it an inch above the table, he smiles at me.

"If you two are done with your boxing match, you might want to look up," Emeric announces, and everyone follows his gaze towards the group of men—the same that are usually hovering around Blane and Dad—get up and leave in a hurry. I spot Sacha in the far corner of the room. We make eye contact just before she follows them out the door.

"What's that about?" Owen hums, but Jaxon has already signalled Nyx over.

"What's going on?" he asks Nyx staidly.

"Blane called for a meeting," Nyx, who I recognise from all the briefings, now hovers over Jaxon. He has a few more lines on his face than Blane, and his dark skin, the same colour as his wavy hair, is covered by his long-sleeved uniform. He's the only one I've seen wearing his shirt tucked properly, his posture a little more seriously held than the others.

"A meeting about?" Jaxon persists.

Nyx looks hesitant to answer, surveying the room, before leaning closer, "All I know is they're holding a vote. For what, I'm not certain, but I presume you'll be clued in soon." He looks at me when he says that last part, and I can't help but feel three sizes smaller.

"When's it happening?" I ask, anger burning my throat. Nyx hasn't said it, but I'm no fool. The vote he's talking about very well might be over my plan.

"Now. Blane just sent word." Nyx's eyes move over the faces at the table. "Don't any of you do anything stupid."

"We won't. Thanks for the heads up." Jaxon nods.

Nyx straightens up. "And don't cause me trouble."

"No promises." Owen smirks from across the table.

"Yeah, that's what I thought." Nyx rolls his eyes and stalks back across the cafeteria. I watch him walk away, my ears burning with this information. More people file out of the cafeteria. Something isn't sitting right. Why hadn't Blane mentioned anything? Why hadn't Dad? I curse that thought the second I have it. Because dad might have told me something, had I not been avoiding him so much. Turning back to face the others, I push up from the table.

"We're going to that vote."

Kale slaps his legs in excitement.

Jaxon's jaw tightens. "I figured you were going to say that."

CHAPTER TWELVE

"Sorry we're late," I announce as we burst into the command centre. The table of eyes in the middle of the room bore our way.

Dad steps forward, him and Blane taking their usual space at the front of the room. "We had the sense you would turn up," he begins. I share a quick look with Jaxon, but he seems as clueless as me.

"And if you wish to stay, you will sit now and speak later," Blane orders, pointing his glare at the empty chairs. The boys don't hesitate to follow command. James and Elle also file in, sitting opposite me. I half expect them to be asked to leave, considering the precautions Blane has been taking, but Dad ushers them in, his eyes lingering on Elle a touch longer than anyone else. And I suspect there's a reason she's here, and James is just the baggage that comes with her.

"What we're about to say can't leave this room," Blane divulges, an eeriness settling over me. I eye Dad, standing just off-kilter from Blane. His foot is still cast as he leans on a stick Cynthia fashioned for him. It's not like him to let Blane take point. Sacha is hanging back too, both of them considerably quiet, which only puts me more on edge.

"We're all aware of how pressing time is," Blane continues. "With Xavier and the others back, Dane's threat only grows. And now that we have insight into his doings in Axiom, he knows we also pose a threat to him. It's only a matter of time before he seeks us out. Within the last 24 hours, the number of Axiom guards seen just outside our radius has tripled, and they're getting closer." Fear grips my chest. "So we have a choice to make." Blane backs away from the table, angling his gaze at Dad, who steps forward.

"Amrey," he says cautiously, regarding me briefly, "proposed a theory—a risky one." He turns his attention to the room. "And while you all went to bed last night, we put it to the test." My heart hammers in my chest. I knew what the meeting was about the minute Nyx mentioned it, but I hadn't expected them to have already acted—not this fast. I watch Dad shift his gaze to the three men standing just behind the table.

"As Blane said, the Axiom guards are getting closer, and last night, Zeal, Herman and Knox came across two while on patrol." All eyes are on the three men, who I recognise from around the Defiance, but whose appearance couldn't be any more dissimilar. Zeal is the tallest, with a shaven head, but Herman's shoulders are the size of both men's put together, and that, with his grey shaggy beard and slit in his right eyebrow, makes him the most intimidating. However, Knox's pale skin and ginger hair only make his blue eyes that much more piercing. The three of them stand shoulder to shoulder, hands pinned behind their backs— stoic, like robots.

"And while one of the guards put up too much of a fight and was put down," Dad continues. I wince over the use of his words. I know we need to protect ourselves from Dane, but it hurts anytime someone from Axiom is killed. Most of them don't even know what they're doing. They're just under Dane's control.

"One of the Axiom guards was able to be sedated and is currently in the repository, being cared for by Cynthia." I sit up straighter, looking directly at Dad, my pulse racing with questions. Kale and the others appear to be in the same amount of disbelief. Elle, however, looks sincerely shaken.

"Are you insane?" James hisses.

Dad ignores him. "The serum still runs through his veins. It will take some time to know how long the effects last."

"But we're hoping, with your help, we could understand it better." Sacha steps forward, addressing Elle, who only blinks in response.

It's James who speaks for her. "She doesn't have to do anything," he says, puffing his chest a little higher. "She just got here. Besides, no one even agreed to Amrey's plan. This whole thing was an experiment. There's no way to know what will happen, what those guards will say or do, and you expect Elle to help you? They know her face. They could hurt her."

Sacha calmly steps closer to Elle's side of the table. "Of course, everything is a risk, but your sister has more knowledge than we do. She worked with the serum." This time, Sacha looks at only Elle. "No one will force you to do anything. And I know you've already done so much. But are you still willing to help?"

Elle lifts her chin so that her face meets Sacha's, her hands tucked in her lap, her shoulders unwavering. She looks placate, unperturbed, but the slight tremble of her lip suggests otherwise.

"I said she's not doing it," James scowls. Elle cuts him off.

"It's fine," she says timidly. "I will help."

"No, you won't," he argues, but Elle, despite the eyes of the room on her, doesn't cower. For the first time since she arrived, I see the girl from the cell—the girl who saved me. Determination burns in her eyes.

"James, I said it's fine." Her voice bites the air in a sharp snap. The room silent as we watch the pair analyse each other, unspoken words passed between them.

I understand James' protectiveness, but right now, he seems less like a brother and more like a keeper with a leash. Though Elle remains steadfast, and with his jaw sewn tight, James eventually subsides.

Sacha nods a firm thanks to Elle.

"With that settled-"

"Wait," I interrupt, slipping forward in my chair. "Are you saying you want to go through with it? That you agree with my plan?" Even though Blane's the one I interrupted, I'm speaking directly to Dad. His face meets mine from across the room. There's still so much unsaid between us, and a part of me isn't ready to hear what he has to say.

"If you let me finish," Blane says, clearing his throat, "I was about to tell you why we're all here tonight." He repositions himself in the front of the room, his eyes drifting to the ten of us who weren't invited. "We're going to be holding a vote. Amrey's theory seems to work, but it has its risks. Going ahead with it means we're setting ourselves up for potential danger. There's no guarantee that the serum or Dane's control can fully be cleansed from the guards. We'll be risking putting our trust in that and because of it, the decision can't rely solely on one party. Everyone deserves a say. So, those of you who are for this plan —for depleting Dane's guard one by one—raise your hand."

The pressure in the room presses down on my chest as I take in everyone's faces. My hand has been raised for what feels like minutes, but during that time, no one has so much as flinched, eyeing each other with inapt scepticism. I sit there, clenching and unclenching my other fist, fury burning through me like lead. Why is no one raising their hand? I'm about to stand up and speak my mind when I see a single hand lift into the air.

Jaxon's.

I turn slightly, his gaze levelled with mine, and it's like his one hand has sucked all the anger out of me. Resting back in my seat, the pressure on my chest eases as I watch more hands go up.

Archer is next, followed by Dad, Sacha, Emeric, Kale and Owen. Griffin hesitates but ultimately keeps his hand down, along with a few more faces I don't recognise. Suddenly I'm more anxious for this vote than before. Looking around the room, I see Zeal with his hand up, but Herman and Knox have kept theirs down, and I wonder if last night's experimental run wasn't as straightforward as Blane explained. James and Elle also have their hands down, but that doesn't surprise me. It's who I see next that shocks me the most. Mags' hands remain firmly held on the table. She barely meets my gaze, her face cast down, and I don't know how to feel. I know we don't share the same beliefs about everything, and even though she can fight, that doesn't mean she loves it when people do. I'm trying to understand where she's coming from, where everyone who's voting against my plan is coming from, but the truth is, we don't have another option right now. This isn't just about defeating Dane; this is about saving Axiom and all the people in it.

Scanning the room, it's clear we're at a standstill and Blane is the decider.

He stands very straight, not oblivious to everyone's stare. The moment stretches out, and I watch him study the room, taking in each person's choice, weighing out his own. I wish he would call it already. He hasn't raised his hand; it's clear where he stands, and I'm not surprised. He's never liked when I take charge, starting from when I questioned him that first day in training. Today he spent the afternoon kicking my arse to show me my place. Whether he means well or not, I know Blane. I know where he stands.

Or at least, I thought I did.

With a hint of a grin, his face locks with mine, and he raises his left hand, swaying the vote to yes.

Chaos.

Uproar.

That's what I expect.

Instead, we're all met with a room of silence. Dreaded, tense silence.

The votes have been cast. The verdict made. And now we have to go through with it. I thought I'd be more relieved, but getting my idea sanctioned was only the first step. Now's the hard part, where our risks can fail us. And then it's on me again. We'll be putting ourselves in the direct line of fire, and if anyone gets hurt, I will carry that guilt in tonnes. I was so focused on doing something, on acting, that I hadn't realised what it meant. Now, I'm staring at a room of faces, of all the people whose lives are hanging in the balance, because of my plan. Because of me.

CHAPTER THIRTEEN

Dad is painstakingly still as I square my gaze with him. Once the vote finished, I thought I finally had my place. The weight of this mission might fall on my shoulders, but I can handle it if it means getting to save Axiom. What I didn't expect was to be completely cut out.

"It's my plan," I repeat, my jaw sore from clenching it. "You can't just tell us to leave while you handle everything. When will you learn? You can't keep this stuff from us. We can help, we have helped." I feel like we've relived this conversation a hundred times over: me wanting to do my part, and Dad keeping me within arm's reach.

"We know what we're going up against. The Defiance needs all the resources it can get. And you'd be stupid not to utilise us," I finish my sentence and heave in several breaths, never tearing my gaze from him. I've spoken for the group, but I know if I didn't, Archer or Jaxon would have. We all feel the same way. "Whether you like it or not, Dane is coming. You can't keep the fight away from us."

Owen eyes me from across the table as Dad observes me

with considerate precision—like I'm a rose in a vase in need of protection.

"I won't have this argument anymore," he dictates. "It's clear that my authority has lost all power over you." I wince at his words. Is that truly how he sees it? That my need to help is only to spite him? Sacha moves then, whispering something in my fathers' ear, a softness touching his features for just a moment. He seems to consider what she says, shifting his weight from his good leg to his bad, briefly, before transferring it back. He looks older than I last saw him—shorter, more hunched. It's probably because he carries his stress in his shoulders, and the weight of it has dragged him down over these past weeks. It almost makes me want to quit arguing. I want to say, *'that's not what this is about,'* but the words don't reach my lips. Even if that is the truth, he won't hear it. We're both so used to fighting each other, battling two ends of a broken relationship.

"Amrey's right," Jaxon affirms calmly. "None of us will stand by and let you fight while we remain here. We have limited time. The more numbers in the field, the more Axiom guards we can detain and rescue from Dane."

"We are well aware of this fact. The statement I was making before my daughter decided to interrupt me..." Dad's pointed glare doesn't go unnoticed. However, I refrain from reacting. "Was that you and your team would take on restricted patrols, without risking your safety, while we let our mature soldiers take the front lines." Dad's gaze brushes over Zeal, Herman and Knox.

"Respectfully, Xavier, if the decision is about safety, then we should be able to choose for ourselves," Jaxon finishes, and before Dad can say anything further, Blane interjects.

"He makes a good point, Xavier," he says pointedly. Dad looks like he's about to square off with Blane when Sacha steps forward again and places a hand on his arm. With one look from her, Dad steps back, giving Blane the floor.

"If you wish to be on the front lines, then you will be." The hum from Blane's words settles over the room as I wait to see if anyone will argue. But there's only silence. "Then we are all in agreement. Assignments will be given promptly." I share a look with Blane. His having my side tonight wasn't an outcome I expected, but one I am grateful for.

AN HOUR LATER, everyone has been given their tasks. Perimeter checks have been on a constant rotation since we came back from Axiom, but for the ten of us who interrupted the meeting, it's new. We have each been assigned pairs for patrols. I'm up for the first shift tonight, so I won't be part of the guard retrieval—that will be Archer and Owen with Knox and Zeal. I know this is Blane's way of keeping the peace, so I don't argue. I've already tested the limits enough—interrupting the meeting, swaying the vote, and demanding my involvement—all of which I scraped through with the skin of my teeth. I can't risk it being revoked, so I suck it up and agree to start on patrol. Besides, at least I'll have a partner to keep me company.

"Catch ya on the flip side." Owen slaps my back, and I watch as he leaves to get prepped for the guard retrieval with Zeal and Knox. Archer's hand hesitates in Griffin's for a moment before he slips out the door behind them. A small wave of nausea rolls through my stomach.

No one dies.

I get ready to leave as well. I'm replacing the patrol shift in less than an hour and I was warned to change into warmer gear and skull a coffee. It'll be a long night, but I don't mind. For the first time since coming back—since my failure at saving the others and getting Emeric taken—I'm getting to be useful again. It might just be patrol and perimeter checks, but it's something. I can work with that.

Looking back over the room, I notice Sacha idling beside

Blane. For a second, I think about thanking them for sticking up for me in the meeting, but I hesitate too long, and the moment passes.

"I said let it go!"

Elle's howl startles me as she bustles past on the way out of the room. I turn to see a pissed-off James left in her wake. It seems she's finally snapped.

"Hey, wait up!" I shout. Elle is already halfway down the hall by the time the door swings closed behind me. "What happened in there?" I ask when I catch up to her, perplexed by the glazed expression she now wears. "Why were you screaming at James?"

Elle sighs, leaning against the wall across from me. "My brother and I have different opinions on things."

"I've noticed."

Elle eyes me curiously. "What do you want Amrey?"

"Just to talk." I move so I'm next to her. "That last time I saw you was in the cells in Axiom."

Elle shudders. "Yes, well, it's hard to keep in touch when you're locked up."

"So you were locked up then? After you helped us?"

"Something like that." Her gaze remains firm on the wall, and I tilt my head so I can see hers. Elle's face is sketched tight, held together by years of practice I'm sure.

"What happened to you that day? Why didn't you leave with us when you got the chance?"

Elle's breath deepens. She regards my question for several seconds. "You weren't the only ones in those cells who needed help that day."

"Did you get to help them, the others?" I ask.

Elle doesn't respond, only holds her jaw tighter.

"If it's any consolation, I'll be forever grateful you stayed back. I'm too scared to think about what would have happened to our people if you weren't there." For the first time since we've stopped to talk, Elle turns to look at me, her dark eyes piercing. I can see up close that, even though she's washed the blood out, her hair's stained with it.

"It seems I saved a budding love." Her cracked lips tear as she smiles. I choke on my breath.

"If you mean Kale, I would not go as far to say love."

Elle's eyebrows raise, her nose pinching with a grin.

"Interesting," she hums, turning back to the wall.

"It's not. I promise. Besides, I stopped you to ask about James."

"What about my brother?"

"Is everything alright between you? He seems a little possessive. Today, in that meeting… It was a lot."

"Don't," Elle growls, cutting me off. "Don't speak about things you don't know."

"Then enlighten me. I'm just concerned. I think all the women in that room were. I understand he doesn't want you to help. That he's protective."

A small laugh escapes Elle's lips. "That's where you're wrong. If it were up to James, I'd be in that repository room right now with that guard. I'm the one that doesn't want to do it."

"So he is standing up for you?"

"In his own way." Elle sighs painfully. "My relationship with my brother was never fluid, even when we were kids. We've always been different. Honestly, I'm surprised he went to the lengths he did to get me back. I thought he would have forgotten about me like my parents. But that's Dane's influence, I guess. He saw an opportunity to use James, and he went for it."

"If you know Dane to be horrible, which I'm assuming you do, then can I ask why you don't want to help?"

Elle looks at me with a cower on her lip. "You won't understand," she stammers.

"Try me?"

I watch her eyes darken as she grapples with whether to talk. Eventually, she turns away, her fingers dug into her sides. "I'm the one who hurt that man, Amrey. I didn't just inject those guards, I tortured them."

My breath escapes me, feeling the guilt rolling off Elle in waves.

"But you didn't have a choice. Dane made you do that." Though she didn't say that outright, I assume it anyway. I may not know Elle all that well, but someone who risks her life to save me and my family isn't a killer.

"It doesn't matter whether I was forced or not. They don't see it that way. Everyone I injected, everyone I hurt, they didn't see my story, they only saw my face. All they felt was pain, and I was the one inflicting it."

I watch her for several seconds, her breath laboured, her skin washed off colour.

"I'm sorry, I never thought of it like that," I say remorsefully.

"Why would you? You don't know me. Up until five minutes ago, we hadn't even spoken properly. Honestly, I assumed you were ignoring me."

"I've been doing that a lot lately. Don't take it personally."

"Well I did. When I arrived, yours and Kale's face were the only ones I knew besides James. And even then, he is, was, a stranger," she corrects herself. "The last time I saw him, I was twelve. I'm sure you remember the day."

"Mrs Morales class," I finish her sentence. "I always wondered what happened to you after that. I never forgot. I searched for weeks."

"And nearly got yourself killed by the sounds of it."

My eyes widen. "What do you mean?"

"There was a bit of time to kill on the walk here. Your dad filled me in. You were lucky to have him. If I had someone like that back then, I never would have failed that damn Axiom test. Things would be so different." Elle's gaze drifts down the hall, her thoughts taking her somewhere else.

"How did it happen?" I ask gently. "Did they just take you from home?"

Elle sighs deeply, and I feel guilty for asking, but I've been wondering for years.

"It was on my way home from school." She breathes. "A guard was waiting for me. They told me my parents were in the city hall, and they were sent to pick me up."

"And you went with them?"

"It was Axiom, Amrey, no one was supposed to be able to lie."

My face steams with the hypocrisy the Governors allowed to infiltrate our city. I was blinded. Everyone is. Serums are put in place to keep us complacent and fearful of our own voice. Yet those in the position of power don't have to hold up to the same rules.

"Do you remember the guard who took you?"

Elle looks like she's a ghost when she turns to face me.

"It was Dane."

I don't know what I expected, but that wasn't it. Even all these years ago, he was still running things. A cold chill races down my spine, the hair on my arms standing on end. It's clear Dane has been planning this for years, and it only makes me that much more terrified of what's to come.

"At first, it wasn't so bad. Dane wasn't so bad. I just stayed in the cell all day, every day. I made friends with the people down there. Two women named Clara and Marg took care of me."

My heart swells at the name.

"Clara, Dane's carer?" I ask.

Elles eyes lift, "you knew Clara?"

"I met her in the cells. She was kind." The memory of her is yet another that now brings forth so much pain.

"Is Clara the person you were going back for? The reason you couldn't leave with Kale and me?"

Elle doesn't speak right away, but her answers are clear. "Marg had died a few years before. Clara was too old to notice, or maybe she did and let herself pretend anyway. When the Defiance came to rescue everyone, she didn't want to go. A part of her still wanted to save Dane from himself, and I couldn't leave her alone."

"I get it." I smile thinly, thinking back to Clara's words, to Marg's empty cell. "Is Clara…?" I don't have the heart to finish the sentence

Elle understands the silence, dipping her head once. "She passed not long after you escaped."

I let out a pained breath. "I'm sorry."

Elle smiles simply. "Having them made my time down there bearable. For four years, the only real horror was the delirium— not knowing whether it was night or day or how much time had passed— but eventually, you get over that too. We would sing together to pass the time."

"You said four years. What happened in the last two?"

"That fifth year, Dane started becoming more erratic. I had assumed the Governors were behind subversive detainment and that they'd only put Dane in charge. But it turns out Dane had told them lies. I was a thief, Clara an insubordinate. Dane was manipulating them. And then Sacha became head of the guard, and he lost it."

"She got that because of her help in the rebel explosion, or what we thought was one. My dad and a few other Subversives blew up a part of the wall to escape Dane."

Something clicks in Elle's eyes. "Makes sense. Dane became another type of manic after that. More and more people began to fill up the cells. He started taking our blood and conducting experiments. Marg was too old to handle it. She died within the year. And then there was me. My blood wasn't what he needed, but I was too strong to be controlled by his weak serum back then. So, he bargained with me. I could come and go from the cells as long as I did what he said. Thinking back, I wish I made another choice, but I was desperate. I'd been locked up for years. I couldn't remember what the sun felt like. So, I made the deal. I did everything he said."

"Can I ask?" I prompt. Everything she's telling me is filling in so many pieces of my taped together puzzle, but one thing still doesn't fit. "Why did you stay for so long? I know you said you were more scared of the unknown than your fate with Dane. But that can't be the only reason."

Elle's breath catches in her throat, her face heavy with pain as she looks at me. "The truth is, I had nowhere to go. I couldn't stay in Axiom where Dane could find me, and I couldn't leave because I didn't even know there was a place to run to. I didn't know about the Defiance back then."

I think back to the day Sacha saved me from the trial, the same trial that took Kale. She had told me to run, to leave Axiom, and I almost didn't. I didn't believe that there was anything outside of Axiom either.

"I'm so sorry." I breathe, unsure of what else I can say.

"Don't be sorry. It's not your fault."

"Still, I'm sorry you had to go through that. To live like that."

"It wasn't all bad, like I said. I had Marg and Clara, and in the early days, Dane wasn't horrible." That shocks me. "I just mean I understood him, that's all. His parents left, and he was hurt."

"But that doesn't make what he's done okay."

"No, of course not. I'm just saying there's another side to Dane. You don't know him like I do."

Suddenly I'm too alarmed to speak.

"Am I completely mishearing you? Or are you defending him? Because it sounds like you're saying he's just done these things because his parents let him. Not because he's a psychotic maniac who kills people in cold blood. Like my mother." I don't know where this intense burst of anger has come from, but I find myself seething, my chest burning with spoiled rage.

"No. Of course not, Amrey. You're right. Forget I said anything." Elle's whole demeanour begins to wilt in front of me, and whatever anger I just had is instantly replaced with guilt.

"Shit, Elle, I'm sorry I didn't mean-"

"It's fine," she says abruptly. "I've got to go." Before I can finish apologising, Elle's gone.

A part of me wonders if I should chase after her, but I don't get the chance.

"What was that about?" Kale walks towards me, his brows knitted at Elle's fading figure.

"How long were you listening?" I exhale.

"Long enough to know you pissed her off." His voice isn't harsh, more condescending. "So what did you say?"

I roll my eyes, leaning my weight against the wall in defeat. "I didn't mean to upset her. She was only telling me about her time in Axiom. It was heart-breaking, but she was opening up to me until I accused her of siding with Dane."

Kale studies me for a moment. "Do you think she would side with Dane?"

"No... I mean, I don't know. She saved Emeric and my Dad but... ahh," I groan, raking my hands through my hair. "It's just, the way she was talking. It was almost like she felt bad for Dane. It was..."

"Creepy," Kale flatlines, finishing my sentence.

"Yes. But I feel bad. I think she told me more than she has told anyone here, and the last thing I wanted to do was scare her into keeping quiet. Something just felt off, like she was protective of Dane. Or maybe I'm reading too much into it."

"You should be reading into it," Kale says gravely. "Amrey, Elle might be the girl you knew once, but she's spent the last six years with Dane. Regardless of her being James' sister, we can't just go blindly trusting her."

"I know. There's definitely something off, I'm just not sure what it is yet."

"We'll figure it out together." Kale's voice is sure, and as I turn to look at him, voices begin taking up space in the hallway.

"Shit," I swear, realising the time. "I have to go to patrol."

Kale's shoulders stiffen. "Right, well, I wouldn't want to keep you."

"Yet, you are?" I question, confusion creeping across my features as Kale's gaze falls to the floor. "If you've got something to say, Kale, just say it, but do it while we walk, or I'm going to be late." I turn around and begin hurrying down the hall, and Kale follows.

"I was just going to say be careful," he offers, though his voice isn't at all convincing. I turn my gaze up at him. "Believe it or not, Amrey, I don't want you to die, and you seem to have a knack for throwing yourself in harm's way."

"Now you're sounding like my father," I groan, my feet moving quicker.

"He has a point. One mention of a fight, and you jump into the lion's den. You're practically hungry for it. And it will get you killed."

"Look, I get that you want to look out for me. But I don't need it. It's not your job to save me. I will be part of this fight, whether you or my father like it or not." With that, I turn the corner and walk right into Jaxon.

"Hey," he stammers, stepping back.

"Sorry," I stutter, straightening my shirt in embarrassment

"No worries. I got you coffee. I figured you'd forget."

"Right, thanks." I smile, and Kale makes a sound as I take the Styrofoam cup.

"That's my cue," he quips, "You two love birds have fun on patrol." If my stare could kill, Kale would be dead. Instead, he walks away and I'm left standing in awkward silence with Jaxon.

"What was that about?" Jaxon asks as we resume walking.

"Just Kale being Kale."

"You sure? It seemed like I interrupted something."

I hesitate, twisting the cup in my hand. "Kale wants me to be careful; he thinks I have a death wish."

Jaxon's face puckers as he takes a slow sip of his coffee. "What?"

"Don't get me wrong, Kale and I don't see eye to eye on much, but I don't completely disagree with him on that one."

"You've got to be kidding. You too?"

"Hey, just because I agree doesn't mean I'd say it or try and stop you." Jaxon looks at me as he walks. "Anyone who knows you knows there's no holding you back. If you want something, you'll find a way to do it. Stopping you will only ever lead to a more dangerous outcome."

"Oh," I say, unsure of what else I should. Jaxon's gaze only intensifies with my prolonged panic until a smile cracks over his lips, and he laughs. "Why are you laughing at me?"

"Because you're funny."

"Jaxon," I scowl, hitting his arm.

"Fine, fine." He shrugs me off, his grin still painted on his lips. "It's just funny to see you squirm. Sometimes I think you believe nobody sees you. Or that you're good at repressing your emotions, but I can always see them."

My heart's pounding at the way Jaxon's looking at me. Like he can see right through me.

"What do you see?" I ask softly, afraid of the question, but more afraid of his answer.

"Wouldn't you like to know?"

"Yes, that's why I'm asking," I quip. Jaxon stops, pivoting so his body is facing mine, his face hovering only inches away. Heat prickles the base of my neck. My lungs become tight. Jaxon's lips part, his gaze teasing mine.

"We should go. We have a shift in two minutes." Jaxon pulls away suddenly and begins walking down the hall.

"Wait!" I call after him, running to catch up. "You have to tell me."

"No, I don't," he taunts, throwing his cup in a nearby bin. I hold his gaze with narrowed eyes, but he just leans his shoulder against the door and walks into the repository room.

THE SKY IS QUIETLY STILL tonight, the stars as clear as a painting. It's a welcomed change from the howling gusts we've been getting, the perfect condition for my first patrol. Jaxon and I headed out at the same time the others left for guard retrieval. We parted ways at the boundary line, the same line Jaxon and I have been walking for an hour. It's 2000 yards from the entrance of the Defiance, but only half as long a stretch, bordering the forest. I step in the indents of my past footprints, hands in my pockets, my gaze locked on the tree's edge. Without the wind, the area is peacefully quiet, almost too still. The slight rustle of the trees is the only certain sign of life.

"You're awfully silent tonight," Jaxon says next to me.

"As opposed to usual?" I mock.

"I'm guessing you disagree." He paces while his stare, like mine, is following the trees.

"Just because I'm opinionated doesn't mean I speak a lot."

"I hate to break it to you, Amrey, but you're not a silent person."

I roll my eyes. "Here we go again with this, 'I know you better than you know yourself' crap."

"Maybe I do," he says with a seriousness that I can't help but laugh at. "What? You think I don't?"

"I think a lot of things. But what you think about me isn't one of them."

"Keep telling yourself that." Jaxon kicks the snow up over my feet. I kick him back. His jaw twitches as he stops and looks at me.

"I'd throw you in this snow if we weren't on patrol right now."

"You keep telling *yourself* that," I tease, and Jaxon shakes his head, picking up his steps. The energy around us is alive, but not in any way that makes me nervous. It's just warm and safe. For the first time in weeks, I feel completely at ease.

"So Mags says you haven't spoken to Cynthia yet; wanna talk about it?"

Jaxon stills, his shoulders tensing with the new breath he draws in. "Do you talk to my sister about me often?" Though his tone is light, I can see the strain in his jaw.

"You're deflecting," I bite.

"So are you."

"I'm just trying to make conversation."

"Fine then. How about you? Have you spoken to your parents since they've returned?" There it goes again, the term "parents," as if I got both back. I didn't. Sacha might be my biological mother, but she isn't my mum. I wish everyone would stop speaking as though she is.

"Sacha isn't my parent," I snap, more sternly than Jaxon deserves.

"Sorry," he stutters. "Your dad and Sacha—have you spoken to them?"

I let my face fall blank, along with my voice.

"That's what I thought."

"So, we're both avoiding our families," I hum.

"Looks like it."

"You don't have to talk about it if you don't want to."

"Okay then, I don't want to," Jaxon says, bending down to

pick up a branch from the snow, inspecting it like it's a weapon. Only the real weapons are what's haltered to our sides. Even though the gun's not in my hands, I feel its weight like an anchor.

"Fine then, if we're not going to talk about our parents, then why don't you answer this?"

Dropping the stick from his hand, Jaxon turns his wide eyes on me right as we reach the end of the stretch. I turn around and begin the walk back, holding onto my question a beat longer, unsure if I even want to say it. I don't want him to think he has that much effect on me, but I haven't been able to stop thinking about it since he said it.

"I'm waiting," he sings.

"You never answered my question earlier."

"And what question was that?" Jaxon looks curious.

"What secret do you think you know about me? What can you see that others can't?"

Jaxon drops his arms, dusting the snow from his hands. His breath shortens as he moves into the space in front of me.

"You really want to know?" he asks, a raised look on his face.

"I really want to know," I repeat.

"Okay then."

I wait for him to answer, but he keeps looking at me. My breath is unsteady as he moves closer, his body less than a foot away.

"Fear, I see your fear."

CHAPTER FOURTEEN

The Sun is rising over the trees when we finish our shift. The last hour was the worst. The wind picked up before dawn, nipping against my cheeks and burning my eyes. My fingers are officially numb, and I lost feeling in my toes several hundred steps ago, but the boundary line remained clear all night. If Dane has his guards searching for the Defiance, they haven't found us yet.

"You ready to go in?" Jaxon asks. I laugh a little when he looks at me.

"Ah… you have…"

"What?" he puzzles, wiping his cheeks. I snort.

"Here." Stepping closer, I brush my fingers over his eyes, dusting the snow from his lashes and brows. Jaxon stiffens under my touch.

"Amrey," he breathes, his hand catching hold of my wrist. I can sense the words resting on his lips, but before I can hear them, something catches my eye. Four men are running towards us, with a fifth hanging like a dead weight in their arms. My pulse spikes.

"Jaxon," I gasp, my eyes widening. He turns around to see what I do, and then we're running.

"It's Owen and Archer," I manage to shout against the wind. Jaxon keeps going. When we get to the boys, we see that the fifth person is a guard, knocked out from a bloody gnash to the head.

"What happened!" I croak, right as the guys slow down. Jaxon takes hold of the guard's arm, replacing Zeal, who I now see has a dislocated shoulder and a busted lip. The others look worse for wear themselves, but Zeal bears the worst of the injuries.

"It was hard tonight. They're hunting us in packs. It was almost impossible to get a jump on them. We only just managed to corner this guy," Owen says, re-gripping the guard's leg. I offer to take his place, but he shrugs me off.

"He beat the shit out of Zeal before we were able to pin him down," Archer finishes, and I look over at Zeal who's wincing with every step.

"Where were you when he was attacking Zeal?"

"It's not their fault. I saw an opportunity and went for it, and forgot to give them the heads up." Zeal looks contrite.

"Yeah, man's crazy. Before we knew what was happening, his whole lip was busted." Owen's narration seems to make Zeal grimace.

"It's not funny." Knox, who had been relatively quiet, speaks up. "It was reckless and stupid." The air grows tense.

"He's right. I shouldn't have been so careless." Zeal winces, tightening his hold on his arm.

"Maybe not, but now we have a guard. I'd call that a success." Owen practically hugs the guard's leg to his chest. They all look as exhausted as I feel.

"We had to knock him out pretty hard. Who's to say he's even going to wake up," Knox scolds. Owen shifts uncomfortably. I can just make out the repository up ahead, the only place in the Defiance that peeks above the ground.

"I guess we'll figure that out now," Archer concludes as the doors to the repository swing open.

"Okay, everyone that's not needed; get out!" Cynthia orders as she rushes into the repository room and over to the section tapered off with curtains. She swings them open to reveal two beds. A woman rests on one—the guard who was brought in last night. She lies unconscious, hooked up to half a dozen wires. And then there's the guard who attacked Zeal, lying where we placed him, on the bed next to her.

"We have to wait until he wakes up and question him. That's our order," Knox sterns, holding his position at the end of the bed. The rest of us have dipped over the far side of the room to make way for the people helping Cynthia. Mags is one of them. She quickly comes over and inspects us before focusing on Zeal's shoulder, which she pops back in without flinching.

"Badass," I hear Owen murmur as she straps him up.

"There won't be any guards to inspect if you don't let me do my job," Cynthia scowls impatiently.

"We're not allowed to leave you alone with them. Unconscious or not." Knox is the only one in the room not suitably cowering to Cynthia, who has now stopped in her tracks.

"Did you strap the guards down?" she whirls on Knox, her voice sterner than I've ever heard it. Knox just nods. I look over at the beds, which have been altered. Four long chains with thick leather straps are attached to each leg and restrained over the guards' wrists and ankles.

"Then we'll be fine," Cynthia bites, moving to grab more equipment. The guard who attacked Zeal is bleeding through the cloth we used to help suppress the wound. "Now leave before this man loses any more blood."

"I'm staying." Knox doesn't waver, and the crease lines on Cynthia's face harden.

"Fine," she barks., "but I won't work with all of you watching me. The rest of you go. Mags come here. I need your help." Cynthia's tone leaves no room for arguments. Mags shoots me a sympathetic look before rushing to her mother's aid, and we all dip out into the hall before Cynthia can start throwing scalpels at us.

"So what do we do now?" Archer asks as the door latches shut behind Zeal, casting us into an echoey silence.

"It's five am. We get some sleep and be back in the command centre by nine," Zeal instructs, his jaw tight, but I can see the exhaustion wrapping his features.

"Sounds good to me." Owen shrugs off his puffed jacket. "I'm dead. Catch ya's later," he says and then heads off down the hall with a yawning Archer following. Zeal, however, takes another look into the repository room, still holding his arm.

"Do you need Mags to take another look at it?" I ask, watching the muscles in his jaw tense. "Nope. I'm not worried about me. It's Knox. He's pissed at what I did. And he should be. I was reckless."

"Don't be so hard on yourself," Jaxon soothes. "Who's to say if you didn't act when you did that we'd even have that guard in there? You saved that person from Dane."

Zeal steps back from the door, an expression I can't read on his face.

"Maybe." He sighs. "But he has to wake up first."

"He will," I encourage, feeling sleep begin to take hold of me. "Now come on. We all need to get some rest. Who knows what's in store for us tomorrow."

"I think you mean today." Jaxon nudges me in the arm. But I don't have the energy to laugh.

ZEAL PEELS OFF FIRST. The repository room is at the start of the Defiance, opposite from where mine and Jaxon's rooms are. By the time we reach the living quarters hall, the silence has dragged for so long, it's unsettling. I can feel Jaxon wanting to say something, but no sound leaves his lips. As tired as I am, I won't be able to sleep until I know what it is.

"Just tell me." I sigh, stopping abruptly in the hall. Jaxon stalls for a second, looking at me with slight concern. "I've sensed it all night. Ever since you told me what you saw in me. I know I froze up, but I can tell you want to say something else. So just say it."

Jaxon locks his jaw, looking like he's battling several thoughts.

"Fine." He grunts. "I'll ask. But so we're clear. You told me to."

"Okay." I shake my head impatiently. "Out with it."

"It's about dinner."

My eyebrows raise. "Dinner? Or what was said at dinner?"

"Archer's question." Jaxon folds, those two words hitting the air with force.

"Archer has a flair for hiding the true meaning of things behind clever words."

"So you got that too."

"I did." Jaxon's eyes meet mine now, intensity burning behind them. But Archer's question is searing a hole in my mind. *Who's your pick, Amrey? Who's on your team? Better yet, who's the one by your side?*

"Don't ask me what my answer would have been," I say suddenly.

Jaxon blinks. "I wasn't going to. I know better than to pressure you before you're ready. I learned the hard way, remember?"

I'm not sure of the exact moment he's referring to, or maybe it's just our situation in general. Everything between us was on my terms. But I'm not the only one who put distance between us after our return from Axiom. And now, I don't exactly know where we stand. He's only just stopped giving me his scowling glares. We've only just begun talking again. Who knows if he still has the same feelings? If I do?

But as his hand lightly brushes mine, a spark warms my chest and I know the answer. It might only be a brief touch, a simple moment. But I know my feelings are still there, burning like coal, suppressed by cider and pain and guilt. Buried by what happened, by what I tied to him, and what he tied to me.

"Amrey," Jaxon breathes.

"Don't," I whisper. His eyes turn cold, and he takes two steps back.

"Fine," he sighs and turns to walk away.

SLEEP EVADES me with no prevail. The only hour I managed was interrupted by nightmares, shocking me awake in cold sweats. The rest of the night I spent in deep thought, my moment with Jaxon playing on a loop in my mind.

I roll over. The tiny, small black clock says it's eight. I've barely been down for three hours. My muscles ache for sleep, but I know it's not coming. Not for a while. So, slowly rolling out of bed, I jump in the shower. The steaming water doesn't wake me up, but it does relax my muscles enough to stop the throbbing.

I wash my face and hair, tying it in a loose plait before slipping on my uniform. My stomach growls, and I know my next course of action. I'm not needed in the command centre for at least another thirty minutes. So, heading out, I swing open my door and almost fall backwards. Kale's standing in front of me, his hand raised like he's about to knock,

"What are you doing?" I accuse, surprised by the sharpness in my tone.

"Headed to the briefing. You coming?

"Yes, but I need food first." I brush past him and close the door, but his stare holds me in place. "That's not what you came to my room to ask, is it?" Kale looks at the empty hall we both stand in. Everyone is tens of metres away in the cafeteria or headed the opposite way to the briefing.

"Not exactly." He stalls.

"So what is it?" I urge impatiently, the growl in my stomach turning into an acidy burn.

"I wanted to know how patrol went."

This time, I do push past him and walk down the hall, my face pinched as he follows.

"Why?"

"I have my reasons," he says, hurrying to catch up.

"Well, you can ask someone else," I grunt. "I'm still mad at you for saying I had a death wish."

"Well, you need to hurry up and forgive me because I want to talk to you."

"Has anybody ever told you you're incredibly pushy?"

"Only every day."

I roll my eyes. The cafeteria's just ahead, which Kales notices too. Sticking his hand out, he grabs my wrist to hold me in place.

"Look, I'm sorry for being condescending and protective. I just don't want to see you get hurt, but I've learnt my lesson, and I'll keep my mouth shut. Now, will you please tell me how your patrol went?"

"You forgot to say, 'Sorry for being a pushy idiot, and I promise to make it up to you.'"

He gives me a dirty look, but the corners of his eyes crease, his lips twisting into a grin. "Fine. I'm sorry for being a pushy idiot, and I promise to make it up to you." He dips his head closer to my ear when he says the last part, sending a chill over my skin. "So, will you tell me?" he breathes, angling his body over mine.

My gaze is fixed on the cafeteria door as I try to hold my resolve. "Patrol was fine. Almost boring, actually."

"You know I don't just mean the patrol." He leans closer, and I wonder if he's asking about Jaxon, but before I can raise the question, he continues. "I heard you brought back a guard last night. Do you know who it was?" I tilt my face up to his, trying to read his expression. He raises his eyes in contest.

"He wasn't wearing a name tag, sorry."

"Well, did anything else happen on patrol?" He pushes, and there it is again: the question with no real point.

I step out of his orbit. "Nope," I bite, pushing past him and walking to the cafeteria.

Kale growls. "You know, for someone who has to know everything about everything all the damn time, you sure as hell don't like to reveal too much about yourself."

"I guess I learnt from the best," I say with a sharp look.

Kale moves into step next to me. "I'm not quite sure what you mean. I'm an open book. You can ask me anything."

"Really?" I challenge.

"Really." His voice curls. I pinch my face in reply. We both pick up a tray of food and walk to an empty table. Kale sits across from me.

"So?" He glares at me while taking a bite of his apple.

"Tell me about your parents," I challenge, splitting my egg over my toast and taking a bite. Kale studies me, his face unflinching. He doesn't look fazed. Unless you've come to know him. Then you'd notice the slight tension in his jaw and the crease between his brows. "Not so easy to judge me now." I quip.

"Touché Amrey X, Touché."

"So, why don't you want to talk about your parents?" I

continue. "I know we just established we're both rather veiled. But-"

"But what?" he goads. "You think we're the same. Our stories might be similar, but our families are not. Besides, it's not that easy for me."

"Maybe not, but it could be better if you spoke to them."

"You're one to talk," he scoffs. "You invented running from family problems."

"Guess we are the same," I murmur, unable to deny how right he is.

"Two bottles of the same cider." He winks, and something about the analogy makes my stomach churn. So, when I see Dad enter the cafeteria and sit with Henry, I get up and walk over.

CHAPTER FIFTEEN

Before I know what I'm doing, I'm halfway across the cafeteria.

"Is this seat taken?" I ask. Dad looks up at me, his fork halfway to his lips.

"Amrey, hi," he gapes. "Of course not. Sit."

I smile and slip into the seat beside Henry, who watches me the whole time, most likely to make sure this is really happening. I can't blame him; I'm just as surprised myself that it is.

"How was your patrol last night?" Dad asks, trying to make it sound casual, but it comes out awkward and disjointed.

"It was fine," I mumble, my mouth half filled with food.

"Good, that's good."

"Yep."

"You guys are being weird," Henry hums, looking between us.

"Who's being weird?" Sacha asks, sitting opposite us at the table. My gaze finds hers for just a second, and when she smiles at me, I find myself smiling back.

"Dad and Amrey," Henry finishes. "They've forgotten how to talk properly."

Dad coughs, swallowing his next bite of bread, and I can't help but laugh.

"Is that so?" Sacha hums, a grin on her face. "Well, why don't we show them how it's done? Henry, what are you doing today?" she asks ardently.

"That would be school." Henry groans.

"School is good for you," I say, tapping my fork on his plate and ushering him to eat his food. "Besides, you're smart. You need to keep nurturing your brain."

"Amrey, do you even know what you do in school? Because maths sucks, and I don't think it helps my brain at all."

"I have to agree with Henry on that one. Math sucks," Dad says.

"Seeeee," Henry sings at me. I shake my head and make him take another bite.

"Even if maths sucks. That doesn't mean you shouldn't learn it. Right, Sacha?" I turn to face her. "Help me out here."

She looks at me a little stunned, like the fact that I'm directly talking to her is a lot to digest. Honestly, it's a lot to digest for me too, but right now, the conversation's light and easy, and I hope it stays that way.

"I'm afraid Amrey's right about this one, Henry. Math is something we all need to learn, even if it does suck."

"Traitor." He frowns, jabbing his finger at Sacha before succumbing to his plate of food, stabbing pieces of bacon and popping them into his mouth.

"Okay, maybe we talk about something else then," Sacha urges. "Amrey, how was patrol?"

"Dad already asked that," Henry grunts.

"Right," Sachs quips, biting her lip in a hum.

"It was pretty straightforward," I say, giving her a sympathetic smile. "I am tired, though."

"You're not out again tonight, are you?" she asks, sounding more concerned.

"No, Emeric and Kale have shift tonight."

Dad looks up from his plate. "Kale?" The way he says his name makes my stomach twinge. "That was the guy who was supposed to be your…"

"Husband," I interject shortly. "That's him."

"Right. And you two are… close?"

"What are you asking?" I hold onto my words, looking at Sacha for reassurance of where Dad's going with this. She only looks back doe-eyed.

"Kale is he? Are you two? I mean-" Dad's words fall short, and Henry snorts so loud I swear the other tables hear us.

"Dad wants to know if he's your boyfriend," he finishes, his voice twisting over the word "boyfriend" like it's a song with an irritating tune.

Sacha makes a point to swallow her food very slowly. Meanwhile, my face has turned beat red. I gulp. I don't want to answer that right now, mainly because I don't know how. And secondly, because this is my family. Who I just started talking to five minutes ago. We haven't even begun discussing the actual elephant in the room, and now they want to know about my love life.

I sit frozen, my cheeks already flushing with embarrassment. The three of them pin me to my chair with their tight gazes. There's no way I can answer this. I don't even talk about Kale to Mags, not in the way they're asking anyway. Yep, there's absolutely no way I can respond to that. So, I figure, answering his question with another is my only way to avoid it.

"Is Sacha your girlfriend?"

But that might not have been my best choice.

Dad's face instantly hardens, his eyes narrowed thoughtfully on me.

"Maybe we should talk about this another time," he suggests, and I feel my entire stronghold melt. Before I know it, I'm sliding out of my chair and picking up my tray.

"Wait, Amrey." Sacha drops her fork, looking at my dad with pleading eyes. "It's okay, we can talk," she insists, but Dad's face remains firm. He's not looking at me, and I realise, I'm not the only one who doesn't want to talk about the hard things. I've been so down on myself for not talking to him—for not being ready or open to the conversation—when all this time, he's been avoiding me too.

"It's fine," I say a little harshly. Sacha recoils as I fix Dad with a cold stare and leave the cafeteria.

"Amrey!" Sacha calls after me. "Can we have a word?" I turn around slowly, holding back the dread from my expression. I don't want another lecture.

"I'm fine." I inhale sharply, hoping she gets the hint. If she does, she ignores it.

"Just let me say this," she insists, her presence unwavering. Though she used to be my instructor, someone I looked up to and admired, right now, all I see is the woman who came between my family. Someone who shares my DNA. That statement alone makes my insides twist. She's not my mother.

"Amrey, I'm not trying to replace your mum or step into your shoes. I just want you to know my story."

"Your story?" I scoff. I know I'm being rude, but I can't help it. This is all so much. "You came into my life. You told me to be careful, that people were deceiving, yet you're the one who has been lying to me since I was born. You were never just my combat teacher. Or my father's friend. You are-"

My voice drops out. Trying to scramble my words together.

"How could you give me up? Why didn't you want me?"

I don't mean to take it this far. I didn't mean to ask those questions, but my words kept tumbling out in a spew of hurt and pain and before I knew it, there it was. The real question.

Dad has his own past to answer for. But with Sacha, lies and betrayal aside, the thing that's been nagging at me, burning behind my chest is two simple questions: *Why didn't you want me? Why couldn't you love me?*

"Oh Amrey, It's not that I didn't want you. I was just young. And back then, I had no clue how to take care of myself, let alone a child. I was lost. Being subversive was only one part of that. But being responsible for a child as well, I couldn't—that fear was debilitating. I wouldn't have been a good mum to you. God knows mine weren't good parents to me. And I don't blame them. They were young. We all are at that time. But I just couldn't put you through that. It never had anything to do with you. You're so bright and beautiful and strong, and I know that's because of your parents. That did an amazing job raising you. But I-"

"But what? All of a sudden you want to be in my life because my mums gone? Just because it was her dying wish, doesn't mean I'm ready for it," I snap.

"Amrey, all I want is to be there for you if you'll allow me, but I won't force it. I just want you to know when you're ready, I'm here."

"How did you even manage to give me up anyway? It's not like Axiom lets you trade babies." I know my words aren't kind, but this situation is bringing out the immaturity in me.

"I think this is a conversation we should have with your dad, and I'll let you take the lead on that. Whenever you want to know, we'll be here."

Sacha doesn't say anymore. Neither do I. There's still so much unsaid between us. I can feel the things she's not saying like a weight over our heads. But thankfully, she keeps them to herself.

When I'm ready. It's up to me.

I just have no idea when that will be. So, with a final, sad look, Sacha turns and walks back into the cafeteria. And I head the other way.

CHAPTER SIXTEEN

THE REPOSITORY ROOM IS STILL WHEN I ENTER, OCCUPIED BY THE sound of machines and heavy breathing. I'm early, but I'm not the first here. Knox stands against the far wall, his eyes trained on the two beds currently hidden behind curtains. He looks like he hasn't slept in days, which I know to be true.

Walking to where he's posted himself, I pull out the granola bar I swiped for later and hand it to him. He moves to reject the offer, but I stern my face, and he takes it without objection.

"Cynthia will be back soon. I told her to get some sleep, but she refused. Settled for a shower and some food instead."

"You should take your own advice. I'm sure someone else can cover your post."

"I can't."

"What do you mean you can't?"

"I have to be here if he wakes up. I have to see if he wakes up." My stare follows to where his lands, on the curtains covering bed two, where the guard from last night lies. I look back at Knox, his shoulders stiff, his eyes strained. The piercing blue I've often noticed is dulled to a stormy grey. He's not just tired. He's sad. And I had forgotten for a moment who he was.

"Do you know him?" My question hangs in the air for several seconds. Knox's breath rises and falls.

"He was my partner."

Suddenly, it all makes sense. Knox isn't just dedicated to rules and procedures. He didn't just stay the night because he thought the guard would attack someone. He's here because he cares for him.

"The boy is barely 21. I took him under my wing. For three years we served in Axiom's guard together. He was a good friend. Our wives were friends. But…" His words fall short.

"You're subversive," I finish for him. He only nods.

SECONDS LATER, the door opens, and a line of people enter, filling the narrowed repository. I stay where I am with Knox, but I feel the weight of the room's gaze.

Jaxon is standing in the far-right corner, Kale next to him, both of them unwittingly glancing in my direction. I'm not particularly fond of either of them right now, our last conversations still burn like a sore in my gut. As I watch them begin to talk, my chest tightens. Something about them getting along and being cordial unsettles me. However, it's better than the alternative.

Dad files in last, behind Blane, with Cynthia. I turn away when he looks at me. It seems something's off with the world's axis. Nearly every conversation I've had in the last 24 hours has ended in more anguish than it began with. I know I'm going to have to face them all soon. Just not yet.

The chatter simmers as Blane walks over and pulls back the curtains to reveal the guards. I shiver. They're both wide awake, sitting up against the bed-frames. Though the sight of their hands and feet strapped is unsavoury, it's their intense gaze that has me the most rattled. They're not looking directly at me or Knox, but I can still sense their stares. We've been in here for minutes talking, a conversation they could clearly hear, yet neither of them said anything. I feel Knox stiffen slightly beside me. He must be realising it too.

"Both suffered concussions and broken ribs," Cynthia states, walking over to inspect the guards' bandages. "Though there appears to be no serious damage. You should be fine to ask questions," she hedges, "as long as they're not too pressing." Then she retreats back to the far corner of the room, likely distancing herself from the situation.

"Thank you, Cynthia," Dad says, though his tone is dry. I guess our conversation this morning still has him unsettled as well.

"Let's begin. What's your name?" Blane asks as he and my father approach the guard from last night, but the man doesn't speak. "I asked you a question." Blane's voice tenses. Still, the guard doesn't say a word nor turn his head in their direction. Instead, he holds his gaze straight, and mumbles through clenched teeth.

"You."

My eyes flick instantly to Knox, wondering if he'll say something, but by his stoned expression, I gather not.

"Do you know him?" Dad asks, addressing only Knox.

Knox's lips thin into a tight line. "I did," he strains. "His name is Ezra."

"Traitor," Ezra sears. Knox flinches as if the word has reached out and slapped him. Blane moves around to the front of his bed, blocking his view of Knox.

"Tell us what your plan is, Ezra." Ezra still doesn't talk. Instead, his face turns almost evil, like he's been possessed. We all watch a little stunned as he bares his teeth in rage and begins writhing against his restraints.

"The serum is injected into the guards before every patrol. If you caught him last night, it will still be fresh in his system. He won't answer questions or orders unless Dane is giving them."

Elle's voice clears the room with an eerie silence. I hadn't even realised she was here. As I look towards the door, where most everyone is huddled, I see her small figure step out from behind James. The last time we spoke, she ran away after I accused her of favouring Dane. But she's here, even though it pains her to be, and I assume it's her way of trying to disprove that very assumption.

"The other guard might be more likely to talk," she concludes.

"Very well," Dad firms, moving away from the sordid guard. They don't pull back Ezra's curtains, they simply turn their backs on him, obstructing him from interacting with the other guard.

"Your name?" Dad asks, still assertive, though a little kinder. The woman sits up straight, stretching her back so that she's closer to eye level with us, only stopping when the restraints on her wrists don't give any more flex. Her hair, thanks to Cynthia, is pinned in a tight bun, but even the firm pull doesn't straighten out the wrinkles that are begging to show on her cheeks and under her eyes. She's older than Sacha. Older than Dad.

"My name's Cora," she says calmly.

"It's nice to meet you, Cora. How long have you been a guard for?"

"Three weeks." Dad's eyebrows go up, as do Knox's.

"That is an odd time for a career change," he queries, looking at her considerately. "Was it your choice?"

Cora's face flinches at the question. The traces of the serum still in her system are hindering her, and I watch as she fights with her mind to answer.

"No." Her voice is like a dagger, sharp and thin. I know from experience how hard it is to fight Dane's serum. I know how badly her throat is burning right now. How painful her thoughts feel. That's why, even though Dad hasn't finished his questions, I walk over and interrupt him. The room hushes still. Dad's voice breaks off in stunned silence, watching me as I hand Cora water from the side table.

She takes it slowly, her eyes glued to mine the entire time. It's as if she's trying to figure me out, wondering if I'll use the water as bait, as a bargaining tool. I simply wait for her to finish it, put the glass back on the bench, and return to where I stood. Only then do I dare return my gaze to Dad, who's looking at me incredulously. When it becomes clear to him I won't be explaining, he turns back to Cora, a new shrewdness to his stance and asks his next question.

"Why were you on our boundary line? Did Dane order you to find us?"

Again, Cora struggles, biting her lips shut until she can force a simple, firm, "yes."

"What is Dane's plan?"

This question is harder. It demands more than a one-word answer and it will take a lot to fight past the serum and give it. Cora blinks slowly, the truth sitting on her tongue, but she's unable to say it. She scrunches up her face, trying to draw her knees into her chest, but the restraints don't allow it. "I can't," she mumbles.

"Try," Dad sterns.

Cora breathes painfully, scrunching the blankets into her fists, "I."

My body lurches, watching her struggle, but Blane's stare holds me in place.

"Just try," Dad says again. It's this side to him, the unrelenting side, that I hate the most. Even though I know he's doing it for us, for the Defiance. Even though I know it needs to be done, it doesn't mean I like seeing it.

Cora squeezes her eyes shut, her head rocking from side to side. She's trying to fight the serum. I see it. I have to help her.

"She needs more time." But it's not me who speaks first. It's Elle.

Pushing past Blane and Dad, she moves to Cora's side and takes her hand. "Give her a few more days. The serum will have started to leave her system, and she can answer your questions."

"You're not in charge here," Blane says in Dad's place.

"You asked for my help. This is me giving it. There's no point asking questions the serum won't let her answer. You're only torturing her." I have to admit, I'm shocked by Elle's rigour. When she was standing behind James, I knew it was because she didn't want the guards to see her face. To see the person who caused them pain. That put them in this position. Yet here she is, and right now, Cora is only looking at Elle with gratitude.

Dad straightens up, turning to share a look with Blane. Neither of them seems too happy with the turn of events. I'll admit, I'm not either. I want, just as badly as anyone, to get the answers we need. Waiting and wondering what Dane has planned is a dangerous game, but hurting Axiom guards to get the answers we need only makes us as bad as him. I'm ashamed I wasn't the one to stop it when I first saw Cora's struggle.

"Okay then. We will resume the questioning in four days," Dad says. "But no longer. We don't have the luxury of time. So, painful or not, the questions will be asked and answered, even if the serum isn't fully out of their system. We know it's possible. Amrey has done it. So, I won't have any arguments on that decision." The room is silent. It's clear Dad's addressing Elle only, her eyes fixed on his. "In the meantime, you will stay with them, and report anything that is said."

She stiffens under his order but doesn't flinch.

"Fine," Elle agrees. "But I won't be a part of making anyone speak against their will or any form of torture."

"That is your choice," Dad says, each word deliberately slow, as if to display to everyone what our options are. You'd never guess from watching them that just days ago, they survived an ordeal together and were grateful for the other's safety.

"As for everyone else, patrols will continue like normal, as will the targeted assignments. If this questioning has achieved anything, it's proved the serum does wear off with time. We will keep bringing in guards, and in two days, we will have answers." Dad's final words conclude the meeting, and everyone shuffles out of the room except for Knox, who Dad insists stay for further questioning.

I want to contest for him, reason with Dad to let him sleep, but something about Knox makes me hold my tongue. He doesn't seem like the type who wants people fighting his battles for him.

"Of course," he says, tiredness creeping into his voice. I give him an encouraging smile before he walks away. A part of me wants to check on Cora before I leave, but she's occupied with Elle, and I don't want to overwhelm her. So, I excuse myself, hoping to sneak in a few more hours of sleep before I'm needed again.

"Amrey!" The sound of my name makes my stomach churn. Foolish to think it'd be that easy. I turn around, weary-eyed, and am confronted by Jaxon and Kale.

"Can we talk?" Jaxon says, sliding his hands into his pockets.

Kale's lips curl into a sly grin. "Funny, I was about to ask that same thing."

CHAPTER SEVENTEEN

Who would have thought shaking off Jaxon and Kale would have been the hardest part of my day? Don't get me wrong, I want to talk to them both, eventually. I just need several more hours of sleep first.

"That situation had disaster written all over it," Mags teases as we walk down the hall. I didn't even realise she was in the repository when she came over and saved me from that nightmare situation. "You looked like a deer caught in the lights."

"Trust me, I was," I groan. Mags laughs. "What's so funny?"

"How clueless you are," she pauses, regarding me carefully. "Let me rephrase that: how purposely clueless you are." My head's shaking, and my eyes are rolling. Mags puckers her lips in a knowing grin. "Eventually you're going to have to pick one of them," she says as we reach the dispensary for her shift.

"Why must you remind me?" I whimper. "And hey! It's not like you can talk. Emeric and Owen?" My eyebrows raise.

"Owen?" Mag's eyes widen. *Shit*. I think I put my foot in it.

"Or maybe I'm just seeing things," I rush to say. Mags narrows her gaze on me.

"That's because you're tired and need sleep. Which you

should get before one of those boys returns and asks you to marry him."

The skin leaches from my face. "You don't think?"

Mags burst out into a laugh. "No, Amrey, you're fine. Trust me, there'll be no more teenage weddings in our future."

"Don't speak too soon," I warn with a smile, backing out of the doorway.

WHEN I REACH MY ROOM, I don't even bother changing. Kicking off my shoes, I walk barefoot to my bed and slide right back under the covers.

"You *are* tired."

I scream. Jumping up and finding the light switch. Kale is reclining against my headboard, hands behind his head, legs crossed lazily over my covers.

"Again? Really Kale," I grate. "What are you doing here? Better question, how do people keep getting in?"

"People?" He raises his eyes. I shake my head and slide back into bed.

"Answer the question."

Kale grins. "I have your spare key."

"I don't have a spare key." I yawn, annoyance bleeding through my words.

"Then, what's this?" Kale removes a key from his pocket, dangling it from his fingers.

I release a deep, tired sigh. "I have no idea how you got that, and I don't want to know. I only want to sleep. So, will you please get out so I can." My voice comes off tired and irate as I slide down and lay my head on the pillow, the adrenaline pulsing out of me in waves.

"And no!" I snap before he can suggest it. "This isn't one of those 'let's have a drink and forget' moments. I'm exhausted. I had three hours of sleep last night. So, if you're not going to move, then at least be silent so I can sleep."

"Fine," Kale says. Moving to pull back the covers, he slides into bed next to me. "Let's sleep."

I roll my eyes, pulling up the blanket and turning away from him, scrunching the pillow under my head. I'm too tired to keep my eyes open. Sleep should come quickly, but Kale's just lying there, breathing so deeply. He's infuriating.

"Aren't you needed somewhere else?" I groan, rolling over to face him.

"Nope." He clacks his lips together at the end of the word. I glare at him as he lies on his back, his hands tucked under his head, eyes closed.

"Fine, let's talk."

"Nah, you wanted to sleep, so we're going to sleep. Goodnight, Amrey."

I growl, long and loud. It's clear Kale's doing this to pester me. But the longer I stay in bed, the more my body relaxes into the mattress, and before I know it, I succumb to the blackness.

THE NEXT TWO days go by tediously slow. The nights are the same, both of which Kale spends in my room, sneaking in after patrol. I blame that as to why my shoulder has been killing me. I'm not used to sleeping with someone, and every time I fall asleep next to him, I'm always sore the following day.

He says it's how I sleep. His exact words, "You sleep like a contorted doll." Whatever that means. Both nights he wanted to move me so I was more comfortable, but didn't want to risk my rage if I woke up. I rolled my eyes at that. Regardless, I still think it's his fault.

At least it didn't affect me too much with training, which

Blane has been drilling us with. If we're not on patrol—or shift with Herman, Zeal or Knox—we're running sprints and sparring or working out with the younger kids. Henry loves it and he's getting pretty good. His face lights up whenever he manages to get a punch in. I feel bad wishing he didn't, but I just don't want that for him. He's so smart. He should be focused on science, medicine, or anything else that won't one day put him on the front lines of a fight. I know Mum wouldn't have wanted that for him. She wouldn't want any of the strain that's been placed on her family. I'm at least trying to ease some of it.

Recently, I've eaten nearly every meal with them, and I feel Dad warming up to me. I feel us warming up to each other. We still haven't spoken about Mum, about what every-thing means. I haven't spoken to Sacha one-on-one either. Though I won't admit it out loud, she's right. I need to talk to Dad. But I'm just not ready yet. My whole life I've known my mum to be one thing, for my parent's relationship to be one way, and now that's gone. I'm not ready to face it, for the memories of my childhood and the picture of my mother to be tainted. One day, I might be, but for now, I won't open up that wound. Not yet. Besides, family issues are not the only drama in my life.

Tonight is my first retrieval mission.

The last groups managed to bring back two more guards, who are now in beds in the repository, with Elle and Cynthia. So far, the plan is working, and that is my focus. It should be an easy task. Except tonight, both Jaxon and Kale are coming with me.

"I TOLD YOU, I don't want to talk about it."

I stop just before turning the corner to the repository room.

Peeking around the bend, I see Kale hovering over someone. Elle. And the conversation looks heated.

"You can't avoid me forever," she hisses.

"Let it go, Elle. I did." Something in the way Kale speaks puts me on edge. I know the two of them have a brief history—they were locked up together—but this feels different. There's no sentiment in Kale's voice.

"I can't, and you know why," Elle blanches. My pulse quickens.

"Things are different now," Kale presses, his posture growing more tense. "I've changed. I've built something here, so don't meddle in it. I'm trusting you because of our past, but one wrong move and I'll take my concerns to Xavier." His shoulders tighten, his fists clench at his sides. He's rattled. Elle's getting to him. I just don't know why.

I watch Elle's face shift then, her big doe eyes, narrowing into something sharper, like those of a siren, piercing Kale with an invisible dagger. "I wouldn't think of it," she hums.

Kale sighs painfully, edging away from her. Seeming to regain some sense of his persona, he says, "You could like it here. I do."

With a final glare, Elle walks away, and I'm left with more questions than before. I've trusted her, even through my doubts. Now I'm worried that was a mistake.

"WE'VE INDICATED Axiom's new patrols here," Blane points to several spots marked on the map. The four of us, not including Elle —who's taken up post next to Cora —hover around the table in the repository, planning our course for the night.

"That's so far from Axiom," I mutter.

"They're getting closer," Jaxon tenses. A shiver works its

way up my spine, fear that I've pushed down now resurfacing, wedging under my ribcage and pressing on my lungs. In the past, Axiom guards never ventured into the forest. It was just their job to patrol Axiom's walls. But since Dane has been in charge, things have changed. He has them hunting the Defiance, and two guards finally found us a few months ago. Luckily, the only one alive to tell Dane is now part of the Defiance. Still, it's an unsettling feeling, knowing they're getting closer.

"That's exactly why we're doing this," Blane yields, handing me the map. "The sooner we get more guards on our side, away from Dane and that serum, the better."

The room's slightly unsettled as Blane leaves, and I'm glad Dad listened to me and stayed with Henry tonight. He needed sleep, and I didn't need another overbearing lecture about safety. The last three nights of retrieval missions have been successful and tonight will be the same.

"You know what to do, so stick to the plan," Knox announces once we've all put on our gear. He hasn't been out since they brought in Ezra. He was stationed with Elle to keep watch of the guards. And though the three of us should have it handled, Dad and Blane won't let any of us go unless Herman, Zeal or Knox are accompanying. And with Zeal still healing from his dislocated shoulder and Herman already sleep-deprived, that leaves Knox, Jaxon, Kale and me.

"You three are on front scout. I'll be heeding from behind. Use me if things get dire, but please," Knox pauses, "don't let things get dire."

"Don't worry, buddy, you won't have to get your nails dirty." Kale walks over and pats Knox on the back.

"Not… the point. And we're not buddies."

"What Kale meant to say is that we understand and we're going to be fine." I eye Kale once more and make sure to give Knox a reassuring smile, which seems to soothe his frustrations slightly. Despite my best efforts to spurn his advances, Kale still manages to invade my personal space.

"Yes, captain." He salutes, laughing at my sour glare. Then, as if we're not standing in a room full of people, he reaches out and moves a sweaty strand of hair from my face. I freeze, certain my entire body has just washed of colour. I don't even try to look at Jaxon, already sure of his response.

"So, what are we waiting for?" Kale frowns as if nothing occurred. I bite down on giving a remark. I've been waiting for my shift all week. I need it to go well. Meaning, I'll deal with everything else later.

"Nothing." I shake my head. "Let's go."

I SHIVER as the breeze picks up. There's an icier sting in the air tonight, biting at my face. So far, the three layers of protective clothes I have on are keeping me warm, but I don't know if I'll say the same in five hours when dawn begins to break—and that's if I even last the next five hours. Who knows what will happen with these two idiots? They look like they want to kill one another or me, and Knox isn't even here to break the tension; he's 50 feet behind, leaving the three of us to walk alone.

"Can we just forget about everything going on between us and focus on the job at hand?" I speak into the night, not turning to face either of the boys. However, that doesn't mean I can't feel the shift that happens when I speak. Kale is now a foot closer to my side.

"And what, per-say, is going on between us?" He speaks with a curly tone, causing Jaxon to scoff. Great. This is exactly what I was trying to avoid.

"Got something to say there, captain?" Kale mocks. I fight the urge to hit him myself.

"Nope. Like Amrey said, nothing is going on between us."

Jaxon's commentary slices through me as his stare pierces mine.

"That's not what I meant," I find myself saying. Though, I don't know why. My words are only adding fuel to the already blazing fire.

"Isn't it?" Kale questions. I take a deep breath, wanting desperately to run back to the Defiance and demand they give me different partners. I would if I knew it would work. If I knew that would solve my problem. Instead, I face forward and pray we all get out of this mission with our limbs attached.

CHAPTER EIGHTEEN

A GIANT SNOW FIELD SEPARATES THE DEFIANCE FROM THE forest, the tree line seeped in darkness. If I were on patrol, this is where I'd stop and walk the border until dawn, but I'm not, so my feet keep going, my boots crunching over leaves succumbed in the snow.

"How close are we?" Kale shouts at Knox, and on instinct, I shove him hard in the chest. "Ouch!" He winces.

"Keep your voice down, you'll draw attention," I warn, fixing Kale with a stern eye as he straightens his puffed jacket.

"We just entered the woods. I think the coast is clear for a bit," he drones.

"Dane could have his guards anywhere," Jaxon chides. "We can't be foolish and risk relying solely on our intel. Keep your wits about you. We could intercept the guards at any moment."

"Intercept is a funny word for kidnap," Kale blunts, and even I don't understand what he's getting at now.

"You got a problem with the mission?" Jaxon queries. "Because if you do, you're free to go back."

"No problem." Kale throws his hands up in a fake surrender, a smirk on his lips. "Just providing commentary."

"Quit the smug act, Kale," I bite.

"You know," he drawls, pointing his raised expression at me, "Him I get. Captain and I aren't built to get along, especially when jealousy is involved. But you." He lets the last word hang in the air, his voice skipping over my nerves, once again making me fight the urge to hit him. "I don't get why you're icing me out. You didn't seem so bothered by my presence when I snuck into your room last night." Just like that, I'm running hot, my stare so sharp I'm surprised it hasn't cut Kale in half.

Jaxon takes that as his moment to hang back.

"Kale, this is not the time." I clip every word with venom.

"Yes ma'am." He eye rolls, speaking in a curly tone, and if I didn't have self-control, I would hit him. Whatever hope I had for an amicable night just went up in flames. My face is red, and I can feel Jaxon's eyes burning a hole in the back of my head.

"It's not what he's making it sound like," I offer, scolding Kale with another glare.

"Your business is your business," Jaxon says, seeming unbothered, and if it wasn't for the slight tension in his jaw, I might have believed it.

"So what is it?" Kale pushes. "Why are you being cold? And don't go blaming it on the snow."

I turn to him, regarding his taunting smirk for several seconds, wondering if this is the place to say what's on my mind. I wanted to wait to have this conversation, but he seems hell-bent on airing our dirty laundry here. So be it.

"What can't Elle let go of that has you so on edge?"

Kale and Jaxon both pause for a considerable amount of time, enough for Knox to get close enough that we see him signalling at us to keep moving.

"What are you talking about?" Kale acts clueless, but I see the pinch between his brows.

"I overheard you talking outside of the repository." My

words seem to temporarily stun him. But then, in Kale fashion, he turns it into a joke.

"You know, it's not nice to spy on people."

"That's your take on what I just said," I snap, and Kale returns his gaze to the forest.

"I don't need to explain myself to you."

Now I'm the one who's heated. I feel a spasm of rage contort my face. This whole time Jaxon has remained silent, quietly listening. If he's watching me, I don't see it because right now, all I care about is getting the truth.

"What was she talking about Kale?" I demand, devoid of poise. He lets out a low grunt, turning slowly to face me. His eyes soften when they meet mine, and I feel the blood drain from my face. I'm watching him, waiting for him to speak, but I have no idea what he will say, and I realise I'm nervous. What if I had been right? What if he and Elle had been together in Axiom? What if the thing she won't let go of are her feelings for him? And now I'm not sure if I want him to answer because I have no idea how I'll react.

"Get down!" Jaxon's voice comes sharp, and Kale pounces on me just as fast. We hit the ground with a thud, scurrying for cover under the trees.

"Guards?" I whisper.

"Just ahead." Jaxons eyes are glued to the horizon, on two blurred figures in the distance.

"That's a lot closer than we calculated," I mutter, feeling Kale's movements next to me. I turn back to motion to Knox, but he's no longer there.

"He'll be hiding," Jaxon says, "but he knows the plan; he'll make his way here."

I hope so.

"How many?" Kale asks, as we move back a few feet, squatting behind a thicket of overgrown shrubs.

"It's hard to make out, but I'd say three, at least." Jaxons voice is tight. My stomach knots. The guys had warned us they were tracking us in groups. I thought I was ready for it, but facing it head-on is different. If we can't split them up and single them out, our orders are to return to base. Though, I have no intention of going back empty-handed.

"What's the plan?" I feel Kale's breath on the back of my neck. "We can't take them all, even with Knox."

"We can if we have to," I stern.

"We're not taking them all on." Knox appears from behind, out of breath but alive.

"We might not have a choice," I argue, pulling out my water and offering it to him.

"Right now, we do. So, we stick to the plan and single one out." Knox's voice is dry against the cold air. "Get one guard. That's the plan. That's what we're doing."

Jaxon's gaze meets mine then, something flickering between us. His eyes are daring, a challenge I'm tempted to take, our past conversation ringing in my ears. '*If you want something, you find a way to do it. Stopping you will only ever lead to a more dangerous outcome.*'

"I know that look," Kale hums, watching the space between Jaxon and me.

"What look?" Knox demands.

"Crazy or smart?" I offer. "Think about it. Three guards mean no risk of one of them tracking us. We take out this quadrant. Dane sees it as a warning, and they back off."

"Or they don't," Kale argues.

"Only one way to find out," Jaxon says in my place.

Knox, who hasn't said a word, looks sternly at each of us.

"Something tells me you'll do what you want no matter what I say." He pauses, looking directly at me. "If we do this. We need a good plan. And fast."

Five minutes later, I find myself in the canopy of a tree, with the boys huddled at the trunk.

"What do you see?" Jaxon asks. I fix my eyes on the forest floor and the three Axiom guards slowly heading towards us. Even from up here, I can't get eyes on any other quadrants. There's no way to know if more guards are coming, meaning we don't have a lot of time to act.

"Three guards, 200 yards away, coming fast," I mouth to the guys as I slide down the trunk and land in Jaxon's arms.

"What's our best angle?" Knox asks.

"If there even is one," Kale says. I give him a look. "What," he protests. "Someone's got to be the devil's advocate, and since it's not Knox…"

I roll my eyes, take off my pack and pull out the map.

"We're here." I point to the middle of the forest, between the Defiance and Axiom. "The guards are here." I indicate to the spot ahead. "If we go around, we can come at them from behind. They won't even see us coming."

"We don't have time for that," Knox interrupts, taking the map to get a better look. "By the time we make our way around, they'll be too close to the forest clearing, and then there's nothing but an open snowfield between them and Defiance. We'll lose the element of surprise the second we're in the open."

"Knox is right," Jaxon agrees, and frustrated silence hangs amongst us.

"What are we supposed to do then? It's not like we can just come at them from here. We might be able to subdue one or two, but not without risking them getting a few shots off and signalling for more guards."

"Then we stick to the original plan. Separate one from the group and take them." Kale stands, peering past the tree to get a better look. "It's our best bet."

"Actually…" Knox grins. "I have an idea, but it might hurt."

AND THAT'S how I find myself in the open, standing face to face with three Axiom guards.

"Ready?" Kale's shoulder brushes mine as he takes up the space beside me.

"Not really."

"Well, I'd like to point out it was your persistence that landed us in this situation," he muses. I shake my head and push him out from behind the tree.

"Better not get killed then. I already have too many deaths to shoulder."

"Now she has jokes." Kale's response is lost to the wind, my attention landing directly on the guards. Just like that, we've been spotted.

"Run!" I yell, my voice a shriek in the night as Kale and I share a final look before turning away from each other and disappearing into the trees.

My feet trample over the ground for several minutes before I even hesitate to look back. *Please work.* My lips whisper a silent prayer as I turn around and see a figure weaving through the trees behind me. *Dammit.* I curse under my breath. Only one guard is chasing me. The other two will be after Kale.

I pick up my pace, heading further into the forest, further away from the Defiance. If we don't run, they shoot, and gunfire will only draw more attention. Attention we don't need. Three guards is ambitious enough. More than that and tonight could go extremely sideways.

I nearly snag my foot on a branch as I jump over a fallen tree. The guard's grunts grow louder behind me as he trips on the same branches I intentionally ran over. His gun smacks against the log as he scrambles over the tree we deliberately placed in his path.

Ten more metres.

I hold my breath, my core tightening as I run and jump over the final log.

Almost there.

But as my feet hit the ground, I stumble forward, the impact rocketing through my shins. I bite down and grunt, pushing back up. I don't have time for this. Ducking to the side, I try to catch my breath. The guard is only metres behind me now, the ground crunching under his feet, his heavy pants filling my ears.

I turn around and lock eyes with him. His hand reaches for his gun just as Knox comes flying out of the tree, landing on top of him. I lunge for the gun. Knox wrestles with him on the ground while I aim the pistol at his head. The guard's eyes widen, fear flashing across his face, but I have no desire to shoot him. Instead, I flip the gun and strike him across the head with the butt, knocking him out cold.

Knox leans on all fours, panting heavily.

"Bloody hell," he grunts, "I swear I saw my life flash before my eyes when I jumped out of that tree."

I scoff, shrugging off my backpack and pulling out the rope. "You looked like a chicken that realised too late its wings were clipped," I mock, handing him the rope.

"Well, that was oddly specific," Knox chuffs, binding the guard's hands and legs. "But hey, at least it worked."

"Yeah," I say, "I just hope Kale and Jaxon had the same luck."

After securing the guard, ensuring he won't yell if he wakes up, we carry him back through the forest towards the meeting point. Doubt starts to creep in my mind about the boys then. If they were on their way to us, we'd hear something. Instead, the only sound I hear is our feet crunching over the forest floor, scuffing through the snow.

"Did you hear that?" Knox stops dead in his tracks, finger to his lip. My breath catches, my grip on the guard slipping. And that's when we hear an ear-curdling scream.

I drop the guard, ready to run, when Knox stops me.

"No," he firms, pulling us behind the shrubs for cover. "You stay here. I'll go and check it out."

"Wait," I protest, but Knox is already gone, silencing me a final time as he slips away.

I HEAR nothing but the sound of the wind for a while. The night is creeping to an end. Daylight will peek through the trees soon, and we need to be back inside the Defiance when it does.

My ears snag on a rustling.

Shit.

I look over at the guard, writing beneath his restraints, his wide, beady eyes glaring at me. He's awake.

The guard's face is older than mine, than Knox's, his eyes wrinkled, but that doesn't hide the fear in them.

"We're not going to hurt you," I say, guilt burning like a low blaze in my chest. The more guards we take, the more we can save from Dane's control, but that doesn't make this part feel any easier. Being held hostage is still being held hostage, no matter the morally perturbed reason.

The man falls still and I find myself fishing for my water bottle. Once I have it, I lean closer but don't remove the tie from his mouth. He watches my movements with sharp sight.

"Like I said, we don't want to hurt you. I'll give you water. I'll remove the tie from your mouth. But only if you agree not to yell. It won't do you any good, and I'll knock you out the second the scream leaves your lips." My hand hovers over the cloth that's suffocating his voice. "Don't yell," I threaten. The man nods once, and I release the tie from his mouth.

My other hand tightens around the branch at my feet, ready to smack him over the head again, but he doesn't make a sound. "There." I tilt the bottle to his mouth, letting him drink. He does, licking his lips dry after.

"What's your name?"

"What's it to you?" The man's voice is as cold as he is old, bitterness biting at the ends of his words.

"I want to know the name of the man I'm protecting."

"Protecting?" he scoffs. "You really are stupid if you believe that."

It's hard for me not to be just as unkind back, but Dane's control has messed with too many heads. I know how painful it is to defy him, to go against his serum, so I can't hold this man's malice against him. But that doesn't mean I have to smile while I take it.

"Never mind then, I'll keep mine to myself as well."

"No need, Amrey," he says with less detest than his previous insults, but with a tone that feels more like a threat. "Everyone in Axiom knows who you are. Dane made sure of that."

"It's nice to know he's still obsessed with me."

"I wouldn't trade places with you even if my legs were falling off and a gun was pressed to my head." I can't deny the chill that races over my skin as I watch a twitching smirk rise at the corner of the guard's mouth.

"Enough," I snap, leaning forward to gag him again. "If you have nothing but innuendos to spout, you're better off mute."

"I do have a question." My hand hesitates inches from his face. He takes that as his sign to keep talking, his smile becoming as sharp as a blade. "For a girl so powerful she can reject the strongest of serums, how does it feel to fall prey to those you should trust the least?"

His eyes are thin, his face twisting devilishly, while mine slams with rage.

"I said no more innuendos. Tell me what you mean, or you won't be able to talk at all." My hand tightens on the cloth, ready to suffocate his words, but the man only snickers.

"I just did." His breath is strawy as he watches me. "So much hatred in those pretty eyes. But are you sure they're directed at the right person?"

"Dane deserves everything coming his way."

"Dane isn't the only one you should be worried about."

"Enough with the lies and games." My voice breaks, the rough edges of my words skidding over the wind.

"Tsk tsk." His tongue clicks. "You're forgetting, I can't lie."

Just like that, something in me snaps. Grabbing the branch at my feet, I knock him over the head.

THE BREEZE HAS BEEN the only sound I've heard in too long, the man's unconscious body bound at my feet. Knox told me to wait, but I've given up patience. Standing, I continue the rest of the way towards the meeting point, guilt worming its way into my chest. Perhaps knocking him out was a bit extreme. It's not his fault he's infected by Dane's lies and serums, but I let him get to me. I reacted out of frustration. I shouldn't have. Though, at least I'm not dragging a conscious weight right now. I can't imagine he'd be making this any easier, but as I pull his body through the snow, back to the boys, I hate to admit how much his words still trouble me. The guard's taunts have etched their way into my mind, and there's no scratching them loose.

"How does it feel to fall prey to those you should trust the least?"

A shiver prickles down my spine. It's just the wind. It's just the cold. But even my own words aren't reassuring me. *"Who shouldn't I trust?"*

"Amrey!" Knox's alarm snaps me out of my thoughts as I come face to face with three panting, sweaty, and bloody boys.

"Are you alright? You look like you've seen a ghost!" Jaxon's eyes meet mine, and for a moment, it feels like no one else is here. His stare pierces mine, questions hanging in the air between us. I want to tell him what the guard said, but something inside holds me back.

"Well, what happened?" Knox interrupts, and I tear my gaze from Jaxon.

"Shouldn't I be the one asking you that?" I exclaim. "What took you so long?"

"Jeez, no, are you okay?" Kale teases, his eyes flirting with mine. "Glad to know you care so much, Amrey."

"You know I care. But I knew you'd handle it." I say the last part looking only at Jaxon. Whatever passed between us has vanished from his face, and instead, he walks past me, his fingers brushing mine as he takes the rope from my hand and the guard from my grasp.

"You've got to be joking." My voice pricks at the eased tension. "You both chose this moment to get along?" We've been dragging the guards through the snow for close to an hour, trying to outrun the fast-approaching sunrise.

"All I'm saying is, we did the hard part. The least you could do is carry the load, right buddy?" Kale says to Jaxon, the two of them sharing a look. Now I'm extra nervous to know what they talked about when I wasn't there.

"It was your idea to snag all three guards instead of one," Jaxon says, handing me the rope.

"Which you agreed with!" I huff, but I take the rope and saddle it over my shoulder, falling into step next to Knox while Kale and Jaxon take point in front and behind. Knox is strong, and I'm not weak myself, but while three bodies alone might not be all that heavy, the further we drag them, the more snow they collect. And by the time we pass the tree line, breaking into the snowfield leading to the Defiance, my arms and legs feel like they're going to detach from my body. Twenty minutes later, I'm about to signal for reprieve and have Jaxon take my spot when I see two figures running towards us. We stop instantly, the four of us budding together, reaching for our weapons.

"Don't shoot, ya morons!" A familiar voice carries over the wind, but my hand remains firm on my gun. "I know it's dark, but surely you know my voice by now!" This time his voice is louder, and only when they're close do I remove my hand from my gun. Emeric and Elle stand panting in front of me.

"What are you guys doing here?" Knox questions as we all ease our stances.

"I was just finishing patrol when I saw ya's. Griff was exhausted, so I sent him back, but Elle-"

"I was in the repository when he came in," Elle interrupts. "No one else was around. I figured I'd help." She says it like it's no big deal, except that Elle isn't trained like we are. She isn't even dressed appropriately. But for some reason, she came barreling out in the snow to help us drag back three guards.

My suspicion must be colouring my face because Elle moves closer, taking the rope from my hand. "I can go back in if you want. Or you can let me finally be of use around here." I hesitate, watching her cautiously. Elle is a mystery to me. Even when I think I have her figured out, I don't.

"Sub, stop your worrying and hand us the reins. You look exhausted, and the last thing we all need is another body to carry back." Emeric's hands grip my shoulders, pulling me out of the way as he takes the rope from Knox. I step to the side and let them take the load. My steps instantly feel lighter, and I stumble slightly.

"Woah," Jaxon says, his hand pressing into my back. "You good?"

"Yep," I mumble, moving out of his hold. Pressing on, I try not to let my suspicions consume me. But as we approach the Defiance—the boys bickering behind me, Knox's tired eyes next to mine, Elle and Emeric carrying the weight of the guards—one question remains burning a hole in my brain. On the other end of this snowfield lies the place I've come to call home. A place we all have. But if what the guard said is true, somewhere within the walls of the Defiance, within the halls I've walked for months, where my brother sleeps, where Mags tends to the broken, where my father strategises and where Sacha worries, is a face I shouldn't trust. What's worse is if that face is not within the walls of the Defiance at all.

What's worse is that they could be out on this snowfield with me.

CHAPTER NINETEEN

THERE'S NOT A MUSCLE IN MY BODY THAT ISN'T ACHING WHEN we arrive back at the Defiance. The cold has seeped through every layer of clothing, soaking my shoes, biting my skin and numbing every part of me.

My fingers fumble over my backpack as I retire my wet things to the floor. The guards, who are worse for wear than I am, are immediately taken into holding. I watch as the man with no name, whose words have etched their way into my skin, gets carried away.

Knox, thankfully, handles the debrief, and I somehow manage not to pass out as he relays the events of the past five hours to Blane, Dad, and a room full of faces I'm too tired to recognise. I hadn't thought I was that exhausted, but as I stand shivering in the command centre, I struggle to hear coherent sentences. Only when Elle enters do my senses sharpen.

"They're awake," she says quietly, her eyes meeting mine as she speaks in hushed tones to Blane and Dad. I can't make out anything else, but I know she's talking about the guards—about him.

I need to know his name. I need to know why he said what he did.

Unfortunately, that won't be happening tonight. Or anytime soon. It'll be days before the serum starts to wean from his system. So, as Blane and Dad rush out of the room, I follow Elle. If I can't get answers from the guard, I can still get answers from her.

"Wait," I gasp, reaching for her arm.

"What do you want, Amrey?" Elle stops, staring at my hand on her wrist.

"What's going on between you and Kale?" I challenge, then let her go.

"You should ask him," she says flatly, her mouth pressing into a firm line.

"I did. He won't tell me."

"Then maybe you should let it go. Just like he told me to."

"I can't. I have to know." My words come out rushed and desperate.

"Sometimes, Amrey," Elle's voice sharpens, "it's better not to know everything."

"You're aware this whole cryptic act isn't helping me trust you."

Elle seems the least bit fazed as she leans closer to me.

"Maybe you shouldn't then." My mouth hangs open. Elle looks like she's about to say more when the moment is cut short.

"What are you two talking about?" Kale enters the hall, his shoulders squared. By the time the door to the command centre shuts behind him, Elle has already left.

"You have impeccable timing," I groan.

"It is a talent," Kale mocks, and either he didn't catch my sarcasm or he's ignoring it. Regardless, I'm exhausted, and if I'm not getting answers, then I will be getting sleep. So, I leave Kale in the hall and walk towards my room, except I've forgotten what time it is. Not even halfway there, I'm trampled by the breakfast rush.

"Ry!" I stop the second I hear Henry's voice.

"Hey, buddy!" I smile as he comes up beside me with Mags and Makin.

"Are you going to join us for breakfast?"

"I think Amrey should get some sleep." Jaxon's voice startles us all as he steps into the space next to me.

"Jaxon," Makin gapes, and I realise the idea of seeing his son alive might not be something he's used to yet.

"Dad." Jaxon's eyes are rimmed red, like mine. His skin is just as blue, but he's doing a better job of hiding his exhaustion.

"Will you join us?" Mags' voice is so sweet you could taste the sugar in it. I know she and Jaxon have become closer, and I also know how much she wants him to be okay with their parents again. I stifle a yawn, yearning to keep going towards my room.

"Only if Amrey does."

I swallow down another yawn. All eyes are on me.

"Come on, Ry!" Henry persists, and though I was ready for bed just moments ago, I nod. Because I should make time for Henry and Mags, and because Jaxon asked. I'd be lying to myself if I said that didn't completely wake me up.

THE CAFETERIA IS BUZZING with people when we enter. Turns out Cynthia will be joining us as well, something Jaxon doesn't seem comfortable with. He sits next to me, furthest away from her, his leg bouncing under the table as she addresses him.

"Jaxon." She smiles. "I'm glad you decided to join us."

"I didn't know you would be here," he says cooly, staring at his food. Cynthia's smile falters slightly. I can tell she's trying not to show hurt over Jaxon's avoidance. But I get why he's doing it. I understand more than a bit about parental disappointment and forced politeness, and this is that. Jaxon's not ready to forgive, and he doesn't have the energy to fake it. I almost feel like I'm sitting in a front-row seat to my own family drama.

"Well, whatever the reason, you're here, and I've been wanting desperately to talk to you."

Jaxon chews slowly.

"I know you want to talk to him, love, but maybe now's not the right time," Makin interrupts, reaching across the table to squeeze his wife's hand. Mags who's sitting next to her mother, tries to reassure her.

"We can leave if you want some privacy?" I say in between their stares.

"No, I think it's nice you're here. You've been through this with Xavier, and you managed to forgive him and move past it. I've watched you all laughing in the cafeteria the past few days."

"I haven't forgiven anyone," I say a little too sharply, and instantly Cynthia's face drops. I hate that I did that after everything she's done for me, but I also won't lie—especially in front of Henry—not again. "I love my dad and Sacha, but I haven't forgiven them yet."

"But I've seen you with them. You all seem to be getting along."

I swallow my immediate words, thoughts racing through my mind that I don't speak, for Henry's sake. Sacha and Dad kept who I am a secret my whole life. I can't just forgive that overnight.

"We're working on it." I smile, bumping my elbow with Henry's. "Aren't we?"

"Yes." He grins, showing off the food in his teeth. "I just wish Amrey would give up who her boyfriend is so Dad would stop asking."

"Henry!" I snap, all the blood in my body rushing to my cheeks. Mags laughs at me from across the table, and I fix my stare on her, trying so hard not to look at Jaxon. Though, every part of me wants to know his reaction.

"I'm happy that's working for you," Cynthia interrupts. "Really." Her smile is genuine, but I can tell she's not ready to drop the subject. "However, our family's different. Our problems are different."

"Not that different," Jaxon mumbles. The firm set of his jaw makes my shoulders tense. There's so much he's not saying, so much hurt he's carrying, and I find myself wanting to take his pain away.

"I just want to talk," Cynthia pleads, "I want our family back."

"Well, maybe you shouldn't have lied about not being my mother for three years." Jaxon's words flatten the entire table. Mags practically chokes on her food. Cynthia deflates, and not even Makin has a reasoning response.

"I think we should go." I nudge Henry in the arm, rising from my seat.

"Don't go." Jaxon's hand clamps over my wrist as I hover above my seat, his eyes locking with mine. So much passes between us in this moment. Questions. Pain. Need. I look at the rest of the table, at Henry. "Stay," Jaxon whispers, and before he can ask again, I sit back down.

Jaxon's lips press together, his hand sliding down my wrist until his fingers are edging between mine, and we're holding hands. I'm still unsure what to do, and I half expect him to let go, but he doesn't.

For a moment, silence descends upon us. Cynthia's head is pressed into her palms as Makin reaches for her again. The cafeteria might be alive with chatter, but it's like we're sitting in a soundproof bubble. The quiet is prickly and remains until Cynthia breaks it.

"I'm sorry," she sighs painfully, her hands moving from her face to her neck, kneading her muscles as if to massage her problems away. "I'm sorry for what I did and for how I've handled things. I'm sorry for assuming with you, Amrey, and lying to you, Jaxon. God, I'm so so sorry for everything. I know I'm not perfect. I know I've messed up. But all I'm asking for is a chance to explain, a chance for forgiveness. Or, at best, understanding. I just want to get to know my son again, for us to be a family." Makin squeezes Cynthia's hand, and Mags' too. All three of them watch Jaxon with such intensity, such desperation that it makes me want to stand in front of him and shield him from it. If he's not ready, he's not ready. I know better than anyone that fake forgiveness is like putting a Band-Aid on a gaping wound.

Jaxon remains expressionless, the table quiet, and I realise his hand is still entwined with mine. So, I squeeze it, and I swear I see his face twitch. Just slightly. And like my touch jolted him awake, Jaxon draws in a deep breath.

"Okay," he sighs, and Cynthia's whole face lights up. Jaxon's only agreed to talk, but it seems that's all his mum needs. That's enough to give her hope. I think of my family and how maybe, if I offer a little more, it might inspire a little hope for Henry and possibly even me.

"Cynthia, you're needed back in the dispensary." Her name is voiced across the cafeteria, and with a strained face, she nods.

"Duty calls," she hums, "But maybe we can have dinner together soon?" Her voice is so gentle you could break it, her offer hanging in the air, waiting for Jaxon to take it.

"That sounds nice," Jaxon says, and when Cynthia stands, I swear she appears taller. The weight of her past is no longer so heavy on her shoulders.

"Come on, Henry, I'll drop you to the school room on the way."

With that, only four of us are left at the table.

"They really should give her more of a break," Makin mutters, pushing away his plate.

"You and I both know why they can't," Mags answers, moving his plate back.

"Is this to do with learning about the effects of this serum? Doesn't it just wear off over time, as Animus did? That's why Dane needs to keep re-administering it, right?" I ask, interrupting their conversation, and Mags stills for a second like she's just realised our presence and her words.

"That's the hope," Makin says in her place. "But we aren't certain yet. We're still trying to determine exactly what makes up his new serum. And if we can figure that out, then we can-"

"You're creating a cure?" I gasp, and Mags hushes me just as fast. Makin's alarmed eyes drag me closer to the table as he lowers his head.

"When I say this is confidential, I mean it." His words are stern, and if you weren't trying hard to hear them, you wouldn't. "Only your father, Blane, and a few of us in the lab know about this. And Mags, of course," he says, glancing at her. "You must keep this between us."

"You have my word," I say, and Jaxon, to my surprise, does the same. If he's hurt about being left out of the family secret, he's not showing it.

Makin runs his hands through his hair. "Alright, the fact is, I've been working on an anti-vaccine, a way to neutralise Dane's serum."

A new fire burns inside me. A cure wouldn't just help us cleanse the Axiom guards. It would give us a way to take Axiom back and end Dane's tirade.

"The idea is that if we can figure out what Dane is injecting his people with, we can find the counteractive drug. We could have a way to stop his mind control."

"Why haven't you told anyone?"

"Because we're not even sure it's possible yet. To do it, we need to know exactly what's in the serum, but we've taken blood samples from every guard you've brought in, and there's one component we can't figure out. Until we do, there's no way we can create a vaccine without risking doing more damage. And both your father and Blane agree that we'd rather not give people false hope right now, not after all we've been through."

The whole time Makin has been talking, my mind has been on overdrive, sifting through every thought, every memory of my time with Dane in those tunnels. In that cell. In that torture room.

His laugh.

His taunts.

The drill.

I can still hear the whirring, the cranking, the loud buzz that completely blocked me from any other sound.

The pain.

The earth-splitting pain.

The numbness.

The dark.

Suddenly, the chair beneath me peels away, and I'm back in that room. I'm back there with him. My heart pounds against my chest, tightening over my lungs.

"Hey, are you okay?" Jaxon's voice snaps me from my thoughts. I stare down at my hands, red dots pooling under the surface of my skin. I close my palms again. "What is it?"

"I think I know what the unknown component is."

CHAPTER TWENTY

Suddenly, I feel very alien. Like I'm being dissected all over again. Except, I'm not in Dane's torture chamber. I survived. Instead, the eyes analysing me belong to those I love, sadness staining their faces as they look at me like I'm fragile and cracked. A wounded deer in the snow field. Helpless. And that's the last thing I want.

The very last thing.

"Would you quit with the pity?" I bite, unable to help myself. "And instead, tell me how this can help. My cells are the missing component you need for your anti-serum. They have to be."

"It's not that easy, Amrey." Makin draws back, his lips pressed in a thin line. "We can't be sure it's your cells we're after, and it's not a simple test to find out. The procedure is taxing."

"And you're exhausted. You should sleep." Mags reaches for my hand, but I pull mine back. I know she's only trying to look out for me, but I don't need that. What I need is to put an end to Dane, to help the people of Axiom, and that won't happen if they keep staring at me like I'm about to shatter.

"I'll sleep later," I snap. "Makin, tell me this isn't the breakthrough you've been searching for." He watches me, still silent.

"It is, and you know it. Test me." Even though the idea of going through that pain again makes every nerve in my body scream, I will. If it means finding a cure, I'll do anything.

Makin presses his hand to his head, his shoulders rising and falling before he straightens up and looks me dead in the eye.

"Okay," he breathes, "Let's go."

So, I rise to my feet, a slight tremble in my steps.

AFTER THE PROCEDURE, Jaxon insists on walking me back to my room. The bone marrow biopsy wasn't as painful as I anticipated, thanks to the anaesthesia. All I'm left with is a sore pelvis, a groggy mind, and the relief that if my bone marrow cells are the missing component and I have to do that procedure again, it won't hurt as much. But that won't happen if I don't fix my blood cell count. According to Makin, he didn't use long-acting agents, whatever that means, so I should have only been out for an hour, max—not three. Apparently, I have low blood pressure, and I'm to keep up my fluids, which would be fine if that's all it was. Except Makin's concern for my health has passed onto Jaxon, who hasn't left my side since.

"Jaxon. I'm fine," I say, trying to wiggle out of his grip.

"You just woke up after being passed out for hours. You could barely stand up. And you might be trying to hide it, but I can see your legs wobbling."

"They are not," I say feebly.

Jaxon sighs, loosening his hold on me. "You can never just agree with me, can you?"

"Someone has to keep putting you in your place." Jaxon rolls his eyes, though his arm remains firmly around me. "Look," I breathe, "I'm exhausted, and I'll admit my eating habits have been less than adequate. The drugs just hit me harder, that's all.

Nothing to stress over, so can we just forget it?" Jaxon does not look like he wants to forget it. "Please," I whisper, making my eyes bigger and puffing out my lower lip. And like that, he lets me go, leaving me to stand on my own, and to his surprise and mine, I don't wobble. I feel almost steady.

"See?" I smile. He only shakes his head.

"Alright, Miss Independent, since you're completely fine, I have a question." I watch his gaze narrowing, his hand held out just in case I fall. I know I can either continue down the path of a broken girl or make things a little fun.

"How about, first to my door gets to ask the questions. What do you say?" I raise my eyes in challenge.

"You shouldn't be running right now."

"What? Scared you're going to lose?" I tease. Jaxon shakes his head, looking from me to the long stretch of hall ahead of us.

"Always with the games." He clicks his tongue, his eyes skimming the surface of my features. I know he's trying to determine my well-being and how much trouble he'll get in if something goes wrong.

"You have three seconds," I say, and his gaze snaps back to mine. "Three."

Jaxon stays still.

"Two."

"You're going down, Amrey X."

I launch into a sprint before the last count even leaves my lips. I hear Jaxon curse from behind, his feet hitting the ground seconds later, and I can't help but laugh. A smile too big for the pain I've been carrying spreads over my lips. Despite being thousands of feet underground—caged in a concrete compound —right now, running through the halls, dodging kids and adults, laughing at those shouting at us to stop, is the freest I've felt since I was up on that ski lift before we fell and everything happened.

But as much as I love the burn in my lungs, the pound of my

heart against my chest, my body does not. My pelvis begins screaming after a few dozen metres, and I'm forced to stop, catching myself against the wall.

"Amrey! Are you alright?" Jaxon rushes to my side, helping me stand straight.

"I'm fine," I wince. "But maybe my legs are a little wobbly now. I should probably lie down, preferably with another painkiller."

Jaxon shakes his head "I shouldn't have let you do that."

"You know better than to stop me. Besides, I won." I smirk, red seeping into my cheeks.

"How do you figure that? we're not even close to your room."

I only shrug.

"You're a pain in my arse, Amrey X," Jaxon groans, though he's smiling. In the same moment, he sweeps his arm under my legs and hoists me into the air.

"A pain that you love," I tease. Jaxon flinches, briefly, then continues walking. I'm suddenly very aware of the words that just left my lips. The air around us becomes tight, a cocoon, and I'm struggling to escape its hold. I need a way out before I'm smothered with emotions I'm not ready to face.

"So, what's your question?" I stammer, biting the inside of my cheek.

"I thought you won. Don't you want to ask me something?" he replies without looking at me. While I do have many things I'd like to ask Jaxon, none of them feel appropriate for this moment.

"Take it as a consolation prize for losing," I quip. And this time, Jaxon does look at me.

"Okay then." He seems to study my eyes and how I hold my lips in a tight smile, not forced, but not comfortable considering the awkwardness. "Why didn't you tell us what happened in the cells with Dane?"

I swallow my breath. The question does the opposite of what I wanted. The tension increases to a new level of discomfort as I dig my nails into my palm trying to push back the memories.

"It's not something I wanted to relive, and it didn't seem relevant until now." Jaxon is silent for a moment. Walking and thinking, I assume. Most likely trying to surmise the right thing to say, when there isn't one.

"I'm sorry you went through that," he whispers, his hands tightening around me. "The idea that you were tortured in that cell..." His jaw clenches, his eyes hardening. "I swear I could kill him. But I won't take that away from you."

Or maybe there is a perfect thing to say, and he just did.

When I don't reply, Jaxon continues, "Sometimes I think locking people up is worse than death."

"I think it might be the only way I could move on," I admit. "If he was gone." I know he understands that I mean it.

The air between us once again feels heavy. Talk of death and potential murder is a lot for anyone—especially those running on minimal sleep. As I look ahead, I see my door, the chipped numbers barely resembling a 38 anymore.

"Thanks for the lift," I say as he places me down. "For the record, I did win, and you better not say you let me this time. Cause I won't believe it."

A smirk dances over Jaxon's mouth as he looks at me. "Trust me, that was the only time I'll ever let you win anything."

"You shouldn't have done it, ever," I say, pulling the key from my pocket.

"We'd just met. Maybe I was trying to impress you."

"The only person you wanted to impress back then was my Dad." Jaxon's laugh fills the silence as I unlock the door.

"Nah, he wasn't the only one." The words are simple, but I find myself flustered as Jaxon leans against the threshold. My pulse quickening as we stand in the silence. It's electric, like a magnet pulling us closer, and I almost lean into it—into him.

"I'll let you sleep," Jaxon says, stepping back.

I don't let the abruptness shake me. Nodding, I walk inside and reach for the handle. It's all I can do to stop myself from saying something. Something like "stay."

And before more words can be exchanged, I shut the door.

CHAPTER TWENTY-ONE

The halls are quiet as I leave the cafeteria. I woke up late today, getting the sleep Makin and Cynthia keep insisting I have, and by the time I arrive at the command centre, it's mid-morning and the door's locked. Muffled voices escape the edges, yet even as I wiggle the handle, it doesn't open. Whatever meeting is happening in there, isn't one I'm supposed to be a part of. Swallowing down my frustration, I force myself to walk away.

The last few days have flown by, and with each passing night, more guards are brought in, saved from Dane. It's been nearly a week since my plan was implemented, and if he's caught on, he's shown no signs of retaliation, which is as scary as it is unsettling. I don't know what he's planning, and I don't like it. The only comfort is knowing that with every guard we save, it's another willing body on our side, though the transition hasn't been smooth. Ezra is fighting it the hardest. He still won't speak to Knox, and I know that's taking its toll. Dane's mind control has a firm grip on the guards, even days later, they remain hostile and insubordinate. The serum may wear off over time, but it'll be weeks before it fully leaves their system. Weeks we don't have. If we want Axiom back, we're going to need an antidote, something that can break Dane's control instantly. Hopefully, with my bone marrow cells, Makin can create and test one quickly, because each passing day puts me more on edge. I can't get the guard's words out of my head. Everywhere I look, every new face I speak to, doubt creeps in. *Is this the person he was talking about? Are you the mole? Are you Dane's sympathiser?*

Then there's the old faces, my friends. I don't want to think that it could be one of them. It can't be. The thought alone melts my bones. Because if it is, I have no idea what I'll do.

"Yo, Sub?" I look up as I pass the dispensary to see Owen walking towards me. "How are you feeling?"

"Better." I smile, but Owen's no longer looking at me. His eyes drift to the dispensary window and the two people inside, Mags and Emeric.

"Where are you headed?" I bump his shoulder.

"Uhh," he mumbles, shaking his head before looking at me. "The training centre. Everyone's in some big meeting, so I'm on babysitting duty."

"Yeah I noticed. Why are we being kept out?"

"Owen's gaze softens. "Don't take it personally, pretty sure it's essential personnel only. We're all in the dark."

"Jaxon as well?" I ask. Owen grimaces. So not all. "What about Kale? Is he there?"

"I'm not sure. The last I heard, he was with Elle, but I saw her go into the meeting alone. I don't know the specifics, but they probably just wanted to let you sleep. We all heard what happened with you giving blood and stuff-" Owen's words fall off, and he doesn't finish his sentence, but I have a pretty good idea about what he's not saying. Everyone knows about what happened to me in the cells. "I'm sure they'll let us know soon," he finishes.

"Sure," I reply. Unsure whether that brings me any solace. If the meeting is about the antidote, they'll need someone who can offer a firsthand account of Dane's testing. Dad's already there, but Elle must know something he doesn't.

"Look," Owen says, squeezing my shoulder, "I might not be able to get you into that meeting, but I can offer you a distraction. Why don't you come babysit with me? I'm stepping in for Blane to teach the kids. I'm sure Henry will be there." Though I'm angry about being excluded from the meeting, I do want to see Henry, so I find myself nodding.

"Lead the way."

No matter how intense life gets, the training centre manages to keep me sane. The sun shines in through the dome roof today, beaming off the water and crystallising the wet cave walls. We put the kids through the basic drills Blane taught us—run, swim, climb, spar. By the end of the afternoon, I'm exhausted for both them and myself. Having a sibling is one thing, but ten kids, full of energy, who each want their turn at beating you is a lot. Though surprisingly, Owen has a knack for it, and I enjoy watching him with his sister Helena, even Henry and Tobias.

"I don't know if it's the fact that these kids had to grow up fast or that you're a giant kid yourself, but you're great with them," I say, handing Owen a drink.

"Thanks, Sub, I'm pretty sure there's a compliment in there somewhere." I smile, listening to the kids bicker behind us.

"I'm pretty sure they have a bet going to see who can kick your butt first."

"Oh, I know they do. My money's on Henry; the kid has skills. He takes after his sister." Owen smirks. Though he means well, that sentiment doesn't do anything but make me feel uneasy.

"Do me a favour, don't tell him that. The last thing I want for Henry is to be running towards danger. He's been caught in the crossfires enough."

"I get that, but you can't hold him back forever. He'll want to fight one day."

"Well, hopefully that day is in the very distant future. One where Dane is very dead."

Owen laughs. "Now that's a future I could get behind."

"Speaking of the future. I've seen how you look at Mags. Why haven't you said anything?"

Owen sighs, sitting next to me on the bench. "I couldn't do that to Ric. Besides, I'm pretty sure he's more her type. I'm a bit too unstable for her. She needs someone like him."

"I don't know about that. But I do know you're selling your-self short. You're a great guy, Owen. Anyone would be lucky to have you."

"Thanks, Amrey. And just between us, whoever you pick, will be damn lucky." My chest seizes as I rest my head on Owen's shoulder. Until now, I've been happily avoiding that thought, but I won't be able to for much longer. Eventually, I'll have to make a decision. Though, right now, I have no goddamn clue.

"Oi, you two." Owen and I look up to see Griffin standing in the door to the arena. "We're needed in the command centre." His voice rings out as the door slams shut, echoing off the cave walls.

"Oh, now we're needed?" My tone is dripping in sarcasm as I straighten up.

"Easy, tiger, give them a chance to explain first." Owen shakes his head, turning off the lights and motioning for me and the kids to exit.

"Don't worry, I will," I sigh. One way or the other, I'll get my answers.

"I MEAN IT. PLAY NICE, SUB," Owen warns as we enter the command centre.

"When have I ever not played nice?" I smile. He only shakes his head, and the second the door closes behind me, I see Kale, leaning against the wall on the far side of the room, Elle at his side.

Everyone's here.

He watches me as I follow Owen and take a place next to Jaxon.

"How you feeling?" Jaxon asks, eyeing me over.

"I'd be better if I wasn't locked out of the meeting today." Jaxon's jaw tightens as he looks at Owen. "Are you going to tell me why?" I say between them.

"That was your Dad and Blane's call, not mine." Jaxon straightens, suddenly serious. My blood boils. Regardless of whose decision it was to keep me out of the meeting, I thought Jaxon was done hiding things from me.

"Fine, I'll talk to you boys later." My snide is clear as I leave them standing there and move to rest next to Kale.

"Having a lover's spat?" he taunts.

"Funny," I snip, making a point to step on his toes. "You gonna tell me where you were today? Or who you were with?" I say the last part pointedly, glancing at Elle. If she can hear me, she's pretending not to.

"Someone's jealous."

"Curious," I correct.

"What? Am I not allowed to have other friends?"

Though we're whispering, I notice we've caught the eyes of multiple people in the room, including Jaxon and my father.

"Better shut up, before you get me in trouble," Kale whispers in my ear. I can practically feel the outline of his smirk on my cheek. In that moment, Dad clears his throat to call everyone's attention and directs us to the interrogation room connected to the command centre. The last time I was here, James was chained up. Dad had just shot and killed his partner. Blood stained the ground. The crack of the bullet ran out in my ears for days, and though the blood's scrubbed clean, the memory still exists. When I look at James, I know the fear does too.

The only solace is that this time, no one's chained up. Instead, Ezra and Cora are seated at a table, their faces devoid of emotion, their arms outstretched in front of them. Sacha walks in accompanied by Makin, his face tired and unshaven, his hair in need of a cut, and when he pulls out a small vile, my eyes widen.

The cure.

Silence descends the room as Makin makes his way over to the chair and sits opposite them. The tension is palpable. The room is still. He places a syringe on the table, and neither Cora nor Ezra bats an eye.

"Do you know what this is?" he asks. The shake of their heads provides the only answer.

"It's an antiserum," Makin continues, a murmur floods the room, a shuffling of feet. Kale's eyes flash to mine.

"Did you know about this?" His breath is tight. I nod. And then we're all watching as Makin takes out another syringe, draws liquid from the vial and injects Cora and Ezra.

They don't flinch, but the sting of the needle is seen in the water pooling in Cora's eyes, in the nail marks on Ezra's palm. I had hoped the antiserum wouldn't hurt, but it's clear it's unpleasant. I wonder if this was discussed in the meeting.

I watch their faces as the seconds slip past, their stone-cold expressions lifting, anxious crease lines forming. Then, like a veil has been removed from their heads, their eyes grow wide, darting around the room.

"I'm going to ask you several questions," Makin begins. "Answer them truthfully." Neither Cora nor Ezra react. "Why did you sign up for Dane's guard?"

"I didn't sign up," Cora says flatly, her stare unflinching.

"Then why did you join?"

"If I didn't, Dane was going to make my son. He is twelve." Her words hit the air like lead on water. Her answer is painful to hear but not surprising. Dane's ruthlessness is no longer a shocking discovery but an expectation.

Makin clears his throat before asking his next question. "What is Dane planning?"

Cora swallows. "I don't know."

"That's not a clear answer."

"It's the only one I can give." Her voice doesn't waver, and I wonder even with the antidote, if it still strains her to speak so openly, or what the sensation feels like at all. In Axiom, we can never lie. Those who aren't subversive physically can't speak false facts. Then there was Dane's serum, which held them prisoners in their own minds. Not only could they not lie or hide anything, they could only speak on what Dane allowed and do what was in the restraints of his commands. Now, to be free from all of that, to have your mind back and thoughts which you can speak without resistance, must be freeing. Yet, Cora looks anything but free as she stares at Makin with hard eyes.

"Very well." Makin turns slightly. "Ezra, can you tell me what Dane's planning?"

Ezra hesitates, expelling air from his legs before deciding to answer.

"All I know..." His voice is shakier than Cora's, and he's not looking at Makin. Instead, he's scanning every face in the room, and I think I know who he's looking for.

"Knox..." he says the moment his gaze collides with his. "I'm so sorry." Knox remains still, but the urge to talk to his friend is there, held back by tight lips.

"You can talk to him later," Dad interrupts. However, Ezra keeps his eyes on Knox, only returning his attention to Makin when Knox offers no more than a nod of recognition.

"All I know is that Dane has mass-produced his serum. New batches every day. And it's stronger."

"How did you come by this information?"

Ezra's gaze wavers from Makin, and he glances at his fingers. "I can't remember."

His words don't sound certain, and I know I'm not the only one sensing that. But, instead of questioning him further, Makin nods towards Blane, and I watch as the door opens, the blood draining from my veins.

The room is wrapped in silence as we watch the guard enter, his grin just as chilling as I remember. His movements are stilted and stiff, his groans painful to hear. The journey from the forest to the Defiance, though trying for me, did more damage to him. Welts and burns lay on his skin from being dragged through snow and debris. He slowly edges into the seat opposing Makin. Exhaustion wraps every inch of his face, but when he tilts his head up, his eyes find mine, and a shiver runs over my body.

"You."

The word trembles from his lips in more of a plea than a threat, and I can barely keep composed. Kale seems to feel the same sense of desperation. Swallowing hard next to me, his face extra taut. I look at the guard again, desperate to ask him what he meant, to demand he tell me who Dane's sympathiser is, but now is not the time nor the place. Not in this room, with this many people. Not when the person he's talking about could be any one of them.

"I warned you." The guard's voice slithers over my skin, and I fight the urge to tremble.

"Enough antics." Makin's voice grips the room. "What is your name?"

The guard slowly turns his attention back to Makin, holding his gaze with a flat expression. But he doesn't answer the question. "Do you know where you are?" Makin persists. Still no answer. "You are at the Defiance. We rescued you."

That makes the guard scoff. "If that's what you want to call it."

"Do you have a better term?"

"A kidnapping. A hostage situation. A beating, by her." He looks at me then, and my stomach drops. I open my mouth to respond, but Kale presses closer to me.

"Don't bait him. That's what he wants," he whispers in my ear, and I have to stop from reacting to his sudden closeness. Re-pinning a blank veil over my face, I don't let the guard see my guilt. Though, it's drowning me in spades.

"I would assume you would have offered a beating of your own had you been given the chance," Makin retorts, and though his tone never wavers from impartial, I sense a hit of pride. "Would I be correct in assuming that?"

"Potentially."

"Great. Now that that's settled, are you prepared to answer questions honestly, without further action?"

The guard's lips trigger into a sly grin. "What do you think?" he quips.

"Very well." Without another word, Makin produces a third syringe.

My eyes go wide, alarm running through me. The needle is barely visible before it's plunged into the guard's arm. The moment the contents are emptied, his face goes blank. His pupils dilate as he blinks once, then twice, as if to clear his vision. The shadow that once crept behind his eyes—the haunting look—is gone, replaced by the same clueless fear I saw in Cora and Ezra. As his reality sinks in, he stares at his shaking hands, searching for guidance in the eyes cast his way. In Makin. In Mine.

Two seconds ago, this man was pulsating with rage and pain. Now, he resembles an empty shell. The difference is palpable. Cora and Ezra have been here for almost a week. They've had blood transfusions, sleep, and time. Dane's serum wasn't as strong in their system when they took the antidote. But with him, the poison that was Dane's serum, surging through his veins just seconds ago, has been wiped out in a single breath, leaving him to piece himself back together.

"What's your name?" Though Makin's voice is steady, the guard struggles to understand it, slowly repeating each syllable in his mind until a single word rests on his lips.

"Pylor."

"Do you remember how you got here, Pylor?"

"Yes," he says with a single nod.

"Good. Now tell me how you ended up in Dane's guard."

Pylor returns his gaze to Makin. His stare a mix of fraught and awe.

"He chose me," he says calmly, narrowing his eyes on the syringe. "What did you do to me? How can I answer you?"

"We gave you a vaccine to counteract Dane's serum."

"An antidote?"

"Yes."

Pylor looks around the room once more, his stare wavering on me, and I swear I see a twitch of fear.

"Why did he choose you?" Makin draws him back to the question. Pylor shakes off whatever it was that triggered the fear I saw.

"I was working as a cleaner, and he needed numbers. We were the first people he recruited." I suck in a breath, wondering just how many people Dane's forced into his guard, how many were threatened like Cora.

"Do you know how Dane is replicating his serum?"

Pylor keeps looking around the room. Keeps looking over at me. And every time the prickles edge higher up my spine. Kale shudders next to me, and I think Pylor's intrepid staring is getting to him too.

"Pylor," Makin urges. I watch the guard's head tilt in my direction, but when he opens his mouth to answer, no words come out.

That seems to shock Pylor. "Ask again," he says sharply. Makin does. He continues to press with his questions, but the more he does, the more I notice Pylor's hands twitch. His foot tapping against the ground. Faster, faster.

"I CAN'T!"

The room is shocked to silence. Everyone staring at a broken down Pylor, his fingers dug into his temples, as he rocks back and forth on his chair. Makin presses his lips together. Another look shared with my father.

"Pylor," he whispers. "It's okay. Take your time. Think of your answer. How is Dane replicating his serum?"

Pylor's frantic eyes meet Makin's, but the calmness has left his face, panic now carved into every feature. "You said you cured me! That whatever Dane injected me with is gone!" Makin only nods. "Then why can't I answer?"

"Try again." Makin's tone is flat and calm. But Pylor is only growing more irate.

"I… I can't." He chokes out each syllable with a sound that makes me think of glass scraped on bone. Nothing pleasant at all. "I can't say what I want to say."

"That's alright," Makin sighs, sitting back in his chair. Then, with a quick word to my father, Ezra, Cora and Pylor are directed out of the room.

Not even ten minutes later, we are all shuffled back into the command centre.

"What just happened?" I growl, my voice overtaking the silence. My father places his hands on the table, leaning over it like the weight of the world is on his back

"One second he was fine, and then he wasn't," Owen adds.

"That was expected," Makin says calmly. "Pylor has only been here a few days. Dane's serum is still so fresh in his system. The antidote was more effective on Cora and Ezra because they've had more time to wean off it, but it's not strong enough for people like Pylor."

"But he reacted, so it worked?" Jaxon says this time, taking the question from my lips.

"Partially. He may have found it easier to talk than without it, but it didn't cure him. The antidote was only being tested today, and now I know it's not ready."

With a heavy sigh, Dad straightens up and begins pacing back and forth. "Makin, please assure me that this wasn't a colossal waste of time."

"It wasn't," Makin says calmly.

"And you can be certain everything he said to us wasn't a bunch of lies strung together in a convincing act?"

"It's hard to be sure. That much is true." Makin thumbs the vile in his hand. "Their hesitancy is warranted and not unexpected, but…"

"But?" Dad sterns.

"But, I believe, for the most part, they were telling the truth."

"Not good enough. If the antidote is not 100 percent effective, then we can't be sure of anything."

"Why would they lie to us?" I step in before Makin can. "Wouldn't they want to tell us everything they can so we can defeat Dane?"

"It's not that easy; they're experiencing true freedom for the first time in their entire life. The choice to speak, or not, it's scary terrain, and they don't know how this is going to go."

"So the conclusion of that experiment was…?" Dad's attitude and demeanour towards Makin makes me uncomfortable.

"The experiment," he says the word with more tenacity than Dad did. "Was a success. We have an antidote-"

"That doesn't work," Dad interrupts.

"That needs to be stronger," Makin corrects.

Dad's jaw clenches. "So, it's as we feared."

"What is as we feared?" My tone rises, and I know I should

simmer down, but I'm not that far on my self-control journey yet. "I understand you had a meeting that I was kept from, but I would like to be clued in now." I watch Dad exchange looks with everyone in the room, like a code is being sent and deciphered with a single blink, and I'm the only one who doesn't know how to crack it. My stomach clenches. "What are you not telling me?"

"To make a stronger serum, we need to run more tests. We need more of your cells."

"I figured that, and they're yours. You can knock me out and take what you need right now. But you knew that already, so can someone tell me the real problem."

"How much?" Kale asks to my surprise. I knew he cared, but not to that extent, and it seems to stun Makin. I, however, notice that Jaxon nor Dad or Blane are asking the same question, and instead, they look at each other—words shared but not said between them. I realise before they answer what they'll say. Makin's antidote is close to working. A few more tests and we could have a way to save everyone from Dane's control. We wouldn't have to lock people up or dry them out. We could save them with one dose, one last injection. But that means making more, that means using me.

"Amrey." Makin's eyes are hollow. "To cure everyone in Axiom, we're going to need to replicate the antidote on a rapid level. And we can't-"

"It's not an option," Dad interrupts.

"What's not an option?!" Kale demands.

"To make enough of the serum, they'd have to completely deplete your cell count. Meaning – "

"I get it." My voice rings through the room. No more cells, no more me.

"You should do it."

CHAPTER TWENTY-TWO

"No."

The word pulses around the room in a steady rhythm.

"What other choice do we have?" I ask flatly. It's not that I want to die. Despite the death wish everyone thinks I have, I don't want to die. I'm just not opposed to it. If it means saving those I love and everyone else. If it means ending Dane and rescuing Axiom. Then, my life is worth it.

"We'll find another way, but that's not happening," Dad affirms, the veins on his face popping out of his skin.

"What we should be searching for is a way to replicate the cure." Sacha, who had become considerably silent in the back of the room, makes her way to the front. "Dane doesn't have Amrey," she says staidly. "Yet he is somehow managing to mass produce her DNA and make his serum. If we can find out how, we can do it too."

"It doesn't matter," Kale interrupts, "trying to make a cure, trying to figure out how Dane's operating and what he's planning, is senseless. It doesn't change the reality. He has an endless supply of the serum, and with every guard we take, he just makes another one. Soon he'll be using kids. We should stand down."

"Stand down?" My whole body tenses.

"It's not the worst idea. Dane's only hunting us because he knows we want to take him down. But if we leave him alone. Then maybe he'll leave us alone, and we can move on with our lives. Isn't that what you all want? To move on with your lives?" Kale speaks so confidently, it's unnerving.

"Not by leaving everyone in Axiom to be used as Dane's puppet. And what makes you think he'll even leave us alone?" I ask him directly, wondering where this has come from. Not once, in all the time we've spent together, did I ever get the sense that he didn't want to fight back. If this is about protecting me, then I don't want it, and he should know that.

"Amrey's right." My eyes are drawn to Jaxon as he speaks. "I don't like it. But Dane doesn't seem like the kind of person to settle peacefully. He'll want revenge for everything we've done. He won't leave us alone. Not without retribution."

"So we make the cure," I repeat. "Put me under, take my cells. As many as you can."

"Amrey enough," Dad sterns. "That's not an option. But doing nothing isn't one either. We have to find another way."

"Xavier's right." Blane steps forward, capturing everyone's attention as he places the empty syringes on the table. "Makin. Tell us what we need to know and what options we have." Makin moves to stand next to Blane, tension creasing his features.

"Right now, we know three things for sure. One, Amrey has strong subversive cells. Two, Dane is altering them for his serum. How? We're not sure, but he's managed to reverse her cells, modifying the part that makes her immune and trans-forming them into the ultimate mind control drug. And three, we know he's managed to replicate those cells rapidly to mass produce his serum." The room is quiet as Makin picks up a syringe and twists it in his fingers.

"To counteract Dane's Serum, I will use Amrey's cells against him, amplifying her immunity into a cure and giving it to everyone. It's ridiculously simple, yet not. We can only harvest one or two quarts of bone marrow cells safely from Amrey every six weeks. To mass produce the cure it would take years. Years we don't have."

"If we knew how Dane was replicating his serum, couldn't you do the same with Amrey's cells? Could you artificially replicate her DNA?" Sacha asks.

"DNA replication is possible. I've done it, but only with the right technology, technology we don't have access to here." Makin places the syringe back down, his fingers drumming over the table in a neurotic way. "And even then, we'd need a way to administer it. It must go directly into the bloodstream."

"Yeah, it's not like we could just sneak into Axiom and start stabbing people with needles," Owen questions, and I find myself nodding along. I hadn't thought about that, but he's right. Our plan has several holes. Right now, it's not a plan at all—just flawed ideas and ill-conceived thoughts strung together.

"Then we need a new objective." Jaxon's voice commands the room, "It's clear, we don't have the sort of time Makin needs to make the antidote, but we can't sit back and let Dane continue his tirade either."

"What do you suggest?" Dad asks. I half expected him to shut Jaxon down.

"We start with the guards," he begins, and instantly the room is clued in. Jaxon explains his idea once and then once more. Dad asks several questions, but I swear I see pride in his eyes. Blane fleshes out the logistics. Makin concludes whether it's possible. Everyone else nods their heads, and then we disperse.

The plan's simple.

In the next hour, Makin will harvest my bone marrow cells— as much as he safely can—tweak the antidote, and produce as many doses as possible. Then, we'll use it to cure the guards we have, enlist them on our side, and together, we'll storm right into Axiom and overtake Dane. Once he's out of the picture, everyone in Axiom will have to listen. Makin can get access to the equipment he needs. We can mass produce the antidote from the lab in Axiom, and administer it to the people. But even with the dozen guards we have already, it's risky. So, there lies the final piece of the plan.

Tonight, we go on one final mission.

One more chance to deplete Dane's numbers and save Axiom. And this time, we're going for the whole damn guard.

CHAPTER TWENTY-THREE

"You shouldn't be coming."

Jaxon startles me, as his hands grab the straps of my pack and pull tight. This moment reminds me of months ago, the night we left for our trek, before we were stuck in a blizzard. A memory of the cabin flashes past my eyes, and I try to shake off the shiver that spills over my skin.

"You know better than to say that," I retort.

"I know, but I wouldn't be me if I didn't," he smirks. "Also, if at any point you feel too tired or sore, let me know. I'll carry you back if I have to." I resist the urge to roll my eyes and settle for a smile and clipped nod. It has only been a few hours since Makin took my bone marrow cells, and even I can't deny I'm a little tired. The anaesthesia is still in my system, but I'm okay with that because once it's gone, the pain sets in, and that's another type of discomfort.

"Ready?" he asks, with a final tug of my pack strap.

"Ready," I breathe.

We leave when dark has settled and a chill has laced the air. Our imprints trail behind us as we trek over the snowfield towards the tree line. Tonight we're going for the entire Axiom patrol, and based on the few cameras we managed to get working again, we gather we'll be intercepting just over a dozen guards—no small feat. We need the numbers, and time is not on our side.

Jaxon and I are the first to reach Axiom's off-base bunker. More memories come to light that I push back. The last time we were here, we needed to get in. This time, we want to blow it up.

I hand Jaxon the explosives Blane gave us, watching as he rigs them to the side of the bunker. With the guards spread out in units over Axiom's boundary line, we needed a way to draw them all to one place. There's no flying under the radar this time. We want attention, and this is how we'll get it.

"Done." Jaxon finishes securing the last IED and we hurry back to hide in the trees, just as the guards on patrol walk past.

"Two minutes," I whisper. Jaxon's finger hovers over the trigger as the guards grow distant. I hear bristles snapping. My gaze lands on a set of eyes a few yards to my right. Backup is here.

It's time.

Jaxon presses down on the trigger, and the bunker goes up in flames and flying debris. If the guards weren't aware of our presence before, they are now.

"No turning back," I whisper.

"The last time I turned back, you were pressing a gun to your head and forcing me to leave. I know better than to look anywhere but forward with you." Jaxon's words hit me with force, and I'd be lying if I said my heart wasn't beating faster.

"Good to know you're learning." I smile, and my breath catches as Jaxon reaches out, his thumb brushing the ash from my cheek. If it weren't for the sound of sticks crunching under pounding feet, the moment might have lasted. But it didn't, and instead we both jump up, alert and ready.

"Our people or theirs?" Jaxon hesitates.

Gunfire erupts.

"Theirs," I say with alarm. That was quick.

I look to my left to make sure we're ready. Emeric steps out of the trees just enough to signal to me. Him, Owen and Mags—who refused to stay behind—are a go. Jaxon looks to the right and nods. Archer, Griffin, and Herman are ready, too. That leaves Sacha and Zeal who are lying in wait ten yards back. Everybody else stayed behind to defend the Defiance, including Kale and Elle. The thought nags at me, but I can't focus on it now. We have a fight to win and people to save.

"Now for the fun part." Jaxon smirks, pulling the flash grenade from his pocket. I smile, reaching for mine and together we throw them into the fray.

In the seconds when the guards are stunned, we move in. The flash grenades take them by surprise, and before they know what hit them, we have four guards subdued and tied up to the trees behind us. It's gratifying to know we've managed it without brute force, but my relief quickly fades as more guards arrive. Time for phase two.

Jaxon pulls me down behind a pile of debris, and thankfully, everyone else has done the same, taking cover in the clearing where the Axiom bunker was just blown apart.

We are protected, but lying in wait.

By my count, there are at least ten guards, with the others still tied to the trees behind us. We outman them by one, but their bullets keep flying, and I'm biting down every bit of willpower not to use my gun. It's a last resort. We all agreed. We want to save these guards from Dane, not kill them in the process.

After a few minutes, the bullets stop. Silence engulfs the smoke-filled air, ash flying off the burning debris.

"Enough games." A voice shouts over the shredded landscape we've claimed as a battlefield. Jaxon's grip on my wrist tightens. The guards sound at least 30 feet away, likely on the outskirts of the clearing, using the trees as cover.

Jaxon presses a single finger to his lips, and I hold my breath. No one from our side talks. Good. Negotiations will lead us nowhere. There are only so many hours left in the night. We can't stay in a stand-off forever. But we do need a way out of this.

"Silence will only cost you, and we have no issue paying retribution on your friend."

Friend? My heart clenches, and I tear my head out from behind the debris to get a better look. Jaxon freezes as Griffin's voice breaks through the air.

"Don't shoot him!" he shouts, and before I can react, Griffin is standing face to face with the Axiom guards, his eyes fixed on the very thing mine are.

Archer.

Angry and wrestling against their grip.

"Don't shoot him," Griffin repeats. I hold my stare on Archer who remains visibly irritated.

"Show yourself," is the guard's only reply. Without hesitation, both Jaxon and I stand. Owen and Herman step out from their barriers as well, but Emeric, Mags and Zeal stay down. They have the same sense I do. We can't let them know how many of us there are. And with a simple nod from Herman, I know Sacha's still waiting in the trees behind us.

"If you want him to live, you'll surrender your weapons and yourselves." The guard's grip on Archer tightens as he presses the gun into the back of Archer's head. My hands shake, palms pressed into my sides, fingers grazing the gun at my belt. We didn't come here to kill, but we may not have a choice.

I focus on the weapon at Archer's head, the guard's finger edging towards the trigger, but before he can pull it, I step in front of Jaxon and raise mine.

Seconds feel like hours as I hold the piece of metal in my

hand—a piece of metal that kills—and with every heartbeat, the gun only feels heavier, the weight suddenly too much. Knowing I have the power to kill someone is too much. My hesitation is all it takes for the guards to draw their guns on me.

A shot rings out.

A casing drops to the ground.

I stare wide-eyed as Jaxon lowers his weapon.

The bullet hits the Axiom guard in the leg. I watch him fall to his knees as Archer's released from his grasp, and unlike me, he doesn't hesitate. Turning around, he shoots the closest guard in a limb that won't prove fatal.

And then it's chaos.

I see Archer make it to Griffin as bullets begin to fly through the air, hitting trees, debris and body parts. Everyone dives behind anything that can give protection.

"Amrey!" Jaxon pulls me down. I can no longer see the others. Angling myself lower, out of the path of the spraying bullets, I try to catch my breath, but my lungs are tight, and panic is beginning to rise in my throat. Every part of me is tense with fear. It wasn't supposed to go this way. I no longer know if we can overtake these guards to cure them. Worse, I don't even know how we're getting out alive.

"Any ideas?" Jaxon shouts as bullets hit the wooden debris we are crouched behind. Owen slides in next to us and begins shooting through the gaps.

"We've got to fish 'em out," he says, looking at me. "Just like training."

"Just like training," I repeat, but the sinking feeling doesn't leave my stomach. Because this isn't training, this isn't 'mudball.' These bullets aren't pellets, and we could really die.

"We need a distraction," I yell over the ring of gunfire.

"What are you thinking, Sub?" Owen meets my gaze and though I haven't suggested anything, I know by the look in his eyes that he can tell exactly what I'm thinking.

"We can't," I breathe.

"We can," Owen affirms.

"What are you talking about?" Jaxon urges, reloading his gun.

"Emeric and Mags have a clear line to the guards on the far left, but there's too much gunfire. It needs to be directed." Owen grabs three more rounds and tops up his load. Then he turns and signals something to Emeric I can't see. "I'm gonna head for the tree line. Cover me." Without so much as another breath, he's up and running. Jaxon and I quickly shoot cover fire, and as the guards direct their aim at Owen, Emeric and Mags make their move.

It's been five minutes, and I'm not sure what happened to Owen. He hasn't come back, not that he could. The bullets haven't stopped, but thanks to him, we managed to secure one side of the clearing, and now three more guards are restrained, the rest being pushed further into the tree line behind them. I feel a little relief, that is until I see one of the guards sneaking up behind Griffin. He raises his gun, and Jaxon notices at the same time I do.

A shot goes off.

My voice rips from my throat, but Griffin only stares at us, stunned. Archer turns around, his reflexes sharper than mine. However, he's not needed. Sacha is there, her gun extended and hovering over a writhing guard. Archer and Griffin quickly cover Sacha with gunfire while Zeal and Herman help her drag the guard behind their barricade and secure him with the others. Another guard secured, another one we can save.

Seconds blur into minutes. Time is becoming mute. My senses dull to sound and sight. If my limbs are aching, I don't feel it. All I know is what's in front of me. The gunfire hasn't slowed. The bloodshed has only increased from both sides. Yet neither is giving up. As I duck to reload my gun, something catches my eye and Jaxon's: the shadow of two guards slipping through the tree line behind us. I don't need a second look to figure out where they're going.

I go over the options in my head, looking at what's left of us. Jaxon has a flesh wound. Zeal has been hit in the leg. Owen's still gone, and even Archer's bleeding from a wound I can't see. We are wearing thin, but I can't let those guards reach the Defiance, where Henry, Dad and everyone else waits. I won't.

My decision must be clear in my eyes because Jaxon simply nods.

"Go! I'll cover you!" he yells, and with a faint smile, I take off running. Bullets spray past me, hitting trees and bouncing off the ground. I stumble forward as one nicks my leg, biting down on the pain that sears through my muscle. But I keep running.

I follow the guards through the trees, dodging branches and twigs as they scrape my legs and cut into my arms. I'm tracking at a good speed, remaining undetected, but my chest burns for reprieve. I don't stop though, the Defiance is only hours away. I can't let them get any closer.

An opening in the trees leads to a small snow hill, and I dredge forward, my calves aching as the snow becomes deeper, the hill steeper. I can no longer make out the two guards—only one—but I'm nipping at their heels.

"Stop or I'll shoot." My voice is hoarse against the wind as I raise my weapon. The guard freezes ten yards in front of me, and I let myself catch my breath. The icy air stings my throat with every intake, the sun beginning to peek above the horizon, tainting the sky with a ripple of orange. It's so secluded up here that I hear nothing but the howling wind, almost like the battle below doesn't exist.

Click.

My head whips around so fast that the strain in my neck is immediate. Instantly, my blood runs cold as I find myself staring down the loaded barrel of a gun. A guard towers in front of me, snow covering their legs, their hands blistered purple. They inch closer. My heart pounds harder. My fingers tighten on my weapon.

And then I see their eyes.

Her hair is shorter, and blood drops from a fresh graze on her arm, but her stare is just as deadly as before. I can't help it. I pull my finger from the trigger.

"Don't go soft on me now, Amrey."

"Kelly." My voice is like dust against the wind.

"Nice to see you too."

"What are you doing here?"

"Did you think you were the only ones who had secret backup?"

I hear the steps of the other guard coming up behind me, taking his place next to Kelly. I don't recognise him.

"What are you waiting for?" he barks. "Shoot her."

"Not this one. Dane wants her alive." My blood runs cold. The gun is still in my grip. But Kelly remains oddly calm.

"Drop the gun," the man yells.

"I don't think so," I breathe.

"Drop it, or I'll shoot you in the wrist. Dane never said anything about injuring you." The other guard is a lot more agitated. I tighten my hold on the cold metal.

"Leave us, Reign. I've got this covered. Go and help the others. That gun show has gone on for too long; it's time to wrap it up."

Reign, seemingly older and angrier than Kelly, holds his disturbing stare on me for a few more seconds before turning around and huffing off.

"Been in the guard for what, a few months? And you already have the men bowing to your orders," I say, aware of the grin breaking out on my lips. My words seem to elicit a hint of a smile from Kelly.

"Did you expect anything else?"

I size her up for a moment. Kelly always had a way of intimidating me, even if I did kick her ass a few times in combat class, that never phased her. No matter who you were, she always stood taller. I notice she hasn't yet asked me to lower my gun, nor has she made a move against me, and she just sent away her only leverage.

"I learnt never to expect anything when it comes to you. But I do wonder why you're so eagerly doing Dane's bidding." Kelly watches me for a second. An answer seems to flash behind her eyes. Her lips twitch ever so slightly, but she doesn't answer. Instead, her stare hardens, and her hold on the gun slips.

That's what the serum does. It takes away a person's free will and moral compass, leaving no room for questions. I knew this when I asked, but I said it anyway. I wanted to push it, to see how far I could bend the strength of Dane's command.

"You don't seem very comfortable holding that thing." I nod towards her grip on the gun and make a display to relax mine a little. "They are annoyingly heavy," I finish.

Kelly flinches, but she still doesn't attack, only continues to size me up, seeming just as curious about what I'll do.

"Dane said I had to bring you in. But he never said how. What do you say we drop these clunks of metal and fight it out like we know how." Heat builds inside me as I watch her steadily lower her weapon.

"Fine with me," I smirk, dropping the gun into the snow. "I much prefer hand-to-hand combat anyway." I launch myself at Kelly.

We're catapulted into the snow, tussling until I can get my footing and pull myself up. Kelly sweeps out her leg, ramming it into the back of mine, but I manage to stop myself from falling and instead drive my knees into her thighs and throw my body on top of hers. This time, I have the upper hand. Pinning her down by the shoulders, I slam my forehead against her skull. There's a crunch of bone, and I'm praying it's Kelly's and not mine. Though black dots threaten my vision, I banish them to the edges and press my forearm against Kelly's throat. I don't want to hurt her. I don't want to hurt anyone. But I need her to pass out so I can drag her arse back to the Defiance and save her. Anything to avoid picking up my gun again.

I'm thrown onto my back.

Kelly manages to drive her knee into my gut and thrust me backwards. The snow hits me hard and makes my chest tight. I'm winded, but that's not what has me frozen in place.

It's Kelly's weight on top of me.

I barely heard the crack against the wind, against our grunts. But I feel her blood, hot and sticky and soaking into my top from the puncture wound in her head.

Time freezes. My scream's silent as I scramble out from under her, frantically scanning the snow for the shooter. My chest pounds as I reach for my weapon.

That's when I see him running towards me.

Reign.

Stupid, stupid, stupid man.

He sees me then, his gun raising once again. My stomach lodges, panic rising to my throat. The bullet cracks through the air. This time I don't hesitate. I watch Reign drop to the ground.

CHAPTER TWENTY-FOUR

After an hour, the shock still grips me, but my tears have begun to dry up as I drag Kelly's body to Reign's, huffing from exhaustion and dropping to my knees. My tears sting my wind-burned cheeks, as I manage to draw in several sharp breaths. Two people lie dead beside me. But one death is my doing. Reign's body is lifeless because of me. I'm just like Dane. I wanted to fight dirtier, and this is what it got me, regardless of my intentions. When he pulled out his gun, I chose me. When it came down to my life or his, I picked mine.

I had no choice.

That's what I keep telling myself as I slowly rise from my knees. The others are still amongst the trees at the burnt-down bunker. And even though it's snowing harder, my feet sinking into deep pots of snow, I have to keep going. I have to make sure they're okay.

The sun has almost risen. I can feel the length of the night in every throbbing limb and tight breath as I pull Reign and Kelly with me. Just as my legs start to buckle, and I fear they can't take me much further, a figure appears in front of me.

"Amrey?" Jaxon's voice melds over the ice.

I squint against the snowy wind. "Jaxon?" I watch him sprint through the snow, making up the space between us in seconds. He pulls me into his chest, his arms engulfing me in a hug so tight it nearly winds me.

"You're alright. You're alright," he breathes, and I realise it's not a question but a statement of relief. His posture eases with every passing moment we remain in each other's arms. I keep my head pressed against his shoulder, but I feel his move, looking at the bodies behind me. At Reign and Kelly. A cry escapes my lips as I look at her.

"He shot her." I tremble. "So I shot him." The words barely make it out, but they do, and Jaxon holds me tighter. "I'm just like Dane."

Jaxon stiffens then. "No, you're not."

"I'm the one who wanted to fight like him, to be crueller so we could win. I'm no better than him."

Jaxon pauses, his hands finding my face as he looks into my eyes, his thumbs brushing my cheeks. "Amrey," he sterns, "You are nothing like him. Nothing." I don't know whether I believe Jaxon—I don't feel like I deserve to—but as I look into his eyes, I realise I want to.

"Okay," I whimper, and with another breath, I pull myself somewhat together.

"Are the others alright?" I ask, "Did you subdue the guards?" Jaxon pulls back slightly, but still holds me close. I watch his eyes. The relief that was there is gone, his face now held tight, and instead of answering me, his gaze falls to my leg.

"You're bleeding!" he rasps. I step back, looking at my thigh and the gore oozing from it. I was covered in so much of Kelly's blood, I forgot some of it was my own.

"I'm fine. The bullet just nicked me." Jaxon seems unconvinced until I move to expose the deep scratch, stifling a wince. "See, no bullet, just a graze. Now can you tell me about the others? What happened?"

With a sigh, Jaxon's gaze returns to my face. "We managed to overpower the guards. Archer, Emeric, Zeal and Herman are keeping watch until reinforcements arrive. Mags and the others carried back the wounded." I can already picture Mags running lead, sewing people up on the way.

"How many people are hurt?"

Jaxon's face folds, the steadiness he had wavering under my question.

"A few."

"But everyone's okay?" I don't know where the sudden need to ask that question came from, but the second it leaves my lips I want to take it back.

"Owen," Jaxon chokes, barely able to say his name.

"What happened?" I ask, hands trembling, panic racing through me. Jaxon studies me with a look I've never seen before. "What happened?" I growl. But my voice has lost all sound.

"He's gone."

My lungs register the truth first, stopping the air from entering. I gasp for a breath but it doesn't come. My hands find themselves buried in my chest. The ground begins to tilt under me, and I fall.

"Amrey!" Jaxon reaches out, and I gasp again, sucking in cold air too quickly. It stings my brain and burns my throat.

"You said you had it covered. You were supposed to have it covered!" I slam my fists against Jaxon's chest. "I shouldn't have left. I should have stayed and helped." My voice stops before I finish my thought because even I know, in truth, someone had to go after the guards; whether we were outnumbered or not, someone had to break off from the group.

"Amrey, don't put this on you. You had to go. We all knew

what we were getting into. This isn't anyone's fault." Jaxon's voice breaks against the wind, his cheeks hot with tears.

"What happened?" I cry. "Was it my fault? My plan?" My voice breaks.

"No. No. Owen made it back after you left, and then we were drawing them out one by one. We were winning. We thought we had it. But they must have had backup." Jaxon's jaw hardens. "They came from behind. We didn't see them in time. Owen didn't see them in time."

I feel my chest getting heavier with every word he says. I look at Kelly and Reign behind me—fatalities in a fight meant to save lives.

"We should go to others." Jaxon's body hardens against me, his face morphing into his usual stoic hold. "It's this way." He slips his hand into mine as we walk, and I let him. I'm not sure if he's holding it for me, himself, or the both of us, but it's the only thing keeping my steps going, my feet moving.

When we reach the clearing, I'm struck by the remnants of the fight. Smoke is still thick in the air, the smell of it burning my nose as I stare at the charred ground, the ash and burned wood, the bullet casings and debris. I know the picture of it will be etched into my mind forever.

Murmurs of pain come for the defeated guards tied up around a tree. There's a lot of them, and I have to remind myself that they're alive. They'll be cured. They'll be okay.

I shift my gaze to the boys who sit nearby, who, despite breathing, look slain. Battered, bleeding, broken. But that's not what catches my attention. My eyes tear from face to face. Emeric, Zeal and Herman. All defeated.

"Where's Owen?" Jaxon asks, pulling me forward. His name hangs heavy in the air. The boys each draw in a shaky, raw breath.

"Griffin wouldn't let it go, man," Emeric nearly sobs. "He

couldn't accept it. Archer went with him." I look over at Zeal, who sits mute, Herman too. "They think he still has a chance."

"Does he?" This time Jaxon doesn't ask Emeric.

"You saw the blood," Herman answers. I see it then, my eyes finally noticing what I was desperate to avoid. The red stains. The blood. There's so much blood.

"He could still have a chance. If they're fast enough," Zeal finally says, and all the air leaves my lungs. Because no matter how fast they are, we're hours from the Defiance.

Jaxon's hand squeezes mine. "Come on," he whispers, tugging me gently towards the guys. I use my free hand to wipe my tears and follow him to the boys, collapsing beside Emeric, who wraps his arm around my shoulders. Jaxon takes the space on the other side of me. And together we wait. While the sun rises and the blood dries, we wait for the others to come. When they do, we will carry all the guards back. We will cure them. We will find a way to make this right, to finally put an end to this. Not just for mum, but for Owen.

CHAPTER TWENTY-FIVE

The thing about hope is that it's fleeting, and without it, a black hole opens. Every ounce of pain you had replaced with faith that somehow something would save you from the dawning reality, comes rushing back. I gave up hoping for things a long time ago. Yet, even then, my mind still manages to trick me into it on occasion. That's why today, standing in a black dress too long, too tight and patched in white thread, I won't cry. The pain hitting everyone today already hit me on that mountain. They carried Owen back. Griffin watched Cynthia pound his chest, trying to defibrillate him. When we finally returned, I watched everyone crumble. I watched Mags and Griffin and Emeric and Jaxon cry. The room fell silent. Owen's heart wasn't beating. It hadn't in hours.

Griffin rises to the podium, standing in front of the lake. I've been at the Defiance for months now and while it's been busier since our raid on Axiom, I've never seen it like this. Everyone, every single person, is in the training centre, facing the water, basking in the light from the moon.

"There's this thing that comes with being a twin that nobody else will ever understand." Griffin's hands shake as he holds onto two small slips of paper. "Everyone is born one body. One person. One mind. But I was born with two. Growing up, Owen was everything I wasn't: outgoing, funny, happy. I struggled a lot for a long time, and though Owen didn't, he understood without words because we were the same. He might not share my pain, but he felt it. He carried it, and he carried me.

"He loved me like nobody else. He might have kicked my arse into the dirt a few times, but he was the first person to pull me back up. And no matter what shit we were going through—hungry, hurt—he would always find a way to make the best of it. He was a light. And the best brother." Griffin's voice cracks as he looks at Helena, so small in the front row, tears wet on her cheeks. Suddenly, the sounds I was blocking out come rushing in —sobs and cries—and when Mags squeezes my hand, I realise some of them are mine.

"If Owen were here today, you know what he'd say. Life can be a bitch. It can suck, and it can be hard. But life is also magic. The kind that gives you flowers, food and pretty girls." I fail at stifling my laugh, but so does everyone. "Life is a bitch and magic, and you get to choose which affects you the most." I'm close to hysterics now. But somehow, Griffin remains poised on that podium.

"Owen was an easy guy to please. Give him a fight and some friends, and he was set. And so, even though I'm not ready to say goodbye to him, I know he went out doing what made him happy. He wouldn't want it any other way. He also wouldn't want us moping around. So, instead of doing that, I want you all to grab a drink and make a toast to my brother Owen, the greatest twin and friend, and to the magic he poured into our lives."

THE HOURS that follow are a blur of sadness. Owen isn't the only one we mourned today. We mourned the guards we lost—Kelly, even Reign and the Defiance soldiers that came before. When the funerals are over, no one's ready to sleep. Especially not me. I want to do something, I need to, but after we got back yesterday, all operations were suspended, including training. I know it's for our safety and to pay respect to those we lost, but with silence comes thinking, and with thinking comes pain. My patrol shift doesn't start for hours. I need something to drown out the thoughts, and I know I'm not the only one.

Cynthia's glued to the repository, Dad too, monitoring the guards, watching them sleep mostly. Blane has locked himself in the command centre, eyes glued to our cameras. He says he's expecting Dane to retaliate, but I know it's more than that. I haven't been at the Defiance all that long compared to others, but I know, despite his hard shell, that Owen was more than just a kid he trained, and his death is hitting him hard. I want to help in some way, but all there is right now is waiting and mourning. I feel like the Defiance has been dipped in darkness, and we're all walking around numb and lost. Nothing feels okay. Nothing feels like it will be. At least not right now.

"Come on." I turn suddenly to see Mags, looping her arm through mine and pulling me forward.

"Where are we going?" I stumble to match her pace. My leg is bandaged beneath my dress, and my range of motion is a little stiff.

"You heard Griffin; Owen wouldn't want this." She wipes the tears from my cheek. "He'd want a celebration. So that's what we're going to give him."

I'm not sure what Mags means, but she offers no further explanation as I follow her to the cafeteria. And it appears I'm not the only one.

"What's going on?" Emeric asks.

"You heard my speech," Griffin begins, "I want to celebrate Owen, not spend all our time mourning him. A giant sad fest is not what he would have wanted."

"So you brought us here to eat?" Jaxon questions, walking into the cafeteria. Our eyes meet briefly, but we don't speak. I still don't know what to say to him after last night.

"We brought you here to drink!" Archer exclaims.

"Found em!" Kale calls out, as he emerges from the back of the kitchen, handing Griffin a crate of cider. The pair carry the bottles over to a table, popping off the tops and passing them around the group.

"To Owen," Archer starts, raising his bottle.

"To Owen," we all say, and though tears still dampen my cheeks, a smile is also on my lips.

"You know, he's gonna be so mad he went out by a gunshot," Archer chuffs, catching us all off guard. I'm about to scold him for being so insensitive when Griffin laughs.

"I think he'll be more pissed he went first. We had a bet, you know. He was convinced I'd get myself killed doing something stupid to impress you." I look at Griffin with wide, teary eyes, holding back a laugh of my own.

"I don't know what's more stupid, that bet or his last words," Jaxon chokes.

"What were his last words?" I ask, and Archer actually snorts.

"He said," Griffin begins, already shaking his head. "He said, tell Mags she's hot." Laughter bursts from Jaxon's lips, snot and tears splattering the air. Mags has gone very silent, red fawning her cheeks.

"You're joking, right? That's what he chose to go out with?" I shake my head with amusement.

"That's Owen for ya," Archer sighs, pulling Griffin closer.

"I think he did have the hots for you." Griffin raises his eyes at Mags before clearing his throat. "Sorry Emeric." Now Emeric is the one blushing, and we're all laughing again.

"I'm really going to miss him." The words leave my lips

without thinking. Jaxon's hand finds the small of my back, holding me tighter. Griffin looks at me sadly.

"He was a pain in my arse, but he was my other half."

We all drink in silence for a while after that, until Griffin starts telling a story which leads to another, and just like that, the rest of the world slips away. We're frozen in this moment, drinking, talking, laughing, and sharing stories about Owen. When I first met him, I hadn't thought much about him—only that he was loud and obnoxious. But after everything that happened in Axiom, he was there for me. With Henry, with Emeric. He had my back. I just never realised how much I depended on his friendship until now.

SOMETIME IN THE LAST HOUR, a radio was found and music started. I'm in Emeric's arms, twisting over the floor. Archer and Griffin move to the left of us, their bodies so close they've become one.

"They're good for each other," Emeric whispers, pulling me closer.

"You know who else could be?" I tease, guiding his eyes to Mags.

"It's not like that," he mumbles, twisting us so we no longer face her.

"I know there's no truth serum here, but that doesn't mean you can lie to me."

"That's exactly what it means." Emeric laughs, dipping me dramatically. "Secrets and lies can be fun."

"Maybe so, but your feelings for Mags are no secret. And I, for one, know she feels the same."

"Is that so?"

"Call it best-friend-tuition."

Emeric eyes me cautiously before whispering something to the person behind me.

"Thanks for the tip," he says with a quick peck on the cheek, and then, before I can react, he spins me out of his grip. I nearly fall, my dress swishing around my legs, when a firm hand lands on my back, another clasping my wrist, pulling me into them.

"Careful there, Sub." Jaxon's voice is smooth and loose. His breath smells of cider. I know mine does too. I stare at his face, a little perplexed. I'm gonna kill Emeric. But even as I think that, I see him whisking Mags out onto the floor to dance and I know I'm not actually mad. I'm happy for them. Owen would be too.

As Jaxon guides us to the slow drum of the music, I watch over everyone in the room. Our hearts are breaking, for Owen, for all we've lost. But right now, we all seem okay. Maybe it's the cider, the music or the company. Whatever the reason, I don't feel pain right now. Instead, I step out of the black hole and let myself feel hope. Hope that we'll get more moments like this one.

"He loves to stare." Jaxon's comment brings me back, and my eyes land on the far corner where Kale watches me with no subtlety. His eyes burn into mine with a gaze I won't call love but something else: jealousy, anger, I can't be sure. We are something, he and I. But Jaxon and I are something too.

"Does it bother you?" I ask. Jaxon only pulls me closer.

"I would lie if I said it didn't." My gut pinches at his omission. The last thing I want is to string people along, to hurt him or Kale, but I have no idea what I'm doing.

"Hey," Jaxon offers as if feeling my shame, "Forget about everything right now and just be in this moment." I smile, looking up at him, falling back into a rhythm. Minutes later, Elle leaves and Kale follows. Now I'd be the one lying if I said part of me didn't want to follow them. Out of curiosity or jealousy, I'm not sure. If anything, it means I'm more lost than ever, especially after…

"About last night." The words drip off my lips, and I half expect Jaxon to pull away.

"We can talk about it later," he breathes, pulling me in so I'm flush against him, my head resting on his shoulder.

"I didn't mean what I said."

"Yes you did, and that's okay." His words are barely a whisper against the music, but they draw me back to last night.

BY THE TIME we made it back to the Defiance, the fight was over. The remnants of it lay in the defeated faces in the room and flatlining machine. Owen was splayed on a table, wires, blood, gauze and medical supplies slain on the ground. Thrown around amidst the chaos. I knew Cynthia would have tried all she could. I could see it in her eyes how hard she fought to hold off death, but it wasn't enough. When she finally made the call, the silence wrapped us all. Griffin let out a guttural cry, so loud it didn't sound human, and it broke me. I ran from the room so fast, down the hall, pushing past anyone in my way. My eyes were foggy with tears, but my feet kept moving, kept slapping over the ground until a hand jerked me back and forced me to stop.

It was Jaxon. His eyes were as red as mine, his face just as broken. Except when he looked at me, he didn't collapse like I did. He held me up and pushed me into the training centre.

"Hit me." Those were the first words to leave his lips. Not, "*It will be okay.*" Not, "*I'm sorry.*" But, "Hit me," he repeated, stepping onto the mat and patting his chest.

"What are you doing?" I sobbed through shaky breaths.

"It will make you feel better."

"How?" I groaned. "How will anything make me feel better?" My questions felt strong when I said them, but they sounded like a whimper—a sad girl's attempt for answers.

"Amrey, this isn't your fault. I know that's what you're thinking, but it isn't. And I also know you won't believe me. You're angry, so hit me. Hit me and get rid of that anger. Get rid of that guilt so you can just be sad. Because that's all this is.

Sadness, pain, but it's not your fault. It's Dane's and Axiom's and Owen's. Because despite everything, he made his own choices—just like Emeric, just like your mum."

Jaxon's eyes were wet too, his own body deteriorating in front of me. But when he looked at me, I realised he was angry. He needed this just as much as me.

"Hit me," he yelled and this time I did.

I lunged forward, anger surging through me, anger I'd been suppressing for three years, since the day Dad left. When my fist collided with his chest, a scream tore from my throat, guttural and inhuman, just like the sound Griffin made. Except mine wasn't followed by tears. It was followed by punches, kicks, pants and pain. Again and again, until Jaxon's nose was bleeding and my knuckles were raw. Until I was pushed against a wall, my arms pinned above my head, Jaxon's chest against mine, heaving in his breath.

"Enough," he grated, and I felt the effort it took him to stop me, but I kept pushing.

"No, hit me. Keep going. I need it, I need…" My words were weak and unfinished, but I kept wrestling him for freedom. If I didn't, if I stopped, I'd have to think and I couldn't think. Not then. Not now. Not ever.

My knee jerked into Jaxon's thigh. He growled, but only held me tighter in place.

"Amrey, that's enough," he said, gentler than before.

"You brought me here to fight. So fight me!"

"No."

"Then why are you here?! If you won't fight me, then leave," I said bitterly, grinding my feet into the ground.

"No." Jaxon's voice was steady as he moves to the space beside me.

"Leave, Jaxon," I spat out each word slowly, wiring my eyes in his direction. "You don't even care about me."

Jaxon recoiled like my words were flames, and they just

seared his skin. I couldn't think about that though. Instead, I turned to leave when the wind was knocked from my chest, and Jaxon's lips crashed against mine.

For a second, I was completely frozen—ice beneath his blaze, slowly melting under his touch. Jaxon's fingers slipped from my hands, sliding up my arms until they cupped my face and strangled my waist, pulling me into him. I thread my fingers through his hair, breathing in his breath.

All the rage. All the sadness. All the pain. Everything I had was pouring out of me and into that kiss. His lips trailed down my jaw and back up again. I sunk my nails into his back, peeling up his shirt and—

Jaxon stopped, jerking back like I somehow stung him.

"What's wrong?" My words lacked air, my face hot as I stared at him, and he stared at the ground. "Jaxon." I reached for him, but he stepped back. Away from my touch. Away from me.

"I shouldn't have done that."

"I don't understand. One second you want me, and then you-" I couldn't finish my sentence, shame and embarrassment flooding my veins.

"You don't want me like that," I eventually found the courage to say, my voice small, and Jaxon dared to laugh. Well, not a complete laugh, more like a low, painful grunt that made my stomach twist.

"If I didn't want that, I wouldn't be here."

"Then why are you looking at me like I'm a sin you've just committed?"

"Because I don't want to be used."

"Used?!" His words hit harder than any of his punches.

"I want to be with you Amrey! If that wasn't already evident. But not like this. I don't want to be a distraction. I'm not Kale."

I was fully clothed yet I felt as if I was standing completely naked in front of him. He sees all of me, and I hate it.

"You used me tonight, too. I wasn't the only one who needed a way to chase away the pain."

"Maybe, but it's not the same, and you know it."

I shook my head, mad he was doing this. Mad that he followed me. Mad that he helped me. Mad that he continues to try and save me when I don't ask him to. I never ask him to, yet he's always here. He's always the one who needs to fix me.

"Maybe it is different. But I'm not the only messed up one around here. Look at yourself. Because you'll barely look at your family unless I'm there. You spend so much of your time trying to fix me, trying to patch me up and make me normal again like that will somehow solve your problems. Well, I hate to break it to you, but it won't."

Jaxon's eyes became stints, staring at me with such intensity that, if I knew better, I'd back down. Or turn away. But I don't know better. Not when it comes to him.

"I might be a mess. I might have no clue what I'm doing but at least I'm honest about who I am and I don't try to convince people otherwise. I don't lie to myself."

"Are you finished?" Jaxon said, and though his voice was sharp, it was calmer than any tone I had managed in the last five minutes. When I didn't reply, Jaxon stepped closer.

"You should go," I shuddered, pushing past him. It was quiet for several seconds, the only was sound our heavy breaths. I felt his eyes boring into the back of my head with every passing second, but I didn't turn around, and he didn't come after me. He didn't say anything else. Instead, I heard his steps as he walked away.

The second the door slammed behind him, the first tear fell.

Jaxon was hurting, too. He used me, too. But as soon as the thought crossed my mind, I knew it wasn't true, and my tears continued to fall. Jaxon might have come to me to escape his pain, but he had never been dishonest with me. He pushed me away, even though I felt how badly he wanted to kiss me—

nearly as much as I wanted to kiss him. He pushed me away because there's Kale. As long as I have him, that can't happen with Jaxon again. I hated myself so much in that moment; Owen was gone, and there I was, crying in a cave over two boys. The only thing that made the tears stop was knowing Owen would have made so much fun of me for it.

"AMREY, YOU WITH ME?" Jaxon's voice coaxes me from the memory, and suddenly I'm back in the cafeteria with him. The music's playing. My feet move over the floor, and Jaxon's hand is on my waist.

"I'm here. Just thinking."

"About last night?"

"Mmhm," I hum.

"We were tired and angry and in pain over Owen. We said things."

"Harsh things," I add.

"True things," Jaxon corrects.

"Maybe, but hurt people hurt people, and that's what I was doing. What you said to me hurt because I knew you were right. I wanted to make you feel how I felt, and I'm sorry."

"It's okay." He breathes tightly.

"It's not." I sigh. "It's just that sometimes it scares me how much you see me, and I don't know what to do with that."

"Same here."

It's two words, but somehow, they make me feel less alone.

"We're each other's biggest critic."

"Maybe we should work on being a little more forgiving then."

"I could do that," I say, and Jaxon pulls back slightly so that our eyes are level with each other, his face washed with intent like he wants to say more, but before he gets the chance, the power cuts out, and we are all cast into darkness.

CHAPTER TWENTY-SIX

For a second it's completely silent, just echoing darkness and Jaxon's arms around me. Then, panic sets in. Kids' screams and parents' shouts filter through the halls.

"It's okay," Jaxon whispers, and I realise how tightly I'm clinging to him. "Everyone stay put. The backup generators will kick in soon, and we should get some light," he reiterates to the rest of the group. And sure enough, within a few minutes, a soft glow comes from the light panels, illuminating the room just enough to see each other. A popping crackle and an earsplitting screech sound just before a voice plays over the speakers, repeating the same message three times then clicking off.

"Everyone remain calm and retreat to your closest safe point to initiate emergency protocols for stage three lockdown. I repeat, everyone remain calm and retreat to your closest safe point to initiate emergency protocols for stage three lockdown."

"Stage three?" Mags asks, and I notice Emeric is still tethered to her side.

"Potential intruder," Archer says casually, though the alarm in his eyes suggests otherwise. We've had lockdowns before, and drills, but nothing like this.

"An intruder? As in, someone's already breached the Defiance? How is that possible?" Mags frets.

Emeric hesitates before saying, "the repository." I mirror the fear in Mag's eyes. Cynthia is there tending to the guards. Dad too.

"We have to get to her," Mags cries, and Emeric is already pulling her out of the cafeteria.

"We'll go too," Griffin says.

"No. You should help with the lockdown," Jaxon insists. "We don't know what's going on, and there'll be a lot of people who need guidance."

With a shared look, Archer takes Griffin's hand and pulls him down the hall.

"Henry." I whisper. "He's all alone in the arena, Dad's in the repository, and I never checked to see where Sacha was. He'll be so scared, I have to get to him." My words come out rushed. Jaxon steadies me.

"It's okay," he reassures me. "Go find Henry, I'll make sure Cynthia and Xavier are fine."

I nod, looking past Jaxon at Mags. "We've got this," she says, giving me a quick hug before continuing with Emeric.

"Will you be alright?" Jaxon asks.

"Yes, I'll grab Henry and retreat to his room; we'll be okay." Jaxon pauses, looking me over. "Go," I say, firmer.

"Okay," he says like it's not. "Just be safe." He lets go of my hand.

"Always am." I smile, but Jaxon shakes his head, and with a final look, I turn down the hall towards the training centre.

The generator has managed to power most of the lights, some flickering, and others so faint that I can barely see a few feet in front of me, but it's enough for me to make my way back. By the time I reach the hallway to the training centre, it's quiet. Almost everyone has retired to their rooms and safe points, already enacting lockdown protocol. When I slip into the arena, I expect to see more people still here from the funerals, but it's empty. The arena isn't a safe point, but I need to check in case Henry stayed to wait for me.

The door creaks shut behind me, casting me into dark silence. The generator's power doesn't reach this area, which makes sense, but also makes finding anyone nearly impossible—especially tonight, with the clouds covering the moon.

"Henry!" I shout, my voice reverberating off the cave walls. If he's here, he'd hear me, yet all that answers is my own echo. "Henry!" I shout again, louder this time, and once more as I move closer to the water. Still, silence is the only response.

"He's not here," Kale says, appearing suddenly. I'm glad I can't see his face, or I'd probably punch it.

"I got that," I grumble, pushing past him towards the door.

"Amrey," Kale says, stopping me in my tracks. "Wait."

"I can't do this now, Kale. I have to find Henry. So, if you'll excuse me." I step aside once more and keep walking. I don't know why I'm being so rude to him, but for reasons I can't explain, everything he's done recently has irked me in some way, and there's no hiding it.

"Fine then, I won't tell you where Henry is." Kale says smugly, and this time I nearly hit him. "Now she pays attention to me." His tone is so casual that I actually growl at him.

"Kale, if you know something, tell me. Otherwise, stop wasting my time."

I turn away a final time, only for him to grab my wrist and hold me in place. "I saw Henry leave with Sacha."

Oh.

My shoulders relent. Kale lets go of my hand. Henry's with Sacha; he's fine. He's safe. But why in the hell did it take Kale five hundred years to tell me that?

"You could have led with that!"

"Can't blame me for wanting to have fun in a time like this."

"When it comes to Henry," I say sternly, "never play games."

"Noted," Kale nods. And though he looks serious, I can never tell if he truly is.

In that moment, the overhead speakers click on.

"Attention, all. The intruder alert has been disabled, and all lives are accounted for. But until we have returned to full power, please remain at your safe points. I repeat, remain at your safe points until further notice."

I breathe a sigh of relief.

"Come on," Kale says, taking my hand as the lockdown alarm rings again. "We need to get back to our rooms." I agree, looking down the hall. My room is still pretty far from here, and the generators are using up their fuel fast. It's practically pitch-black for the rest of the way.

"You can come to my room. It's closer," Kale offers, as if I didn't already know that, like I haven't spent nights there. Though that was a while ago. Usually, it's him slipping into my room and that thought makes me hesitate to respond.

"Amrey, it's just for the lockdown. We can talk. No funny business," he adds, and even though I can only make out the outline of his features, I know he's smirking.

"Fine then. But only because I'm too tired to walk to my room right now."

"Of course," Kale taunts, and I let him lead me towards his room.

When we enter, it's even darker than the hall. I can barely make out the edges of the furniture, let alone Kale, but I remember his layout, a bed and a bathroom.

"Do you want some water?" he asks.

"Sure," I reply, unmoving, afraid I'll knock into something or worse, fall over, and give Kale something else to taunt me about.

"Here." He grabs my hand and places the cup in it. The glass is cold against my fingers, but I welcome the water happily, realising it's the first I've had all day. As it refreshes my mouth from the cider, I relax a little.

"Did you have anything to drink tonight?" I ask. Those first weeks after we came back, Kale and I would drink together a lot, but it's been a while since I let that happen.

"I did," he whispers. "I saw you did too."

Ignoring his comment, I move to the side, just making out the small table as I place the glass down. "I'm surprised you saw much, considering you disappeared with Elle for most of the night."

Kale's breath catches slightly, and I only notice because he is suddenly inches closer. Too close. "I'd say jealousy isn't a good look on you, but I'd be lying."

Though I just drank water, my mouth is dry. The tension between us is crackling. "Jealousy has nothing to do with it. Curiosity has always been my fault."

"That and your ability to with-stain from bad impulses. You know Jaxon and I might not see eye-to-eye on much, but it seems even we can agree on that."

"I didn't realise this was a therapy session. Gee, Kale, why don't you tell me more things I'm bad at."

"Why would I do that when I could list the things I like instead." Like that, my heart is in my throat. Kale pushes me back against the door, the handle digging into my side, sending my pulse spiralling. Goosebumps climb up my neck where his breath hits my bare skin.

"You're breathing heavy," he taunts. "Is something wrong?"

"*Many, many things,*" I want to say, but the words never leave my lips. I shouldn't be here. I don't want to go backwards, and I don't want to get caught up in our distraction games again, but I can't deny his breath is intoxicating, and my body is reacting to it.

"I like it when I make you nervous." Kale dips his head closer to my collarbone. I can practically feel the outline of his words as he talks into my shoulder, working his way up my neck. "I like it when you fight me." His lips trace the line of my jaw. "I like it when you put me in my place." He kisses me. For a second, I'm lost in the moment, the senses in my body trying to take over. I'm furled with a desire to be wanted, but I can't not like this. I'm done being Kale's distraction. I want more than that. I deserve more than that.

Sliding my hands up Kale's chest, I push him away.

"What's wrong?" he asks so sweetly I have to remember it's Kale and not Jaxon.

"I don't want to be a distraction anymore." My words come out breathless, but the intent is there, and Kale steps back.

"What do you want?"

"I think…" I fumble over my thoughts, catching my breath to give me more time. "I want something more," I finally manage to say. "More than just our usual back and forth. Our kisses that block out the voices, the pain. I want more than just a means to an end." My words must sting because for once, instead of a witty remark or a taunt or insult, Kale is silent.

It's still for a while, just our breaths and our thoughts between us until I can no longer take it. We might be in a lock-down, but I can't be in this room; I should never have accepted the invite in the first place. I knew the trap I was walking into. Turning around, I turn the door handle, but before I can pull it open, Kale's palm is flush against the metal, pushing it closed.

"Don't go." His voice is in my ear. His arm rests next to my head as his other hand finds my waist and turns me around to face him.

"Why, Kale?" My voice is harsh, but this boy has barely looked at me in the past few days. Instead, he's spent all his time with Elle. And even if that wasn't what bothered me, it's the fact that we spent the last month drinking and sharing a bed, yet I feel like he wasn't ever completely honest with me. This boy who shares so much of my pain still feels like a stranger, and I don't know why he won't let me in.

"Tell me what's going through your mind. Tell me something."

Kale forces himself to meet my gaze. I can see him wrestling with his thoughts, thoughts I want him to share. Yet, he still says nothing. Shaking my head, I turn back around.

"I think I love you."

I stop.

My hand hesitates on the handle, my heart is in my throat.

Where is this coming from?

That was the last thing I expected him to say. The very last thing.

I stay still as he creeps closer. His fingers lightly trace over my arm, tickling my skin and sending my senses spinning.

I can't breathe.

I want to move, but I no longer know how, and as he steps forward, his body pushing mine against the wall, it feels different. Like if I fall into this, into him, there's no going back this time. I don't know how I feel about that. We've been revolving doors for so long, coming into each other's space but always leaving, never staying for long enough to get hurt, to get attached. I don't know what I am to him. A distraction? That's what I've thought for so long, and that's what I tell myself now as he edges even closer, his body pressing into mine, his fingers caressing my cheek.

I tilt my head to avoid his gaze, but his fingers press into my chin, forcing me to look at him. To see him. Oh god, here it comes, that stirring feeling inside my chest, pulling me into him. He's caught my senses now, and I can't turn them off. Every part of me wants this, even though it shouldn't. Should it?

"Amrey," his soft voice brushes against my ear as he whispers, "say the word."

I know the word he means. *Stop*. He's telling me to stop him, but I can't. After everything, after Owen, I need this.

When I don't speak, his eyes light with a fire I haven't seen before. I feel my entire stomach drop as his hot breath tickles my neck. "Say it," he whispers again. This time his other hand digs into my hip, rising as I draw in a deep breath, his fingers edging under my shirt.

"I can't," I murmur, unable to make my voice any stronger.

"Say it," his voice weakens as his nose slides against mine, his lips just a breath away.

"I-" This time my voice is inaudible, his lips teasing me with a bare touch. I wait for him to pull away, like he has many times before. But he doesn't.

Sucking in a breath, I watch his gaze shift from my lips, to my eyes, my heart pounding. This is uncharted waters, and the thrill doesn't escape me. I keep my words at bay and without anymore hesitation, Kale slams his mouth against mine, knocking the air from my chest.

Minutes pass, and neither of us pulls away. One of his hands cradles my neck, while the other slips to the small of my back, pressing me closer. Our bodies move in sync, feeling our way through the darkness, holding onto as much as we can.

I don't know when it happened, I can't quite remember, but soon enough, we're moving. Kale's arm wraps around my back and pulls me up. My legs straddle his torso as he walks me over to his bed.

"Amrey," Kale pulls away slightly, whispering again, but I push my lips back against his.

"Don't stop."

So, he doesn't.

He doesn't stop when I pull off his shirt or when I take off mine. He doesn't stop when we pause for a breath or when we lie there with only the thin layer of undergarments between us. Not when I sigh against his lips as his fingers brush over every part of my body, causing my hips to arch against him. Not when he gently moves on top, his body moving with mine.

"I love you," he whispers again, and it's like the fog clears from my brain. My hands are still in place as I pull back and realise all that separates us is the air and the sheets.

"What's wrong?" Kale pulls back, watching me with gentle eyes, but there's nothing soft about my expression. Suddenly I feel wrong, very, very wrong.

"I have to go." My words are as frantic as my movements as I scramble out of his grip and off his bed, almost tripping as I twist myself free of his sheets.

I don't know what I was thinking.

"I just told you I love you."

"I know." It's the only thing I can think to say. I know what he wants me to say but I can't. I'm not sure how I feel right now. Owen just died, my blood levels are lower than what one would classify as safe, joined with one too many glasses of cider, and we're in lockdown. I shouldn't be here. I shouldn't be doing this. Not now, not with Kale. As those thoughts make it to my brain, I realise something even bigger. Something I'm sure is written all over my face but will never find my lips. Not as long as I can stop them.

Throwing on my clothes, I leave Kale's room. I don't look back, and he doesn't stop me. Once, in another life, Kale was supposed to be my husband—my arranged match. But now, I think it's time I make that decision for myself.

CHAPTER TWENTY-SEVEN

Slowly, I click the door shut, resting my forehead against the frame.

"Ahem." A clearing throat startles me, and I turn towards curious eyes.

"Jaxon," I squeak. "Are you alright? Is everyone okay?" My voice is barely a whisper.

"Yes, everyone's fine and accounted for. It was a false alarm." His words are clipped, devoid of emotion.

"That's good," I whisper, not finding the heart to smile.

We stand there, eyes locked, unmoving in an empty hall, the lights flickering above us. I fight the urge to straighten myself. I can only imagine what he's thinking as his eyes trail over my messy hair, my top—which I'm sure I put on inside out—and my hand still clasped around Kale's door handle.

"Jaxon," I say again, but he only shakes his head and turns around.

My heart lurches.

"Jaxon, wait." I hurry to catch up, grabbing his hand. "Please."

I don't know if it's my plea or my hand holding him in place, but Jaxon turns around, his face sewn tight as he breathes me in, not meeting my gaze.

"Can you look at me, please?" I say painfully. The idea of him hating me is too much to bear. "It's not what you think."

"But it is," he says flatly. I can't hear any anger in his words. I can't sense any emotion at all, and I fear that's worse than if he were to break down and yell at me.

"Okay," my voice is like liquid melting off my tongue and spilling like acid on the ground. The way Jaxon recoils when I speak makes me think my every word is stinging him. I don't want it to.

"Archer isn't asleep yet. I'll ask him to join me on patrol." Jaxon moves to leave, attempting to tear his hand from my grip. Dammit, I forgot we had patrol.

"No. Just let me explain." I hold his arm tighter.

"You don't need to explain anything," he sterns, and now I hear it: the anger, the resentment, the hate.

I let him go.

"You hate me." My voice is small. Jaxon looks at me as if I've slapped him.

"Since the moment I met you, you've had a knack for speaking out of turn. For making some pretty dumb assumptions. But that might be the most infuriating."

"I don't understand?"

Jaxon's breath deepens, his eyes darkening. Before I can react, he steps forward, grabs my face, and slams his lips against mine.

The air's knocked out of me. My senses spinning.

I kiss him back, a moan escaping my lips as he pulls me closer, grazing my tongue with his. In this moment, we're all that exist. All that matters. Until he pulls away.

"If only I hated you," he whispers.

"What are you two doing in the hall?" Blane's voice shatters the moment between us like a rock thrown against glass. We each step back. How much did Blane see? Hear? Questions I don't dare ask, but from the look Jaxon shares with me, I know he has them too.

"Never mind," Blane grunts. "Come on, we're needed in the repository." Blane answers his own inquiry, and his suspicions—whatever they are—aren't voiced. "Hurry up," he shouts, already halfway down the hall. Jaxon and I share another look before rushing to catch up with him.

"What's happening?" I fret, trying hard not to trip over my feet to keep up with Blane.

"Did someone trigger the intruder alarm?" Jaxon asks.

"Can't be certain. But our power was cut off, and it wasn't from the storm."

"Did the cameras pick up anything?"

"No."

"Then it must be someone on the inside." Blane considers my comment for several seconds, our feet still shuffling over the ground.

"That seems the most likely."

WHEN WE BURST through the repository, I see where all the generator's power has been directed. The room is brightly lit, the hum of a dozen conversations filling the space. Dad stands in the corner with Sacha and another woman who looks vaguely familiar.

"Henry?" I shout. The conversation between them halts immediately, and Sacha's steady eyes grip mine.

"He's with the other kids in the command centre. He's fine." The coils wrapped around my chest loosen, and I manage a deep breath.

"Amrey!" Blane scolds me from behind as he and Jaxon come over and meet us. "You really have no restraint."

"Sorry," I mutter, even though I'm not. Not when Henry's concerned.

"No time for that," Dad interjects. "We have much to do." Turning, he directs us to a table, now covered by a large canvas and moving chess pieces.

"What is this?" I ask, picking up a bishop.

"Improvisation," Dad starts. "With no cameras, we are relying on our patrols to keep us in the loop of Dane's movements. The bishops represent the tree line, and the pawns represent our people on patrol. The black checkers are where our cameras are positioned-"

"I'm working on them, but I need more time." I look up at the new voice entering the room. Rowan stands tall, but her usual sleek look is ruffled, her shirt worn and stained. It seems I'm not the only one deprived of sleep. I haven't seen her in a while—she's always tucked away in the tech room. I wonder if she's spoken to Kale. But before I can engage in conversation, word comes in from patrol. Dad takes the king and places it on the table.

"What do we need to do?" Jaxon and I say at once.

AFTER THE BRIEFING, we're given a section to patrol. There are already eight Defiance members surveying our borders, including Emeric and Mags, who volunteered after they found Cynthia. Rowan is working with Makin to get the power back, but until then, our eyes are our best tool. And patrols will continue to be tripled and extended. After seizing a dozen Axiom guards, we have to be prepared for retaliation.

"Ready?" Jaxon looks at me, his eyes meeting mine with the same intensity they always do, but he shows no hint of what transpired between us earlier tonight, only focus for our current task.

Looking back over the room, I notice Rowan hunched over

half a dozen broken cameras, most of which she's already fixed and converted to battery power. Jaxon told me once she was a wizard with technology, and now I'm seeing it first-hand.

"One sec," I motion to Jaxon before slipping past him and over to the far corner of the room.

"Rowan," I breathe, and somehow my gentle whisper manages to startle her. Fixing her glasses, she looks at me over the lenses, her grey-tinged hair tied messily in a bun, loose threads tucked into her collar.

"Amrey? Do you need something?" Her voice is sharp as she places the camera on the table.

"No, I, uh…" I stumble on my words, unsure how to even bring up the topic. She is Kale's mother, yet they could not seem more unalike. Though, considering she left him to be raised by strangers, it makes sense.

"Out with it, hun. I have cameras to fix." She ogles me curiously, her stare fixed between my eyebrows.

"I'm sorry, I don't mean to interrupt. I just wanted to say that, even after everything, forgiveness is possible. No one blames you for the choices you felt you had to make, and there is still time to reconnect. I think he could use it right now. He's smart like you, a little closed off and foolish, but a skilled fighter. I think you would love him if you got to know him. And if losing Owen and my mum has taught me anything, it's that life's too short to hold grudges and resentment. Even though he doesn't show it, I know he'd love it if you reached out to him."

Rowan looks at me with a strange twinge in her eye, her jaw held tighter than before, and I feel I may have hit a nerve.

"I'm sorry, Amrey, but can I ask who it is you're referring to? Who I'm supposed to be reconnecting with?"

Ouch.

Is she so far removed from her own son that she can't even make the connection? Have I stepped over the line? Maybe she isn't the mother Kale needs.

"Amrey?" Rowan persists right as Jaxon moves to my side.

"We have to go," he speaks into my ear, his hand loosely grabbing my arm. He means to pull me from this room if I don't leave this second—Jaxon and his duty. Following his steps, I turn once more to face Rowan.

"It's Kale, your son. If you want a relationship with him, I would try before it is too late." I don't wait to hear what she has to say next, I've said my piece. Turning, I let Jaxon pull me out the door, into the biting wind and the waiting cold.

"WHAT DID you say to make her look like that?" Jaxon asks when it's only us and hundreds of feet of snow.

"Nothing bad. I don't think."

"I see," he hums to himself like he's found the last piece of a puzzle.

"Stop analysing me, it's completely infuriating."

"I wouldn't need to analyse if you told me things more clearly."

"Yeah, well, life's more interesting when there's intrigue. You'd be bored if you knew everything all the time."

"Is that really how you see it?" Jaxon doesn't stop walking. Neither of us does, but his head tilts towards mine. I can feel his gaze on the side of my face. I do well to ignore it.

"Life has never given me the answers I needed, so why should I be so obliging?"

"You really are a mystery to solve, Sub." My heart jumps a little at the nickname. It used to be all he called me. Now, it's rare that I hear it. But when I do, I can't hide the smile it invokes.

"But I'm more fun that way, right?" This time, I do turn to face him, a wink and a smile accompanying me. Jaxon watches me for several seconds before shaking his head and refocusing his gaze straight ahead.

"I take it back. You're not a mystery, just a girl with many secrets she's been forced to keep and walls so high she has trouble freeing them." The air is quite literally sucked from my lungs. Never has anyone been able to see me as sharply as Jaxon. The feeling isn't a comfortable one. I grew up always keeping part of myself hidden. It protected me. I liked it that way, or maybe it's just that I didn't know any different.

Minutes pass, and another cold snap comes through, stinging my nose and biting my cheeks. Water leaks from my eyes, which I reach to wipe. The movement uncoils an old pain in my shoulder, a dull ache that begins to grow stronger. Readjusting my backpack, I let it hang from my left arm.

"Everything good with you, you know, besides the obvious?" Jaxon asks.

"Yeah, just a twinge in my shoulder, it's fine."

"Let me see."

"I said it's fine."

"Amrey, I've watched you rub that shoulder for weeks. Somethings up, let me have a look." Jaxon stops walking, and I know the look he wears well. He's not budging. Better get this over with so we can keep going.

"Fine," I huff, dropping my backpack, "but I'm telling you, it's nothing. Probably just tweaked it in training." Jaxon rolls his eyes, moving behind me as he peels off my jacket. The air hits my skin, sending shivers down my spine and to my toes.

"Sorry," he breathes. "I'll be quick."

He tugs the edge of my top, pulling it as far down as it will go without me taking it off. I tremble, no longer concentrating on the pain but his hands on my bare shoulder.

"See, it's nothing," I bite, clenching my teeth to stop the chattering.

"I don't know about that." His words confuse me, and I try to move out of his hold, but Jaxon's grip only tightens as his thumb brushes over a tender part. I wince.

"That hurts?" Jaxon asks unsurprisingly.

"Yes," I manage, fighting the urge to flick my heel up and knock him to the ground. "I told you, I must have pulled a tendon or something."

"First," Jaxon says, "You have no idea what that sentence even means. Second, you didn't."

"And how do you know?"

"Because I can see it, and this isn't a training wound."

"Wound?" This time I snap back, turning around and using my free hand to feel over the space on my shoulder. "Don't you mean bruise?"

Jaxon watches me carefully.

"No, it's more like puncture marks, like you've been bitten or stung. You've bled. I can tell that much for sure, and the bruises surrounding the marks are tinged purple and blue, almost black. There are a few in different stages, almost like you've been bitten repeatedly over a few days. How long have you had a sore shoulder?"

"A few weeks."

Jaxon doesn't say anything, just continues his stare, making me more uneasy as the seconds grow. "You think there's some type of bug that's been biting me for weeks?"

"I didn't say bugs."

"Well, you didn't *not* say it."

"The marks are so small, a few tiny dots, but they made you bleed, and they've swollen, so it makes me think…" Jaxon's eyes cloud over, his face tightening with alarm.

"Jaxon, what is it!" Before he can finish, there's a sharp *swoosh* in the air, and then something hits him from the side. I watch Jaxon grab his arm, a red dart sticking out of his skin. He rips it free, but it's too late. Whatever it was loaded with has already sunk in. Jaxon's eyes turn glassy, his legs wobble and before I can catch him, he falls face-first into the snow. I scream, terror ripping from my throat as I fall onto the ground towards him. Rolling him over, wiping the snow from his face.

"Jaxon, wake up!" My voice scratches against the icy wind as I yell, hoping the others will hear me. "Jaxon!"

"Amrey."

I blink, wiping at my tears to get a better look at his face. "Jaxon, it's me, I'm here." Except that wasn't Jaxon's voice, and I realise it too late.

Something cold and hard crashes against my skull.

And the world turns black.

CHAPTER TWENTY-EIGHT

I WAKE UP DRENCHED AND COLD, THE SHARP PRICKLE OF frostbite nipping at my skin. Snow lies over and under me, but it's not what trickles down my cheek. Hot blood warms my temple as it slowly drips onto the snow, and from the look of the red stains on the ground, I've been bleeding for a while—losing blood I can't afford to.

My senses sharpen as I tear my eyes back and forth across the trees and snow surrounding me. *Where am I?* My hands are bound, vertigo gripping my stomach when I try to stand. My skin stings, burning with each struggle against the rope. I start to wobble. *Not enough blood. Too dizzy. Can't balance.* I catch myself against the tree and slide back down.

"Easy there, you'll only make it worse." The voice scrapes at the very corners of my brain, seeping from my memories and materialising as a face.

No.

Heat creeps up the back of my neck.

It can't be.

Because that would mean I was wrong. That would mean I

was fooled. That the truth I thought tied us together was never there.

It was all a lie. Everything was a lie.

"Kale."

His name tastes like taffy with too much salt, sticky, foul and rotting my teeth.

"You know, if you had just played your cards right, you'd be soundly asleep in my room right now." His lips shift from an evil curl to a flat line as he steadily moves in front of me, kneeling so his head is level with mine. "Dane wants me to do this quickly, but I know how much you like your answers, so I figured I'd entertain you with some first."

"You're working with Dane?" I remain as passive as I can, lifting my chin so that my gaze locks on his, and I hold it there. I won't let him rattle me. Not like this, not after everything.

"Surely you have smarter questions?" Kale snipes, and for five seconds I just stare at his face, searching for a sign that this isn't real. That it's a joke, that I'm not some foolish girl who fell for a boy's lies and was so easily trapped in them. I trace my memory, searching every moment we shared for a hint of the person who's standing in front of me, but I come up with nothing. The Kale who looks at me now shows no semblance of the Kale from only hours ago, the same one that said he loved me, the same one I thought I might love.

"What did you do to Jaxon?" I hiss, clenching my jaw to stop my teeth from chattering. I won't let him see my fear—at least, not yet. Not until I know which emotion to play off, which will help me more.

"Your boyfriend will be fine," Kale groans, his annoyance clear. "I wanted to kill him. I've been aching to do that for months, but it was unproductive. Pistols draw more attention than darts."

"You sedated him?"

"I did." Kale sounds pleased with his actions.

"How did you even-?"

"How do you think?"

Dane.

"Why are you doing this?" The question is vague, but Kale bites.

"For gratification, of course. Really, Amrey? For someone desperate for knowledge, your catechism for answers needs work."

My jaw locks.

Everything in the way he speaks to how he looks at me feels awfully vile. Prickles seize my skin at the thought of our time together mere hours ago, but the sadness I feel for the loss of a person I cared for can wait. Right now, all I feel is rage. I squeeze it with every cell in my body.

"So Dane managed to fool you into his control. That tracks," I mock, my voice bristling with detest.

Kale's face sharpens at the edges. "I am no fool. Dane didn't deceive me. I chose this."

"Is that what you think?"

"Oh, Amrey, that's what I know."

I stare back at a loss for words, too stunned to comprehend this reality. Kale knows everything about the Defiance. He was let into nearly every meeting. We trusted him. I trusted him. But everything he's done since the moment we met has been for Dane. Everything I told him, everything I said, was a direct line to Dane. What happened to my mum, Owen, and the others was all because I let Kale in. I trusted the wrong person.

"Don't be so hard on yourself; you couldn't have known. I am an excellent liar." His tongue rolls over the last word, and bile rises in my throat. "It's just like I told you on the day we were arranged to be married."

When everyone's made to tell the truth, no one questions whether you really are.

My mind flashes back to that day—the day in the closet. I

was naive to find relief in hearing his name. I thought I finally wouldn't be alone. I had someone like me, someone to confide in and share my fears with, but I couldn't have been more wrong. I was paired with the devil, and I let him right in.

"You know," I seethe, writhing my hands against the restraints. "You may have tricked me and the others into buying your orphaned act, but it seems you've also managed to trick yourself. Dane doesn't care for you. You are just a pawn to him. A piece he moulds and moves as he sees fit. You are no better than one of his guards." My words must slice deep because Kale's sneer slips, and instead, his teeth flare.

"You don't know what you're talking about!" I feel the blood drain from my face as he roars with a burst of savagery I haven't witnessed before.

"Don't I?" My mouth twists as I raise my eyes in challenge. "Has anything you've done been your choice, or was it all Dane's? Befriending me, running away with me. Was that your idea or his?"

Kale's features tighten with rage, the red of his cheeks deepening by the second.

"Coming here, was neither my choice nor Danes," he snaps. "Had insufferable Elle not been so bothered by her conscience, none of this would have happened in the first place. But since she put me in that position, I was forced to continue my act, and lucky for you, I didn't hate it here. I even convinced Dane to let you stay longer."

I watch him with steady breaths as he paces in front of me.

"Why would you do that?"

Kale considers me and the question for a moment. "You might be something Dane needs, but a fight with the Defiance wasn't, not after your last attempted attack. It would be wasteful, and Dane isn't one to waste life."

"All Dane does is waste life." I scoff. "He killed my mother and Owen, tortured innocents, and now he wants to use me to help. And if you think there won't be resistance from taking me, you're as obtuse as him. This is only going to get more people killed."

Kale stops walking and turns to look at me. "Well, that's on you! It didn't have to happen like this. I could've just kept taking your bone marrow. Dane had a special syringe made for it. I'd do small aspirations that barely left a mark, and with you passed out from the cider, you never even woke up. I'll admit, at first I wasn't sure what I was doing and accidentally took your blood. My bad with the low count. But eventually, I got the hang of it and got enough of your bone marrow for Dane to replicate."

The realisation hits me like a knife in the chest.

I suck in a breath. My being weak, my low blood pressure. My aching shoulders. The puncture wounds. It's all making sense. I swallow hard against the bile that threatens to rise in my throat. Violated. I feel violated.

"Because of me, the Defiance stayed untouched. But you had to agree to make that damn cure. We can't have that. Your bone marrow cells are too valuable to Dane. He won't have you sharing them."

Kale's words pierce my ears, but I can't process them. My stomach churns as I cling to the realisation of his deceit. "All this time," I breathe, the rest of my words falling short. It's finally hitting me just how far Kales' deception goes. How much of our time together was a lie? All of it.

"Oh, don't pretend to be sad," Kale grinds. "It's not like you weren't using me too."

"I didn't use you," I say, though my voice is much softer than Kale's and when his gaze catches mine, my breath becomes lodged in my throat.

"Didn't you, though?" he seethes, decreasing the space between us with two strides. "You never loved me, Amrey, not like I did you. It was always Jaxon."

"It wasn't always Jaxon. I met you first, and even then, you speak of love like you know the emotion. I'm not even completely sure what love feels like, but I know this isn't it. If you truly loved me, Kale, you wouldn't do this."

"Don't talk to me like that," he scowls furiously, his face locked so tight I can make out the veins beneath his skin. The colour of the cave water, of midnight and strain. Of hurt and maddening.

"What about your parents, Kale?" I say in a whisper this time. "How could you do this to them?" His anger fades, just slightly, enough so I can see beneath it. But instead of sadness, I see humour. A smile?

"My parents?" He scoffs, standing up. "God, you know nothing." Relaxing his fists, he massages his temples before storming off to grab a gun.

My heart stops. My stomach flips and flips.

This is it.

Kale continues to move in erratic patterns, stomping in a circle, pacing back and forth, juggling the gun between his palms like a circus act. I keep expecting his fingers to slip, for the trigger to puncture and for my head to roll back. But he keeps moving, his mouth mumbling, with no sound coming out, like his words are battling his mind even as he says them. His expression is wild when he finally turns to me, and all I can think is how did I miss this? This person, this frantic shell of messy thoughts and crazy ideas, is not Kale. Not the Kale I knew. Or maybe it is, and I never knew him at all.

I watch Kale with fear in my eyes, not knowing what he's going to say next, wondering if the next shake of his hand will be the one that kills me. I look at him like I did the first time I laid eyes on him, curiosity and fear rolled into one. Except this time, when I watch Kale, I don't inspect with admiration or anticipation. This time, I fear for my life.

"Are you going to kill me?"

Kale turns to me, a dull look in his eyes, and instead of

answering, he laughs—a scratchy chuff that drags as he wheezes against the icy air. It does nothing to keep my fear at bay, and when he rubs his thumb over the blunt of the pistol, my chest tightens.

"Do you want to be killed?"

"No one wants to die."

"On the contrary, I've known many people who beg for just that."

"People who were suffering at the hands of Dane. Subversives who were tortured. How about that, Kale, those nights in the cells, where you cared for me, warned me. Was that all fake too? Did Dane ever lay a hand on you, or a needle or a hammer? And if he did, wouldn't you want to hit him back?"

I don't know where my sudden brashness comes from, but I hold it steady in my chest. Kale pigeons his gaze at me before turning and scanning the forest. I sit still, watching him scratch at a familiar spot on his arm, a wound similar to the puncture Jaxon described on my shoulder. The realisation hits me, clear as day.

A bruised needle mark.

He's being drugged with Dane's serum.

I don't know how I never noticed it before.

The air around me manages to grow colder in the space of a second. The hair on my arms stands on end. Kale is not Kale, not really. How long has he been controlled by Dane? Since the cells? Since we met? Or even before then? A heavy sadness plagues my heart as my mind tumbles back through my memories, trying to remember when I might have seen him before we met. All I can come up with is the funeral. His parent's funeral. Dane must have latched his claws into him then, three years ago, when he was vulnerable. When he was only a child. And, like a spirit possessing a body, my own becomes mad with rage. The urge to make Dane suffer is stronger than ever.

I just have to get out of here first.

"If you won't answer questions about yourself, answer this then. What does Dane want?"

Slowly, Kale turns around, the smallest hint of amusement on his lips.

"You, of course."

This much I knew already—my blood cells, my DNA, is the key. The only way for him to make his serum. To gain his control, his power. So why has it taken me until now to realise there is a way out of this? A way to stop Dane? It's wildly obvious.

"Why haven't you brought me to him then? What are you waiting for?" Though my words are merely points for stalling, I do wonder why I am here, tied up to a tree and not swung over Kale's shoulder, on my way to Axiom.

Kale halts. "Maybe I'm tired."

"Or maybe you don't want to see me hurt?"

His gaze narrows on me. "What I want or don't want plays no role here."

I'm fairly certain Kale is under the influence of Dane's serum, and if that's the case, his choices don't matter. But I have to try. If I can break free of the compulsion, maybe Kale can too. And if I can reach him, my plan might just work.

"I don't believe that. Dane relies on you, but you have a choice. You don't have to play his games anymore," I say, my voice firm.

"How quick you are to call me a pawn when you are the master of your own game. I heard you talking to Jaxon in the halls tonight. You left my bed and went right into his arms."

My stomach coils at the memory. Guilt and shame written over me in permanent ink.

"Kale, I never meant to hurt you or him."

"Enough. Save your lies and woes. You're right; it's time. I'm taking you to Dane." As Kale steps forward, the gun raised above my head, I brace for impact, anticipating the brunt of it colliding with my skull. Blood still trickles from the last wound he gave me, an instant reminder that sharpens my reflexes. With the last scraps of energy I have, I dodge his swing, ram my shoulder into his chest, and spring to my feet. My hands might be bound; I might not win this fight, but I don't need to. I just have to hurt him enough so that he can't take me back to Dane. Enough that he needs help. Help he has to fetch.

KALE'S LEG wasn't broken when he left, but it wasn't bent right either. His limp made his steps slow and stilted, and as I watched him disappear into the thicket of trees and snow, I finally let myself relieve a breath, filling my lungs with icy air that burns the whole way down.

My body's so cold I feel the chill in my bones. Shaking is uncontrollable, but it's no help in preserving heat. I am at the thin end of a timer with minutes to go. My eyelids fall closed, too heavy to keep open. It goes against all my training not to stay awake, to keep my gaze locked on the tree line and potential threats, but I can't fight the disease that is exhaustion.

The sound of Kale's steps no longer reverberates in my ears.

He's gone.

I'm alone.

As the minutes trickle by, my breathing becomes laboured, the icy air like shards down my throat. I let my mind fall quiet, and my wound bleed out.

CHAPTER TWENTY-NINE

"She's over here!"

"Amrey! Stay with us."

"She's lost so much blood."

"Where is he?"

The low drum of voices pulls my mind from the black. "Emeric?" I breathe, trying to open my eyes.

"I'm gonna kill him."

"Archer?" I murmur. This time a slither of light takes over my vision, but it's gone in seconds, and my head falls heavy. Right as something scoops under my legs, and the ground falls away from me.

"Kale," I stammer, "Kale he-"

"Hey, shhh, we know, we know." I recognise Emeric's voice clearly, soft against my trembling words. "We've got you, Sub. We've got you."

"Jaxon?" I ask.

"Who do you think sent us after you? The boy dragged himself back to the Defiance, half sedated." Emeric pulls me closer, and relief sinks in. Words form on my lips, but the exhaustion takes me before I can say them.

My legs shake as I make my way to the command centre. In the last 24 hours, I've had at least four units of blood transfused. While my cell counts have risen, and I'm no longer in danger of death from blood loss, I'm still a little light on my feet.

"Amrey," Dad stresses as I enter the room, "you shouldn't be out of bed."

"I'm fine," I say without a hitch of breath. "Cynthia said I could leave."

Technically, she said I should wait another day, but when I stood up, she didn't stop me. Dad gives me a side eye but lets me make my way over to Jaxon who pulls out a chair for me, his hand brushing mine as I fall into the seat next to him. We share a smile but nothing else. The sedation Kale stung him with wore off after a couple of hours, and besides some ice burns from dragging himself back to the Defiance, Jaxon looks pretty unscathed, even less than when he visited me last night. We didn't speak then. I just held his hand. I'm still not even sure what to say to him. Or how to make sense of any of this.

"Now that you're here, we could use your help piecing together the details." Blane circles to the front next to Dad, "We need to know exactly what Kale had access to and what he plans to do with that information."

"He's going to feed it to Dane if he hasn't already," I say matter-of-factly, and by the puzzled expressions I receive, I realise that while they know Kale attacked us, they may not have connected him to Dane. "He's under Dane's control. I saw his needle marks. Dane's probably been injecting him with his serum for months. Not only that," I reach my arm to my opposite shoulder and expose my skin. Jaxon's gaze hardens. "Kale's been taking my bone marrow almost weekly and giving it to Dane. That's why I had such a bad reaction when I went under anaesthesia, why I've been so weak." The mouths in the room fall silent, their looks more intense. "Dane must have got to him when Rowan and Magnus left Axiom. He's been using him for years."

"Amrey," Dad interrupts my tumble of thoughts, and that's when Rowan steps forward. My face pulls tight.

"Amrey, after our conversation in the repository, I was worried. You said some things that triggered me."

"I'm sorry," I say and leave it there. Even though I don't like that my words caused someone stress, I still feel like I needed to say them.

Rowan's gaze only grows more distressed as she shifts her eyes back to my father's.

"What is it?"

"Amrey, Kale isn't my son."

"I know you're not close, and while Kale might have made some horrible choices, he's under Dane's control," I spew, trying to rationalise.

"Amrey, he's not my son because I never had a son."

"But the funerals, your tombstone. Kale was there. He mourned you," I stutter, shuffling through my memories. I'm not wrong. I know I'm not. Kale was there. We spoke about it. The boy who lost both his parents. The orphan taken in by friends.

"Magnus and I never had a son. We couldn't conceive a child. It's why we both left Axiom. We had nothing to lose. I never would have left my child behind." Rowan's words ring clearly through the room, and I cast Dad a small look. While I don't like that he left us behind, I'm past it now. I won't make him suffer forever for the choices he felt he had to make back then.

"Well if he's not your son," Blane asks, "Then whose is he?"

Just then, the door bursts open and in comes Zeal and Herman, with a ragged and beady-eyed Elle.

"She was in the repository like you said," Zeal quips, his voice sharp.

"What's happening? No one's telling me anything," Elle says in fits and starts, sweat trickling down her forehead. Aside from the strain on her face, she isn't resisting their restraints.

"What's going on?" I shout, looking at Dad for answers.

"The details of Elle's rescue were always under scrutiny," Blane says steadily. "And earlier tonight, Cynthia overheard her talking to one of the guards. She has a past with Kale. For all we know, she's a mole too." All eyes in the room turn to Elle, including mine, but this isn't new information to me.

"I'm not a mole!" Elle pleads. "I can prove it."

"You will have time to prove yourself in questioning. Lock her up in the back room." Blane motions to the small door within the command centre. It's not a cell like Axiom, but that room has had its share of bloodshed and gruel.

The boys begin leading Elle over, and no one protests. I'm starting to think James being on tonight's patrol shift was intentional. I watch as Elle gives up her fight, letting her head drop with a defeated sigh. Suddenly, all the moments I witnessed between her and Kale flash through my mind. My selfishness had me so consumed with jealousy, I believed they were together, that it was romantic. I never thought to look past that, but now that I think about it, Elle always seemed on edge around Kale, her stare curious, wary. And I remember how Kale looked at her the day she arrived at the Defiance, almost as if he hadn't expected to see her.

Suddenly, I find myself standing.

"Let her speak," I command.

Dad's strained gaze meets mine, but with a firm nod, he agrees. The tension in the room is thick, the air dry as we watch Elle shake free from Zeal and Herman's grip. Straightening her shoulders, she looks me square in the eye.

"Kale is Dane's son."

CHAPTER THIRTY

THE ROOM WAS A ROCKET OF CHAOS AFTER ELLE'S REVELATION. Dad let her speak and I watched fury lines etch deeper onto his face, ones I know too well. I always had suspicions of Elle, but I didn't expect this. She might not be a mole, but she's in no way innocent either. Elle has known who Kale is this whole time and said nothing. She let me get swept up in his lies and charm. She watched him pretend to love me, confusing me with feelings and distracting me with cider and hazy nights. And what's worse is she loved him first.

Everything she said after that only made me feel more like a fool.

Kale's birth was a secret. His real mother, a Subversive who had an affair with Dane, died during childbirth, leaving him to be raised by Dane in secrecy within the cells of Axiom. And then at twelve, there was Elle. She spent years with Kale, two children wrapped up in Dane's vendetta. She fell in love with the boy who kept her company, a boy she thought was just like her. Over time she pieced it together, forced to watch the boy she loved be controlled and manipulated by Dane.

When my father and the other Subversives blew a hole in

Axiom's wall to escape, everyone thought they had died, but Dane knew the truth. This infuriated him, leading him to send Kale out into society to track down more Subversives. Rowan and Magnus are not Kale's parents; they are merely names on a tombstone, providing evidence for his fake identity. Elle was forced to watch Kale betray and manipulate, luring people into exposing their subversiveness. All in an effort to find the right match for Dane—to find me.

And he nearly had me. If Sacha hadn't gotten me out of Axiom, he would've had me. She even tried to save Kale too, before he was caught. Not that that did anything. Dane got him out. They were in on it together, always have been, because Kale was never Kale. Not one single moment with him was real.

"And there lies the real reason it took me so long to leave," Elle finishes, pulling me back into the room and the moment. Yet, my blood still bubbles with rage, my mind still fighting off the memory of my time with Kale.

"What I said before wasn't a lie, but it wasn't the whole truth. I thought I lost Kale to Dane's serum, but when I saw him tending to you in the cells, being kind…" She looks only at me now, and her words bring about more memories, more lies, more pain. "I wanted to believe he was back, that he was himself again and not Dane's mindless droid. But I also wasn't ready to face him, to face the fact that maybe he wasn't himself. Because I knew then what the consequences would be, and I still loved him. I didn't want him hurt. So, I stayed in Axiom, in denial, as long as I could.

"And when I finally came to the Defiance, I hoped he'd be the Kale I once knew. For a while, it seemed like he was. But then I started noticing things—his behaviours, his patterns. He was acting just like he did in Axiom. I confronted him. I wanted to say something, but it would have just been his word against mine, and no one trusted me yet. You still don't."

"That is not an excuse for letting Dane's son roam these

halls!" Dad fumes. "You saved us. I vouched for you when people doubted your loyalty. And yet, you let that boy get close to my daughter, to hurt her and everyone here. You should have said something. At the very least, we would have listened."

"I know. I'm so, so sorry." Elle's voice is shaky, her eyes beginning to shine with tears. Throughout her whole confession, I kept watching Dad. His face falls, and his fists clench. He's seething. Everyone is angry. I am, too. But mainly, I feel stupid because everything Elle said makes sense.

Kale was the first person I opened up to. He got me in ways I thought nobody did. He drew me in, sought me out, and started private conversations, but all of it was to get me to admit my secret. And it worked. He even escaped with me back to the Defiance to keep up his ruse, to keep me in his sights. He's played me from the beginning, and I fell for it. I trusted the wrong person, and now Pylor's words echo in my mind. *How does it feel to fall prey so easily to those you should trust the least?*

It was Kale. It's been him all along. I had this coming.

I believed the boy who could lie.

CHAPTER THIRTY-ONE

Pushing the door open, I step out into the hall, the chorus of voices still in argument behind me.

"Why did no one question this boy's presence earlier?" Dad's voice is harsh, but I know it's because he's putting this all on himself. I read it in his face the moment Elle told us. *How didn't he see it? How didn't I?*

"There were too many refugees from Axiom. We didn't think concerning ourselves with the eligibility of one boy, whom your daughter trusted, was a top priority."

I groan, rolling my eyes as the door clips shut behind me, and I'm locked out in the hall's silence. It's the early hours of the morning. Everyone in Axiom is either in the command centre, the repository with Cynthia and the guards, or in bed. I wish I was the latter. But sleep won't solve my problems, and I don't think it would come even if I tried.

With a deep sigh, I slide to the floor and rest my head against the cold wall, closing my eyes. Sleep might not come, but I need to quiet my thoughts, so I let myself fall into a memory of Mum.

It was my first day of combat class. I came home with

bruises all over my arms and a black eye. Sacha had made us all jump into it head first, literally. It was a lot, but I appreciate her for not coddling us. We were as tough as the guys, and she treated us as such. It was refreshing. And somehow Mum, even though she'd lost her husband to being a guard, didn't chastise me for choosing the same path. Instead, she patched me up, asked me questions and even smiled when I relayed how happy it made me. She spoke highly of Sacha's teachings and never told me to stop.

Knowing what I do now only makes my heart ache for her more. I went from a quaint life, having no contact with my biological mother, to her holding the weight of my future and my literal bones in her hands. And Mum never said anything, she never acted out of the ordinary. Everyone likes to tell me I'm a strong fighter like my mum, and I never understood why, but I'm starting to. She wasn't a combat fighter, but she was strong. She let her daughter grow closer to the woman who gave her life, and not once did she complain. Even after we lost Dad, she held us together. She might have been colder, less inclined, but she made sure Henry and I were always okay. She was a good mum, and I miss her more than I ever thought I could.

"Amrey, are you alright?" Dad startles me, and I open my eyes to see him hovering there. I hadn't even heard the door to the command centre open.

"I'm okay," I say quietly, watching the space between us for a few seconds. "I was just thinking about Mum." Dad's expression softens and he lowers himself to sit beside me. His movements awkward with his injured foot.

"You know, she'd be so proud of you," he says.

"I don't know about that," I mumble, "I've made some pretty crappy decisions."

"Our decisions don't define us."

I turn to face Dad. "Then what does? Because right now, I

feel like a total screw-up. Everything that's happened feels like this huge weight on my shoulders—a weight I've put on everyone else's too."

"You can't really believe it's your fault?"

"Of course I do. I was Kale's assignment. I brought him back with me. I spent all that time with him. I let him distract me, he was taking my goddamn bone marrow for weeks, and I had no idea because I was too preoccupied with drowning in my pain to realise. I gave him access to everything. And when he did act suspiciously, when I started to notice things, I was too wrapped up in jealousy to see clearly. I was stupid."

"You are young."

"Young and stupid."

"No, Amrey, just young. Naïve maybe, but you should be. I only wish you could be more. I know you're tough. You put up a good fight when you want to." Dad rubs his jaw, his skin still bruised from his time in Axiom. "But being tough doesn't protect you from everything, especially when you open your heart to people. You care fiercely. It's who you are, Amrey, and it's what I love about you. What your mother loved about you."

My heart clamps tight and I let out a broken sigh. "I wish she was here."

"Me too."

Dad rests his head next to mine, breathing in the silence.

"You and Sacha seem happy," I say the words before I can rethink my decision to speak them.

Dad immediately sits straighter, eyeing me hesitantly. "It's okay. I'm happy for you two, honestly." I don't know why I chose this exact moment to have this conversation, especially after talking about Mum, but it feels right.

After another beat of silence, Dad's shoulders ease. "We are," he finally confesses, relaxing against the wall. "I want you and Henry to know I'll always love your mother."

"We know, but that doesn't mean you can't be happy now. It's what Mum would want."

Dad's face softens. "Amrey, I know we haven't spoken about any of this yet. I've wanted to give you space, and honestly, I wasn't sure I was ready to talk about it either. But if you're open to it, I'd like to talk to you." My heart beats a little faster as Dad's voice becomes rigid. I think he's expecting me to shut down the conversation, but for the first time, I don't want to. Even though the timing is considerably off, I finally feel ready to talk.

"I'd like that," I say, though the smile on Dad's face quickly fades.

"I was unfaithful to your mother," he begins.

I blink twice. The ease I felt melts away.

No sugar-coating it then. And though my heart hurts, it's a truth he must know I've realised, because the way he says it is devoid of sentiment. There are no excuses or "buts." It's a fact, and he's not denying it. While I respect him for being straightforward after all the lies, a part of me wants to scream at him for the blatancy. Instead, I draw in a heavy, heavy breath and try not to punch him for acts he committed before I was born.

"I was young. I didn't understand why I was different from everybody else. And then there was Sacha. Somehow, we had found each other. We were the same, and it felt better dealing with everything with her. But I was arranged to marry your mother, and that was it. That is until we found out Sacha was pregnant with you. I told your mother everything. She could have turned me in right then, but she didn't. I never understood that until I saw how she held you in her arms. She would do anything for you and Henry. You were hers, and neither Sacha nor I ever denied that."

"But how?" I manage to ask, holding back my tears. "How did you not get caught?"

"I was a guard by this time. The serum didn't work on me or

Sacha, and no one knew much about subversives back then. So, your mother faked a pregnancy, and Sacha managed to hide hers. With a few lies and a fake serum to give your mother, you came into our life, and Sacha went about her own."

I sit further back, taking this all in. It's so much. How they even managed it is beyond me, but it makes sense. Things were different back then. Dane wasn't around. It was easier to be subversive. Easier to lie.

"I know Sacha has already spoken to you," Dad continues, "but I want you to know she's always loved you too. She just wasn't in the position to have a child, and I respected that, just like she respected your mother and kept her distance. But she was always there, in the background."

My gut sinks as I listen to Dad's words. When Sacha explained her story to me, I was rude and standoffish. I didn't want to deal with it. I was immature and I regret that. My hurt clouded my judgment, but after hearing this—knowing what I do now—I don't judge my parents for the choices they made. They were only my age, and everyone knows I'm not making great decisions when it comes to love. I can't imagine caring for a child now as well.

"Did you ever love Mum?"

"Of course I did," Dad stammers. "I might not have been in love with your mother, but that didn't mean she wasn't a significant love in my life. You and Henry are the greatest lights in my life, and I would never have given that up. Not even for Sacha."

"Are you in love with Sacha now?" I ask straight.

Dad seems to consider his words for a moment, and the weight behind them. "I am," he smiles. "I believe a part of me always has been, and I think your mother knew that. Genevieve was a brilliant woman. Heaven knows I didn't deserve her kindness, but through everything, she remained with me and loved you before you were even a baby to hold. She always said you were half mine, and how could she not love any part of me."

My lungs feel tight. Hearing those words—knowing Mum said those things—mends my heart in so many ways it's hard to breathe.

"I know so much has happened. There was a lot more to your mother and I's story that you didn't know, but all that's important right now is that we both loved you. And when it came to it, your mother wanted Sacha in your life. She wanted you to know her." My chest aches, thinking back to Mum's last words.

I want you to know you're not alone.

I wipe the tears that escape my eyes. Mum was right. I'm not alone. I have Dad and Henry, Jaxon, Emeric, and Mags.

And Sacha.

And after all of this is over, though it will take time, I'm ready to let her in.

Just then, the door to the command centre swings open.

"Sorry to interrupt." Blane bursts into the hall. "But you need to see this."

Within seconds, Dad and I are up and hurrying into the room, leaving the moment, the past, and all the resentment behind us. I'm hopeful we'll have more time to talk about everything, but that time isn't now.

Commotion quickly envelops us as we enter, and I notice the monitors right away. Everyone is staring at the security camera footage, focusing on one screen in particular.

"Is that?"

"Dane and Kale," Blane finishes for me. My breath becomes stuck in my throat. Dad's skin washes of colour as he stands beside me, his eyes glued on Dane.

"What are they doing?" I shiver.

No one answers. Then, one by one, every screen cuts to black —all but one. A lone image buzzes on the remaining screen, shaking, blurring, and distorting with static, until there's no doubt what we're looking at.

Dane.

His eyes rattle the deepest parts of me, his face pressed into the lens, his taunting sneer sending chills down my spine. We might not get sound through the camera, but we don't need it. I watch each syllable twist over his lips.

"I'm coming for you."

Drawn out like a threat.

And I swear he's looking directly at me.

CHAPTER THIRTY-TWO

"Tripwires rigged!"

Emeric shouts down the hall as I look over Henry once more. The Defiance is in orderly chaos while we prepare for the next few hours.

"I want to help," Henry whines.

"You are. You kids have a very important job." I'm trying to be upbeat and play up his role, but Henry can pick up on the sugary coat of my voice. He's young, not stupid.

Henry rolls his eyes with an exaggerated sigh but doesn't protest. He knows that if it were up to me, I'd have him far away from here, safe from Dane and his approaching army. But we need all the help we can get, and there wasn't time to evacuate. We can't risk Dane's guards following the kids. So, we hunker down. When the time comes, we'll make our move. There may be only one entrance into Defiance, but there are two exits.

In just over an hour, Dane and his army will be here. When they breach, those who aren't needed will slip out the second exit to safety; the rest of us will fight.

We have a plan. It's good—if it works.

"Go get into position." I pull the zipper of Henry's jacket higher up his neck. "Stay with others, and no matter what happens, don't leave Sacha's side. Promise me." Henry looks up at me with his big eyes, and it takes everything in me not to cry, not to grab him and run far away from here.

"I promise," he says, giving me a quick hug.

"Go go." I smile at him one last time as he races down the hall towards the repository with Helena and Tobias.

"Sacha will be with them. She won't let anything happen to him," Mags says in my ear, squeezing my hand.

"I know."

"And they're the first to evacuate." That does offer me some relief. Right now, the kids, Sacha, and a few parents are soaking the repository—the only entrance we have—in oil and setting up tasers and sedation darts before heading to the evacuation point, while we are rigging the rest of the compound in traps. We aim to take down as many guards as we can at the start. The moment they breach, the kids will already be at the exit on the other side of the Defiance. If we're going to lose our home, we'll do it on our terms. And we're taking Dane with it.

"After today, there won't be a Defiance," I whisper.

"Not true. We are the Defiance. We're not going anywhere," Jaxon says, joining Archer, Griffin and Emeric.

"Actually, we're going back to Axiom. And setting things right," Mags says firmly, squeezing my palm.

"I like how you talk, woman," Emeric chuffs, taking her other hand, and the two share a look I feel guilty for watching.

"But first, we get to kick some ass." Archer stands a little taller.

"Tell me why you actually sound excited." Griffin shakes his head and leans closer to Archer, who simply shrugs with a smile.

"Just promise me, whatever happens." Griffins' voice is softer. "No one else dies." There's a second of silence as we all look at one another.

"No one else dies," we say in unison.

"This is for Owen." Archer takes Griffin's hand.

"And for my mum," I say with a heavy sigh.

"For everyone in Axiom," Mags says finally.

267

CHAPTER THIRTY-THREE

The repository is blown apart.

The floor shakes beneath my feet, the lights flickering before we're cast into darkness. Muffled voices and shouts echo, screams piercing my ears, sending chills down my spine. And then rounds and rounds of gunfire.

It takes everything I have not to run towards it.

Dane and his guards have breached the repository, blowing through the walls and deep layers of snow. We saw this coming. We're prepared for it, but that doesn't mean the idea of the Defiance being blown to bits is any less hard.

I'm waiting in the halls, listening to the sound of the falling guards, the shouts and the shots going off. No one was in the repository, just oiled floors, rigged darts and tasers. It won't subdue them for long, but hopefully, it takes down the first line of their defence, sheds a few numbers, less for us to deal with. If everything is going as planned, the kids should be evacuating right now with Sacha.

When I said we had a second exit, I may have embellished slightly. The repository was technically the only official way in and out, but that doesn't mean we don't have a backup plan.

The training arena is built into the chamber of a cave, a cave which, if you look hard enough, has small passageways. Most of them are sealed, but there is one that leads directly to the outside. It's a tight squeeze, but doable. One at a time, the kids and anyone not needed will climb out of the Defiance and up to the surface, where Sacha will lead them to the safety point. If all goes according to plan, we'll join them. But for now, our job is to hold off the guards and keep them away from the training centre long enough for everyone to evacuate.

"They're on the move," Archer calls out, and I position the gun in my hand, feeling the weight of the bullets. My heart twinges with the thought that I could kill someone again, but we can't risk it anymore. Kale might be the enemy, but he was right when he said Dane doesn't fight fair. We've tried to protect the guards, to minimise casualties, but now Dane is here, invading our home and threatening the lives of the Defiance—threatening my family and friends. We can't afford to fight fire with rocks anymore.

Unfastening the safety switch, I shake the reckoning thoughts away and recount the flash grenades strapped to my belt. I hear more gunfire up ahead right as Archer, Knox, Zeal and Emeric disappear into the smoke and rubble, along with Cora, Ezra and a few Axiom guards. Despite the time shortage, Makin was able to manufacture a few more doses of the cure, and those strong enough insisted on fighting by our side.

"Soon," Jaxon whispers as we slip into the command centre, wedging the tips of our guns between the door and the frame.

My grip on the weapon tightens. And we wait.

BANG

A flash grenade goes off—one of the many we rigged the halls with— providing only an echo of moans and a distant ringing in my ears. No voices, no bullets. Jaxon tugs on my arm. It's time.

"Go, go!" His orders echo through the hall as Archer,

Emeric, Zeal, and Knox run past, dusty and bleeding, but alive. They'll head to Mags to help her and the others finish setting up the traps, which Jaxon and I will set off when we leave. We're the last to go.

"That's it," Emeric says as the last guard runs past us. I nod sharply, doing the mental count. Three men down. Cora never ran past. Or Ezra. The thought stabs at my heart.

"Don't think about that now," Jaxon speaks into my ear, his shoulder pressed against mine. "Tomorrow we can grieve. Now we fight, so no one else dies." I don't speak in response, only swallow down the tears that were burning in my eyes and step out into the hall. Emeric disappears the opposite way, and I realise there's still no sound of Axiom guards. They're being discreet, trying to worm their way into the Defiance—just like we planned.

I keep moving towards the cafeteria. It's the easiest place to get to from the repository and the only room in the Defiance big enough for an army to recoup. It's also the only route we didn't booby trap. We want Dane and his men there, and judging from the scuffle of feet I now hear through the halls, they've fallen for the bait.

We just need to get there first, and that won't be easy. The hallway is clogged with smoke, and I hold back my cough as we make small, quick steps. The few lights still working create a glow in the darkness, and with every crack or spark, I flinch, squeezing my muscles so tight that my movements become stiff. But we make it.

Just.

The rhythmic squelch of wet boots stomping over the ground gets louder, and Jaxon pushes me through the doors.

"Quick!" His voice is urgent as he hands me another cartridge of bullets, and both of us duck into the kitchen, dropping behind the bench.

"How many?" I ask steadily, trying to calm my racing pulse.

"Too many."

The probabilities of what could happen next lay in the space between us, but we ignore them and top up our pistols. I check my waistband for the flash grenades; I've got two, so does Jaxon, and these aren't just smoke and nuisance. These are filled with sedative gas, so we have to time them right and hope we don't get shot in the meantime. Until then, we only have two cartridges of bullets and sedation darts.

"Any minute now," Jaxon breathes. I notice the stiffness in his neck, the way he keeps looking over our shoulders even though we haven't heard the door to the cafeteria open.

And then it does.

Slowly, it creaks forward, the eeriness unsettling. There's one set of footsteps, and another. Boots begin clipping the ground, voices muffled and soft filling the room.

"See you on the other side?" I smile, nudging Jaxon with my elbow. But instead of offering anything sweet, Jaxon looks at me hard in the eyes.

"Don't do anything stupid. Don't deviate from the plan."

My stomach knots. My chest strained.

"I promise," I whisper, quiet and with slight intent. Lying may be threaded through my veins, but that doesn't mean I like doing it.

"HEY!" A guard's voice bellows through the room.

We've been made.

Jaxon and I don't hesitate. Leaping from behind the kitchen, guns in hand, we fire with fury at the guards.

They aren't expecting it, and half fall before one round is through. But the others start firing back. I do my best to aim at non-fatal limbs, taking the guards down by the legs or arms so they can't shoot. This gets harder when all their guns are aimed at our heads.

Even harder when I'm hit.

I feel my skin tear as it's grazed by a bullet, blood trickling down my arm. It's not deep enough for me to care, but it still stings like hell and causes me to lose focus for a split second, just enough to get nicked a second time.

"This is ridiculous," I snap, ducking to reload my gun, wincing at the blood spilling from my arm and shoulder. "There are too many of them."

Jaxon looks at me, and with unspoken agreement, we rip flash grenades from our belts, pull the pins, and toss them into the fray. Then, grabbing our dart guns, we shoot the stunned guards.

"We should go before more of Dane's guards find us," Jaxon says during a break in the gunfire.

"But it's too soon," I fret. "We have to buy the others more time."

"If we wait any longer, we won't get out of here alive."

I barely have a moment to contemplate our options when we hear more footsteps.

"Dammit," Jaxon curses, glancing at our dwindling ammunition. "We're almost out of everything. We have to go now." He's right. I won't let him die.

"Let's go," I decide, taking the lead as we hurry out of the cafeteria while the guards are down.

When we reach the hall, the voices grow louder. Their backup has arrived, and they're getting close. We won't outrun them, and I refuse to lead Dane's guards to the others. It leaves us with one option.

I reach for a flash grenade on Jaxon's belt and toss it behind me as hard as I can. It detonates in seconds, and we both drop to our knees. There's one left. Fidgeting with my belt, I feel the weight of the last grenade. It won't be enough to hold the guards back. We need more time to set off the rigs and traps—more time for everyone to escape without being followed.

Jaxon is finally coming to the same conclusion I have. The one I've known all along.

"No," he says, but it's faint, and with the ringing in my ears, I barely hear it. So, instead of arguing a pointless argument, I lean forward and press my lips against his, soft and tasting of smoke. Jaxon wipes a tear from my cheek.

"I'll be right behind you," I say, because what else is there? I won't lie again. It's too late. Jaxon knows me, and I won't pretend to be anything else, so I say what I hope is true: "See you on the other side." Then I turn and run into the smoke. I don't look back to see if Jaxon's following me. I know he's not. Regardless of what he feels for me, of what we feel for each other, he has a job to do. The safety of those in the Defiance is worth more than my singular life. I only hope that whatever I can do now, whatever time I can buy them, is enough.

CHAPTER THIRTY-FOUR

My palm slams against the cafeteria door, sticky with smoke and ash. I push it open and tumble inside, gasping for fresh air.

"Look who finally decided to show her face."

My blood runs cold.

"Dane," I breathe, but it's not his eyes I see.

"I should have known you'd be the last one standing."

Kale.

My eyes narrow on his, trying to remember if the bruises that batter his face were there before. His busted lip definitely wasn't, nor his right eye that's swollen shut. He leans all his weight on one leg, and I know that's from me. But aside from his new marks, he still looks like Kale. That is until Dane steps into view, the two of them sharing a look that makes my insides twist, and I realise the similarities. How did I not see it before? Was I so blinded by Kale's attention that I didn't see the poison he was feeding me?

"Now that doesn't look like the face of a girl missing her boyfriend," Kale taunts.

I scoff. "I don't know what serum Dane's injected you with

recently, but the closest you ever got to being my boyfriend was when Axiom was forcing me to marry you." Kale's face hardens, and I feel a spark of satisfaction. He may have had me fooled once. I may have felt something for him, but I know now that the boy bleeding and seething in front of me was never the one I cared for.

"Enough of this stupid chit-chat," Dane spits. "We have what we need. It's time to go, and we're taking you with us, sweetheart." The nickname prickles my skin, and I fight the urge to gag. Kale looks at the space between us before directing his stare to Dane. The more I look at them, side by side, the more the similarities become undeniable. Dane is his father, and that thought alone gives me chills.

"We haven't finished here yet," Kale urges. "The others might have scattered, but we'll find them."

"Don't let yourself get wrapped up in petty revenge, boy. Having the girl is our retribution. The rest is a problem to be dealt with later." Dane's eyes trace over me and I dig my nails into my palm.

"It's sad that your only way of gaining people's allegiance is to drug them," I taunt, the edges of my voice dripping with ire.

Dane's sneer deepens.

"People are too dim-witted to make their own decisions. It's best this way."

His words boil my blood, and though rage for him burns in my throat, I swallow the urge to lunge at him because I want to keep him talking, to keep his feet rooted to this room for as long as I can. If I can buy enough time, not only will Dane not return to Axiom, but he won't ever see outside the Defiance again.

"You would know. You are drugging your own son."

Kale flinches. Dane only laughs.

"Is that your cheapest shot? Of course I'm drugging him. You can't rely on anyone to do what you need. This boy went soft the minute I took in that cleaning girl. I even kept her alive at his wish. All the good that did me."

I understand without clarification that he means Elle, and I wonder now if the love she felt for Kale was reciprocated.

"Is that true?" Kale has fallen very still next to him, his voice weaker than I've ever heard it.

"Forget it, boy. She's the one we want." Dane groans, his tone so irate I swear the room shakes.

"I won't go with you. Not as long as I'm breathing." I step back, my fingers skimming over my belt. A jolt of fear races down my spine. My gun's missing. I must have dropped it in the hallway. Before I let them see me panic, I grab the grenade at my waist. Dane seems to consider me then, eyeing the weapon in my hands, before releasing a deep, tight breath.

"Have it your way. It all ends the same. I don't need you compliant. I don't even need you conscious."

My lips press into a hard line as my hand tightens around the flash grenade. Dane's growl shifts into a smirk. He's relishing the challenge.

"Well, Miss X," he says, reaching for his gun. My hand trembles slightly. He might not kill me, but that doesn't mean he won't hurt me. "It's been a pleasure hunting you down."

I hold my breath as Dane aims his gun at me with sharp precision, my pulse roaring in my ears. My grenade won't stop a bullet.

Then Kale screams.

"You can't kill her!" His voice rips through the cafeteria as he steps in front of Dane, the barrel of the gun now aimed at him. But Kale isn't looking at his father; he's looking at me. And when our eyes meet, for a split second, I feel like I'm seeing the boy I met in Axiom, the one who caught me in combat class and cared for me in the cells. The Kale I saw in the flickers of our drunken nights when he caressed my face and told me his fears. The Kale who must resurface when the serum is weak in his veins. The person Dane is trying so hard to destroy.

"You stupid boy," Dane growls, "I'm not going to kill her. Now get out of my way!"

I hear the thud as Kale hits something hard, but I don't see it because I'm already running, tossing the flash grenade over my shoulder. Dane might not think much of his son—I definitely have my own feelings towards him—but even though he didn't save me, he gave me time to save myself. If only that was my plan.

THE HALLS ECHO as I run through them, broken lights flickering overhead as I dodge the debris that muddies the floors. My eyes water from the thick dust that clings to the air, and my ears still ring from the grenade, but I keep moving, hoping it was enough to give me a head start. Praying that everyone made it to the rendezvous point safely. Because no one can be here for what happens next. No one but Dane.

I hear his footsteps echoing down the empty halls. He's getting closer. The shimmer of the trip wire we set this afternoon catches my eye, and without further thought, I leap over it, my body sailing forward. I forgot about the greased floors. My feet slip and I barely manage to stay upright, crashing into the doorframe. Pain slices down my arm as my shoulder takes the brunt of the impact, but I shake it off and keep moving.

When I make it to the dispensary, I suck in a breath. This is it. Everyone's gone, everyone except Dane, his army and me. If I leave, they'll follow. I won't let that happen. I won't let him find a way to keep making his serum. Because as long as he can make his army do his bidding, he won't stop. No matter how many guards we save, how many people we pull from his clutches, he'll just keep going. There's only one way to make sure he never gets what he wants.

I find what I need on the far bench. Cynthia's medical tools lie discarded next to an unmade bed and a knocked-over chair. The room is the remnants of a hasty exit, but at least the people here did exit. I hold onto that thought. Those I love are far from here.

As my fingers twist over the scalpel, a sound like a hundred plates shattering crashes in the halls, followed by a scream, grunts of pain and feet crunching over broken glass. Dane must have set off one of the traps. It was Griffin's idea to hang the crockery on the ceiling, attached to a little tripwire. One wrong step, and it rains down over the entire hall. But if Dane's tripped that, then he's getting closer.

Retreating to the far side of the room, I press my back against the wall, holding out the scalpel. I don't hesitate. The pain's immediate. The sting that comes with running a blade over tight skin threatens to bring up my dinner, but I swallow it down. Squeezing my eyes shut, I hold onto the black, the dots blurring behind my eyelids as I dig the scalpel into my other wrist.

We've spent so long trying to find a way to stop Dane, to end his tyrant. When the answer has been clear all along. He can't control Axiom without his serum. And he doesn't have a serum without me.

By the time Dane reaches the dispensary door, the knife has already slipped from my hand and clattered to the floor, smeared in my blood.

"A rebel base emptied because of me. How flattering." His voice drips with contempt as he steps through the threshold. "If only you didn't have so many weaknesses. Maybe then, you would've stood a chance the first time you tried to escape, instead of playing right into my hands." His snicker dies the moment his eyes land on me, and I'm grateful I still have enough life left to see it.

"WHAT HAVE YOU DONE?!" His roar is more pained than angry, and the only satisfaction I can offer is the faint smirk on my lips. But I revel in it. I might have weaknesses, but so does Dane. And he forgot—I was his biggest one.

Within seconds, Dane's rough hands lift me from the ground and throw me onto a bed. I don't fight back, I can barely summon my eyes to stay open. So, I lie there as his grunts and barks grip my ears, the sound of metal trays and furniture clashing filling the silence as I fade out.

I see flashes of drawers flying open, Dane stomping around the room. If he's looking for a way to save me, he won't find it. The only thing that could save me is a person, and I made sure she was long gone from here.

Dane returns to my side, attempting to bind my wrists, but it's too late. The final piece of the plan will go off soon. There's no saving either of us. The thought of death doesn't scare me. I'm okay with leaving life this way. The ones I love are safe, and this will make sure of that. So, as my eyes draw shut, I don't fear the black. I welcome it. With a final breath, I no longer hear whatever absurdities Dane is shouting. Time is up.

The bomb will kill us both.

CHAPTER THIRTY-FIVE
JAXON

"SHE SHOULD BE OUT BY NOW!" I SHOUT. MY VOICE SLAMS against the still, waiting air. I know I shouldn't be yelling at Xavier. He's our leader. He's her father. But to hell with it. Amrey is still in the Defiance with Dane and a ticking bomb.

I knew leaving her wasn't a good idea, but she didn't give me much choice. I had to set off the remainder of the traps, and she had her mind made up. I know better than to stop her. I also know she's not stupid. She stayed behind to give me and the others a better chance, but she knew how much time she had. Dane was never supposed to leave the compound, and as the minutes pass, I realise Amrey won't be either.

God, that girl boils my blood.

The moment the plan was finalised, I saw the flicker in her eyes, one I'd seen too many times, and I felt the pressure under my ribs, waiting to be cracked open. Amrey always seems to have a backup plan that only she knows about. She did it in Axiom when she pressed a gun to her head and sacrificed herself. I wanted to strangle her for her *stupidity*, but she did it for her brother. I can't fault that. This time though, I'm not going to stand by. I may know better than to stop her, but I'll be damned if I leave her. I refuse to let her die.

Before anyone can stop me, I'm running towards the repository, gun in hand. Xavier shouts after me, but no one else says a word. Most of the Defiance is at the safety point; the rest of us are hiding in the trees, waiting for Amrey. But I think we all know she's not coming

What's left of our old entry is a room of rubble, half buried in snow from the approaching blizzard. All that remains is the door frame, blown open, creating a wide entrance into the Defiance. As I clamber over the cement and ashen snow, I feel the bile rise in my throat. Amongst the burnt oil barrels, discarded sedation darts and bullet casings—are bodies, slain in the chaos. Blood splashed over the scene. I tear my gaze from the red, fighting the urge to check all their vitals. Minutes are burning, and Amrey's still inside.

A strong gust pushes me from behind, my hair whipping in the wind as I step into the hallway. The darkness is almost encapsulating, even with the broken lights flickering above. I make my steps slow and light, saying silent prayers. *Where are you, Amrey? What is your plan?*

Aside from the howl of the wind and the cracks of broken glass crunching under my feet, the Defiance is as quiet as I've ever heard it. I press my back against the wall, trying to make out any sounds, but there's nothing. No footsteps, no voices. Only the rattle of loose rubble and the remnants of chaos.

I hurry towards the cafeteria—the last place I saw her. Even if she's not there, maybe I can get a sense of what happened.

The halls remain hollow, my footsteps echoing as I enter the room we used to eat in, now full of stale air and the residue from the grenades. The same floor I slow danced with Amrey on is covered in blood and bullets. I chase away the thoughts of her body pressed against mine, the way my heart raced and how her skin felt. I will see her again. I will feel those things again. So, with a heavy breath, I scan the room.

At first glance, the cafeteria looks like the rest of the Defiance, deserted. But then I see it. As I edge into the room, I see a shape on the ground.

A body.

My heart plummets.

"Amrey." Terror rips from my throat in the sound of her name. I rush over and collapse beside her body, but as I roll her over, I realise it's not her at all. Blood is smeared across the face, and though the light is minimal, I know who it is without a doubt.

"Kale."

He twitches under my hands, and I freeze as the edges of a shadow surround me.

"DON'T MOVE!"

My stomach clenches. Slowly, I turn to see Dane, his eyes wide, face frantic. A figure is draped over his arms, and a gun is pointed in my direction. Suddenly, the flickering bulbs spark to life from above, lighting up the room and illuminating Amrey's blood-soaked body.

"What did you do to her?" My voice is thick.

"Not at all what I wanted. It seems she tried to make her death wish come true. If only she were so lucky."

My blood runs cold, my body stricken as I stare at Amrey, unconscious in his arms. I want to kill him for hurting her. And I want to yell at her for being so stupid. Why couldn't she stop being a hero for one day?

Finding my feet, I slowly reach for my gun.

"Don't take another step," Dane growls.

"You're not taking her," I bite. Dane only laughs, but it's lost to the latest howl of wind and with Dane's slight distraction, I rip the gun from my sidearm and point it at Kale. "Let her go, or I kill him." The room echoes with my words, but Dane barely flinches. "Surely your black heart has some love for your only son."

For a second, I think he's considering my threat, but just as my grip begins to loosen, Dane barks out another laugh.

"You think I care about him?" He cocks his head, amused. "The stupid boy has caused me more trouble than he's worth. He grew fonder of this Subversive brat than of his own father." My hand flinches slightly on the trigger. Disgruntled family relationships seem to be a recurring trend.

"If you want Amrey to live, you'll hand her to me," I demand, but my resolve is wavering. If Dane doesn't care for Kale, then all leverage is his.

"I'll do no such thing. Tell me how to get out of here." He pauses, his tone threatening. "Without triggering any more of those vexing traps. Or she'll die in my arms."

A smile peeks at the corner of my lips as I notice, even in the dark, the cut on his cheek, the tears on his clothing. "Axiom's too far," I speak in a tone that matches his. "If she goes with you, she'll never make it. Give her to me, and I'll ensure she lives, and you can keep making your serum." I stare at the space between us, listening as the wind continues its torrent. The blizzard's getting closer, and the timer's running out.

"You're not getting it, boy. Either she lives with me or not at all. Make your choice before I make it for you." Dane raises the gun, stiff under Amrey's weight. He's tired and angry, and we're running out of time. There must be only minutes left until the bomb goes off. We have to get moving. I don't have another choice.

"Fine." I concede. "I'll get us out of here." I begin to move but stop as Dane's stare hardens.

"I won't be tricked into an ambush, boy. She'll die before I let that happen. That is a promise." I watch his gun shift, no longer pointing at me. Instead, the nub rests against Amrey's temple.

My heart lurches.

"It's not a trick," I insist. "Trust me; I want her alive." Dane watches me with steady precision, his grip on the gun tightening as I bend down and pick up Kale, throwing him over my shoulder.

"What are you doing?"

"Just because you're fine with letting people die, doesn't mean I am."

"He's unconscious, not dead." The look Dane gives me is one of complete disinterest. Dane might not know about the bomb. But even if he did, I doubt he'd be rushing to save Kale. Despite everything Kale has done, a part of me pities him. At least he's not awake to see how little his father cares.

WITH DANE on my heels and his gun still in hand, I direct us back towards the exit, avoiding the traps we set, though most have already been triggered. The wind is stronger at this end, its bite stinging my cheeks and clawing at my eyes. Thoughts of Amrey's lifeless body play on a loop in my mind. *She can't die. She can't.*

My steps quicken. Though the lights have been torn apart, daylight has begun to peek through the clouds, filtering in from the giant hole in the repository. A cold sweat breaks out over my skin. If morning is here, then we've run out of time.

The wind has grown into a torrent when we enter the repository—what's left of it. Half the walls are obliterated, the other half crumbling and sprayed with bullet holes. The oncoming blizzard has covered the ground in a fresh layer of snow, almost like a white veil has been placed over the fallen guards, protecting them. If the sight of it disturbs Dane, he doesn't show it. Instead, his pace increases, his strides heavier – making it harder to match with Kale's weight in my arms. He begins to stir as more snow slaps against his skin. I brace myself for him to wake up, but he doesn't. His body remains limp in my arms.

"You better not be lying, boy."

Dane's words press against my throat, and I swallow down the bile in my mouth. His threats don't shake me. As long as he follows me, I'll let him bark orders.

God, I hope this works.

Minutes later, the Defiance is still intact, which means I either got the timing wrong or something happened. But I can't worry about that now. Dane has Amrey and a gun pointed at my head; I have to focus on staying alive. He could kill me at any moment, and I'm surprised he hasn't tried already. But the further we walk, the deeper into the blizzard our steps take us, the more I realise Dane is lost.

I can work with that.

As we approach the tree line, it becomes clear that I'm leading the way. My steps grow sluggish under the weight of Kale's body in my arms, but I don't stop. Dane is still behind me, gun poised, showing no sign of slowing down. I wish I could take him right now. The image of Amrey drooped in his arms, her head swaying back and forth, boils my skin. Blood is soaked through her clothes, leaking out of Dane's poorly wrapped bandages. He's sick. But even though his reasons for wanting Amrey alive aren't the same as mine, right now, they're working in my favour. As long as he keeps following me, she has a chance.

"What was that?" Dane growls, and I stop as the sound of a branch snapping echoes through the trees.

"Nothing," I bite back, pretending I didn't hear it. The knots in my chest tighten.

"What games are you playing at, boy?" Dane's voice is low, his finger digging into the trigger of his gun as he looks at me through slanted eyes.

"No games, just trying to keep her alive." My throat burns as

I direct my gaze to Amrey. She's running out of time, if she hasn't already.

Dane takes a discerning look between us, a smirk reaching his lips.

"Oh, she'll live." His voice thins, turning oddly sweet. "Too bad you won't." Before I can react, he pulls the trigger, and a bullet cracks through the air. Dane's gun hits the ground before him.

I try to reach for Amrey, but Kale is in my arms. I yell her name, watching her fall, and then Archer is there, catching her just as the ground rumbles beneath me, smoke and snow bursting into the air. Everyone is thrown to their knees as the Defiance goes up in flames.

An explosion of rock and ice rains down with a thundering force. My friends emerge from the trees, rushing to mine and Amrey's side, and we watch on shaky ground as billows of smoke rise up behind us. The Defiance collapses, mounds of snow and debris caving into a giant hole. The sound rings in our ears, but no one moves. No one speaks at all. Instead, we stand in the glow of the fire, watching as the place that became our home, our safe haven, burns down—waiting for Amrey to breathe again. And when she does, I'll tell her that the Defiance is now nothing but a heap of rubble and ashen snow.

CHAPTER THIRTY-SIX
AMREY

THE WORLD IS A DULL, THROBBING PULSE AS I SLOWLY COME back to consciousness. The lone beep of a machine is the only sound of life. But I hear it, and I feel the itch from the bandages wrapped over my wrists, the stiffness in my neck from the brace.

I feel pain. Which means I'm alive. I didn't die.

A slither of light breaks through the dark as I open my eyes. I recognise the room, the same white walls, the same white ceilings. I'm in the school's infirmary.

I'm in Axiom.

Panic lodges in my throat, and I force myself to sit up. I have to get out of here before Dane comes back.

"Amrey!" Cynthia is at my side in seconds. "Sit back down and let me take a look at you."

"Cynthia?" I question, letting her look me over as I take note of her face. There are no bruises. She's not hurt. So why is she here? "What's going on? Why are we in Axiom? Did the bomb go off? Did Dane-?"

Before I can finish my question, she shushes me.

"We're alright, everyone's safe. Dane won't be hurting

anyone anymore. Now let me clean those dressings." I'm stunned quiet as she begins unwrapping the bandages from my arm—making quiet work of it. To my surprise, Cynthia doesn't comment about the cuts that run deep across my wrists. She says nothing as she cleans the gauze and re-dresses them.

"Time for the neck brace," she hums, helping me sit up to remove it. "Not to worry. It was just a precaution. You are a rest-less sleeper." The words surprisingly make me smile as I remember the last time I was told that. I was in this very room on the day that changed everything. The day I met Kale. The day I met Dane.

My smile falls.

I look around the infirmary, it's dirtier than it was, older. Everything feels off. The last year's events have left their mark.

"I suspect you want to know about Henry," Cynthia inter-rupts my spiral, her gaze softening as she takes my hand.

"Please," I beg.

"He's doing fine, as are your friends. Everyone's trying to get back to some normalcy. Henry's even started at school."

"School, already? How long have I been unconscious?"

Cynthia sighs. "Almost five days. I know it's soon, but the kids need it. Despite what the Defiance has been through, the kids here know no different and it should stay that way for a while. Until we have a story to tell them."

"We're going to tell the truth. We're going to tell everyone the truth," I say sharply. Cynthia only looks at me, and I get the sense she knows something I don't, but I don't get the chance to find out what.

"Jaxon." She smiles, looking past me towards the door.

"Hey, Mum."

His voice is just how I remember it, soft and kind, and the warmth that spreads over Cynthia is palpable. "I'll leave you to it then," she simpers, squeezing both Jaxon's and my hand before exiting the room.

There's a moment of silence between us, and I have to hold my breath as I look at him. He's so clean, so shaven and new. Yet, he's still Jaxon—my Jaxon.

"Hi," he says finally, his eyes sweeping over my body, and I fight the urge to hide my arms.

"Hi," I reply, weaker than I'd like, but Jaxon doesn't fret. Instead, he hands me the cup of water from the nightstand.

"We've got to stop meeting like this," he teases, my fingers brushing against his as I take the cup.

"I guess I have a thing for bleeding out in the snow."

"Not a funny joke." Jaxon's eyebrows knot as he watches my throat while I drink. His eyes trail over my body again, stopping at my wrists. He doesn't say anything else.

"Let's go for a walk," I insist. With a nod, he extends his arm for me to take.

I lead him through the halls of the school. I feel like a ghost walking through this place. Memories keep resurfacing with every turn I take, and it's hard to ignore the tightness in my chest that comes with them. The rooms are filled with kids in class, just like Cynthia said, and for a moment, it feels like nothing ever happened. Like I'm back in time, with no fear of Dane, no battle for power—no Defiance, no death. Except there was, and I can't go another second without knowing what happened.

"I need to know," I say breathlessly, holding my body up with the little energy I have. "The last thing I remember, I was with Dane in the dispensary."

"I found you." Jaxon stills, his grip on me tightening. "When you didn't show up, I knew something was wrong, so I went back, and that's when I saw you hanging almost dead in Dane's arms." His voice catches, and I wince at the picture his words create. I figured when I woke up alive that someone had saved me, but the idea that Jaxon ran back into the Defiance, with the bomb still active, and saw me in that state, pains me more than words can describe.

"Dane wouldn't give you up, but he couldn't navigate his way out of the Defiance without me. I used that to my advantage and managed to guide him all the way to the tree-line, where your dad, Archer, Mags, and Cynthia were waiting. And then the bomb went off." Jaxon's expression darkens. "The Defiance is gone."

I take a moment to process his words. I knew this. I signed off on the plan. The Defiance was always meant to be the casualty, but I guess I just assumed I wouldn't be here to live without it.

"But what about the others?" I ask. "Why were they there? They should have been at the safe point."

"They stayed behind. A few of us did. We weren't leaving without you."

My heart feels heavy. I don't know what to say—or feel.

"We were out of the blast range," Jaxon continues, "but right in the middle of an incoming blizzard. It was touch and go. I'm so grateful Cynthia and Mags were there, but even then, watching them try to revive you was the most terrified I've ever been. You weren't breathing. They had barely enough blood or equipment for a transfusion. The Defiance was up in flames. For five minutes, no one moved—until you started breathing. Then it was a race to get you back here."

Chills race over my skin at the thought.

"But even though Dane and Kale were down, we couldn't just walk into Axiom. Dane's guard was still under command and primed to shoot. It was a bloody fight. On both sides." Jaxon hesitates for a moment. "Herman didn't make it. It was a relief any of us did."

"How?" I tremble, tears brimming.

"Makin managed to make a batch of the antidote before we left. It wasn't enough to cure everyone, but enough that a wedge opened up in the guard, and we were able to stop the bloodshed and force our way in. Though, it was hours before we broke through the wall and got control of Axiom—hours of fighting and not knowing if you'd make it to the next minute. Even then, we hadn't secured the hospital, so Emeric and I ran to the infirmary with you in our arms, hoping it would be enough."

I don't know what I expected to happen after the bomb went off. I never let myself think about it. All I wanted was for my loved ones to be safe, and they are. But at what cost? I don't regret the choices I made, but I'm still sorry for everything that happened, for all everyone went through.

I'M NOT sure when we started walking again, but as our steps echo in the halls, I catch sight of a familiar face through the windows. Henry is sitting at his desk, absorbed in his book, concentration wrinkles creasing his forehead. Seeing him like that fills my body with so much warmth.

"Thank you." My voice is barely there as I turn to Jaxon. "Thank you for giving me this." If Jaxon hadn't shown up, I'd be dead, and though I was okay with that, it doesn't mean I'm not grateful to be here now—to be given the chance to see Henry grow up.

Jaxon's eyes pierce mine with an intensity the old me would have run away from, but now it's nice. It's everything I feel for him in a look. Jaxon doesn't say anything else. Pulling me closer, we keep walking.

"Let me guess, you kicked a few butts in this room?" My arm comes loose from Jaxon's as we stop in front of the gym, our old combat class. Mats lie scattered on the floor. There's no class in session, but the evidence is still there.

The last time I was here, I practically signed my death sentence with Dane. Kale had been there. He had tried to protect me, or so I thought. Now, every memory I have of that day—of him, is tarnished. The questions I have grow by the second. *Was he ever himself? Was any part of our relationship real? Or was everything a lie?* If it was, I can't even be mad. Kale was always honest that he could lie. He was never restricted to the truth. I was just naive. I wanted to believe him.

"What happened to Kale?" The question is quiet as it leaves my lips, afraid of the answer. Did he go up in flames with the Defiance?

"I made sure he made it out," Jaxon tells me, and a feeling I want to call relief laced with pain, leaves my body in a sigh. "Do you want to see him?"

I turn to Jaxon. "He's here?"

WALKING into Axiom's hospital is jarring. Bodies fill every bed. I knew the fight at the Defiance would have casualties, but I didn't let myself think about it at the time. I couldn't. If I had, I wouldn't have been able to do what I needed to. I wouldn't have survived. But now, seeing bed after bed of the injured, it's suffocating. How many of them are here because of injuries I inflicted? I might have been fighting for my family and everyone's freedom, but that doesn't change the fact that I hurt people. People who were just as much victims of Dane.

We come to a stop at the end of the hall, in front of a room with bars on the windows and two guards positioned out front. I don't remember the hospital ever having bars on the windows. I never knew someone to be watched by guards. But this isn't the same Axiom, and Kale isn't just anyone.

The glass might be blurry, but I can still make out Kale sitting on a bed, his face unshaven and his eyes droopy. He's sedated and barely moving. But he's there. It's Kale.

"He isn't himself," Jaxon begins, not wavering from the spot beside me. "You were right about Dane injecting him. Makin found incredibly high trace amounts of the serum in his system. Dane's been giving it to him for years. That's taken a toll. It's a wonder Kale managed to be sane at all. And now, without Dane, he's just become numb. He hasn't spoken much. Cynthia thinks he'll need months of extensive therapy and treatment before he'll ever start to feel like himself again. If he even knows who that is."

"I just don't understand how. He's been with us the entire time."

"Rowan managed to access Axiom's security, and from what we've seen, Kale was meeting with Axiom guards every few days, swapping your blood for serum injections. He's gotten so used to it that he just took it like a regular dose of medicine."

"But if Kale was Dane's secret weapon, then they've known where the Defiance is for months. Why didn't they attack sooner?"

Jaxon watches me for a moment.

"My guess is Dane's greedy. He wanted more power, and he knew a fight with us wasn't a sure win. He was probably waiting until his numbers tripled ours, but then we started taking his guards."

"So why attack us?"

"I don't think he planned on taking out the Defiance. I think he just needed a distraction. You've always been what he wanted."

I don't realise I'm squeezing Jaxon's hand so tightly until I hear him wince.

"Sorry," I murmur, letting go.

"Don't be. I'll take you squeezing my hand over bleeding out any day."

My throat feels tight as I look at him. So much has happened. It feels like years have passed in the span of one. And yet, standing this close to Jaxon, it's like I just met him yesterday, with his crooked smile, his brown eyes piercing mine. Mere inches separate us, and suddenly, my heart is racing in a way I missed, my stomach flipping under that stare of his. I almost move closer, but quick footsteps jar us apart, as a nurse enters Kale's room.

Jaxon clears his throat.

"So, any more questions?" he asks.

I think for only a moment. "Dane. Is he here too?" Jaxon's breaths grow quiet.

What is it?" I dread. *Tell me he didn't get away.*

"Amrey, Dane's dead. Griffin shot him. It was fatal."

I don't think my brain knows how to take in that information. For a moment, my lungs stop constricting, and it's like the blood in my body stops moving. Everything's just still. I'm frozen. And then, slowly, I begin to defrost, as does my new reality. One without Dane.

He's dead.

The words echo in my head like the boom from a cannon. Dane is dead, and Kale is here, and it's over. It's really over.

A scream rips through the air. Metal clatters on the ground and I spin around to find Kale arguing with the nurse.

Before I can step in, guards rush to subdue him, and as I stare at him through the glass, I feel like I'm looking at a stranger. I don't know what parts of Kale were him and what parts were the serum, but I choose to believe he's not all bad. That deep down, part of him did care. He's just a scared boy trapped by a horrible father. I hope over time he can find himself again, and maybe we can be friends.

"What will be done with him?" I notion. Jaxon follows my gaze to the window and the beaten-down boy sitting behind the glass.

"He's awaiting trial, but Cynthia suggested we wait a while and let the serum leave his system."

"Why don't they just give him the antidote."

"They will, but there are more important people to give it to first, and we don't have a lot right now, so we are prioritising based on need."

That's when it clicks. They need me to make more of the antidote.

"We have to go find Makin," I fret, turning to leave, but Jaxon holds me in place.

"Amrey, it's okay," he says, settling me. "Right now, your only focus is healing."

"But they need my bone marrow."

"They still have some left. The only reason they're not using it is that Makin is working on replicating it. We have better technology here, and once he learns how, Makin can rapidly replicate your bone marrow cells and the antidote."

"So they won't need me anymore?"

"Makin will explain everything, but no, they'll never need your blood or bone marrow again. And once everyone's cured, serums of any kind will be banned." Jaxon's voice is so sure, so safe, and for the first time, I'm not afraid of what the future holds in Axiom. It's a lot to take in—I haven't even begun to process it all. But as I stand here, looking up at the boy who's been with me through it all, I know it'll be okay.

"So, how was school today? Learn anything cool?" I ask Henry before he can stuff his face with more food. We're sitting around the kitchen table at a different house. Ours is still there. I walked by it today, but none of us have the heart to live in it again, at least not now.

"I don't know how much he was learning," Sacha smirks. She lives with Dad and Henry now. "When I checked on him, he was busy talking to Helena."

"Helena?" I ask. Mags caught me up on most of the new changes in Axiom, including gender-inclusive classes. It makes sense, but for the kids who've never known any different, it'll be a big adjustment.

"I thought you were closer with Tobias." I finish, my comment making Henry's cheeks flush as he puts down his utensils to stare at me.

"I like them both." He huffs, pointing his fork at me. My eyes meet Dad's, and we both can't help but laugh.

"Leave him be. Someone has to show the new kids around," Sacha says, rubbing her arm with Henry. It's clear who she's trying to win brownie points with.

"Exactly, and I'm turning eight soon."

"Didn't you just turn seven?" I gasp, rolling my eyes, Dad stiffens next to me. He wasn't there for it. Henry's birthday was almost two months ago, but we haven't spoken about the time that passed while he and Sacha were gone. It was hard, losing Mum, losing them. Henry was so strong, but he shouldn't have had to be. He shouldn't have to grow up so fast. That's why I was determined not to let his birthday pass by. He deserved a celebration. So, Mags baked a cake, and Owen played games with Henry and the kids in the arena. I smile at the thought of Owen as I look up at Henry, all smiley with attitude towards Dad. I'm grateful for this moment. We still have a lot of healing to do, but we will, as a family.

"Well, I'm seven, which means soon I can have a boyfriend or girlfriend if I want." Henry finishes his sentence, bringing me back to the moment.

"Hey now!" Dad coughs. "You can have no such thing."

"Amrey does!" Henry argues.

"She does?" Sacha asks, turning to look at me.

"I saw her and Jaxon walking together in school today. They were holding hands."

"They were?" Sacha continues her commentary, her smile deepening while Dad only stares at me. I want out of this conversation so bad, but something tells me this time it won't be so easy.

"No one has a boyfriend… yet," I mumble, shovelling food into my mouth to avoid everyone's stares. When I swallow my bite and look up, Dad raises his brows at me.

"I promise if there's something to say, I'll say it."

After a second, he nods, and I release a heavy breath. It's not that talking about Jaxon is that anxiety-reducing, although with Dad, it definitely adds a layer. It's more that with everything that's happened, I barely know which way to turn, let alone who I want to date. Dating was never a concept in Axiom. It was simply no contact and then an arranged marriage. I spent my whole life with girls, my family and Makin, but then the Defiance threw me right into the deep end, and now some of my best friends are boys. I wouldn't have it any other way, but for the moment, I'm happy with it staying that way. Friends first, and with time, we'll see.

"Do you need my help with it?" My thoughts disappear as I catch the end of Sacha's and Dad's conversation.

"With what?" I ask, finishing off my vegetables and looking between them.

"I'm going to Axiom's command centre tonight to see what we're dealing with," Dad answers.

"And you're sure you don't need me?" Sacha asks again. Dad looks up from his plate, his eyes meeting hers.

"I'm alright, I promise. You've been teaching all day. You need rest." Sacha looks like she's about to protest, but Dad gives her a soft look that melts it away.

"If you're sure," she sighs, "though, I am pretty tired."

"I am. Besides, Rowan will be there to help with the technical stuff. Something tells me Dane has some advanced hijinks I won't understand."

"Why can't you just do it tomorrow?" I question, watching Dad stifle a yawn.

"I need a basic understanding first, before the meeting tomorrow with the temporarily elected counsel. We're discussing how to further proceedings."

"Proceedings?" Henry looks puzzled.

"It means what comes next," Sacha explains.

"What is next?" I ask, staring at Dad. He sets down his fork, finishes his drink and then meets my gaze.

"We rebuild."

CHAPTER THIRTY-SEVEN
FIVE YEARS LATER

DREAMS WERE NEVER SOMETHING THAT FILLED MY NIGHTS. Nightmares often plagued my mind instead. Fear, loss and pain. Running and wandering and searching and falling short. Time and time again. For years, the same torment. Until I found my dad, and then a different nightmare came. A gunshot. Pools of blood. Mum's last words.

Eventually, that stopped too, leaving me with nothing.

My sleep was black.

Desolate.

Dreamless.

But as time in our new Axiom passed, as we rebuilt and I grew older, that changed again. One dream bled into another, and now my sleep is sweet. Filled with hopes as I grow to want more. Now, when I wake, I often miss my dreams. Not because they're better than my reality, because Mum is in them and she's happy, and it's on mornings like this when I wish she were still here.

Marriage was never something I wanted. It was something I tried so hard to run from, something I feared would only ever be an obligation, a duty.

But now, it's a choice.

"If I knew you talk this much in your sleep, I would have opted for a different living arrangement." Jaxon's voice tickles my ear as his arms snake around my bare waist, pulling me flush against him.

"You still can. Archer, Griffin and I will be just fine," I say with as much snark as I can muster, though I feel myself melting completely in his touch.

"And leave you to suffer Griffin's cooking? I might be sleep-deprived, but I'm not a monster. Besides, they'll be even more insufferable after today. I have to stick around, or you'll have no one to talk to."

"Is that so?" I raise my brows in a challenge. "Sounds like you're stuck with me then."

"How horrible." His voice grumbles as he bites my ear, and I flip myself around, wrapping my legs with his, threading my hands through his hair. It's hard not to lose my breath. Even first thing in the morning, he looks too good to be real.

"You're staring again."

"It's not my fault. Blame your parents. They made you look too pretty."

"Pretty?" Jaxon's eyes raise, one of his hands sliding under the covers and down my stomach. "I'll have to remember to thank them at the wedding." He smirks, and I don't wait a second longer before I meld my lips with his. His strong arms pull me closer, fusing us. His touch is like fire over my skin, and I sink deeper into his kiss.

Jaxon tastes like mint and chocolate and all things right in the world. I know he managed to sneak out and brush his teeth this morning. Months ago, I would have done the same, but that faded. Jaxon's mine, bad breath and all, and I'm his.

And mornings are ours.

When everything happened, I didn't think he'd want me, especially after he saw me leaving Kale's room. The look on his face broke my heart, and even though I never completely went there with Kale, the idea that I almost did was a heavy weight between us. The realisation that I might have lost Jaxon forever was worse. No matter how much I thought Kale was my answer, that Jaxon and I were too dissimilar and Kale was the one who got me, I was wrong. For when the moment came, and my clothes were on the floor, Jaxon was the one taking up all the room in my brain, not anyone else. When I escaped to the hallway and saw him, it felt as if life was showing me I'd made the right choice. Jaxon wasn't my arranged husband. He isn't subversive. He's Mag's brother. He's the boy who chased me into the forest. He's the boy who saved me time and time again.

He's mine.

PETALS LIE at my feet as I walk down the aisle, the soft silk of my dress swishing around my legs. The flowers in my hand drip water, the stems rough on my hands, but I don't care. The roses smell of perfume, fresh and glistening in the light. The city square looks beautiful in the sunset, with the newly built fountain trickling behind the altar and twinkling lights strung up all around. This is a perfect moment—one I'm so glad I get to share.

When I reach the altar, Jaxon is standing to the right, his suit fitted, his smile as warm as ever, and as our eyes meet, it's like we're the only two people who exist. He nods his head ever slightly towards me, *'I love you'* twisting over his lips. Just like in the beginning, the butterflies that fill my chest are still there, still buzzing, and even more alive today.

Though it's not practice, I step closer, kissing him firmly on the lips.

"I love you," I whisper back.

I hear Emeric laugh next to us and step towards him, giving him a quick peck on the cheek. With a final look at Jaxon, I walk over to the left and join Helena. The older she gets, the more parts of Owen I see in her, and I know he would be so happy for this day. I drift my gaze to the empty chair in the front row. A single rose rests over it. Owen might not be here, but he is with us, always.

The room is alive with hope. It's the first wedding in Axiom since everything happened, the first wedding of pure choice, made from two people's decision to be with each other. No government, no laws, no status.

Just love.

The next footsteps clip down the aisle, and everyone watches Mags, elegant as ever, walking towards us, her blond curls bouncing around her face. They've grown considerably in the last five years, and it was trickier to do than when we were kids. Cynthia had helped me pin them up this morning, leaving a few to fall and frame her cheeks. Her deep blue eyes shine so clearly as she looks at Emeric. Her skin glows against the soft pink of her dress, the colour of roses mixed with snow. She is stunning. It will always baffle me that she ever thought she was bland. She could never be bland.

"Weddings are beautiful. I'm so sorry I missed yours," I say as Mags stands beside me, flowers glistening in her hands.

"Maybe I'll just have to have another one." She smiles, but not at me. When I trace her gaze, I see Emeric staring right back at her, just before the music changes.

Mags and I share a squeal of excitement as everyone stands, and we all turn towards the groomsmen walking hand in hand down the aisle. It's a moment Axiom's never seen, and I make sure to take everything in: the look of happiness shared between Sacha and Dad as they stand wrapped in each other's arms. I know Mum would be so happy for them. As am I, and Henry, who's 12 now and too young to know what love is—in my opinion. However, whenever Tobias is around, his smile becomes greater, his eyes bigger, and I don't think he's too unfamiliar with the feeling at all.

I watch Kale next as he whispers something to Elle that makes her smile. He's no longer bruised, lost or torn, but happy—something that he's only recently allowed himself. The serum was buried so deep in his mind, years' worth of injections and manipulations warping his every thought. It was hard to undo, but Elle was there every step of the way. I was too, when he let me. It took a lot before Kale was able to face me. The guilt shone deep in all his features. I accepted the first apology, though he showered me with hundreds more. And when he was ready to speak, he told me there were moments when the serum would fade, and he would find himself again. The moments of clarity were brief, but our time in the cell was one of them. When Kale told me about Dane's hunt for bone marrow, about his torture, it was real. Dane punished him for it. I know that's why he nearly died that day. I'm just so glad he lived. Kale's been through so much. He experienced more of Dane's manipulation than anyone else. So, when the chance came for him to live freely, he took it, giving back to Axiom in every way he could.

Jaxon also keeps me updated on Kale ever since they were both made combat teachers. Now, anyone can learn defensive skills, not because we have walls to defend or need guards, but because it's fun. That and because Blane's annual mudball competition has sparked a lot of rivalry in Axiom—the winners' bragging rights last all year.

Axiom's guard was abolished along with Dane, and as head of the newly stated peacekeepers—with Knox and Zeal to keep me in check—I am a referee of Mudball, which I find just as fun and less painful. Henry's team won last year. In a way, I got the best bragging rights of all. Peacekeepers also maintain regular patrols of the wall at the Governor's request. Now that Dane is gone, Dad's obsession has shifted to threats beyond Axiom. I think he's paranoid, but I won't tell him that, just like I won't run for the board of governors, even though he keeps pushing me to. I know it's because he can't discuss anything with me unless I am, but I have no interest in politics. Besides, I know Axiom is in great hands with those already on it. Dad, Emeric, Rowan, Sacha and Blane, along with Dawn, a representative from the old Axiom, have it under control.

The kids are in safe hands with Mags running the school and its infirmary. No more gender segregation, just one cohesive unit. Plus, I know Henry loves having Mags in charge and Makin as a science teacher. I've heard a few stories already about special treatment, but I'll let Dad handle that one.

THE MUSIC BEGINS to fade out as Griffin and Archer reach the altar. I can't help but smile like a cheesy fool. Marriage was always something that plagued my mind, something I was running from. But now, I'm so honoured to stand up here and witness such beautiful love.

It's inspiring.

I never thought I'd want a wedding or a marriage, but with Jaxon, the idea isn't terrible. Who knows what could happen? I have time after all. And I know, looking at Griffin and Archer, their love strong enough to carry them through everything, that they have so much goodness ahead.

Everyone does.

For we live in Axiom, where you're free to be who you want, how you want. Where our lies don't define us and our secrets are ours if we choose. As I watch Archer and Griffin recite their vows, their faces alive with each other's love. I place one hand over my stomach. My secret, for now.

EPILOGUE
FIVE DAYS AFTER THE
DEFIANCE RECLAIMED AXIOM

IN A SMALL ROOM INSIDE THE AXIOM GOVERNOR'S QUARTERS, six people sit at a table built for ten. Squaring his shoulders, Xavier looks across the table at Makin and two other women, Dawn and Trista—Axiom's representatives. Blane and Rowan exchange cordial nods as they shuffle into their seats—the Defiance representatives.

"I'm sorry to call on you all in the middle of the night, but this is a matter for the council," Xavier speaks over the room in a hushed tone. He doesn't know that the layers of drywall Dane installed years ago keep his voice, and the words spoken in this room, sealed away from outside's prying ears.

"You mean temporary council. We were nominated out of necessity, not voted in. Xavier, shouldn't we abstain from discussing anything dire until a proper election is held?" Makin argues, his posture rigid and tense against the leather chair. He doesn't like this position any more than he originally thought, but he was nominated by his wife and saying no to her has always been impossible.

"If time was on our side, I would have held off." Xavier draws in a deep breath, waiting as everyone settles in. The moon is at its peak now, a harsh chill in the air, felt even inside. The crease in Xavier's brow deepens. His hopes of returning home before Amrey falls asleep are improbable. But at least she's awake. She's alive. They had dinner together. His relationship with his daughter is a work in progress, but for the moment, he has more pressing things to worry about.

"What is it, Xavier?" Dawn intercedes, her tired eyes piercing his. "And can it be quick?" Xavier doesn't take her tone personally; she's tired. Sleep isn't something anyone in this room has had much of in the last week, since Dane's takedown and the merging of the Defiance with Axiom. Plus, Dawn—as Xavier has come to know her—doesn't have the greatest social skills.

"That is not something I can say I'm afraid." His words spark an eerie ambience that even Makin finds uncomfortable.

"On with it then." Blane says, and Makin finds it odd that he isn't already in the know.

Xavier straightens his stance, his shoulders squared so tight they could serve as a foundation for bricks.

"Earlier tonight," he begins, "Rowan was helping me understand the electrics and wiring of this place, when we received a transmission."

"A transmission?" Trista leans forward on the table, folding her hands.

"Call it a video message," Rowan replies, shaking her head. She can already see the creases forming on Xavier's face from the technicalities of the explanation. And if there's one thing she hates, it's men explaining things they don't understand. "It was sent electronically, by a form of technology we've never seen. I'm still trying to decipher the exact source."

"What was on the video?" Makin asks.

"That's the thing," Xavier jumps in, his voice thin, his eyes narrowed on the screen. "It's not so much what we saw, but who." The image blinks a few times before a room materialises, revealing a man at a desk.

All the faces at the governing table turn their stares to the man in a tailored suit, who is sitting at a desk rather casually. There's a clicking of a camera and a whirring sound, some background noise, and then his voice, which makes Dawn's mouth zip shut and Blane's shoulders tense.

"If you're seeing this, then you're not Dane. And I can tell you that is as much a relief to us as it is to you."

Us? Makin questions but stays silent.

"The Governors in Axiom Seven seem to have grown rather… stale, for a lack of a better word."

The term *'Axiom Seven'* sends a severe chill through the room that Blane cannot ignore. The hair on the back of his neck has been standing on end since the screen flashed on. He keeps his pulse steady as he watches the old man press his lips together, mulling over his choice of vocabulary as if it were premeditated. Blane can tell from the position of the man's hands and the way he watches the camera rather than looks at it that it is. Whoever this man is, whatever he wants, one thing's for sure: he's meant to intimidate.

"Dane became a problem. His greed for power and recklessness with the serum caused quite a stir here. And I thank you greatly for your efforts in cleaning up his mess."

This is not the first time Xavier has heard this message, not even the fifth. The simple word *here*, still haunts him when he hears it. Where is here? And what do they want?

"I can only assume that whoever is watching this message has no idea who I am or what interest I could possibly have in the prosperity of Axiom. While I don't have enough time to answer all your questions, I will tell you what you need to know for now. I am Deaton Newark, the fourth, great grandson to Gregory Newark, the creator of Axiom cities. And yes, you've been hearing me right. You are not the only Axiom. There are more than a dozen cities exactly like yours, with the same rules and regulations implemented. Axiom cities were an experiment we began as a way to control corruption when the war ravaged our world. The truth serum was effective, it has been until Dane decided to take things into his own hands."

Rowan leans back in her chair. Her skin itches just like it did the first time she watched this. The only way for anyone to know the goings on in Axiom is if they've been watching. The whole city, everyone in it, has been under a microscope, an experiment, and they're not the only ones.

Deaton's chair creaks as he leans closer to the camera. The glint in his eye and the tug of his lip unease the entire room.

"I welcome you all to the Governing table. We have much to discuss."

ACKNOWLEDGMENTS

First and foremost, I want to thank my parents for their endless love and encouragement. Independent publishing isn't for the faint of heart, and I'm incredibly fortunate to have such a strong support system in them, along with the rest of my family. I know many of my first sales came from you, and I couldn't be more grateful.

A special thanks to my wonderful cousins, Emily and Olivia, who were not only the first readers of *Axiom II* but also the very first to read *Axiom*. I still remember how excited I was to receive their feedback.

To my beautiful Grandma, the matriarch of our family. I'm so blessed to have you. Thank you for your prayers and for caring for Grandpa. Though he's not here to read this, I feel his presence with me always.

Nicole, you're probably sitting right next to me as you read this, so I'll keep it brief: I feel incredibly lucky to have a partner who's also my best friend. Thank you for listening to my rants about potholes and publishing woes, and for being patient when I kept the manuscript from you. I can't imagine annoying anyone else.

To Jules and Tia, thank you for your constant support, even if *cough* Jules still hasn't read *Axiom*. I can't imagine getting through my days without our calls. And Molly, who quickly became my 'call a doctor' friend—thank you for helping with everything from explaining blood transfusions to solving plot holes. Your map design for *Axiom* surpassed my wildest dreams. You're multi-talented, and I couldn't ask for a better friend.

I also want to give a special mention to the wonderful Dana Alsamsam, who edited *Axiom II* and did an incredible job, and to one of my lovely beta readers, Gemma, whose feedback was invaluable.

Lastly, a heartfelt thank you to my amazing readers who discovered me on BookTok, sent messages, and shared videos of *Axiom*. This book exists because of your support.

I'm incredibly proud of this series and where it's taken me. While Amrey's story might be finished, there are still more tales within the *Axiom* world to be told, and I can't wait to share them.

ABOUT THE AUTHOR

Madison Rose is an Australian author best known for her *Axiom* series, which is an Amazon Best Seller in children's and teen dystopian fiction.

Currently residing in Barcelona, Madison has a passion for all things dystopian and romance. When she's not teaching English to kids or diving into the world of BookTok, she's often writing with a glass of wine or a cup of coffee in hand. Her love for books is second only to her family, and on the rare occasions she's not writing, she's likely book shopping, or sleeping in and dreaming up her next story.

Dear reader,

Did you wonder what happened in those five years after the Defiance reclaimed Axiom? Visit my website and sign up for my newsletter to have a bonus chapter sent straight to your inbox!

To stay up to date with new releases, Axiom news, my upcoming projects and all things book-related, you can follow me on social media @madisonrosebooks.

Thank you for taking the time to read my books! If you enjoyed Axiom, I would greatly appreciate it if you could leave a review and share your thoughts.

With love,

Madi x